GRAPHIC
NOVEL

GODDESS GIRLS

ARTEMIS THE BRAVE

CREATED BY
JOAN HOLUB &
SUZANNE WILLIAMS
ADAPTED BY **DAVID CAMPITI**

✳

ILLUSTRATED BY **MARTINA DI GIOVANNI**
AT GLASS HOUSE GRAPHICS

Aladdin
New York   London   Toronto   Sydney   New Delhi

ALADDIN
AN IMPRINT OF SIMON & SCHUSTER CHILDREN'S PUBLISHING DIVISION
1230 AVENUE OF THE AMERICAS, NEW YORK, NEW YORK 10020
FIRST ALADDIN EDITION FEBRUARY 2023
TEXT COPYRIGHT © 2023 BY JOAN HOLUB AND SUZANNE WILLIAMS
ILLUSTRATIONS COPYRIGHT © 2023 BY GLASS HOUSE GRAPHICS
COVER ILLUSTRATION BY MANUEL PREITANO
LAYOUTS BY DAVE SANTANA
INTERIORS ILLUSTRATED BY MARTINA DI GIOVANNI AT GLASS HOUSE GRAPHICS.
ASSISTANTS ON PENCILS ONOFRIO ORLANDO AND MARTINA RITANO.
COLORS BY NATALIYA TORRETTA, VANESSA COSTANZO, GAETANO INGALISO, FRANCESCA INGRASSIA,
CHIARA SPINOSO AND MARZIA MIGLIORI.
SUPERVISION BY SALVATORE DI MARCO/GRAFIMATED CARTOON.
LETTERING AND ADDITIONAL ART BY MEMY MEDIA.
ALL RIGHTS RESERVED, INCLUDING THE RIGHT OF REPRODUCTION IN WHOLE OR IN PART IN ANY
FORM. ALADDIN AND RELATED LOGO ARE REGISTERED TRADEMARKS OF SIMON & SCHUSTER, INC.
FOR INFORMATION ABOUT SPECIAL DISCOUNTS FOR BULK PURCHASES, PLEASE CONTACT
SIMON & SCHUSTER SPECIAL SALES AT 1-866-506-1949 OR BUSINESS@SIMONANDSCHUSTER.COM.
THE SIMON & SCHUSTER SPEAKERS BUREAU CAN BRING AUTHORS TO YOUR LIVE EVENT. FOR MORE
INFORMATION OR TO BOOK AN EVENT CONTACT THE SIMON & SCHUSTER SPEAKERS BUREAU AT
1-866-248-3049 OR VISIT OUR WEBSITE AT WWW.SIMONSPEAKERS.COM.
THE ILLUSTRATIONS FOR THIS BOOK WERE RENDERED DIGITALLY.
THE TEXT THIS BOOK WAS SET IN ANIME ACE 2.0 AND STEINANTIK.
MANUFACTURED IN CHINA 1022 SCP
2 4 6 8 10 9 7 5 3 1
THIS BOOK HAS BEEN CATALOGED BY THE LIBRARY OF CONGRESS.
ISBN 9781534473966 (HC)
ISBN 9781534473959 (PBK)
ISBN 9781534473973 (EBOOK)

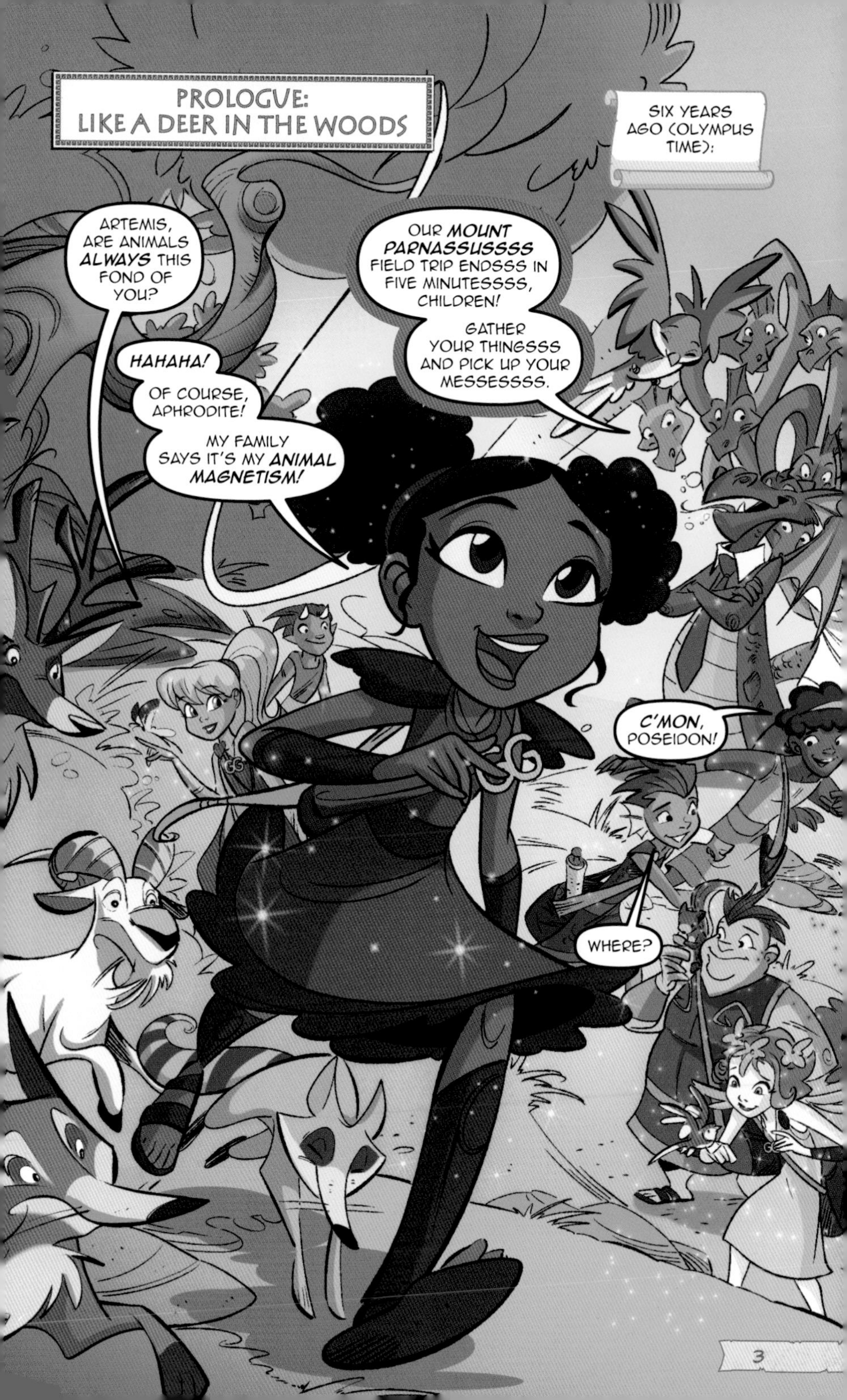

PROLOGUE: LIKE A DEER IN THE WOODS
SIX YEARS AGO (OLYMPUS TIME):
ARTEMIS, ARE ANIMALS ALWAYS THIS FOND OF YOU?
OUR MOUNT PARNASSUSSSS FIELD TRIP ENDSSS IN FIVE MINUTESSSS, CHILDREN!
GATHER YOUR THINGSSS AND PICK UP YOUR MESSESSSS.
HAHAHA!
OF COURSE, APHRODITE!
MY FAMILY SAYS IT'S MY ANIMAL MAGNETISM!
C'MON, POSEIDON!
WHERE?

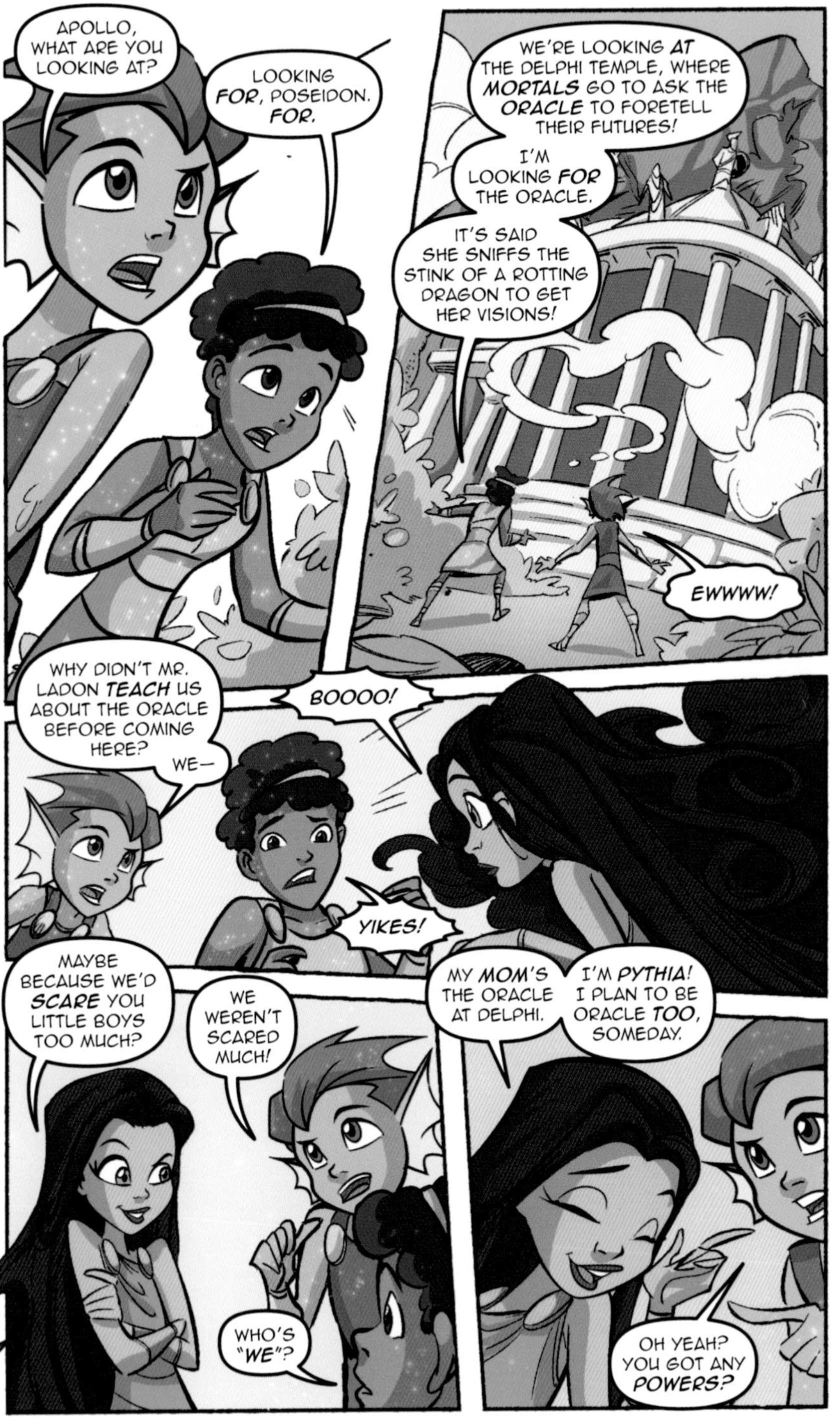

APOLLO, WHAT ARE YOU LOOKING AT?
LOOKING **FOR**, POSEIDON. **FOR.**
WE'RE LOOKING **AT** THE DELPHI TEMPLE, WHERE **MORTALS** GO TO ASK THE **ORACLE** TO FORETELL THEIR FUTURES!
I'M LOOKING **FOR** THE ORACLE.
IT'S SAID SHE SNIFFS THE STINK OF A ROTTING DRAGON TO GET HER VISIONS!
EWWWW!
WHY DIDN'T MR. LADON **TEACH** US ABOUT THE ORACLE BEFORE COMING HERE? WE—
BOOOO!
YIKES!
MAYBE BECAUSE WE'D **SCARE** YOU LITTLE BOYS TOO MUCH?
WE WEREN'T SCARED MUCH!
WHO'S "**WE**"?
MY **MOM**'S THE ORACLE AT DELPHI.
I'M **PYTHIA**! I PLAN TO BE ORACLE **TOO**, SOMEDAY.
OH YEAH? YOU GOT ANY **POWERS**?

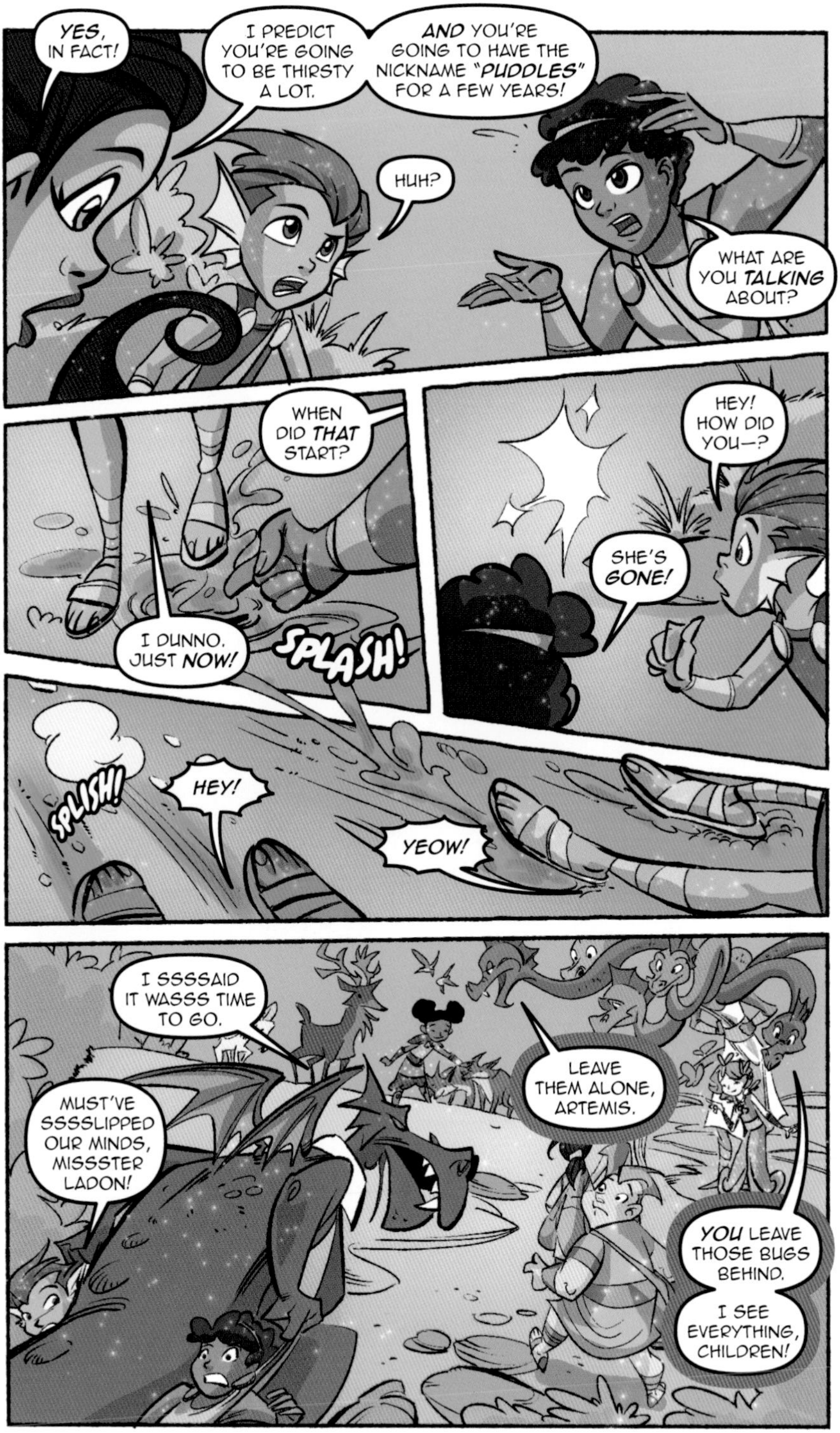
YES, IN FACT!
I PREDICT YOU'RE GOING TO BE THIRSTY A LOT.
AND YOU'RE GOING TO HAVE THE NICKNAME "PUDDLES" FOR A FEW YEARS!
HUH?
WHAT ARE YOU TALKING ABOUT?
WHEN DID THAT START?
I DUNNO. JUST NOW!
SPLASH!
HEY! HOW DID YOU—?
SHE'S GONE!
SPLISH!
HEY!
YEOW!
I SSSSAID IT WASSS TIME TO GO.
MUST'VE SSSSLIPPED OUR MINDS, MISSSTER LADON!
LEAVE THEM ALONE, ARTEMIS.
YOU LEAVE THOSE BUGS BEHIND.
I SEE EVERYTHING, CHILDREN!

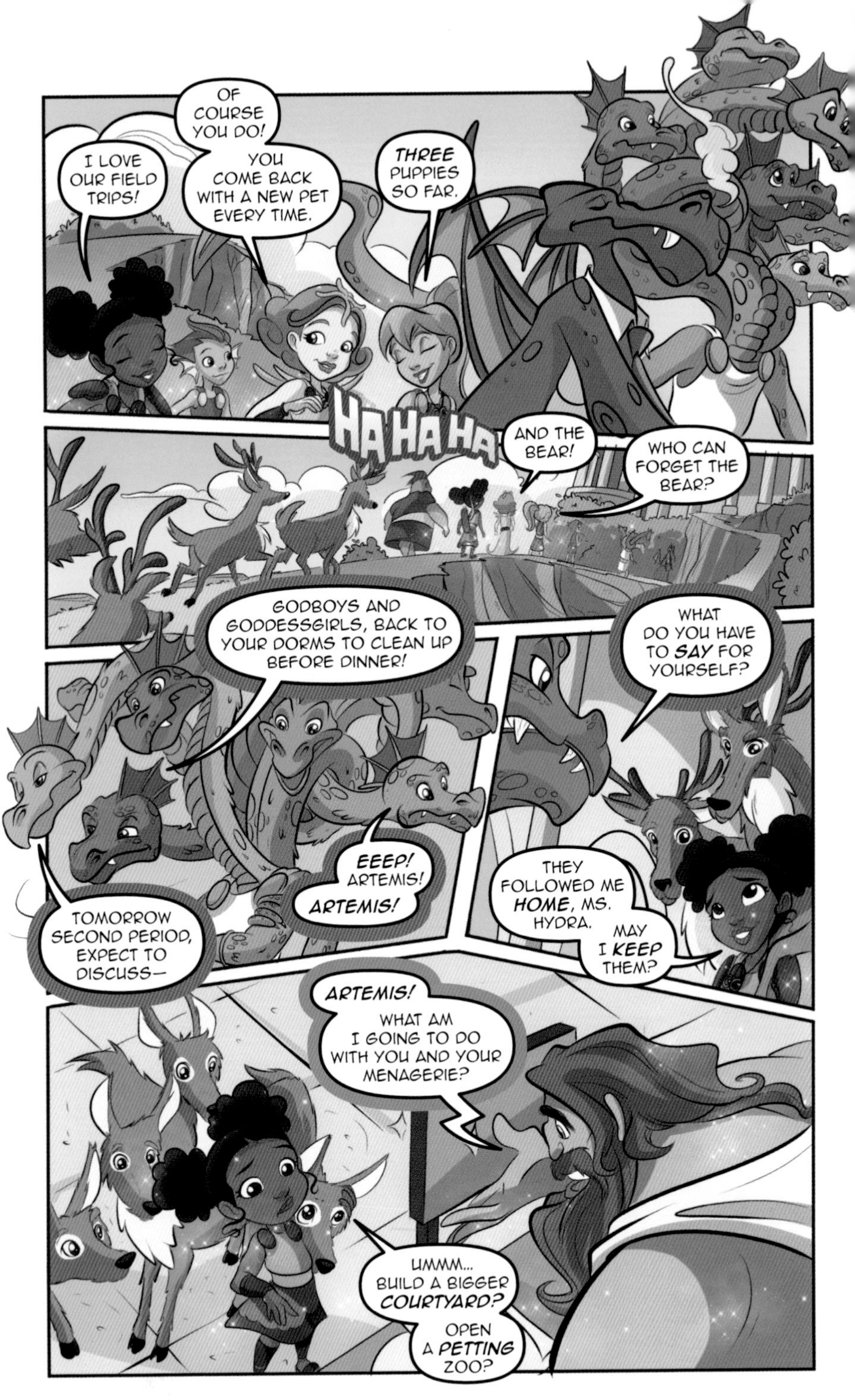
I LOVE OUR FIELD TRIPS!
OF COURSE YOU DO!
YOU COME BACK WITH A NEW PET EVERY TIME.
THREE PUPPIES SO FAR.
HA HA HA
AND THE BEAR!
WHO CAN FORGET THE BEAR?
GODBOYS AND GODDESSGIRLS, BACK TO YOUR DORMS TO CLEAN UP BEFORE DINNER!
EEEP! ARTEMIS!
ARTEMIS!
TOMORROW SECOND PERIOD, EXPECT TO DISCUSS—
WHAT DO YOU HAVE TO SAY FOR YOURSELF?
THEY FOLLOWED ME HOME, MS. HYDRA.
MAY I KEEP THEM?
ARTEMIS!
WHAT AM I GOING TO DO WITH YOU AND YOUR MENAGERIE?
UMMM... BUILD A BIGGER COURTYARD?
OPEN A PETTING ZOO?

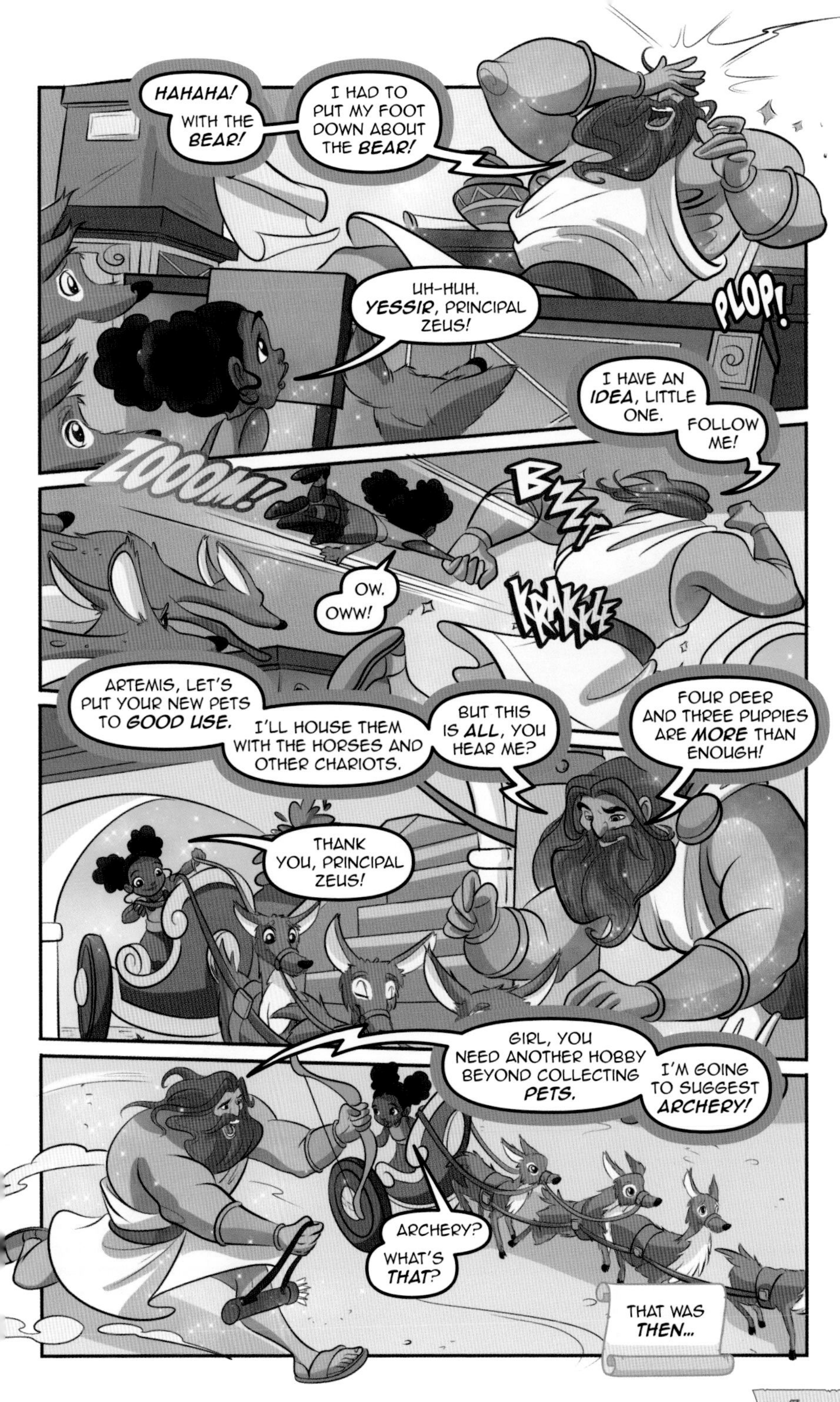
HAHAHA! WITH THE BEAR!
I HAD TO PUT MY FOOT DOWN ABOUT THE BEAR!
UH-HUH. YESSIR, PRINCIPAL ZEUS!
PLOP!
I HAVE AN IDEA, LITTLE ONE.
FOLLOW ME!
ZOOOM!
BZZT
OW. OWW!
KRAKKLE
ARTEMIS, LET'S PUT YOUR NEW PETS TO GOOD USE.
I'LL HOUSE THEM WITH THE HORSES AND OTHER CHARIOTS.
BUT THIS IS ALL, YOU HEAR ME?
FOUR DEER AND THREE PUPPIES ARE MORE THAN ENOUGH!
THANK YOU, PRINCIPAL ZEUS!
GIRL, YOU NEED ANOTHER HOBBY BEYOND COLLECTING PETS.
I'M GOING TO SUGGEST ARCHERY!
ARCHERY?
WHAT'S THAT?
THAT WAS THEN...

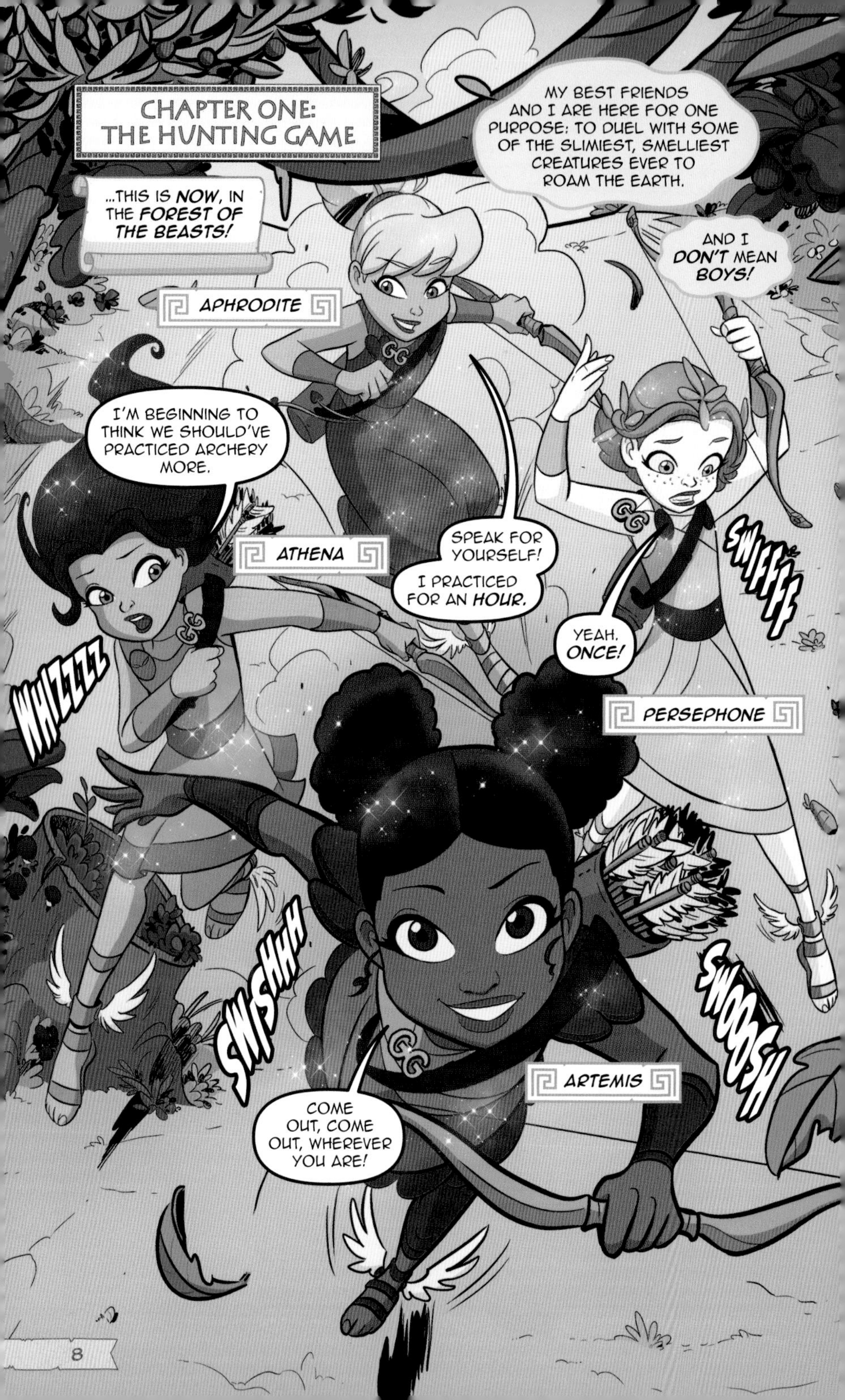
CHAPTER ONE:
THE HUNTING GAME
...THIS IS NOW, IN THE FOREST OF THE BEASTS!
MY BEST FRIENDS AND I ARE HERE FOR ONE PURPOSE: TO DUEL WITH SOME OF THE SLIMIEST, SMELLIEST CREATURES EVER TO ROAM THE EARTH.
AND I DON'T MEAN BOYS!
APHRODITE
I'M BEGINNING TO THINK WE SHOULD'VE PRACTICED ARCHERY MORE.
ATHENA
SPEAK FOR YOURSELF!
I PRACTICED FOR AN HOUR.
YEAH. ONCE!
SWISSSS
WHIZZZZZ
PERSEPHONE
SWISHHH
SWOOOSH
ARTEMIS
COME OUT, COME OUT, WHEREVER YOU ARE!

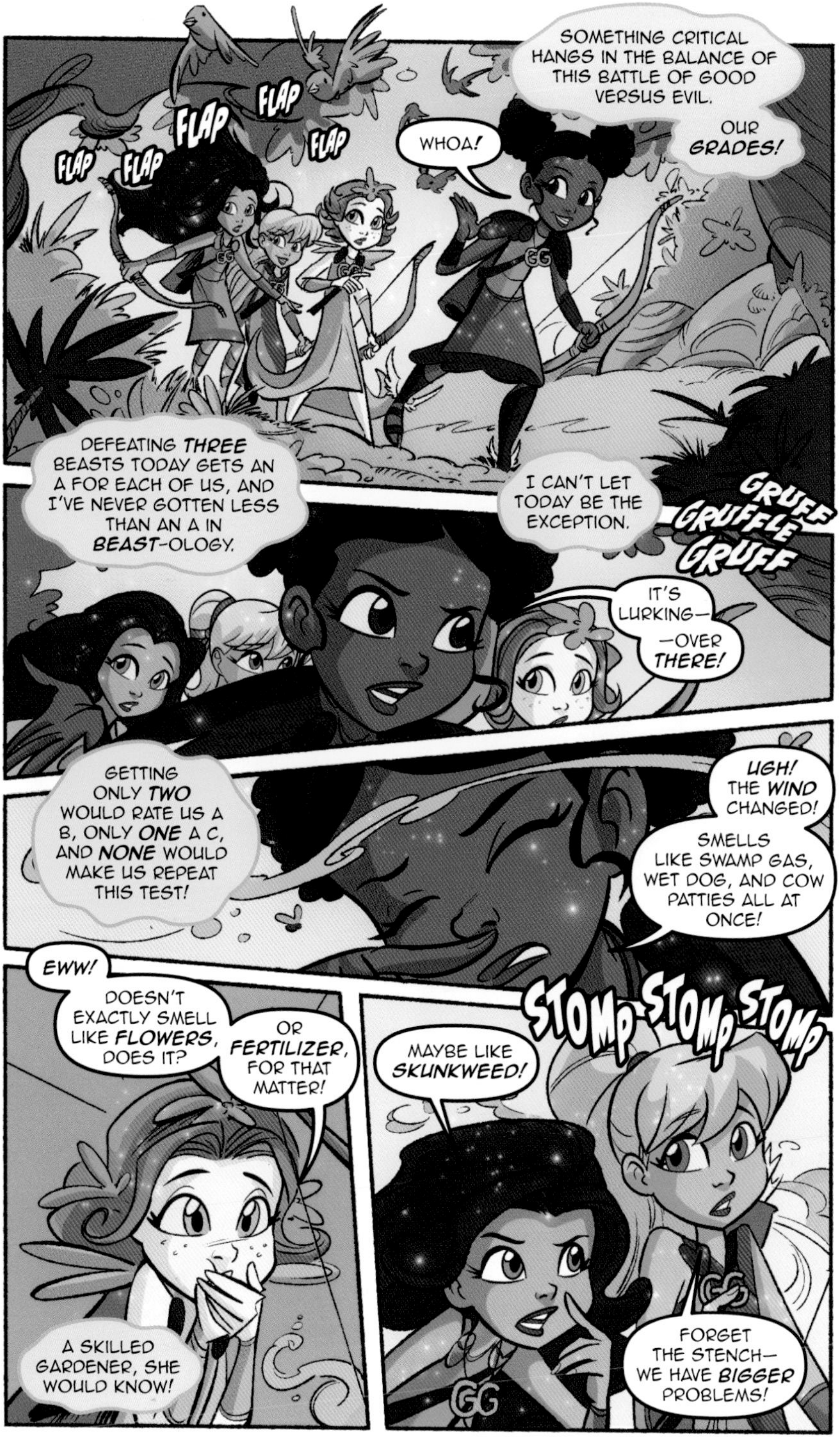
SOMETHING CRITICAL HANGS IN THE BALANCE OF THIS BATTLE OF GOOD VERSUS EVIL.
OUR GRADES!
FLAP FLAP FLAP FLAP FLAP
WHOA!
DEFEATING THREE BEASTS TODAY GETS AN A FOR EACH OF US, AND I'VE NEVER GOTTEN LESS THAN AN A IN BEAST-OLOGY.
I CAN'T LET TODAY BE THE EXCEPTION.
GRUFF GRUFFLE GRUFF
IT'S LURKING—
—OVER THERE!
GETTING ONLY TWO WOULD RATE US A B, ONLY ONE A C, AND NONE WOULD MAKE US REPEAT THIS TEST!
UGH! THE WIND CHANGED!
SMELLS LIKE SWAMP GAS, WET DOG, AND COW PATTIES ALL AT ONCE!
EWW!
DOESN'T EXACTLY SMELL LIKE FLOWERS, DOES IT?
OR FERTILIZER, FOR THAT MATTER!
A SKILLED GARDENER, SHE WOULD KNOW!
STOMP STOMP STOMP
MAYBE LIKE SKUNKWEED!
FORGET THE STENCH— WE HAVE BIGGER PROBLEMS!

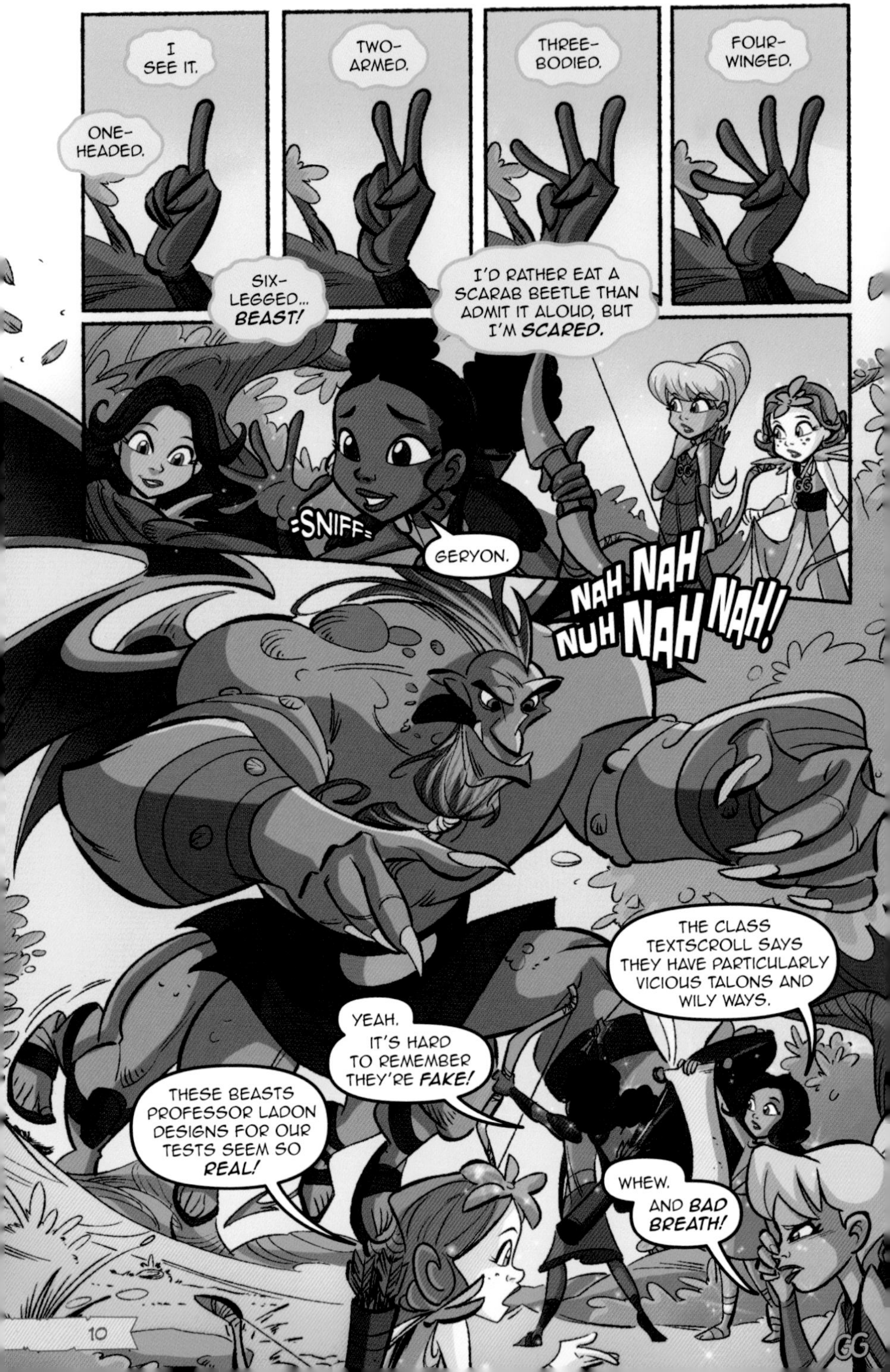
I SEE IT.
ONE-HEADED.
TWO-ARMED.
THREE-BODIED.
FOUR-WINGED.
SIX-LEGGED... BEAST!
I'D RATHER EAT A SCARAB BEETLE THAN ADMIT IT ALOUD, BUT I'M SCARED.
=SNIFF=
GERYON.
NAH NAH NUH NAH NAH!
THE CLASS TEXTSCROLL SAYS THEY HAVE PARTICULARLY VICIOUS TALONS AND WILY WAYS.
YEAH.
IT'S HARD TO REMEMBER THEY'RE FAKE!
THESE BEASTS PROFESSOR LADON DESIGNS FOR OUR TESTS SEEM SO REAL!
WHEW.
AND BAD BREATH!

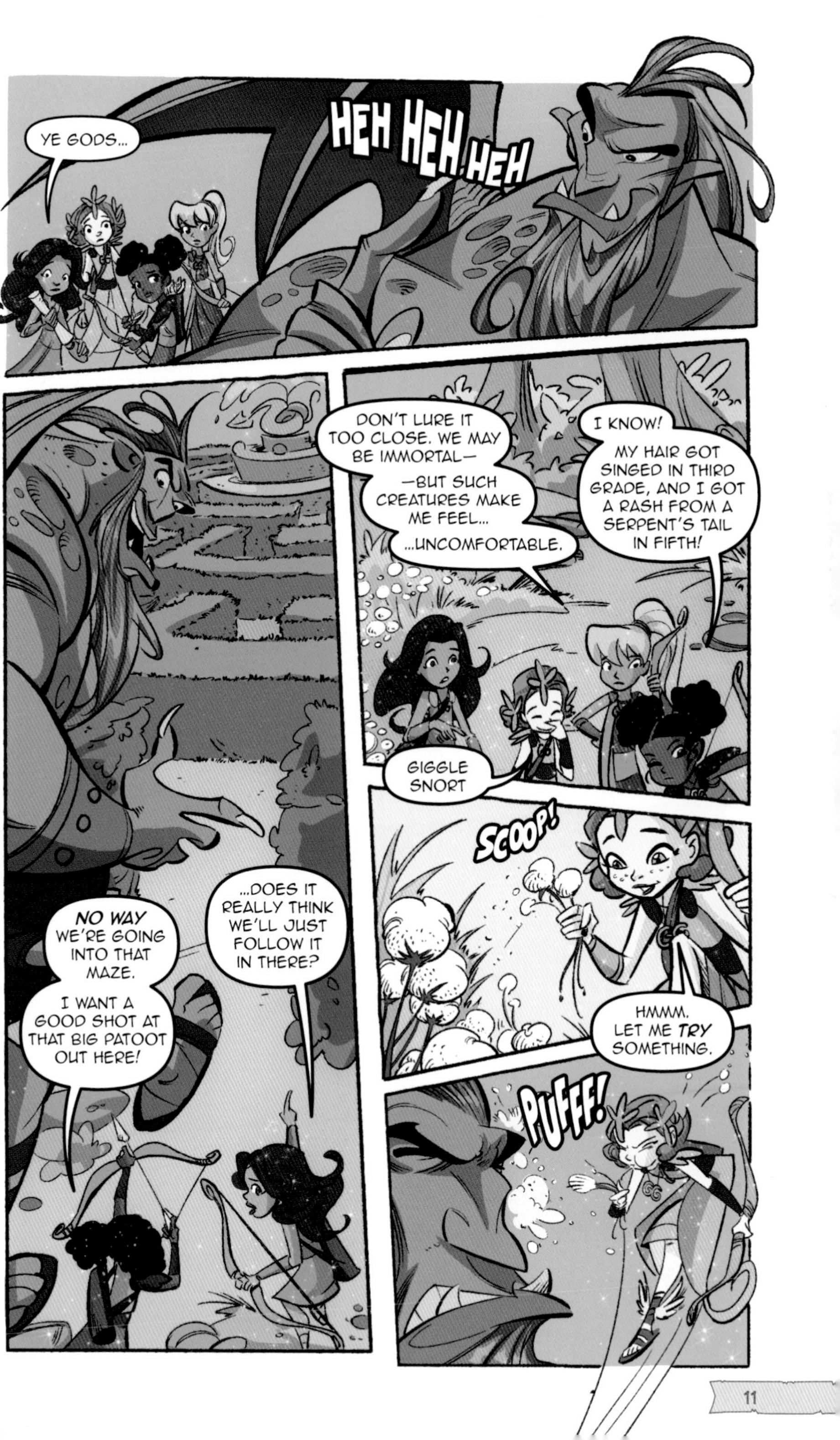
YE GODS...
HEH HEH HEH
NO WAY WE'RE GOING INTO THAT MAZE.
I WANT A GOOD SHOT AT THAT BIG PATOOT OUT HERE!
...DOES IT REALLY THINK WE'LL JUST FOLLOW IT IN THERE?
DON'T LURE IT TOO CLOSE. WE MAY BE IMMORTAL—
—BUT SUCH CREATURES MAKE ME FEEL...
...UNCOMFORTABLE.
I KNOW!
MY HAIR GOT SINGED IN THIRD GRADE, AND I GOT A RASH FROM A SERPENT'S TAIL IN FIFTH!
GIGGLE SNORT
SCOOP!
HMMM. LET ME TRY SOMETHING.
PUFFF!

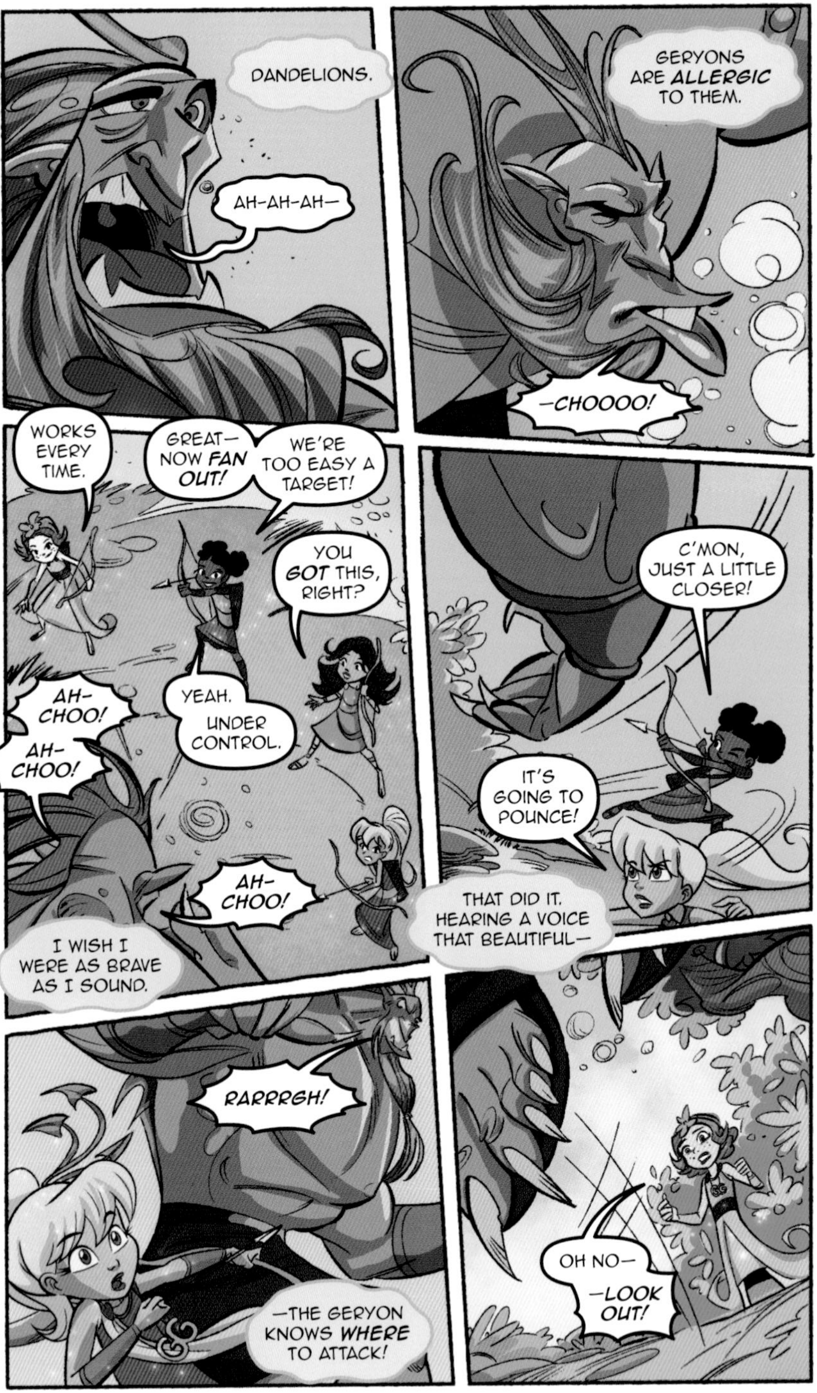
DANDELIONS.
AH-AH-AH—
GERYONS ARE ALLERGIC TO THEM.
—CHOOOO!
WORKS EVERY TIME.
GREAT— NOW FAN OUT!
WE'RE TOO EASY A TARGET!
YOU GOT THIS, RIGHT?
YEAH.
UNDER CONTROL.
AH-CHOO!
AH-CHOO!
AH-CHOO!
I WISH I WERE AS BRAVE AS I SOUND.
C'MON, JUST A LITTLE CLOSER!
IT'S GOING TO POUNCE!
THAT DID IT. HEARING A VOICE THAT BEAUTIFUL—
RARRRGH!
—THE GERYON KNOWS WHERE TO ATTACK!
OH NO—
—LOOK OUT!

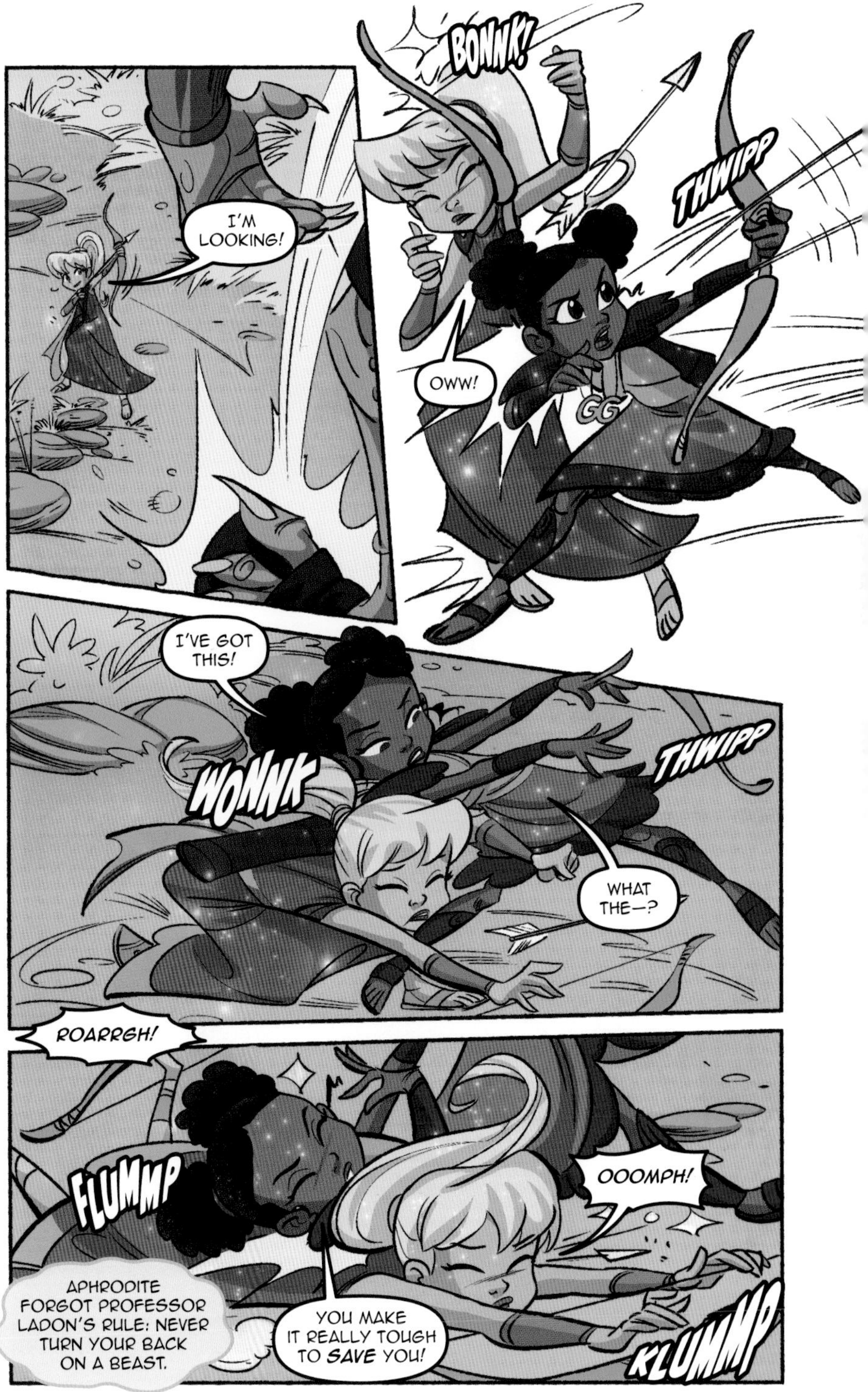
BONNK!
I'M LOOKING!
THWIPP
OWW!
I'VE GOT THIS!
WONNK
THWIPP
WHAT THE—?
ROARRGH!
FLUMMP
OOOMPH!
APHRODITE FORGOT PROFESSOR LADON'S RULE: NEVER TURN YOUR BACK ON A BEAST.
YOU MAKE IT REALLY TOUGH TO ***SAVE*** YOU!
KLUMMP

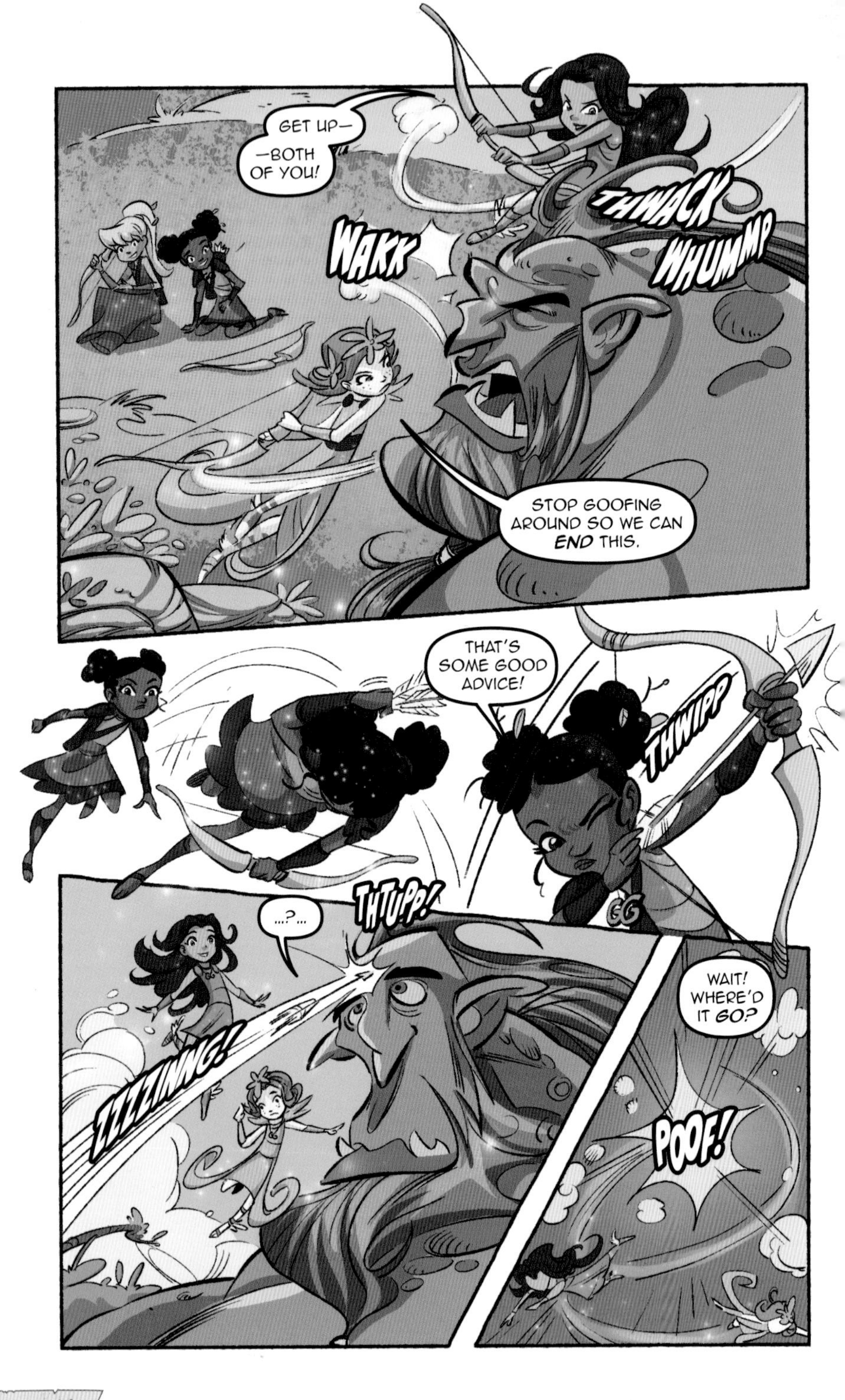
GET UP—
—BOTH OF YOU!
THWACK
WHUMMP
WAKK
STOP GOOFING AROUND SO WE CAN END THIS.
THAT'S SOME GOOD ADVICE!
THWIPP
GG
THTUPP!
...?...
ZZZZINNG!
WAIT! WHERE'D IT GO?
POOF!

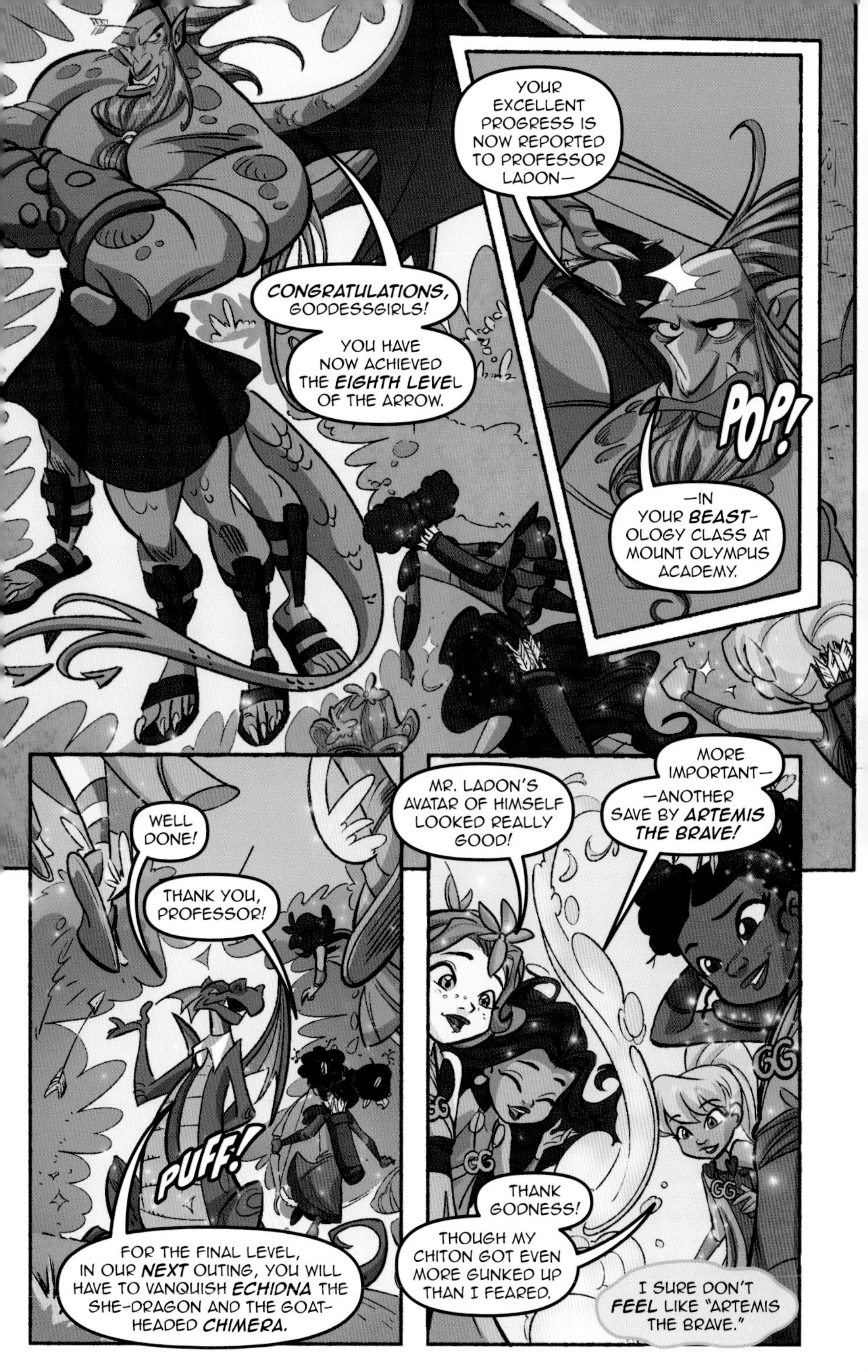

CONGRATULATIONS, GODDESSGIRLS!
YOU HAVE NOW ACHIEVED THE EIGHTH LEVEL OF THE ARROW.
YOUR EXCELLENT PROGRESS IS NOW REPORTED TO PROFESSOR LADON—
POP!
—IN YOUR BEAST-OLOGY CLASS AT MOUNT OLYMPUS ACADEMY.
WELL DONE!
THANK YOU, PROFESSOR!
PUFF!
FOR THE FINAL LEVEL, IN OUR NEXT OUTING, YOU WILL HAVE TO VANQUISH ECHIDNA THE SHE-DRAGON AND THE GOAT-HEADED CHIMERA.
MR. LADON'S AVATAR OF HIMSELF LOOKED REALLY GOOD!
MORE IMPORTANT—
—ANOTHER SAVE BY ARTEMIS THE BRAVE!
THANK GODNESS!
THOUGH MY CHITON GOT EVEN MORE GUNKED UP THAN I FEARED.
I SURE DON'T FEEL LIKE "ARTEMIS THE BRAVE."

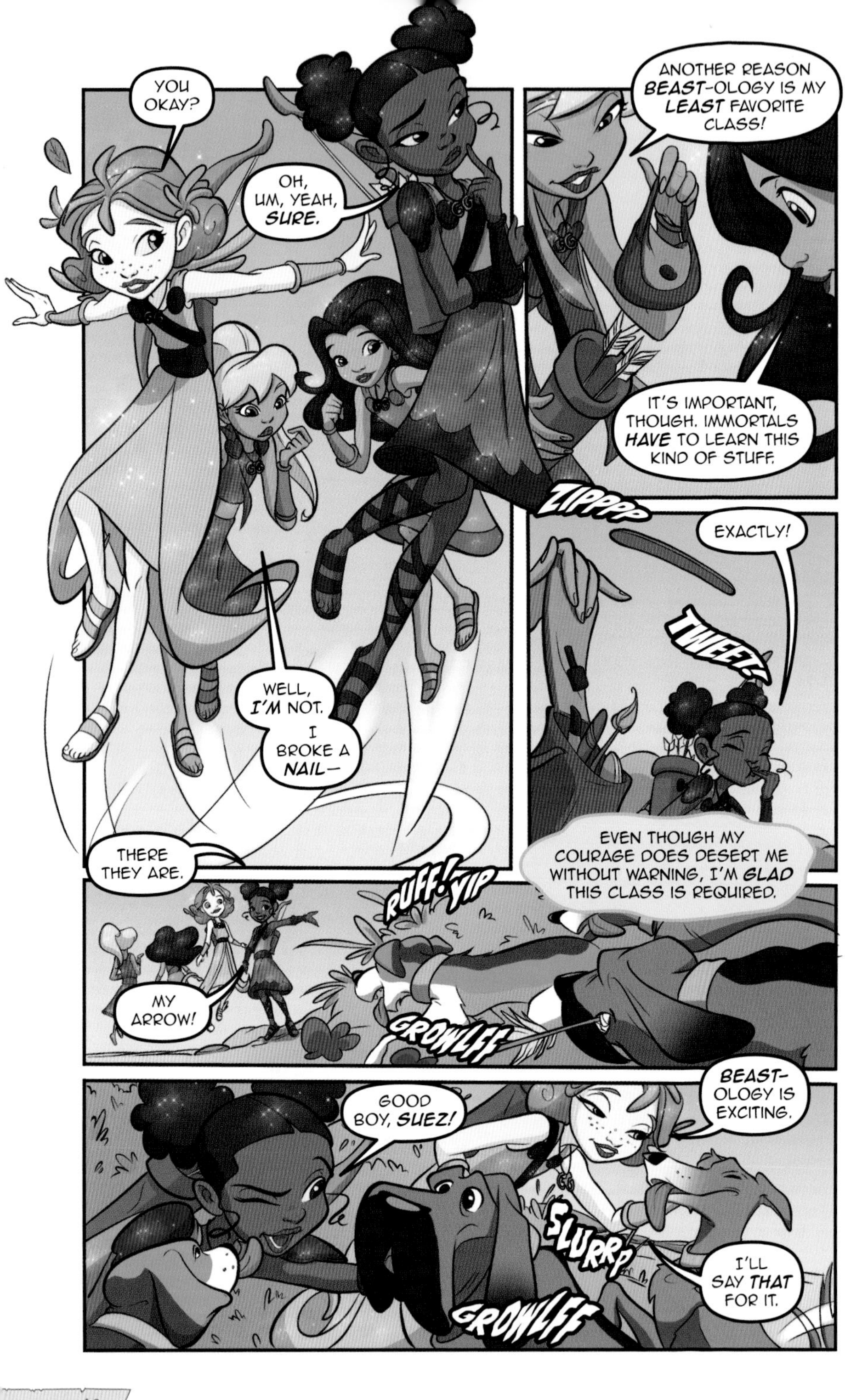

YOU OKAY?
OH, UM, YEAH, SURE.
WELL, I'M NOT.
I BROKE A NAIL—
ANOTHER REASON BEAST-OLOGY IS MY LEAST FAVORITE CLASS!
IT'S IMPORTANT, THOUGH. IMMORTALS HAVE TO LEARN THIS KIND OF STUFF.
ZIPPPP
EXACTLY!
TWEET!
EVEN THOUGH MY COURAGE DOES DESERT ME WITHOUT WARNING, I'M GLAD THIS CLASS IS REQUIRED.
THERE THEY ARE.
RUFF! YIP
MY ARROW!
GROWLFF
GOOD BOY, SUEZ!
BEAST-OLOGY IS EXCITING.
SLURRP
I'LL SAY THAT FOR IT.
GROWLFF

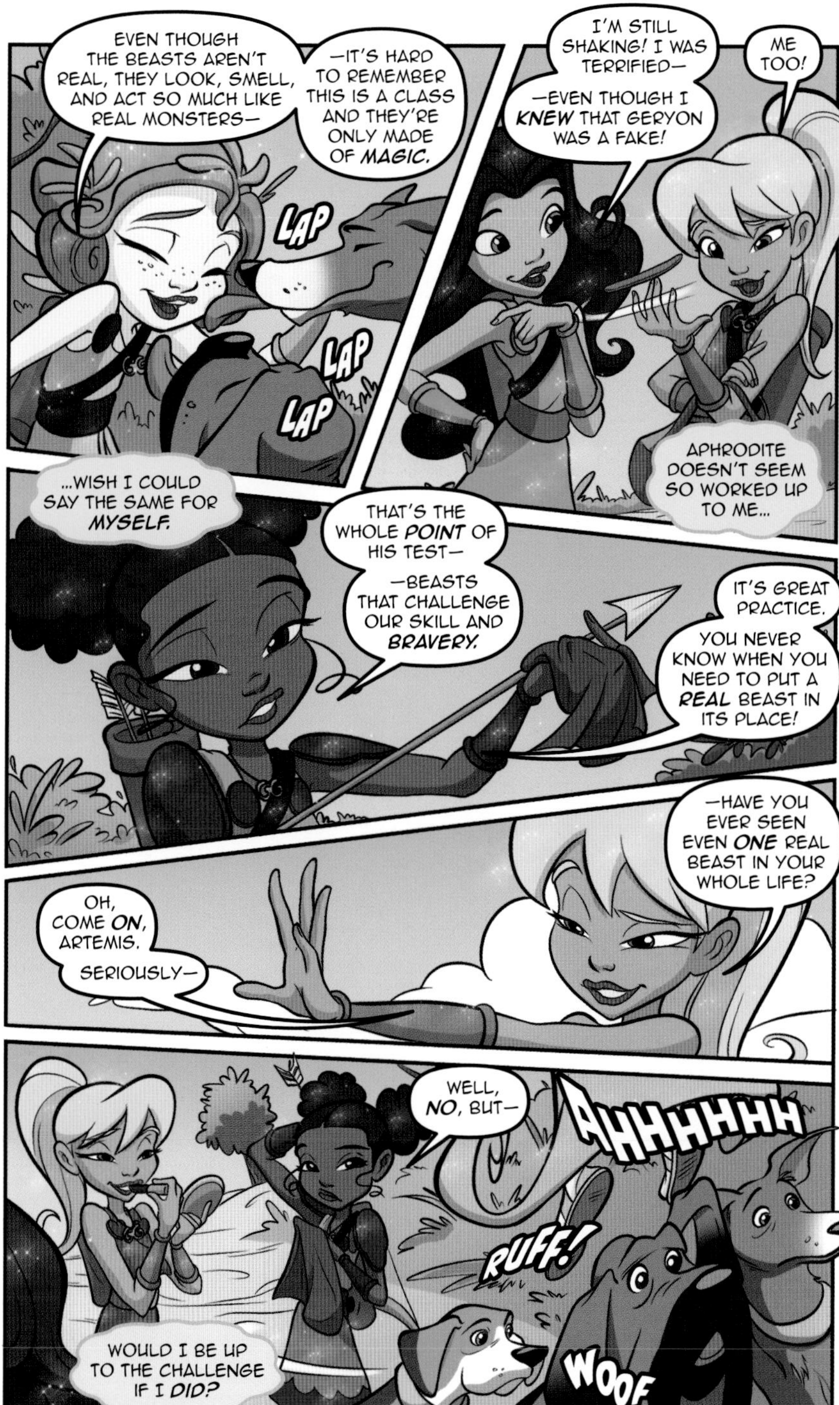
EVEN THOUGH THE BEASTS AREN'T REAL, THEY LOOK, SMELL, AND ACT SO MUCH LIKE REAL MONSTERS—
—IT'S HARD TO REMEMBER THIS IS A CLASS AND THEY'RE ONLY MADE OF MAGIC.
LAP
LAP
LAP
I'M STILL SHAKING! I WAS TERRIFIED—
—EVEN THOUGH I KNEW THAT GERYON WAS A FAKE!
ME TOO!
APHRODITE DOESN'T SEEM SO WORKED UP TO ME...
...WISH I COULD SAY THE SAME FOR MYSELF.
THAT'S THE WHOLE POINT OF HIS TEST—
—BEASTS THAT CHALLENGE OUR SKILL AND BRAVERY.
IT'S GREAT PRACTICE.
YOU NEVER KNOW WHEN YOU NEED TO PUT A REAL BEAST IN ITS PLACE!
OH, COME ON, ARTEMIS.
SERIOUSLY—
—HAVE YOU EVER SEEN EVEN ONE REAL BEAST IN YOUR WHOLE LIFE?
WELL, NO, BUT—
AHHHHHH
RUFF!
WOULD I BE UP TO THE CHALLENGE IF I DID?
WOOF

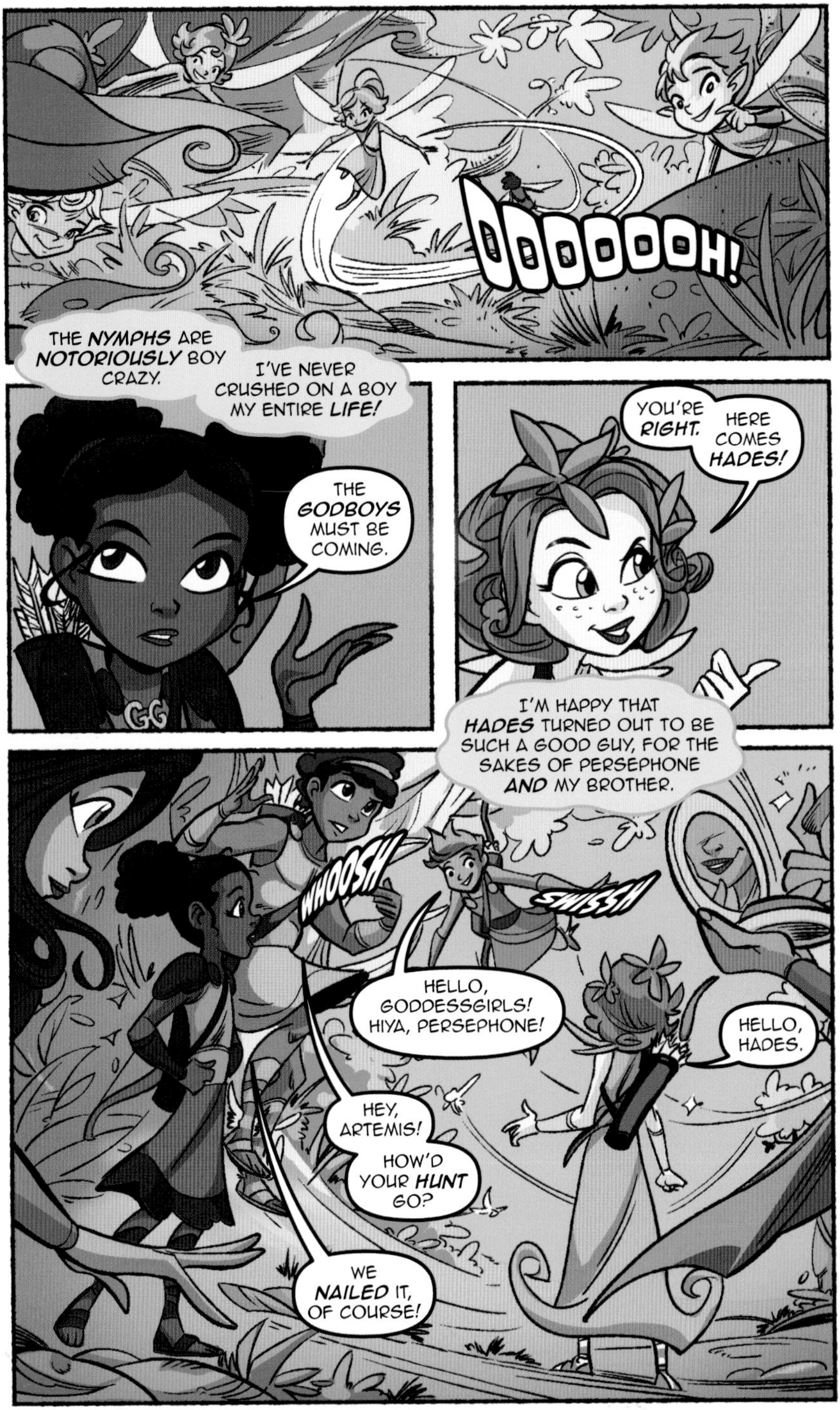
OOOOOOOH!
THE NYMPHS ARE NOTORIOUSLY BOY CRAZY.
I'VE NEVER CRUSHED ON A BOY MY ENTIRE LIFE!
THE GODBOYS MUST BE COMING.
YOU'RE RIGHT.
HERE COMES HADES!
I'M HAPPY THAT HADES TURNED OUT TO BE SUCH A GOOD GUY, FOR THE SAKES OF PERSEPHONE AND MY BROTHER.
WHOOSH
SWISSH
HELLO, GODDESSGIRLS! HIYA, PERSEPHONE!
HELLO, HADES.
HEY, ARTEMIS!
HOW'D YOUR HUNT GO?
WE NAILED IT, OF COURSE!

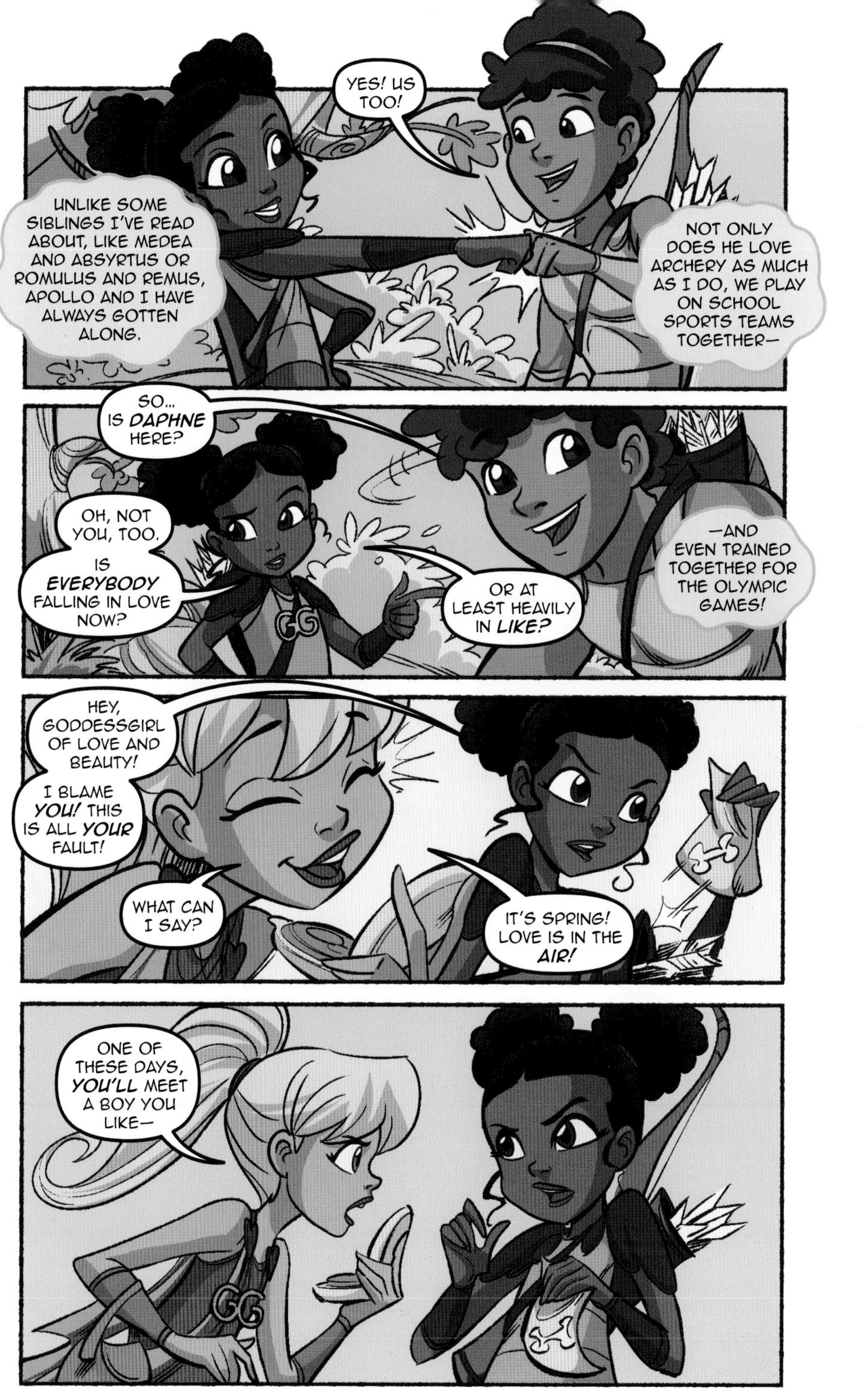
YES! US TOO!
UNLIKE SOME SIBLINGS I'VE READ ABOUT, LIKE MEDEA AND ABSYRTUS OR ROMULUS AND REMUS, APOLLO AND I HAVE ALWAYS GOTTEN ALONG.
NOT ONLY DOES HE LOVE ARCHERY AS MUCH AS I DO, WE PLAY ON SCHOOL SPORTS TEAMS TOGETHER—
SO... IS *DAPHNE* HERE?
OH, NOT YOU, TOO.
IS *EVERYBODY* FALLING IN LOVE NOW?
OR AT LEAST HEAVILY IN *LIKE?*
—AND EVEN TRAINED TOGETHER FOR THE OLYMPIC GAMES!
HEY, GODDESSGIRL OF LOVE AND BEAUTY!
I BLAME *YOU!* THIS IS ALL *YOUR* FAULT!
WHAT CAN I SAY?
IT'S SPRING! LOVE IS IN THE *AIR!*
ONE OF THESE DAYS, *YOU'LL* MEET A BOY YOU LIKE—

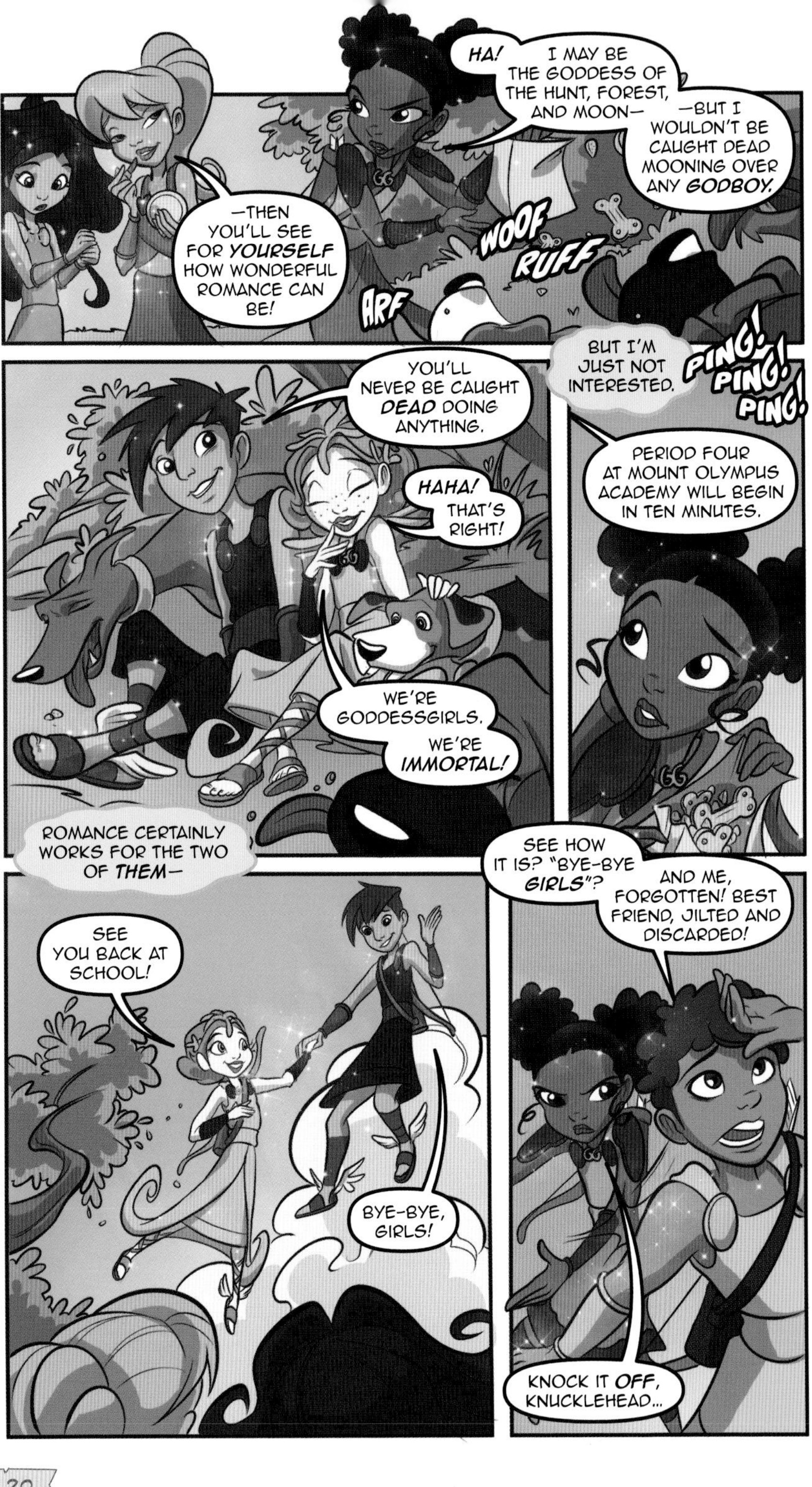

HA!
I MAY BE THE GODDESS OF THE HUNT, FOREST, AND MOON—
—BUT I WOULDN'T BE CAUGHT DEAD MOONING OVER ANY GODBOY.
—THEN YOU'LL SEE FOR YOURSELF HOW WONDERFUL ROMANCE CAN BE!
WOOF
RUFF
ARF
YOU'LL NEVER BE CAUGHT DEAD DOING ANYTHING.
HAHA! THAT'S RIGHT!
WE'RE GODDESSGIRLS.
WE'RE IMMORTAL!
BUT I'M JUST NOT INTERESTED.
PING! PING! PING!
PERIOD FOUR AT MOUNT OLYMPUS ACADEMY WILL BEGIN IN TEN MINUTES.
ROMANCE CERTAINLY WORKS FOR THE TWO OF THEM—
SEE YOU BACK AT SCHOOL!
BYE-BYE, GIRLS!
SEE HOW IT IS? "BYE-BYE GIRLS"?
AND ME, FORGOTTEN! BEST FRIEND, JILTED AND DISCARDED!
KNOCK IT OFF, KNUCKLEHEAD...

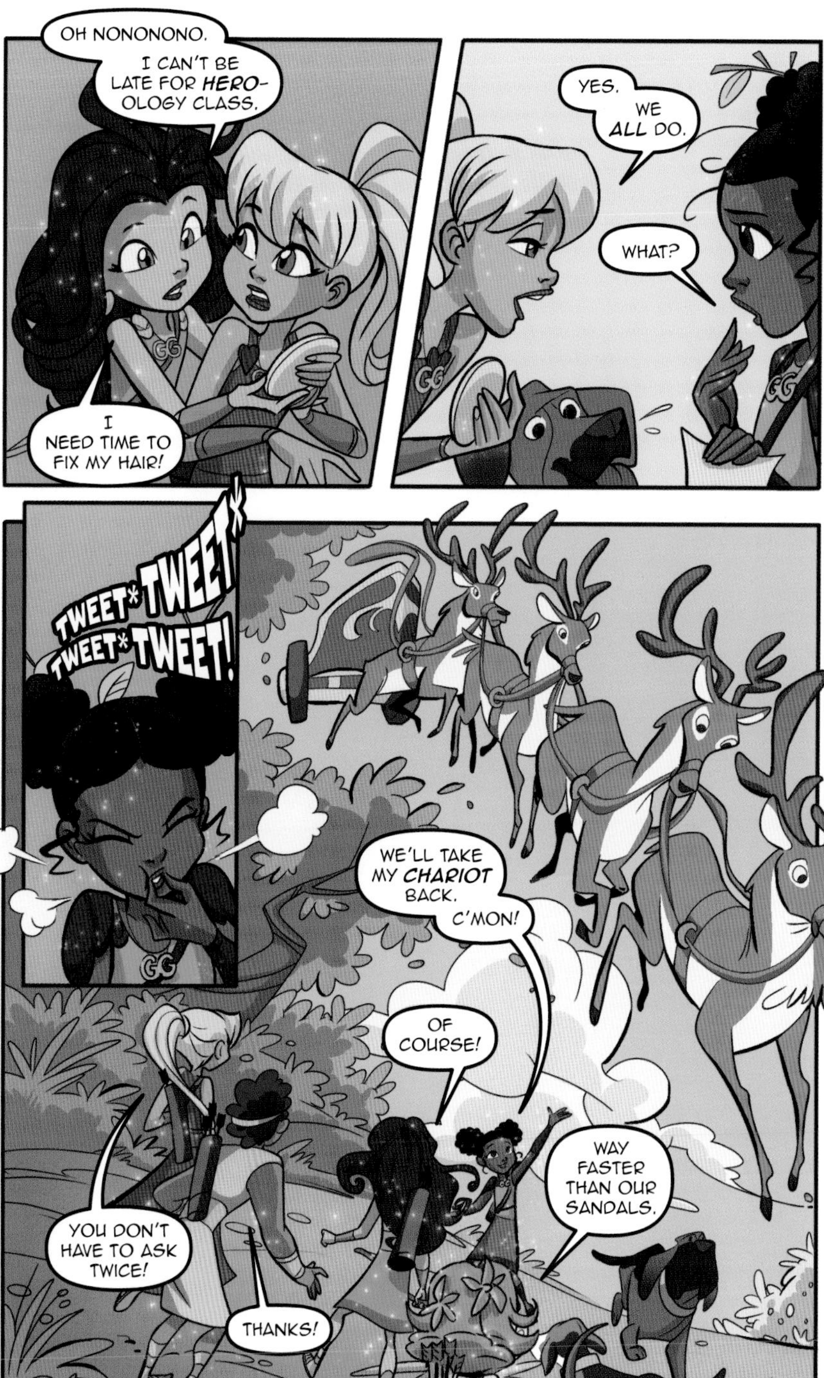
OH NONONONO.
I CAN'T BE LATE FOR HERO-OLOGY CLASS.
I NEED TIME TO FIX MY HAIR!
YES.
WE ALL DO.
WHAT?
TWEET* TWEET* TWEET* TWEET!
WE'LL TAKE MY CHARIOT BACK.
C'MON!
OF COURSE!
WAY FASTER THAN OUR SANDALS.
YOU DON'T HAVE TO ASK TWICE!
THANKS!

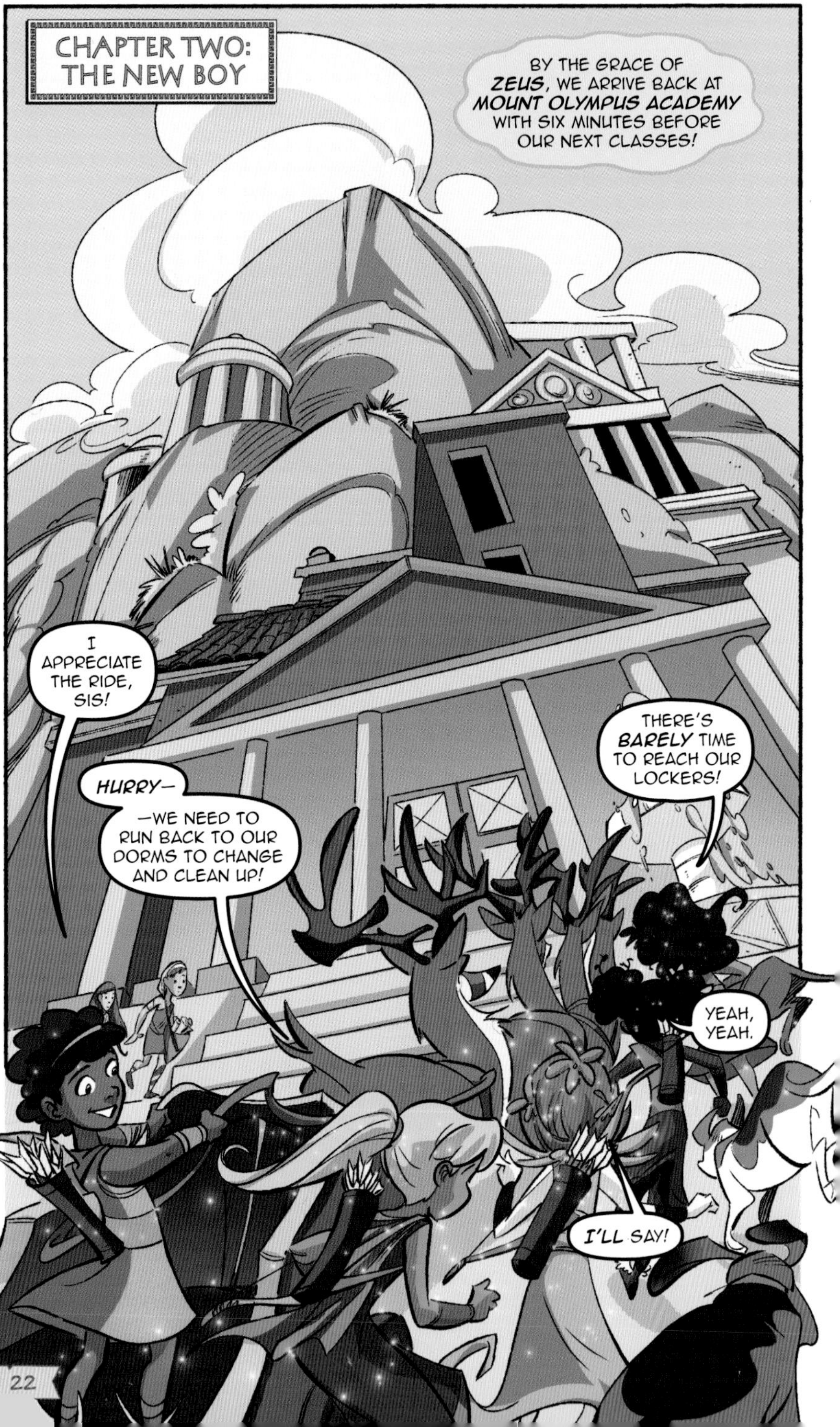

CHAPTER TWO: THE NEW BOY
BY THE GRACE OF ZEUS, WE ARRIVE BACK AT MOUNT OLYMPUS ACADEMY WITH SIX MINUTES BEFORE OUR NEXT CLASSES!
I APPRECIATE THE RIDE, SIS!
HURRY—
—WE NEED TO RUN BACK TO OUR DORMS TO CHANGE AND CLEAN UP!
THERE'S BARELY TIME TO REACH OUR LOCKERS!
YEAH, YEAH.
I'LL SAY!

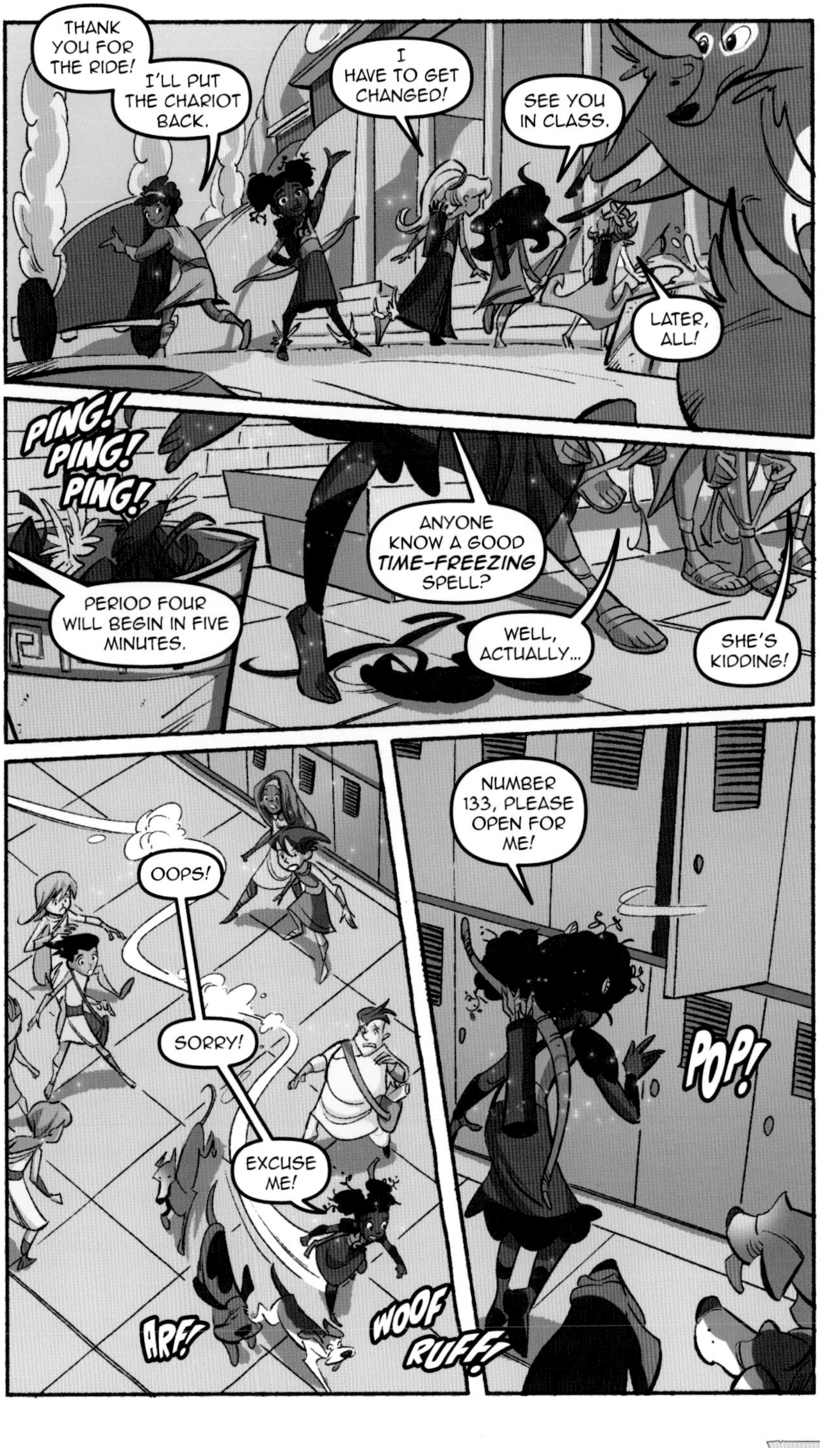
THANK YOU FOR THE RIDE!
I'LL PUT THE CHARIOT BACK.
I HAVE TO GET CHANGED!
SEE YOU IN CLASS.
LATER, ALL!
PING! PING! PING!
PERIOD FOUR WILL BEGIN IN FIVE MINUTES.
ANYONE KNOW A GOOD TIME-FREEZING SPELL?
WELL, ACTUALLY...
SHE'S KIDDING!
OOPS!
SORRY!
EXCUSE ME!
ARF!
WOOF
RUFF!
NUMBER 133, PLEASE OPEN FOR ME!
POP!

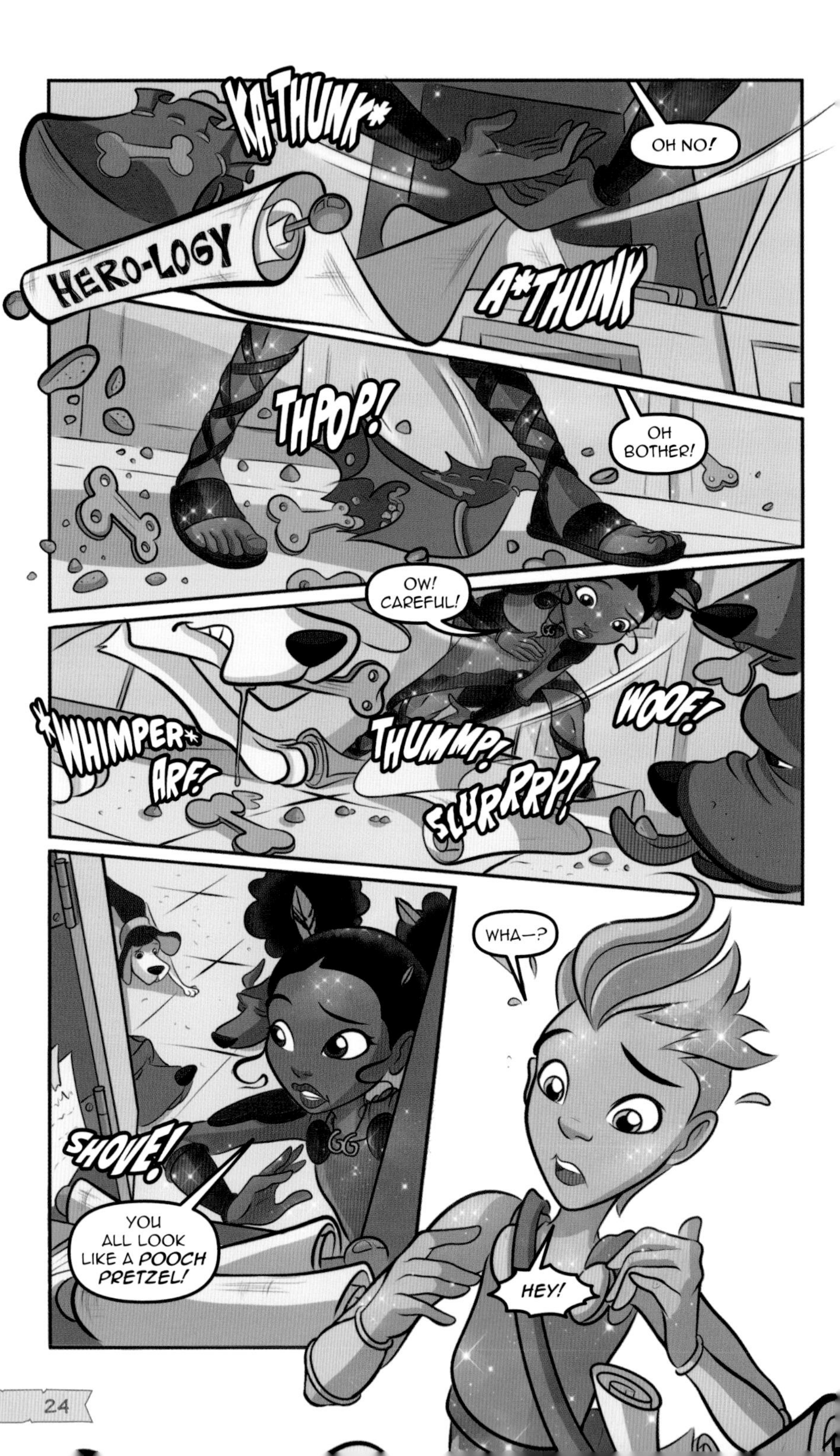
KA-THUNK*
OH NO!
HERO-LOGY
A*THUNK
THPOP!
OH BOTHER!
OW! CAREFUL!
WHIMPER
ARF!
THUMMP!
WOOF!
SLURRRP!
WHA—?
SHOVE!
YOU ALL LOOK LIKE A POOCH PRETZEL!
HEY!

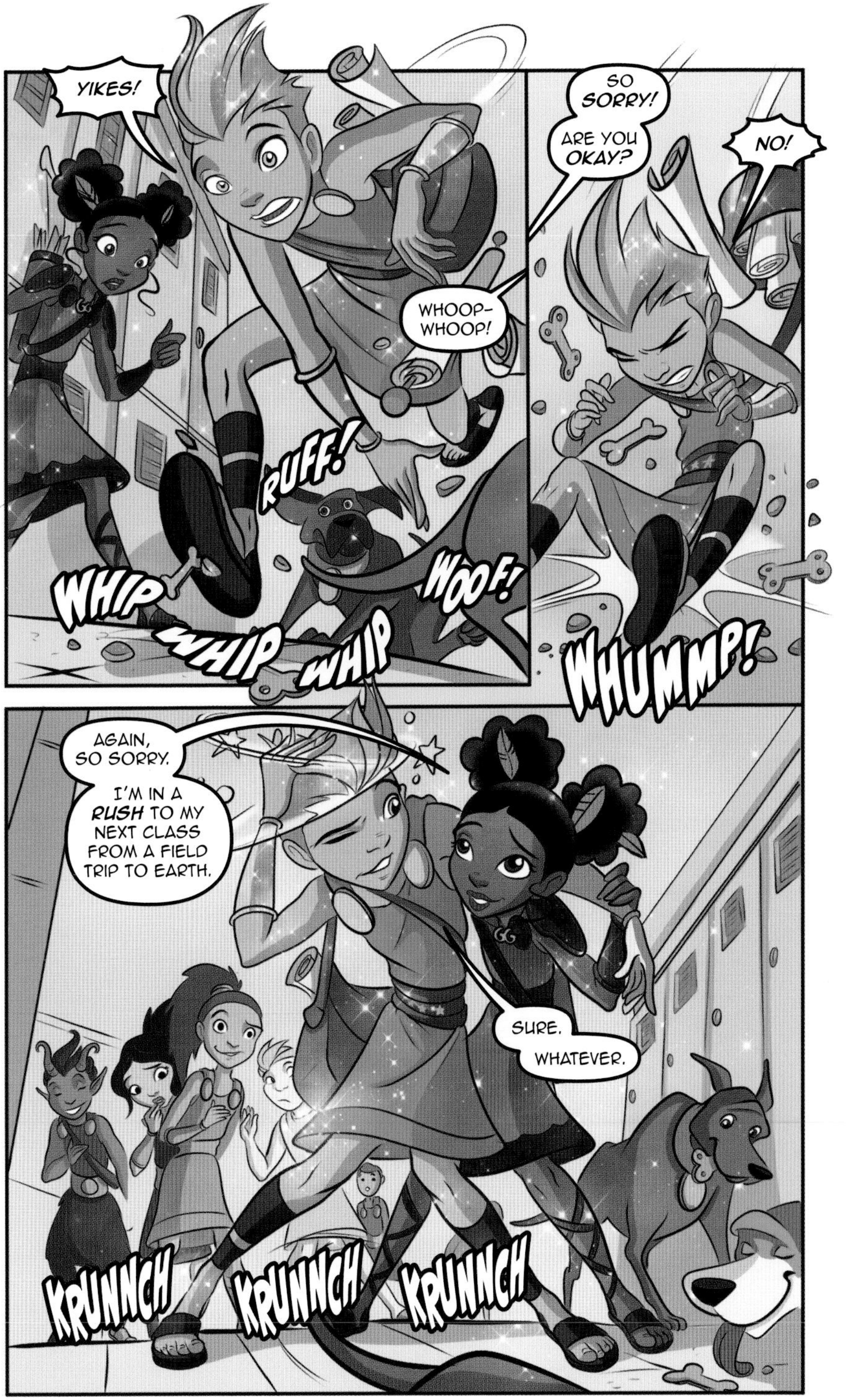
YIKES!
WHOOP-WHOOP!
RUFF!
WHIP
WHIP
WHIP
WOOF!
SO SORRY!
ARE YOU OKAY?
NO!
WHUMMP!
AGAIN, SO SORRY.
I'M IN A RUSH TO MY NEXT CLASS FROM A FIELD TRIP TO EARTH.
SURE.
WHATEVER.
KRUNNCH
KRUNNCH
KRUNNCH

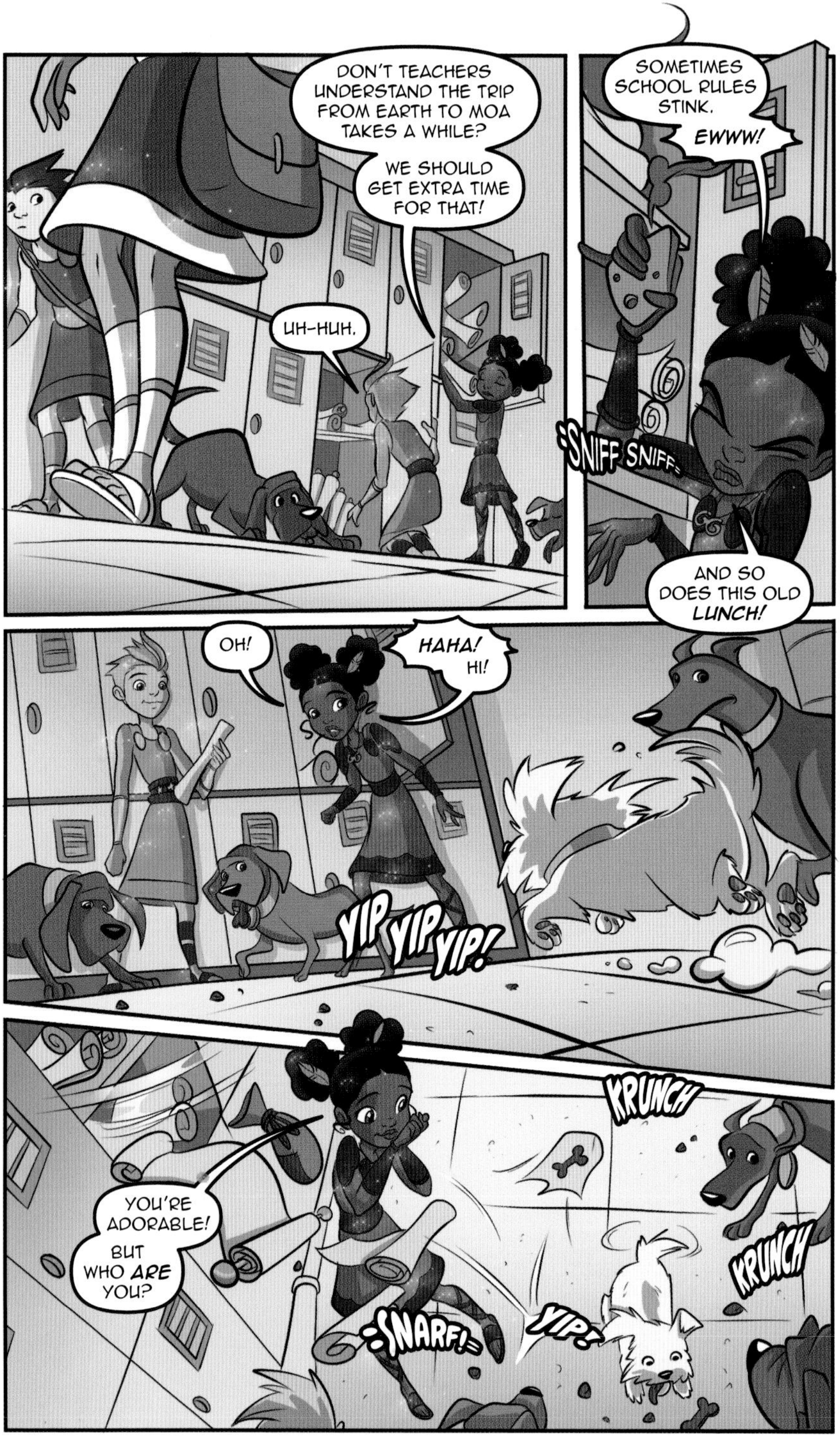
DON'T TEACHERS UNDERSTAND THE TRIP FROM EARTH TO MOA TAKES A WHILE?
WE SHOULD GET EXTRA TIME FOR THAT!
UH-HUH.
SOMETIMES SCHOOL RULES STINK.
EWWW!
SNIFF SNIFF
AND SO DOES THIS OLD LUNCH!
OH!
HAHA! HI!
YIP YIP YIP!
KRUNCH
KRUNCH
YOU'RE ADORABLE!
BUT WHO ARE YOU?
SNARF!
YIP!

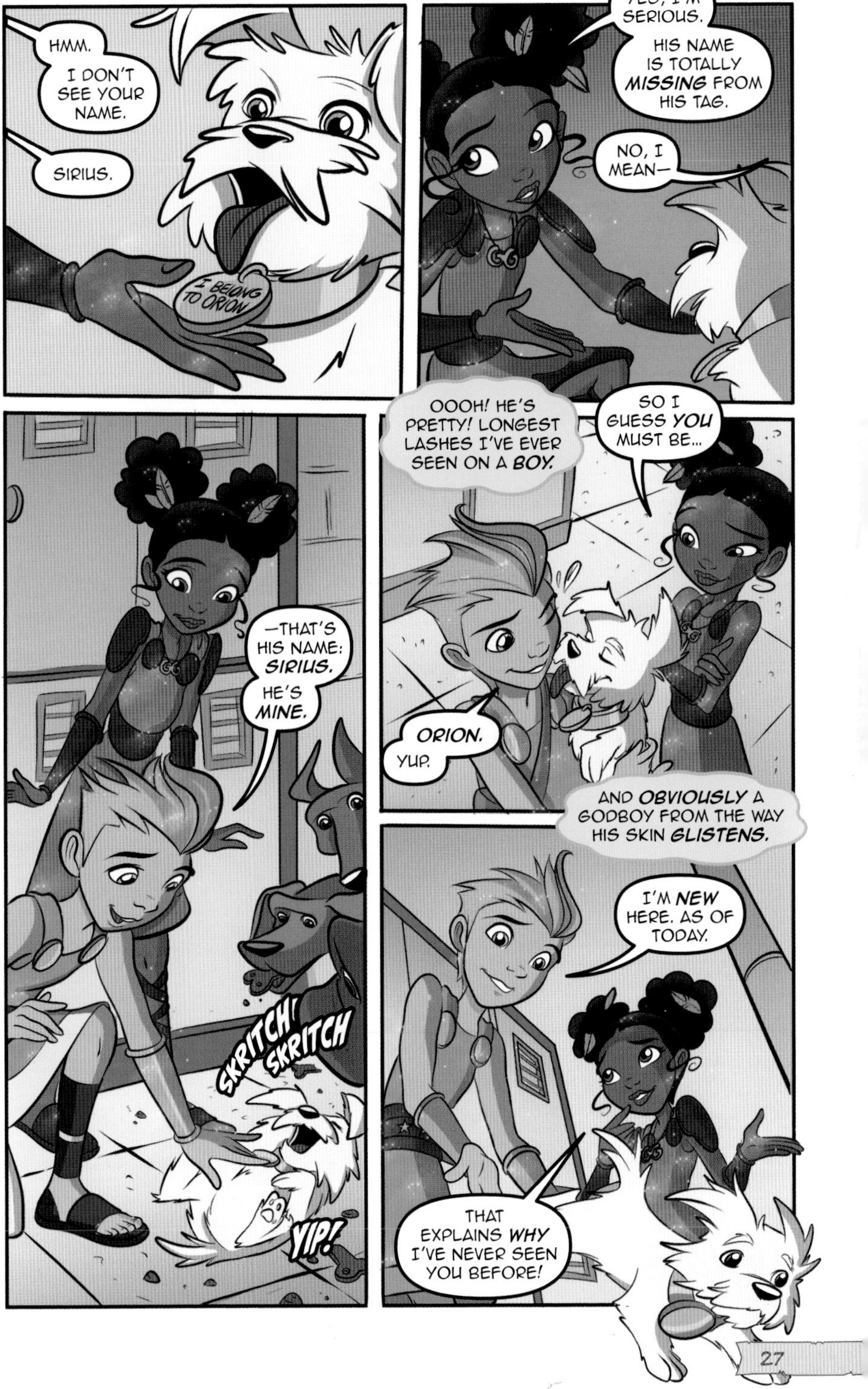
HMM.
I DON'T SEE YOUR NAME.
SIRIUS.
I BELONG TO ORION
YES, I'M SERIOUS.
HIS NAME IS TOTALLY MISSING FROM HIS TAG.
NO, I MEAN—
—THAT'S HIS NAME: SIRIUS.
HE'S MINE.
SKRITCH! SKRITCH
YIP!
OOOH! HE'S PRETTY! LONGEST LASHES I'VE EVER SEEN ON A BOY.
SO I GUESS YOU MUST BE...
ORION.
YUP.
AND OBVIOUSLY A GODBOY FROM THE WAY HIS SKIN GLISTENS.
I'M NEW HERE. AS OF TODAY.
THAT EXPLAINS WHY I'VE NEVER SEEN YOU BEFORE!

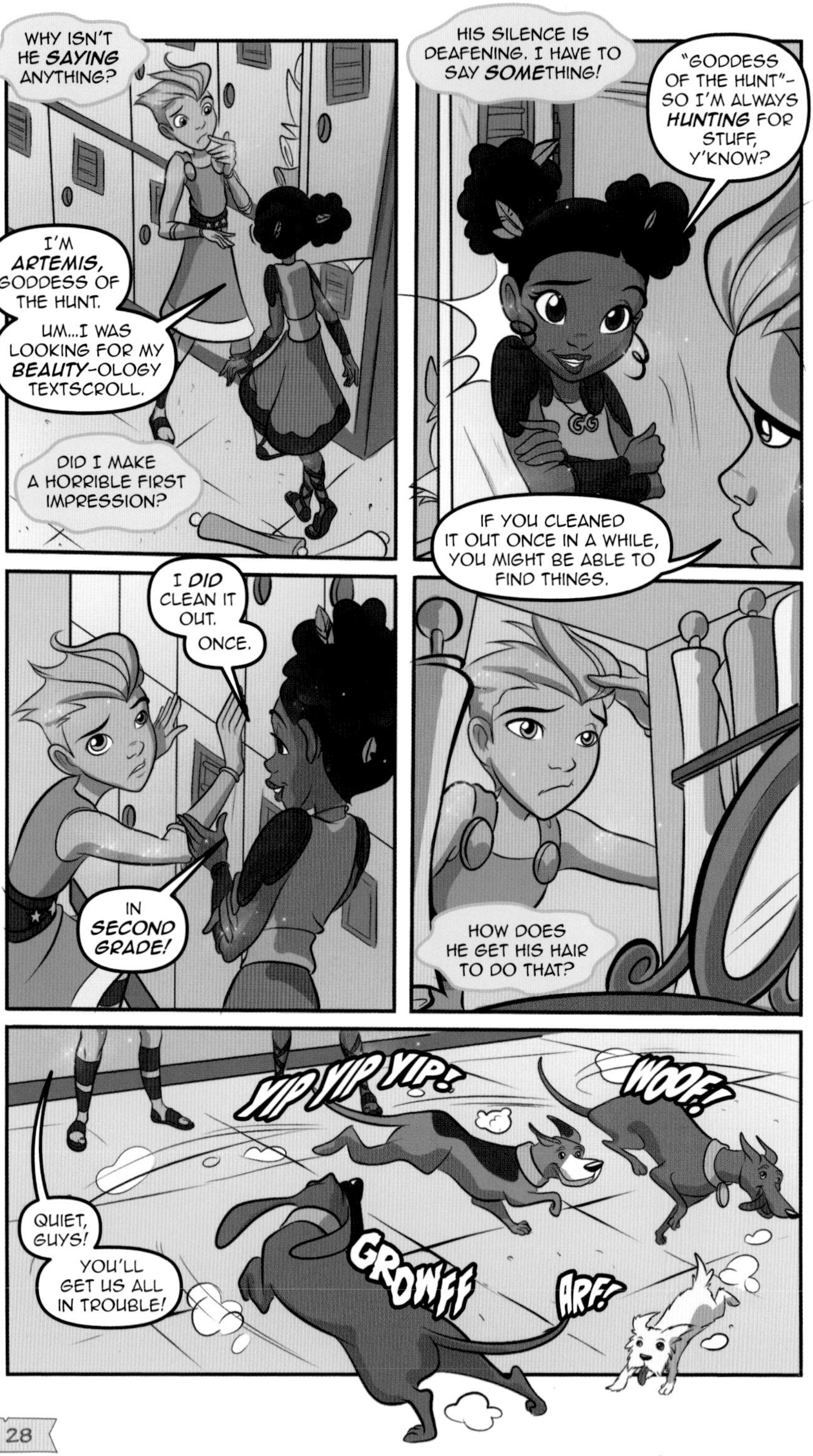

WHY ISN'T HE SAYING ANYTHING?
I'M ARTEMIS, GODDESS OF THE HUNT.
UM...I WAS LOOKING FOR MY BEAUTY-OLOGY TEXTSCROLL.
DID I MAKE A HORRIBLE FIRST IMPRESSION?
HIS SILENCE IS DEAFENING. I HAVE TO SAY SOMETHING!
"GODDESS OF THE HUNT"- SO I'M ALWAYS HUNTING FOR STUFF, Y'KNOW?
IF YOU CLEANED IT OUT ONCE IN A WHILE, YOU MIGHT BE ABLE TO FIND THINGS.
I DID CLEAN IT OUT.
ONCE.
IN SECOND GRADE!
HOW DOES HE GET HIS HAIR TO DO THAT?
YIP YIP YIP!
WOOF!
QUIET, GUYS!
YOU'LL GET US ALL IN TROUBLE!
GROWFF
ARF!

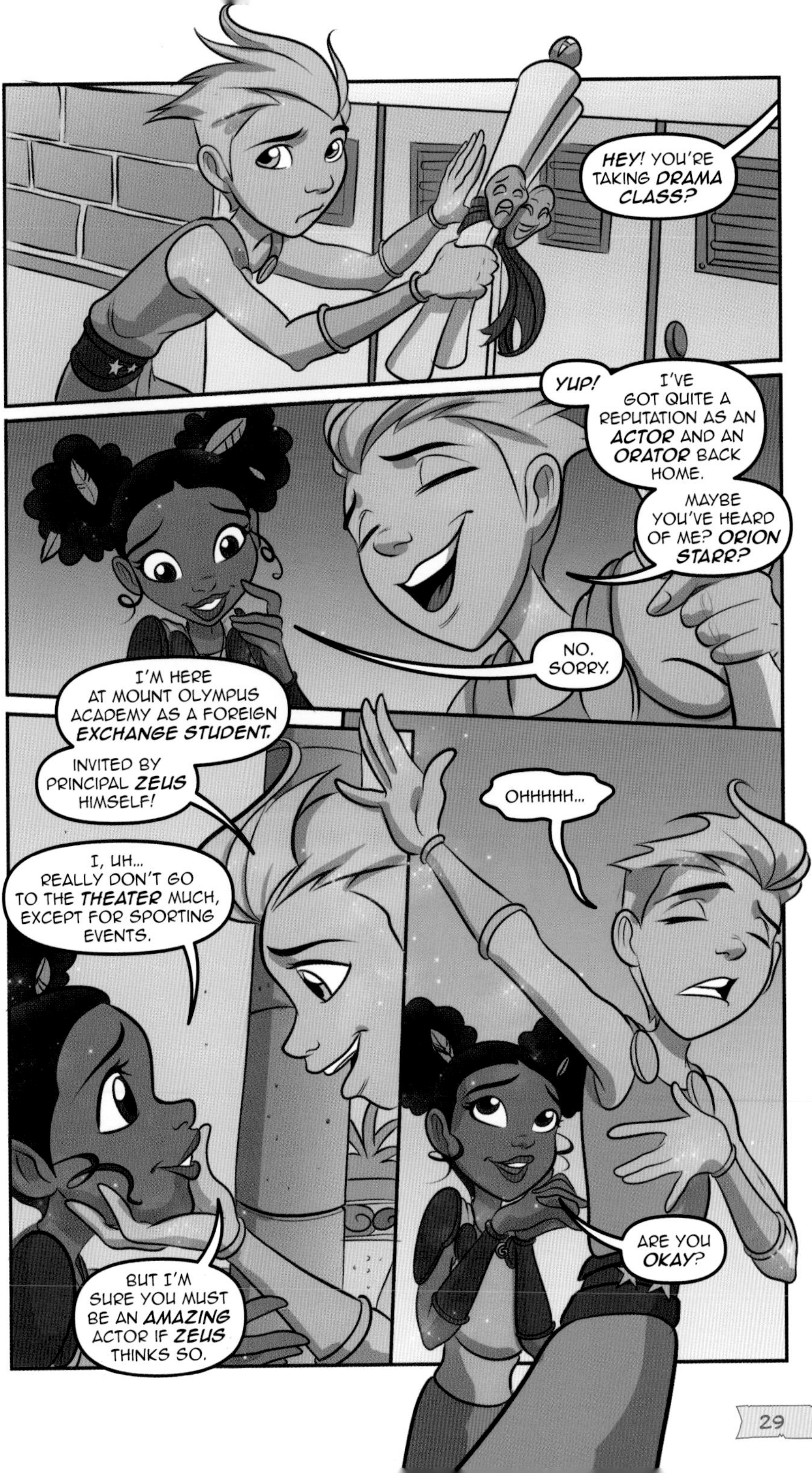
HEY! YOU'RE TAKING DRAMA CLASS?
YUP!
I'VE GOT QUITE A REPUTATION AS AN ACTOR AND AN ORATOR BACK HOME.
MAYBE YOU'VE HEARD OF ME? ORION STARR?
NO. SORRY.
I'M HERE AT MOUNT OLYMPUS ACADEMY AS A FOREIGN EXCHANGE STUDENT.
INVITED BY PRINCIPAL ZEUS HIMSELF!
I, UH... REALLY DON'T GO TO THE THEATER MUCH, EXCEPT FOR SPORTING EVENTS.
BUT I'M SURE YOU MUST BE AN AMAZING ACTOR IF ZEUS THINKS SO.
OHHHHH...
ARE YOU OKAY?

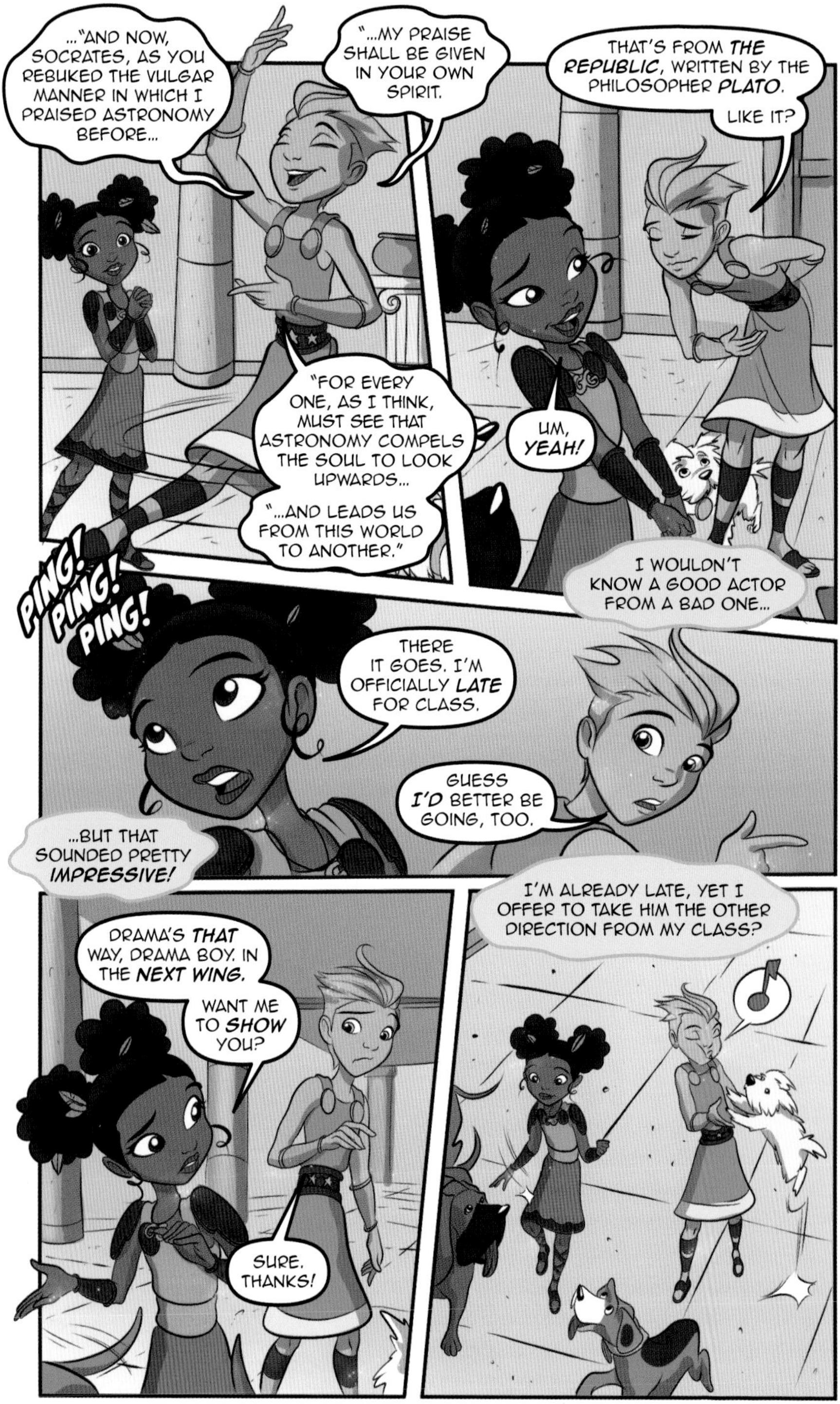
..."AND NOW, SOCRATES, AS YOU REBUKED THE VULGAR MANNER IN WHICH I PRAISED ASTRONOMY BEFORE...
"...MY PRAISE SHALL BE GIVEN IN YOUR OWN SPIRIT.
"FOR EVERY ONE, AS I THINK, MUST SEE THAT ASTRONOMY COMPELS THE SOUL TO LOOK UPWARDS...
"...AND LEADS US FROM THIS WORLD TO ANOTHER."
THAT'S FROM *THE REPUBLIC*, WRITTEN BY THE PHILOSOPHER *PLATO*.
LIKE IT?
UM, *YEAH!*
PING! PING! PING!
I WOULDN'T KNOW A GOOD ACTOR FROM A BAD ONE...
THERE IT GOES. I'M OFFICIALLY *LATE* FOR CLASS.
GUESS *I'D* BETTER BE GOING, TOO.
...BUT THAT SOUNDED PRETTY *IMPRESSIVE!*
DRAMA'S *THAT* WAY, DRAMA BOY. IN THE *NEXT WING.*
WANT ME TO *SHOW* YOU?
SURE. THANKS!
I'M ALREADY LATE, YET I OFFER TO TAKE HIM THE OTHER DIRECTION FROM MY CLASS?

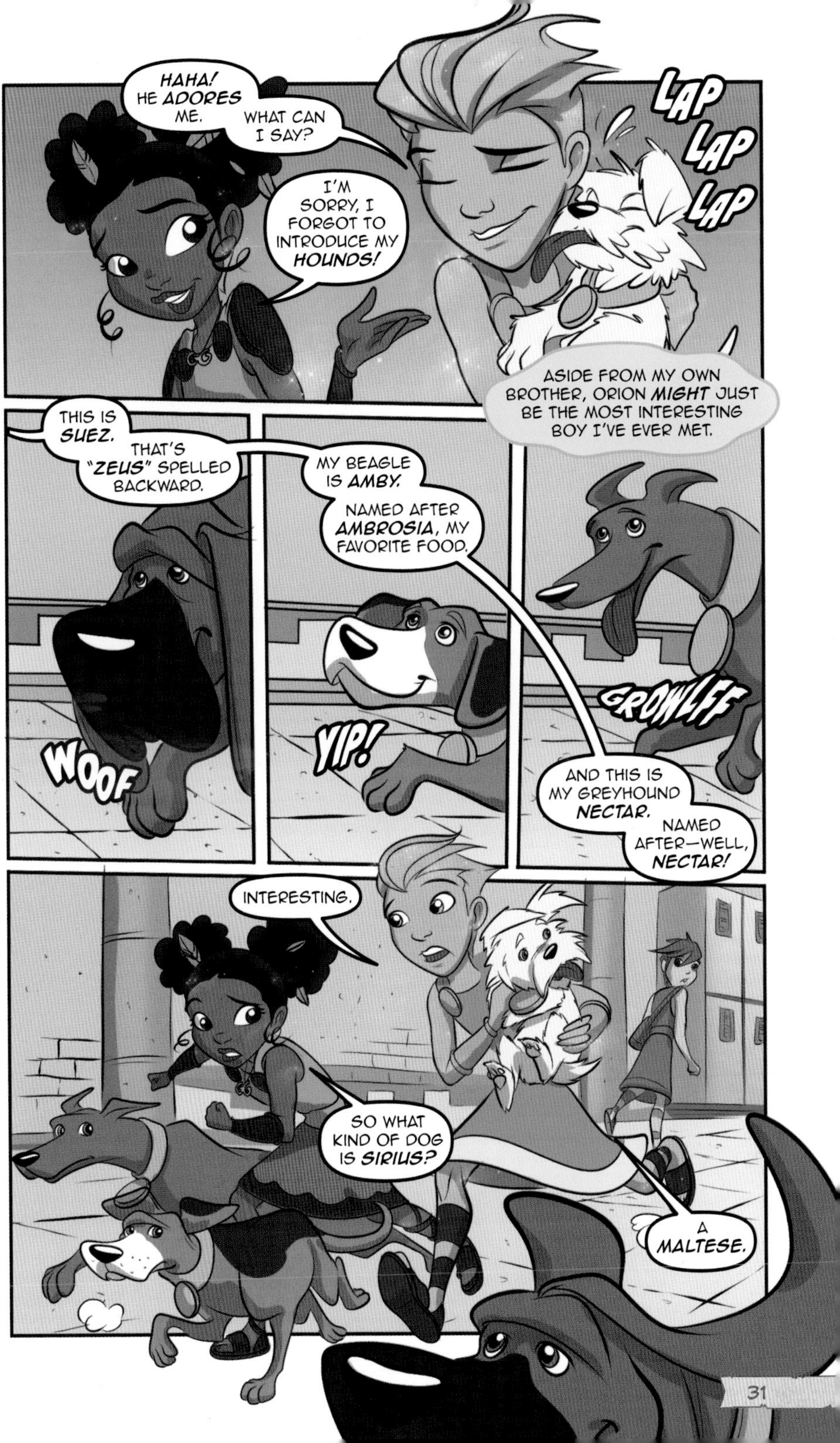

HAHA! HE ADORES ME.
WHAT CAN I SAY?
LAP LAP LAP
I'M SORRY, I FORGOT TO INTRODUCE MY HOUNDS!
ASIDE FROM MY OWN BROTHER, ORION MIGHT JUST BE THE MOST INTERESTING BOY I'VE EVER MET.
THIS IS SUEZ.
THAT'S "ZEUS" SPELLED BACKWARD.
WOOF
MY BEAGLE IS AMBY.
NAMED AFTER AMBROSIA, MY FAVORITE FOOD.
YIP!
GROWLFF
AND THIS IS MY GREYHOUND NECTAR.
NAMED AFTER—WELL, NECTAR!
INTERESTING.
SO WHAT KIND OF DOG IS SIRIUS?
A MALTESE.

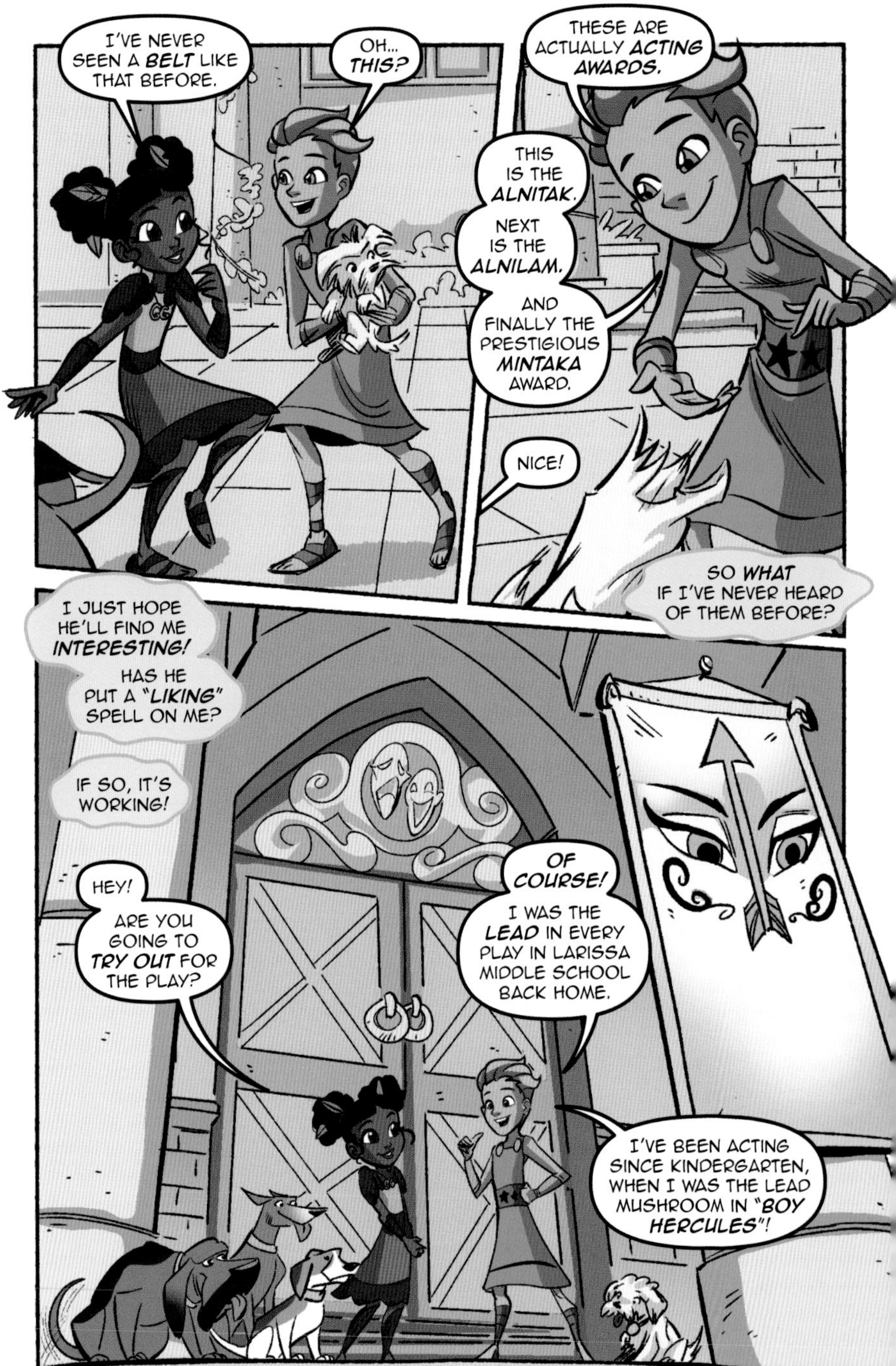
I'VE NEVER SEEN A BELT LIKE THAT BEFORE.
OH... THIS?
THESE ARE ACTUALLY ACTING AWARDS.
THIS IS THE ALNITAK.
NEXT IS THE ALNILAM.
AND FINALLY THE PRESTIGIOUS MINTAKA AWARD.
NICE!
SO WHAT IF I'VE NEVER HEARD OF THEM BEFORE?
I JUST HOPE HE'LL FIND ME INTERESTING!
HAS HE PUT A "LIKING" SPELL ON ME?
IF SO, IT'S WORKING!
HEY!
ARE YOU GOING TO TRY OUT FOR THE PLAY?
OF COURSE!
I WAS THE LEAD IN EVERY PLAY IN LARISSA MIDDLE SCHOOL BACK HOME.
I'VE BEEN ACTING SINCE KINDERGARTEN, WHEN I WAS THE LEAD MUSHROOM IN "BOY HERCULES"!

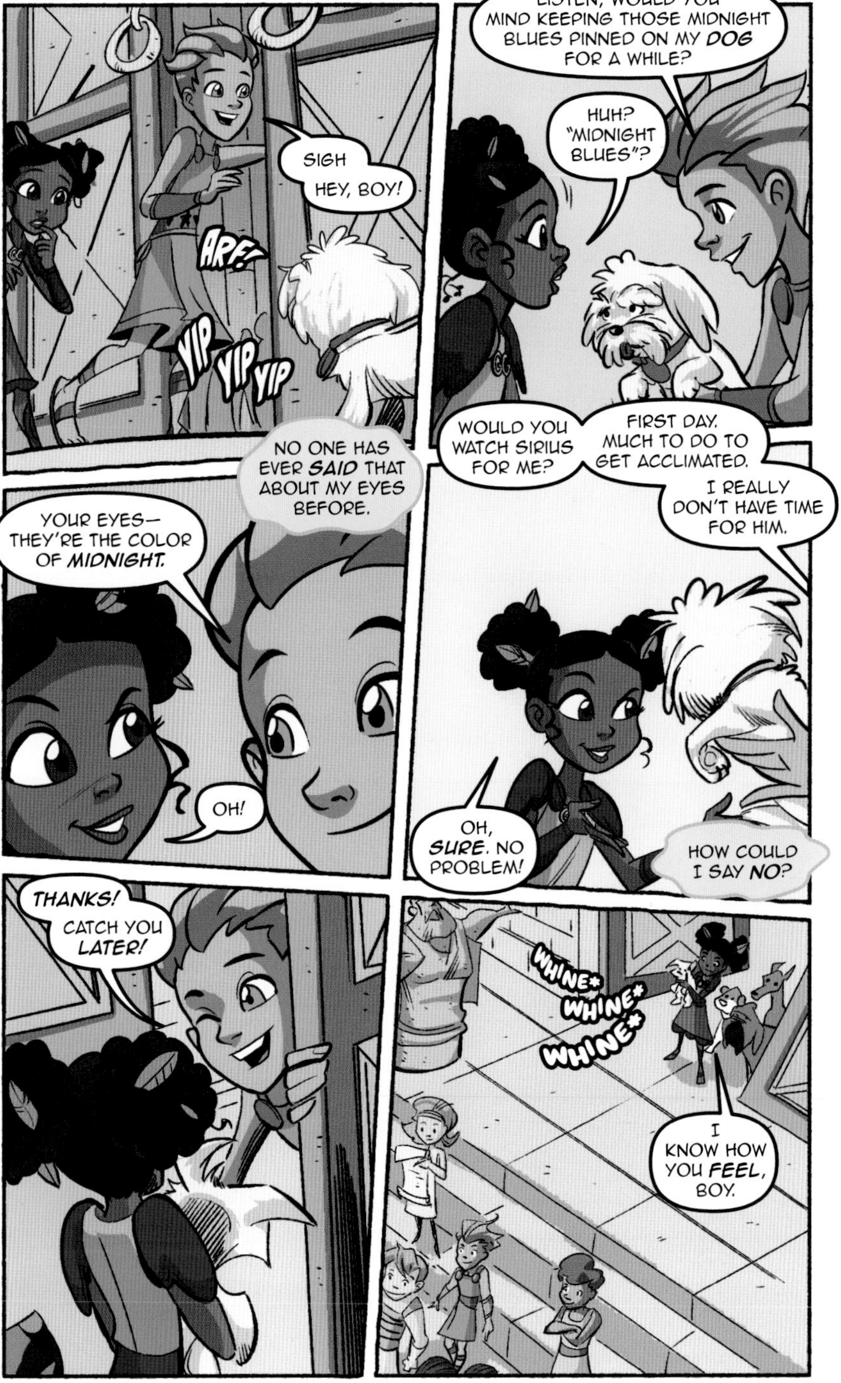
SIGH
HEY, BOY!
ARF!
YIP
YIP
YIP
LISTEN, WOULD YOU MIND KEEPING THOSE MIDNIGHT BLUES PINNED ON MY DOG FOR A WHILE?
HUH? "MIDNIGHT BLUES"?
YOUR EYES— THEY'RE THE COLOR OF MIDNIGHT.
NO ONE HAS EVER SAID THAT ABOUT MY EYES BEFORE.
OH!
WOULD YOU WATCH SIRIUS FOR ME?
FIRST DAY. MUCH TO DO TO GET ACCLIMATED.
I REALLY DON'T HAVE TIME FOR HIM.
OH, SURE. NO PROBLEM!
HOW COULD I SAY NO?
THANKS!
CATCH YOU LATER!
WHINE
WHINE
WHINE
I KNOW HOW YOU FEEL, BOY.

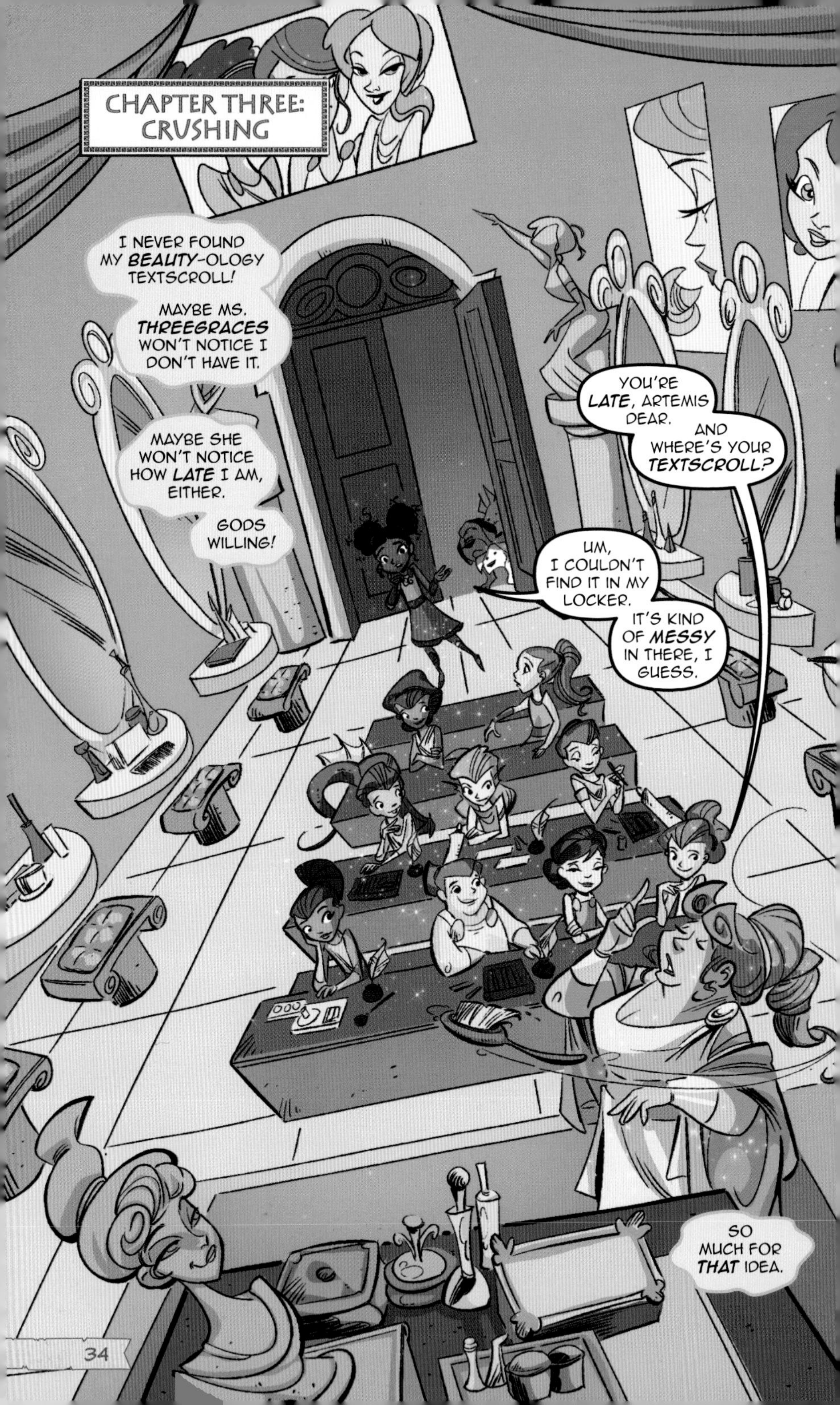

CHAPTER THREE: CRUSHING
I NEVER FOUND MY BEAUTY-OLOGY TEXTSCROLL!
MAYBE MS. THREEGRACES WON'T NOTICE I DON'T HAVE IT.
MAYBE SHE WON'T NOTICE HOW LATE I AM, EITHER.
GODS WILLING!
YOU'RE LATE, ARTEMIS DEAR.
AND WHERE'S YOUR TEXTSCROLL?
UM, I COULDN'T FIND IT IN MY LOCKER.
IT'S KIND OF MESSY IN THERE, I GUESS.
SO MUCH FOR THAT IDEA.

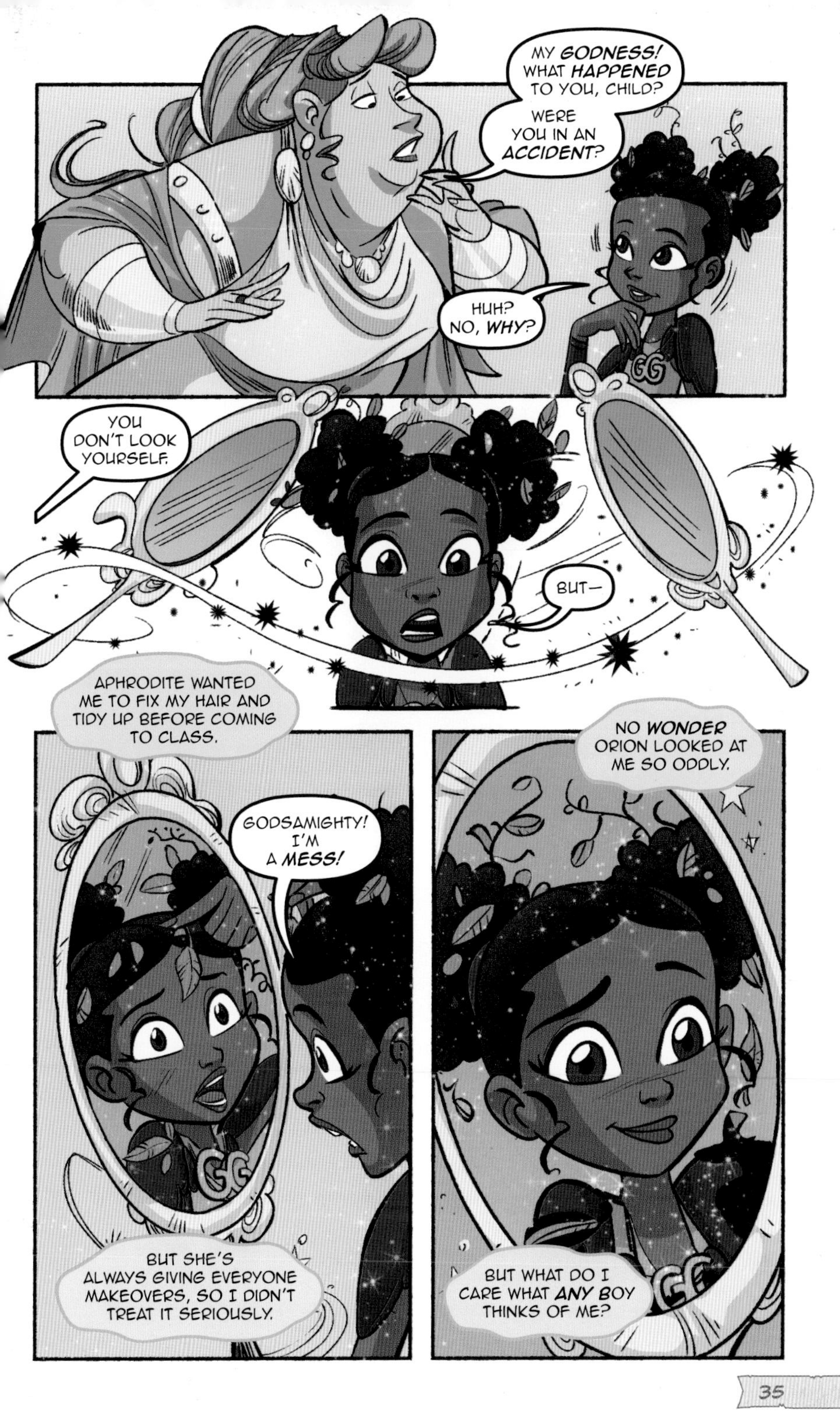
MY GODNESS! WHAT HAPPENED TO YOU, CHILD?
WERE YOU IN AN ACCIDENT?
HUH? NO, WHY?
YOU DON'T LOOK YOURSELF.
BUT—
APHRODITE WANTED ME TO FIX MY HAIR AND TIDY UP BEFORE COMING TO CLASS.
GODSAMIGHTY! I'M A MESS!
BUT SHE'S ALWAYS GIVING EVERYONE MAKEOVERS, SO I DIDN'T TREAT IT SERIOUSLY.
NO WONDER ORION LOOKED AT ME SO ODDLY.
BUT WHAT DO I CARE WHAT ANY BOY THINKS OF ME?

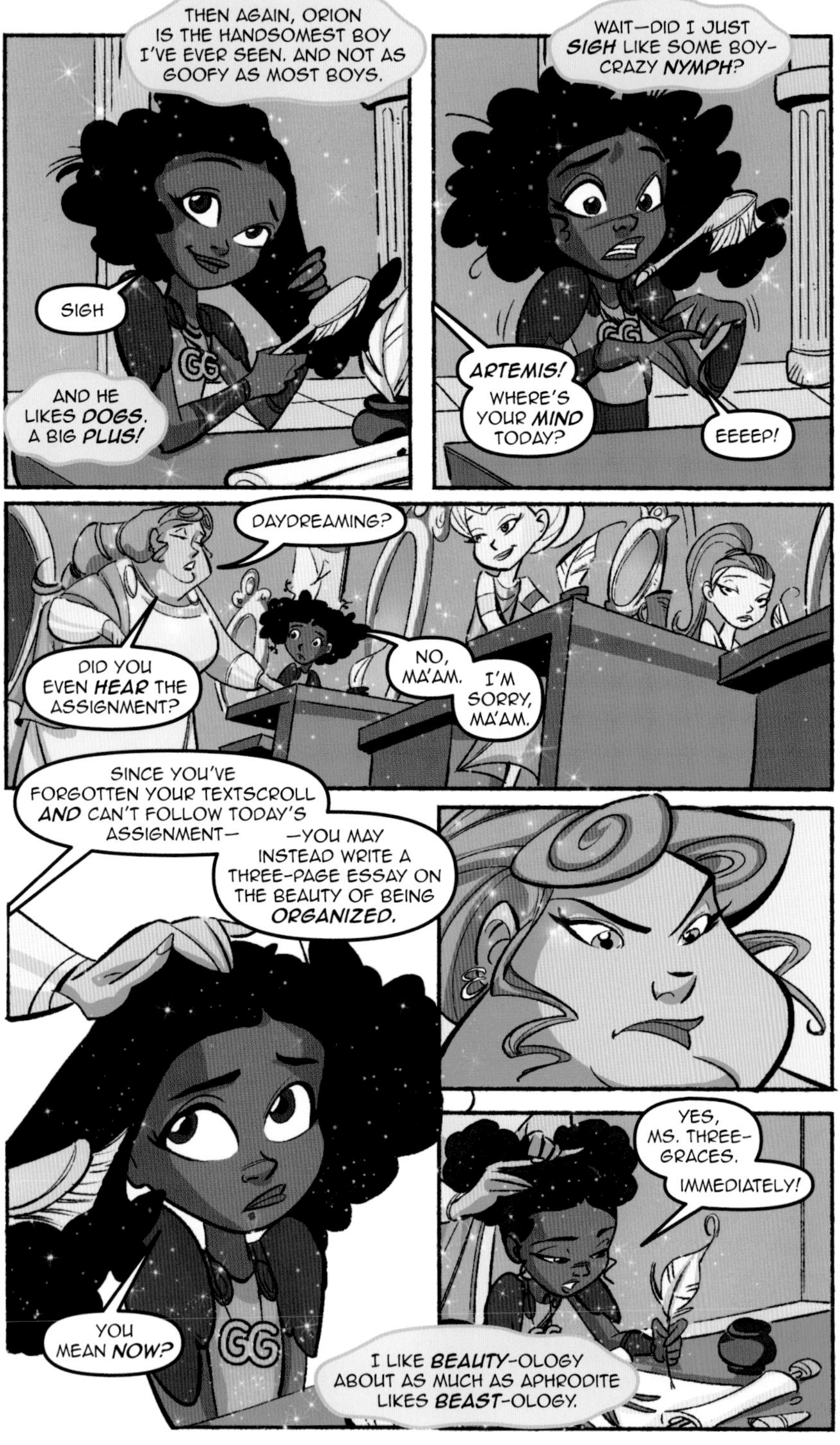
THEN AGAIN, ORION IS THE HANDSOMEST BOY I'VE EVER SEEN. AND NOT AS GOOFY AS MOST BOYS.
SIGH
AND HE LIKES DOGS. A BIG PLUS!
WAIT—DID I JUST SIGH LIKE SOME BOY-CRAZY NYMPH?
ARTEMIS! WHERE'S YOUR MIND TODAY?
EEEEP!
DAYDREAMING?
DID YOU EVEN HEAR THE ASSIGNMENT?
NO, MA'AM.
I'M SORRY, MA'AM.
SINCE YOU'VE FORGOTTEN YOUR TEXTSCROLL AND CAN'T FOLLOW TODAY'S ASSIGNMENT—
—YOU MAY INSTEAD WRITE A THREE-PAGE ESSAY ON THE BEAUTY OF BEING ORGANIZED.
YOU MEAN NOW?
YES, MS. THREE-GRACES.
IMMEDIATELY!
I LIKE BEAUTY-OLOGY ABOUT AS MUCH AS APHRODITE LIKES BEAST-OLOGY.

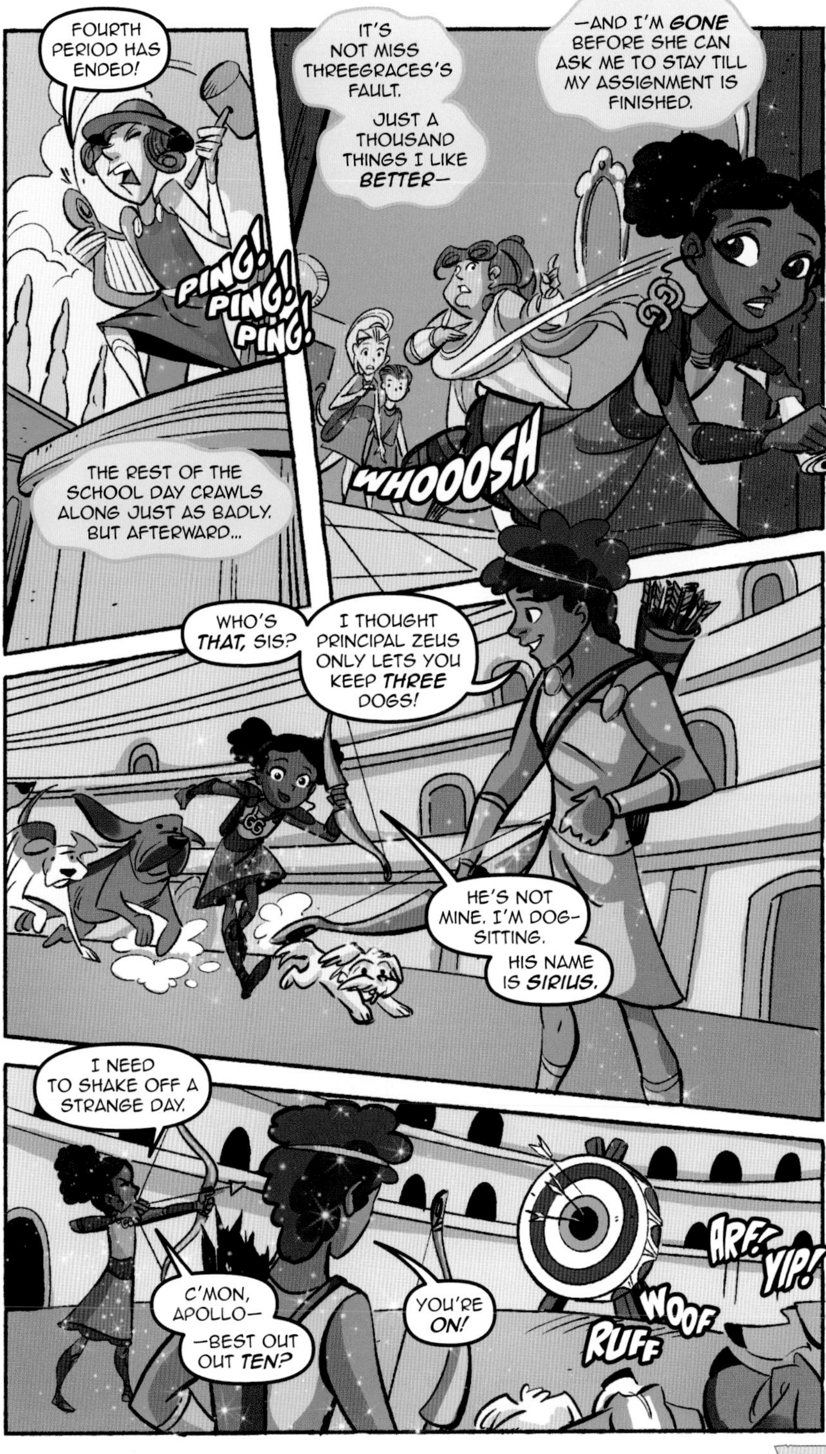
FOURTH PERIOD HAS ENDED!
PING! PING! PING!
IT'S NOT MISS THREEGRACES'S FAULT.
JUST A THOUSAND THINGS I LIKE BETTER—
—AND I'M GONE BEFORE SHE CAN ASK ME TO STAY TILL MY ASSIGNMENT IS FINISHED.
WHOOOSH
THE REST OF THE SCHOOL DAY CRAWLS ALONG JUST AS BADLY. BUT AFTERWARD...
WHO'S THAT, SIS?
I THOUGHT PRINCIPAL ZEUS ONLY LETS YOU KEEP THREE DOGS!
HE'S NOT MINE. I'M DOG-SITTING.
HIS NAME IS SIRIUS.
I NEED TO SHAKE OFF A STRANGE DAY.
C'MON, APOLLO—
—BEST OUT OUT TEN?
YOU'RE ON!
ARF! YIP!
WOOF
RUFF

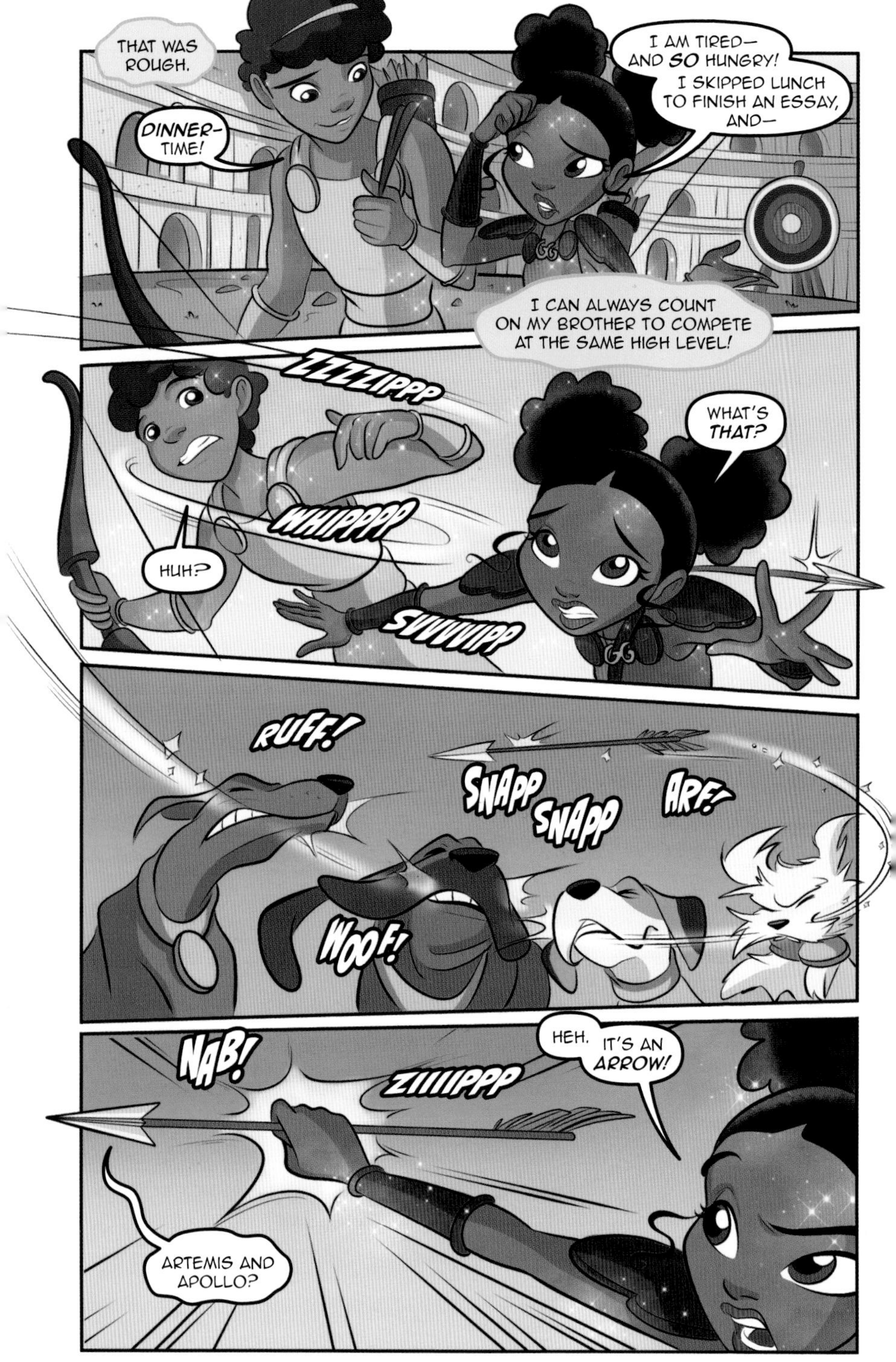

THAT WAS ROUGH.
I AM TIRED— AND SO HUNGRY!
I SKIPPED LUNCH TO FINISH AN ESSAY, AND—
DINNER-TIME!
I CAN ALWAYS COUNT ON MY BROTHER TO COMPETE AT THE SAME HIGH LEVEL!
ZZZZZIPPP
WHAT'S THAT?
WHIPPPP
HUH?
SVVVVIPP
RUFF!
SNAPP SNAPP
ARF!
WOOF!
NAB!
ZIIIIPPP
HEH.
IT'S AN ARROW!
ARTEMIS AND APOLLO?

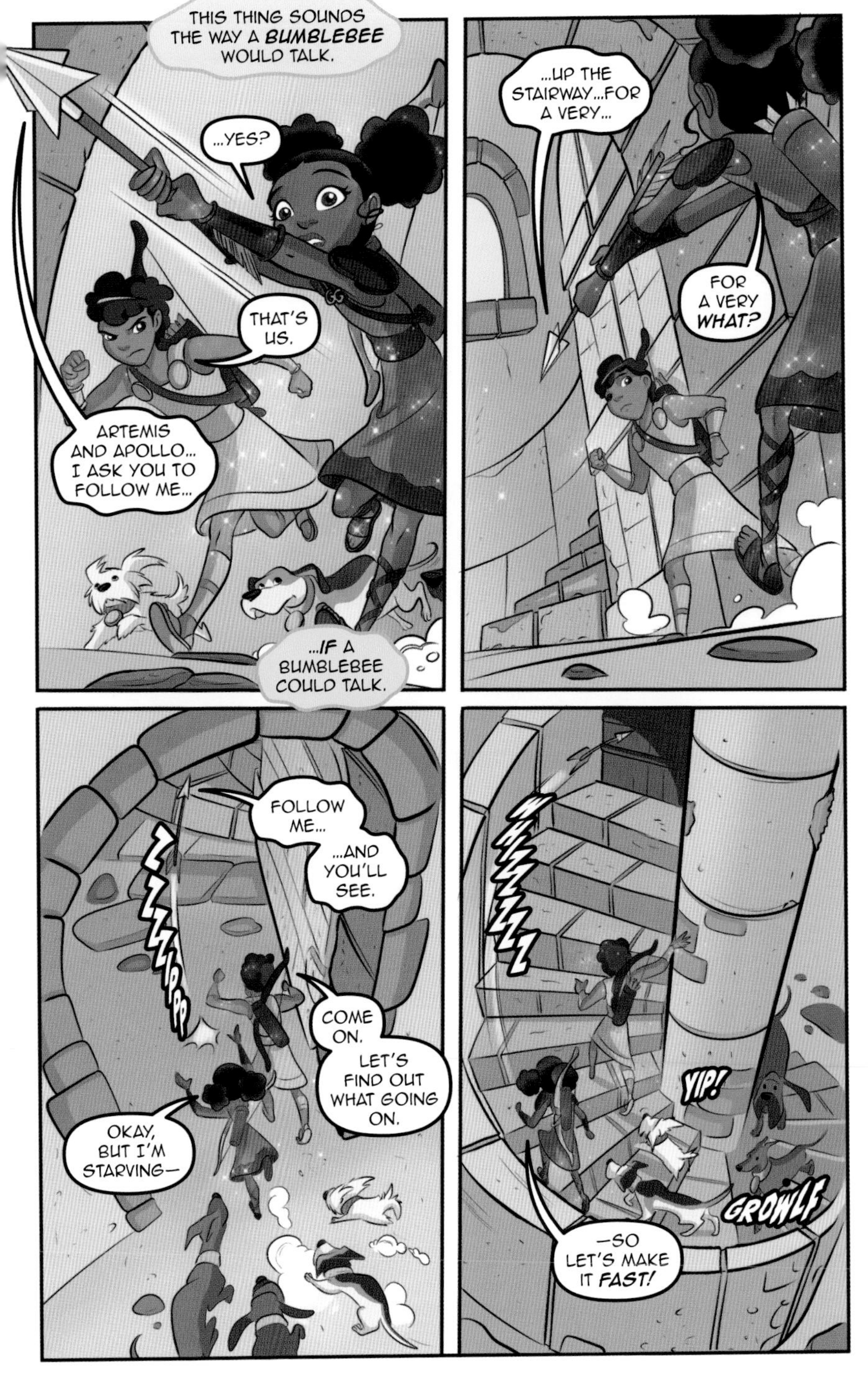
THIS THING SOUNDS THE WAY A BUMBLEBEE WOULD TALK.
...YES?
THAT'S US.
ARTEMIS AND APOLLO... I ASK YOU TO FOLLOW ME...
...IF A BUMBLEBEE COULD TALK.
...UP THE STAIRWAY...FOR A VERY...
FOR A VERY WHAT?
FOLLOW ME...
...AND YOU'LL SEE.
ZZZZIPPP
COME ON.
LET'S FIND OUT WHAT GOING ON.
OKAY, BUT I'M STARVING—
WHZZZZZZ
YIP!
GROWLF
—SO LET'S MAKE IT FAST!

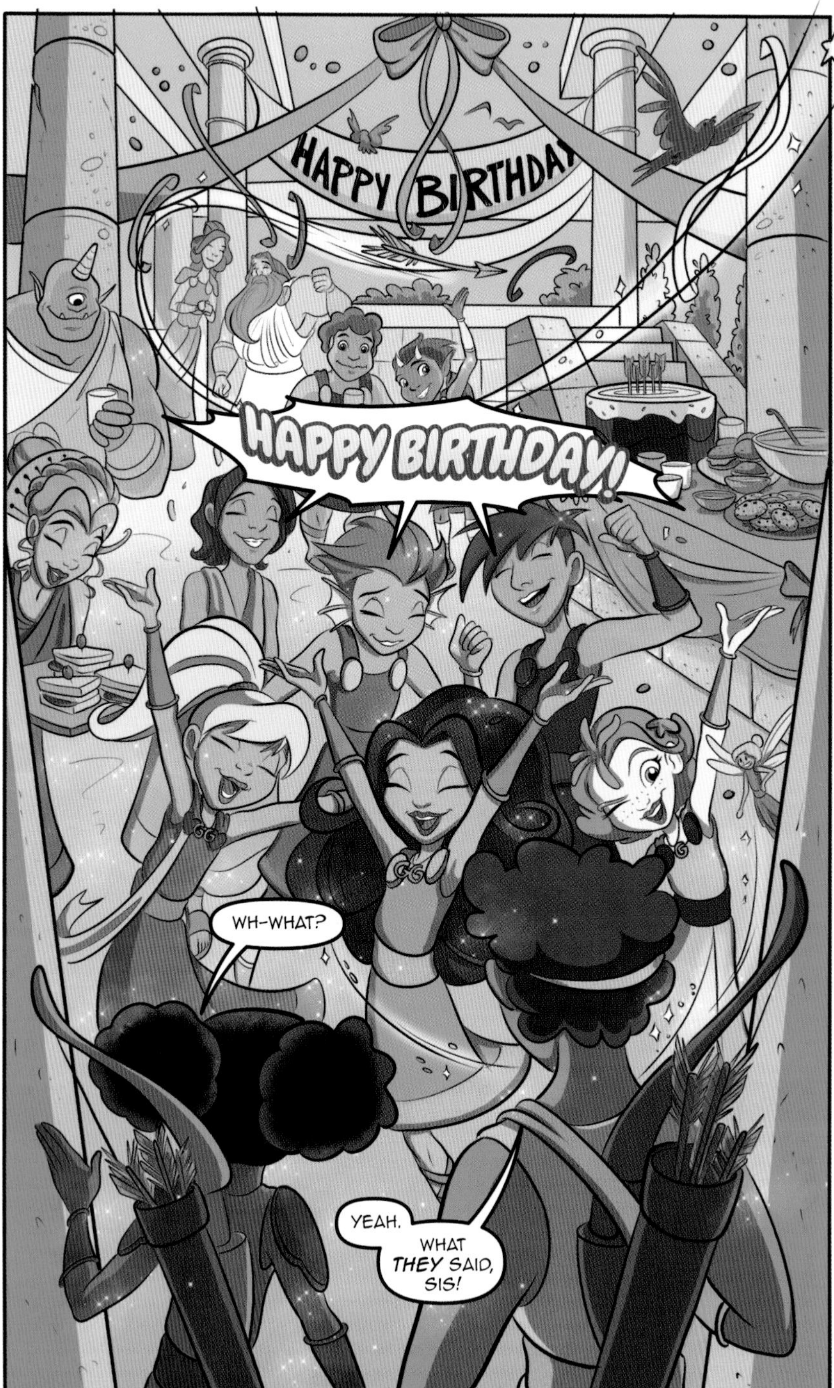
HAPPY BIRTHDAY
HAPPY BIRTHDAY!
WH-WHAT?
YEAH.
WHAT *THEY* SAID, SIS!

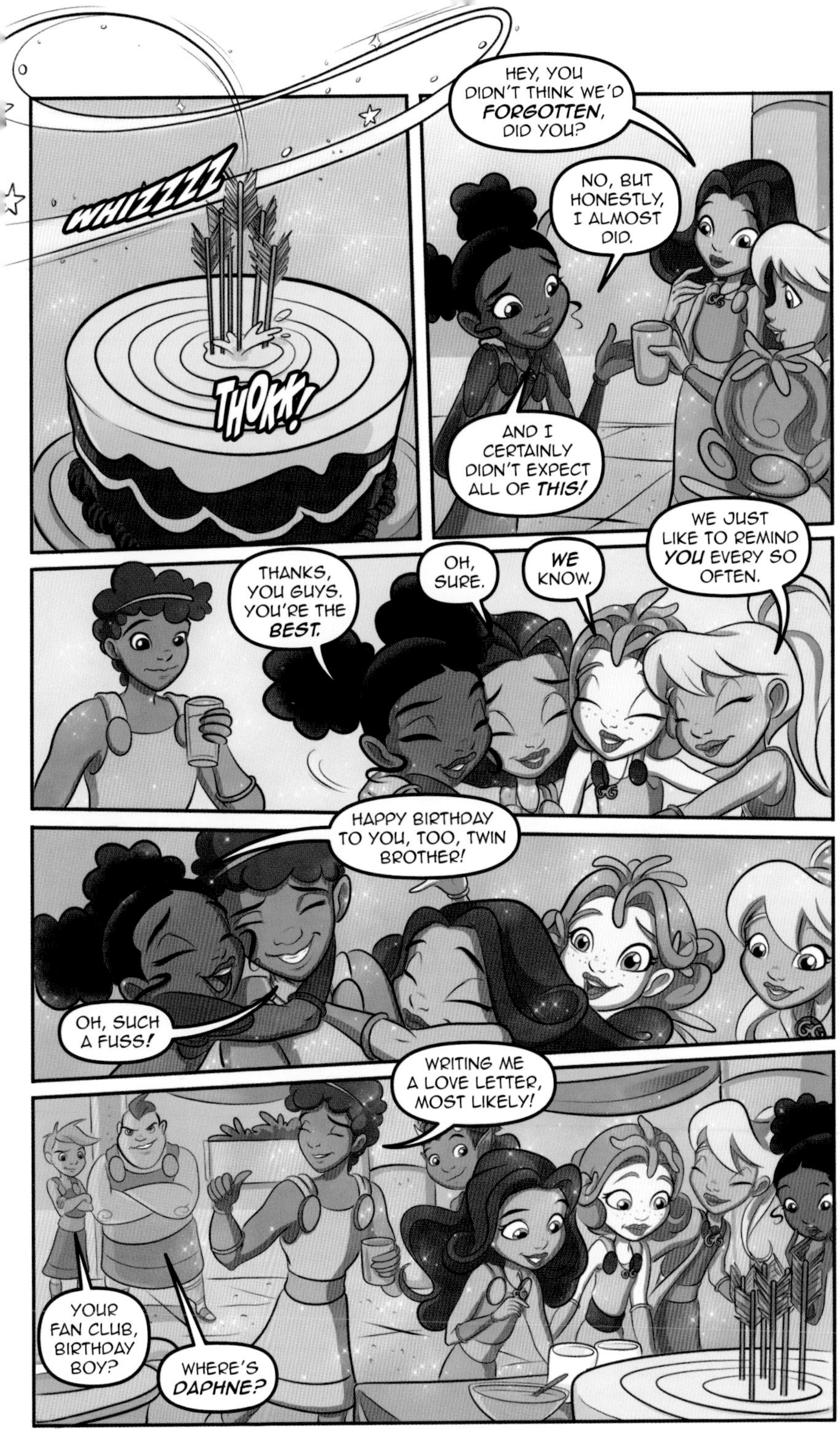
WHIZZZZ
THOKK!
HEY, YOU DIDN'T THINK WE'D FORGOTTEN, DID YOU?
NO, BUT HONESTLY, I ALMOST DID.
AND I CERTAINLY DIDN'T EXPECT ALL OF THIS!
THANKS, YOU GUYS. YOU'RE THE BEST.
OH, SURE.
WE KNOW.
WE JUST LIKE TO REMIND YOU EVERY SO OFTEN.
HAPPY BIRTHDAY TO YOU, TOO, TWIN BROTHER!
OH, SUCH A FUSS!
YOUR FAN CLUB, BIRTHDAY BOY?
WHERE'S DAPHNE?
WRITING ME A LOVE LETTER, MOST LIKELY!

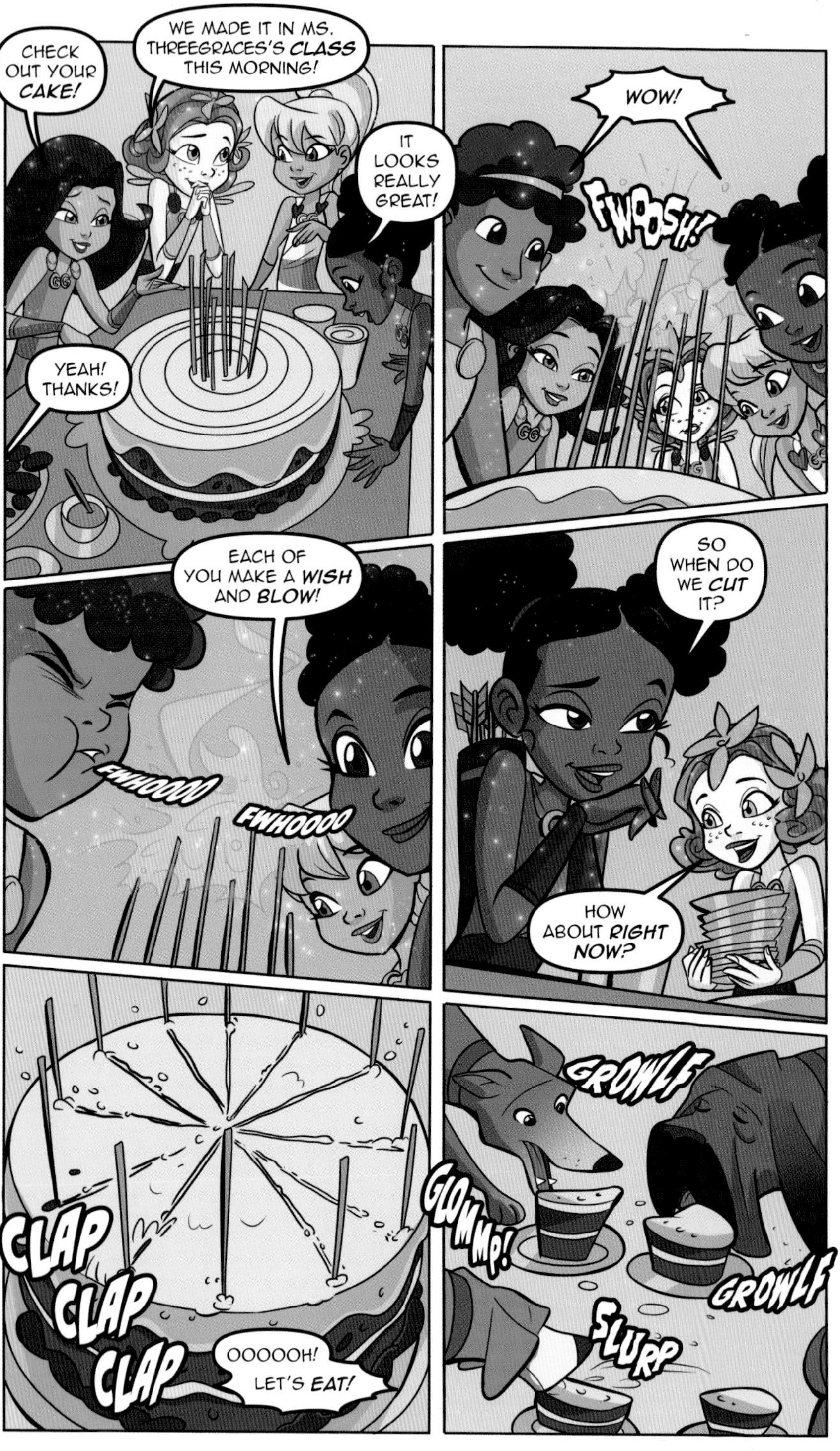
CHECK OUT YOUR CAKE!
WE MADE IT IN MS. THREEGRACES'S CLASS THIS MORNING!
IT LOOKS REALLY GREAT!
YEAH! THANKS!
WOW!
FWOOSH!
EACH OF YOU MAKE A WISH AND BLOW!
FWHOOOO
FWHOOOO
SO WHEN DO WE CUT IT?
HOW ABOUT RIGHT NOW?
CLAP
CLAP
CLAP
OOOOOH! LET'S EAT!
GROWLF
GLOMMP!
GROWLF
SLURP

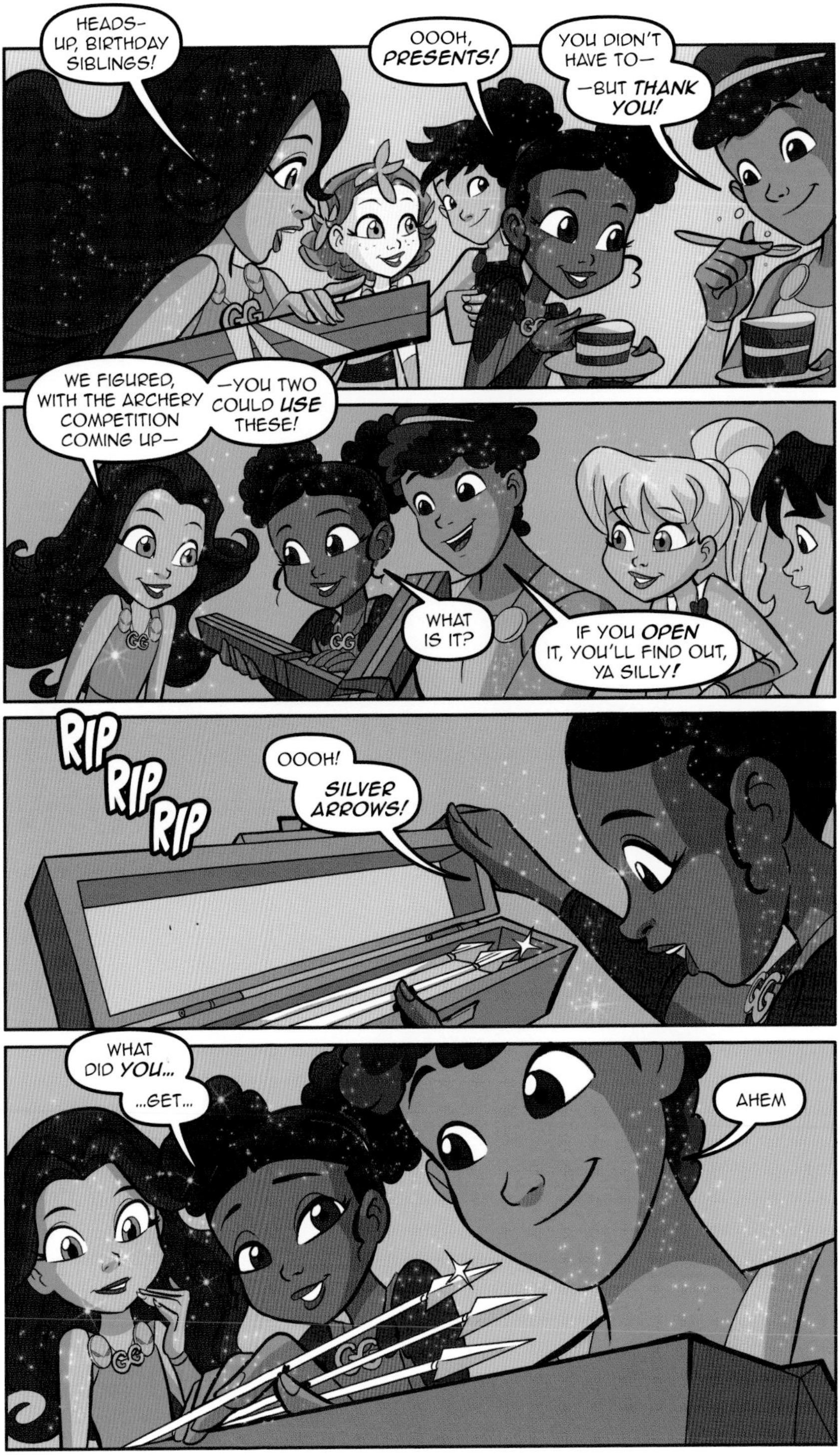
HEADS-UP, BIRTHDAY SIBLINGS!
OOOH, PRESENTS!
YOU DIDN'T HAVE TO—
—BUT THANK YOU!
WE FIGURED, WITH THE ARCHERY COMPETITION COMING UP—
—YOU TWO COULD USE THESE!
WHAT IS IT?
IF YOU OPEN IT, YOU'LL FIND OUT, YA SILLY!
RIP RIP RIP
OOOH! SILVER ARROWS!
WHAT DID YOU...
...GET...
AHEM

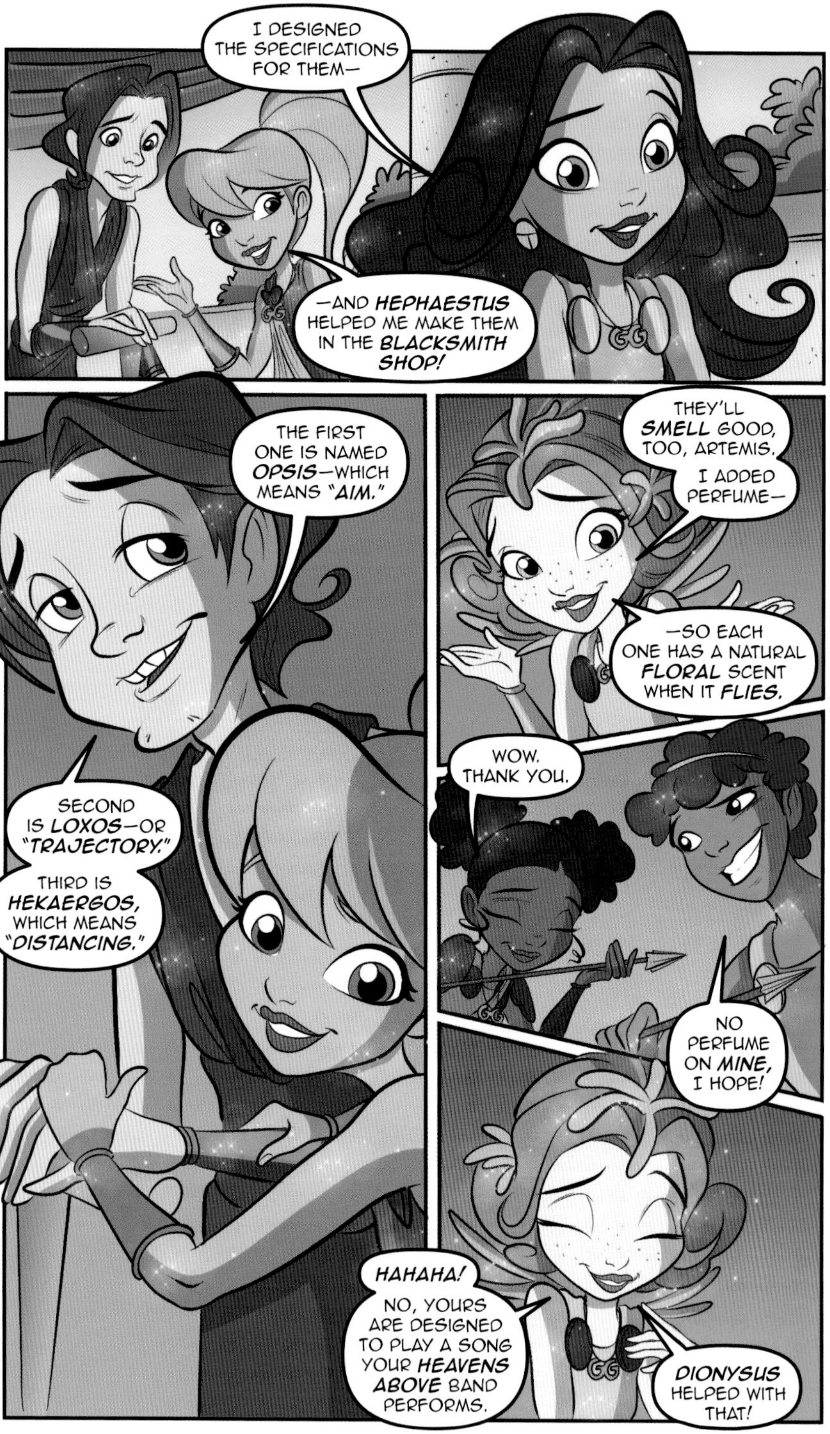
I DESIGNED THE SPECIFICATIONS FOR THEM—
—AND **HEPHAESTUS** HELPED ME MAKE THEM IN THE **BLACKSMITH SHOP!**
THE FIRST ONE IS NAMED **OPSIS**—WHICH MEANS "**AIM.**"
SECOND IS **LOXOS**—OR "**TRAJECTORY.**"
THIRD IS **HEKAERGOS,** WHICH MEANS "**DISTANCING.**"
THEY'LL **SMELL** GOOD, TOO, ARTEMIS.
I ADDED PERFUME—
—SO EACH ONE HAS A NATURAL **FLORAL** SCENT WHEN IT **FLIES.**
WOW. THANK YOU.
NO PERFUME ON **MINE,** I HOPE!
HAHAHA!
NO, YOURS ARE DESIGNED TO PLAY A SONG YOUR **HEAVENS ABOVE** BAND PERFORMS.
DIONYSUS HELPED WITH THAT!

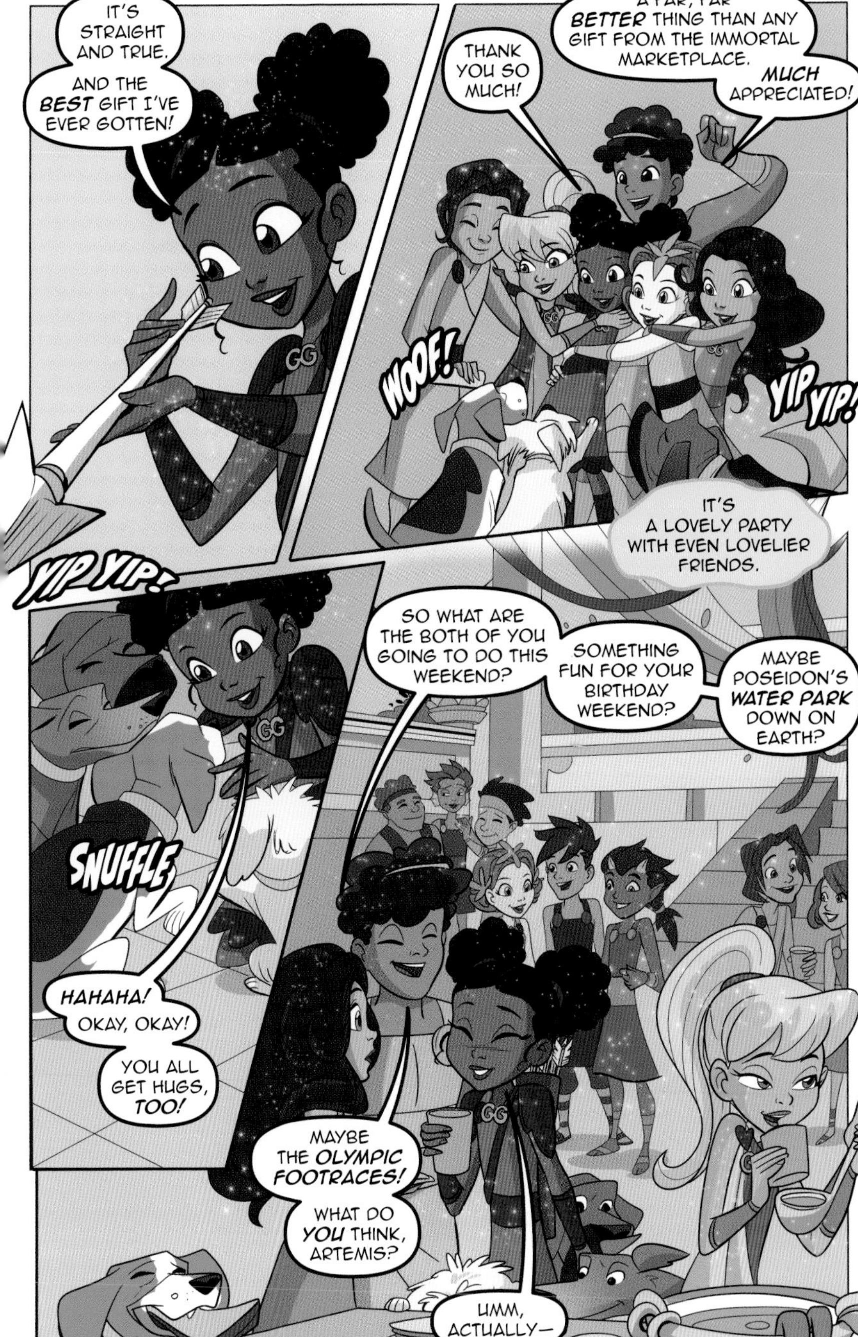

IT'S STRAIGHT AND TRUE.
AND THE BEST GIFT I'VE EVER GOTTEN!
THANK YOU SO MUCH!
A FAR, FAR BETTER THING THAN ANY GIFT FROM THE IMMORTAL MARKETPLACE.
MUCH APPRECIATED!
WOOF!
YIP YIP!
IT'S A LOVELY PARTY WITH EVEN LOVELIER FRIENDS.
YIP YIP!
SNUFFLE
HAHAHA!
OKAY, OKAY!
YOU ALL GET HUGS, TOO!
SO WHAT ARE THE BOTH OF YOU GOING TO DO THIS WEEKEND?
SOMETHING FUN FOR YOUR BIRTHDAY WEEKEND?
MAYBE POSEIDON'S WATER PARK DOWN ON EARTH?
MAYBE THE OLYMPIC FOOTRACES!
WHAT DO YOU THINK, ARTEMIS?
UMM, ACTUALLY—

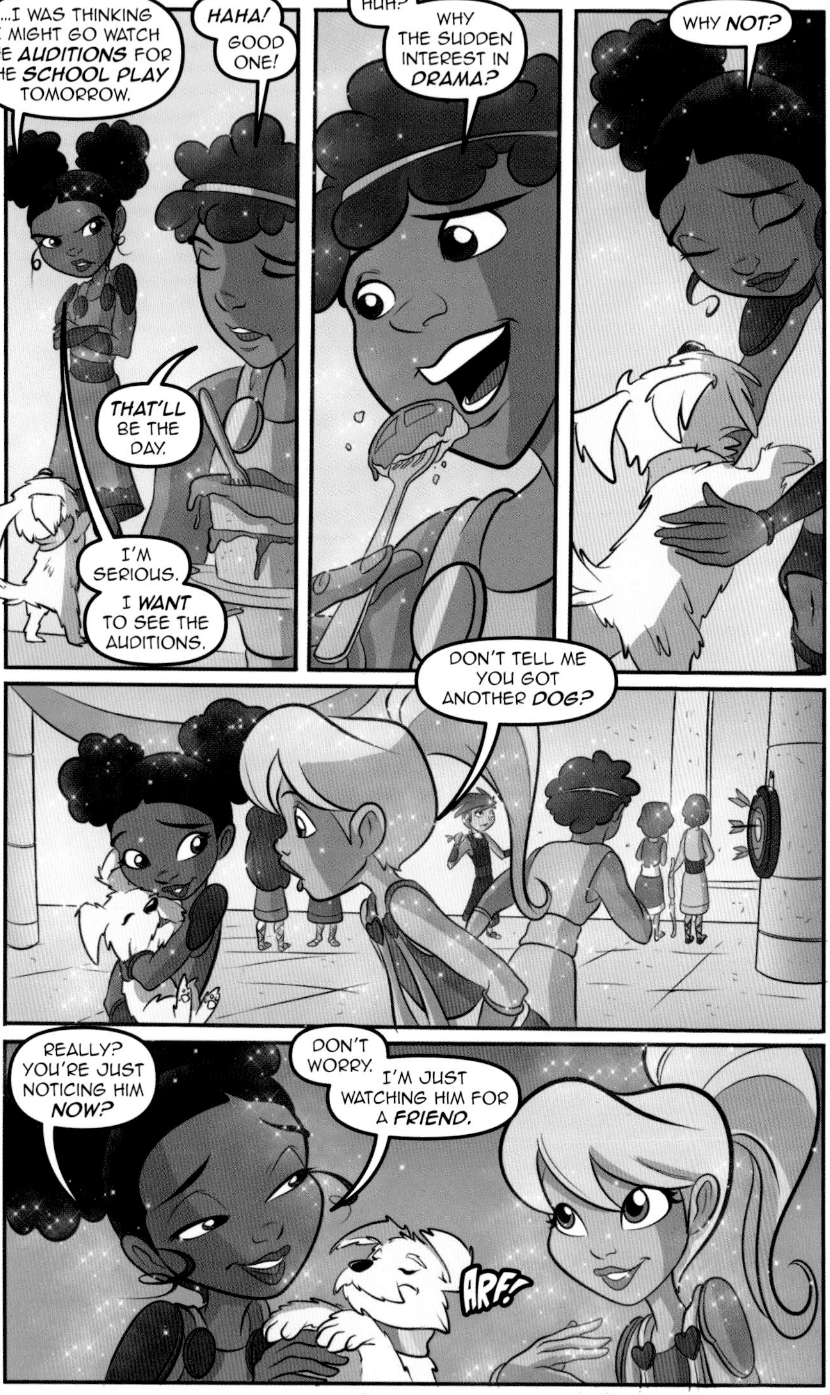

...I WAS THINKING I MIGHT GO WATCH THE AUDITIONS FOR THE SCHOOL PLAY TOMORROW.
HAHA! GOOD ONE!
THAT'LL BE THE DAY.
I'M SERIOUS.
I WANT TO SEE THE AUDITIONS.
HUH?
WHY THE SUDDEN INTEREST IN DRAMA?
WHY NOT?
DON'T TELL ME YOU GOT ANOTHER DOG?
REALLY? YOU'RE JUST NOTICING HIM NOW?
DON'T WORRY.
I'M JUST WATCHING HIM FOR A FRIEND.
ARF!

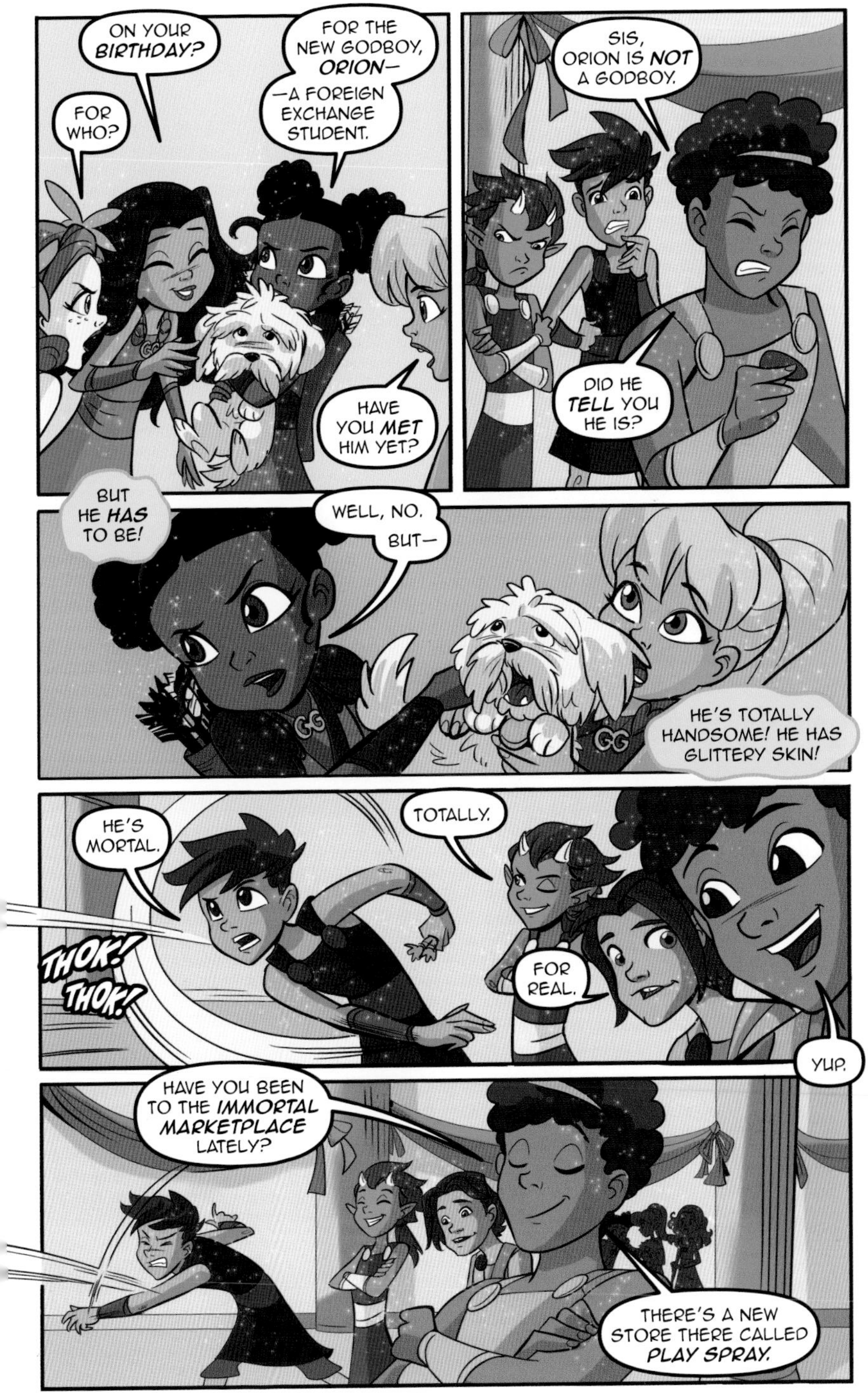

ON YOUR BIRTHDAY?
FOR WHO?
FOR THE NEW GODBOY, ORION—
—A FOREIGN EXCHANGE STUDENT.
HAVE YOU MET HIM YET?
SIS, ORION IS NOT A GODBOY.
DID HE TELL YOU HE IS?
BUT HE HAS TO BE!
WELL, NO. BUT—
HE'S TOTALLY HANDSOME! HE HAS GLITTERY SKIN!
HE'S MORTAL.
TOTALLY.
FOR REAL.
YUP.
THOK! THOK!
HAVE YOU BEEN TO THE IMMORTAL MARKETPLACE LATELY?
THERE'S A NEW STORE THERE CALLED PLAY SPRAY.

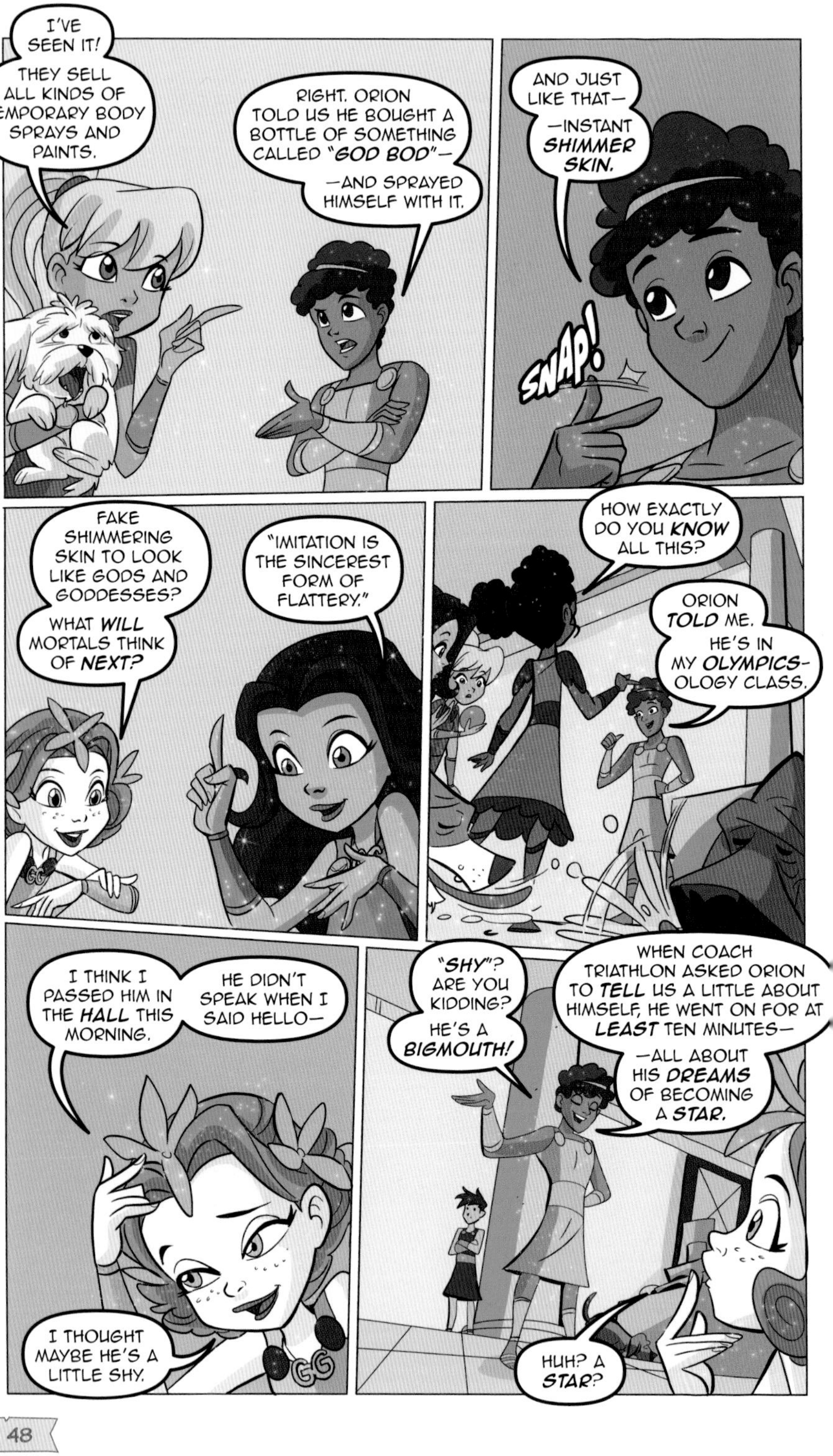
I'VE SEEN IT!
THEY SELL ALL KINDS OF TEMPORARY BODY SPRAYS AND PAINTS.
RIGHT. ORION TOLD US HE BOUGHT A BOTTLE OF SOMETHING CALLED "GOD BOD"—
—AND SPRAYED HIMSELF WITH IT.
AND JUST LIKE THAT—
—INSTANT SHIMMER SKIN.
SNAP!
FAKE SHIMMERING SKIN TO LOOK LIKE GODS AND GODDESSES?
WHAT WILL MORTALS THINK OF NEXT?
"IMITATION IS THE SINCEREST FORM OF FLATTERY."
HOW EXACTLY DO YOU KNOW ALL THIS?
ORION TOLD ME.
HE'S IN MY OLYMPICS-OLOGY CLASS.
I THINK I PASSED HIM IN THE HALL THIS MORNING.
HE DIDN'T SPEAK WHEN I SAID HELLO—
I THOUGHT MAYBE HE'S A LITTLE SHY.
"SHY"? ARE YOU KIDDING?
HE'S A BIGMOUTH!
WHEN COACH TRIATHLON ASKED ORION TO TELL US A LITTLE ABOUT HIMSELF, HE WENT ON FOR AT LEAST TEN MINUTES—
—ALL ABOUT HIS DREAMS OF BECOMING A STAR.
HUH? A STAR?

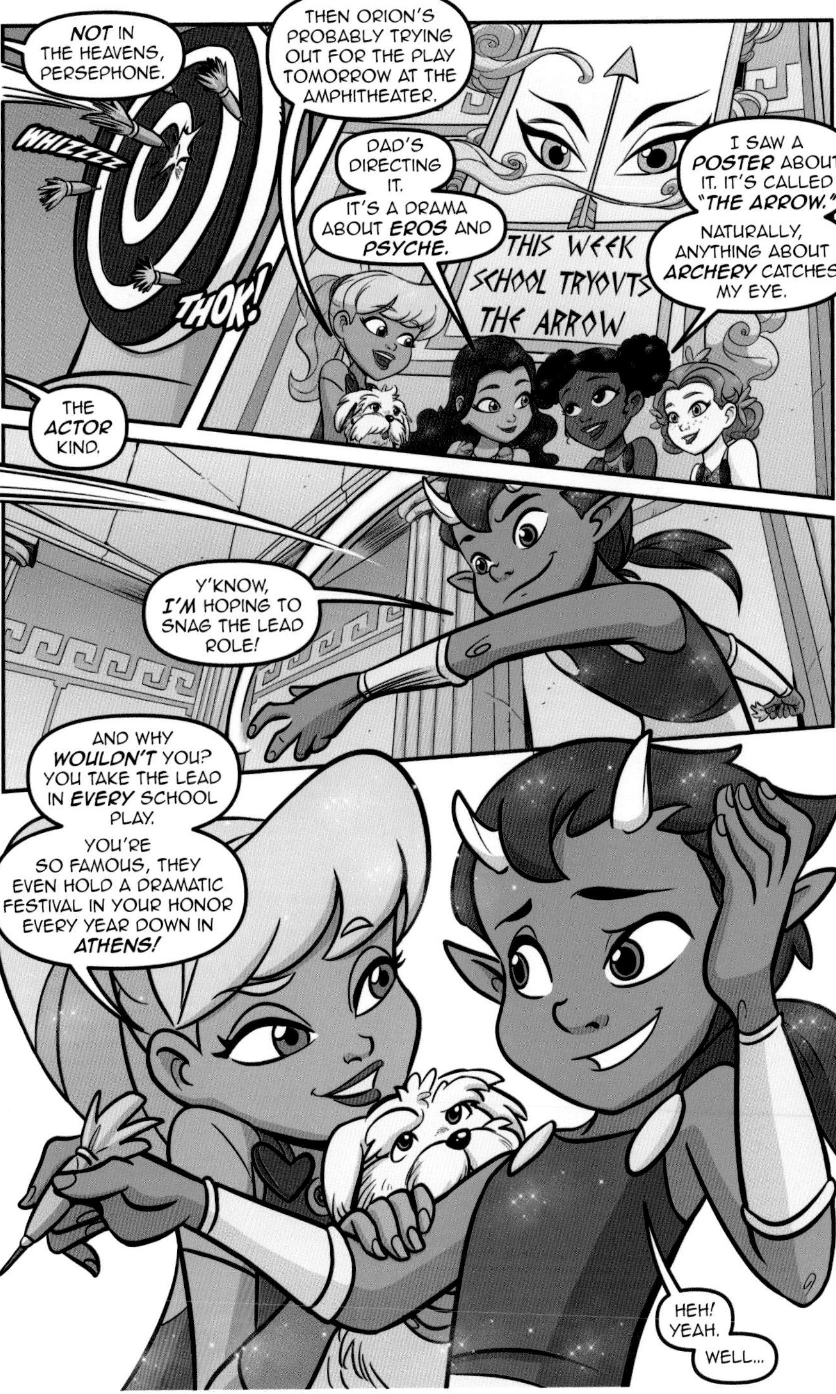
NOT IN THE HEAVENS, PERSEPHONE.
WHIZZZZZ
THOK!
THEN ORION'S PROBABLY TRYING OUT FOR THE PLAY TOMORROW AT THE AMPHITHEATER.
DAD'S DIRECTING IT.
IT'S A DRAMA ABOUT EROS AND PSYCHE.
THIS WEEK SCHOOL TRYOUTS THE ARROW
I SAW A POSTER ABOUT IT. IT'S CALLED "THE ARROW."
NATURALLY, ANYTHING ABOUT ARCHERY CATCHES MY EYE.
THE ACTOR KIND.
Y'KNOW, I'M HOPING TO SNAG THE LEAD ROLE!
AND WHY WOULDN'T YOU? YOU TAKE THE LEAD IN EVERY SCHOOL PLAY.
YOU'RE SO FAMOUS, THEY EVEN HOLD A DRAMATIC FESTIVAL IN YOUR HONOR EVERY YEAR DOWN IN ATHENS!
HEH! YEAH.
WELL...

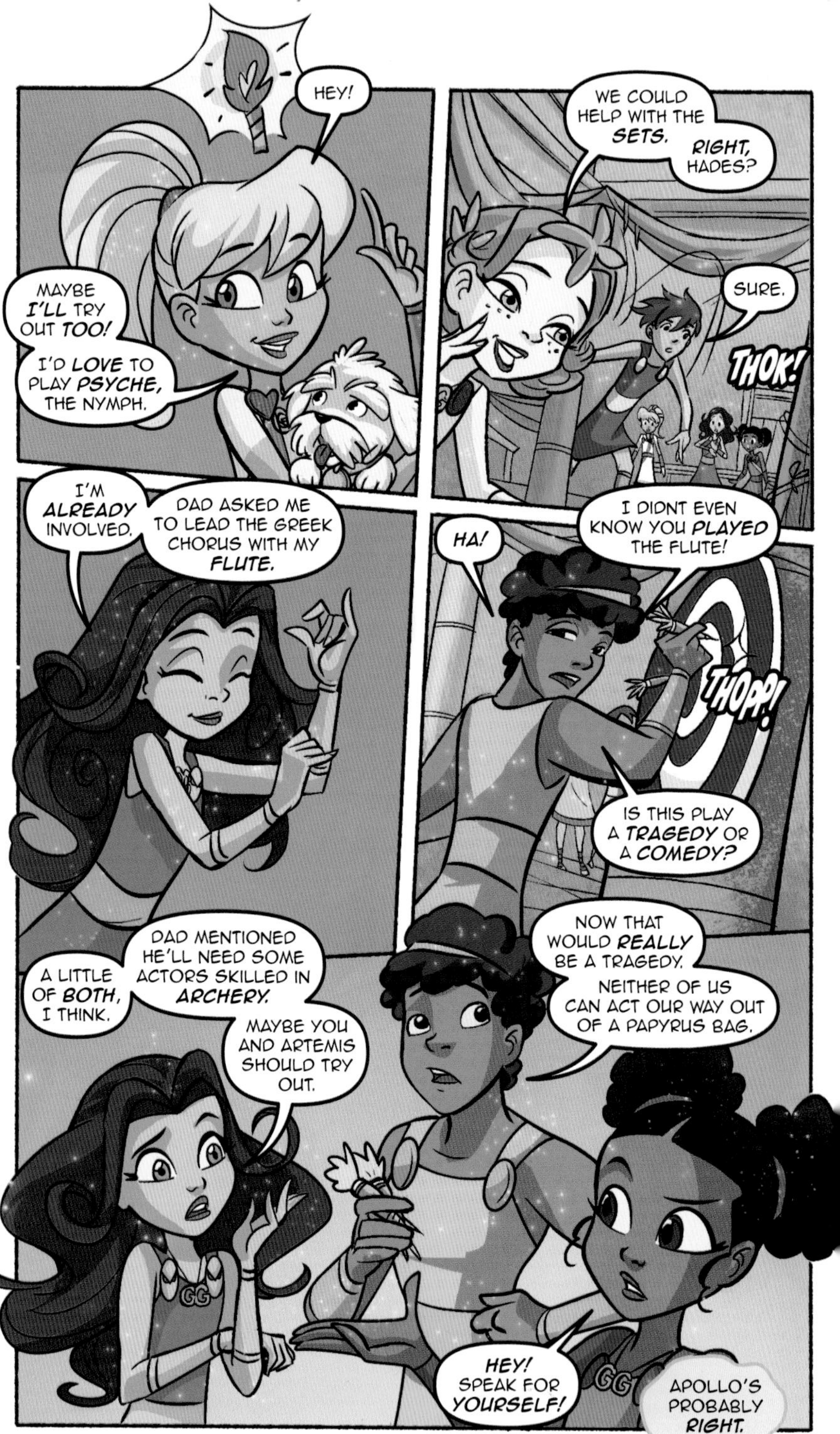
HEY!
MAYBE I'LL TRY OUT TOO!
I'D LOVE TO PLAY PSYCHE, THE NYMPH.
WE COULD HELP WITH THE SETS.
RIGHT, HADES?
SURE.
THOK!
I'M ALREADY INVOLVED.
DAD ASKED ME TO LEAD THE GREEK CHORUS WITH MY FLUTE.
HA!
I DIDNT EVEN KNOW YOU PLAYED THE FLUTE!
THOPP!
IS THIS PLAY A TRAGEDY OR A COMEDY?
A LITTLE OF BOTH, I THINK.
DAD MENTIONED HE'LL NEED SOME ACTORS SKILLED IN ARCHERY.
MAYBE YOU AND ARTEMIS SHOULD TRY OUT.
NOW THAT WOULD REALLY BE A TRAGEDY.
NEITHER OF US CAN ACT OUR WAY OUT OF A PAPYRUS BAG.
HEY! SPEAK FOR YOURSELF!
APOLLO'S PROBABLY RIGHT.

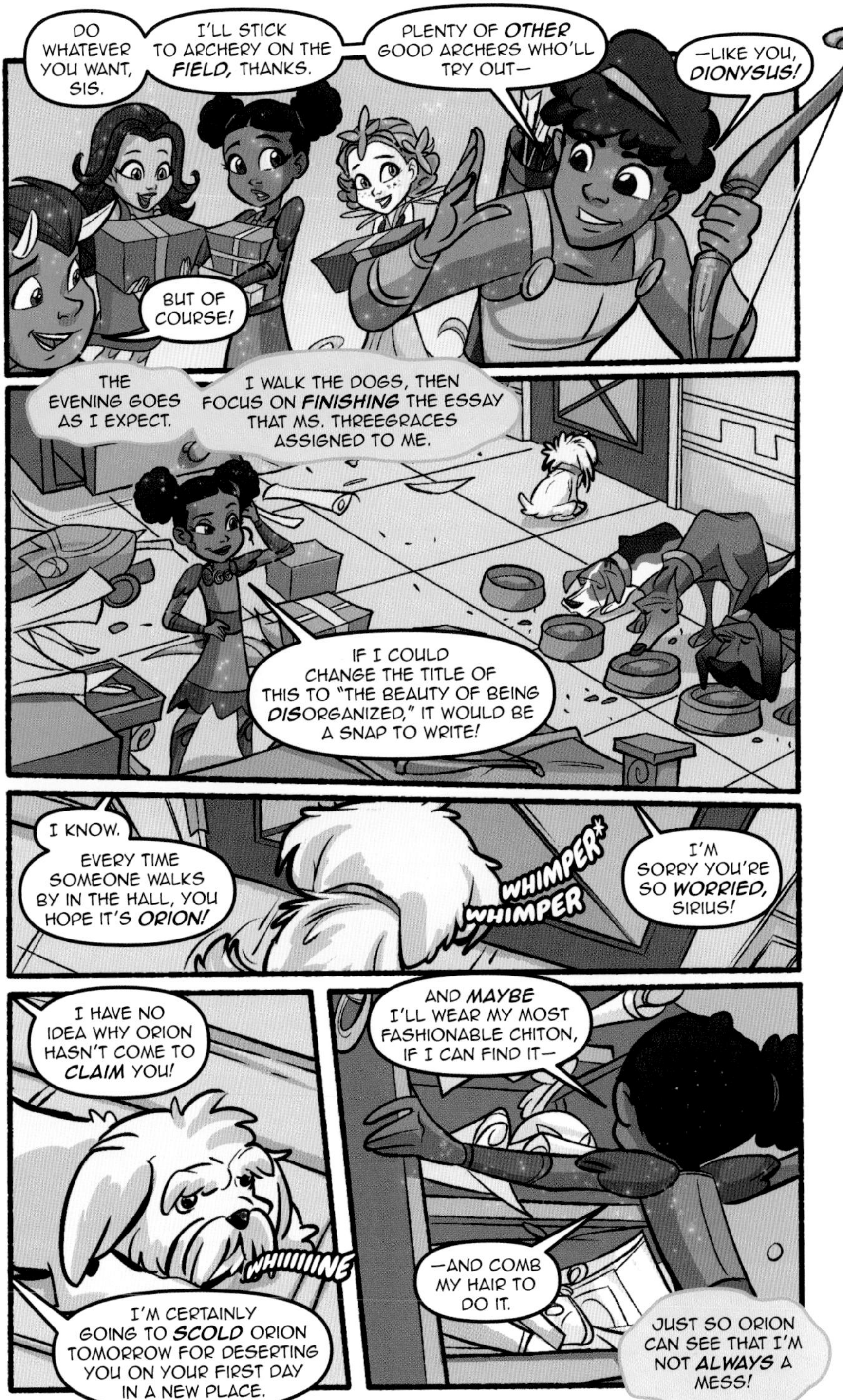

DO WHATEVER YOU WANT, SIS.
I'LL STICK TO ARCHERY ON THE FIELD, THANKS.
PLENTY OF OTHER GOOD ARCHERS WHO'LL TRY OUT—
—LIKE YOU, DIONYSUS!
BUT OF COURSE!
THE EVENING GOES AS I EXPECT.
I WALK THE DOGS, THEN FOCUS ON FINISHING THE ESSAY THAT MS. THREEGRACES ASSIGNED TO ME.
IF I COULD CHANGE THE TITLE OF THIS TO "THE BEAUTY OF BEING DISORGANIZED," IT WOULD BE A SNAP TO WRITE!
I KNOW.
EVERY TIME SOMEONE WALKS BY IN THE HALL, YOU HOPE IT'S ORION!
WHIMPER* WHIMPER
I'M SORRY YOU'RE SO WORRIED, SIRIUS!
I HAVE NO IDEA WHY ORION HASN'T COME TO CLAIM YOU!
WHIIIIIINE
I'M CERTAINLY GOING TO SCOLD ORION TOMORROW FOR DESERTING YOU ON YOUR FIRST DAY IN A NEW PLACE.
AND MAYBE I'LL WEAR MY MOST FASHIONABLE CHITON, IF I CAN FIND IT—
—AND COMB MY HAIR TO DO IT.
JUST SO ORION CAN SEE THAT I'M NOT ALWAYS A MESS!

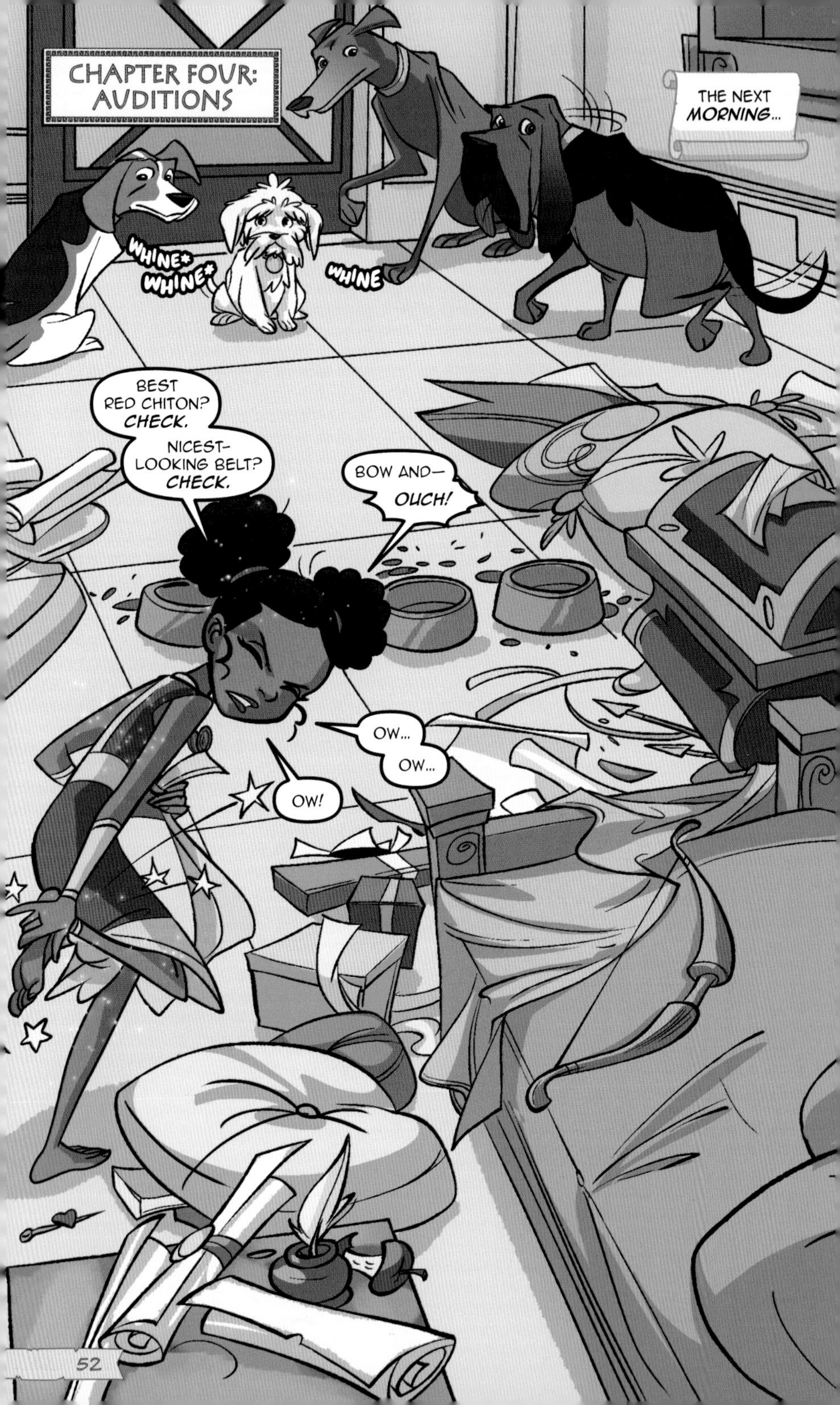
CHAPTER FOUR:
AUDITIONS
THE NEXT MORNING...
WHINE* WHINE*
WHINE
BEST RED CHITON? CHECK.
NICEST-LOOKING BELT? CHECK.
BOW AND— OUCH!
OW...
OW...
OW!

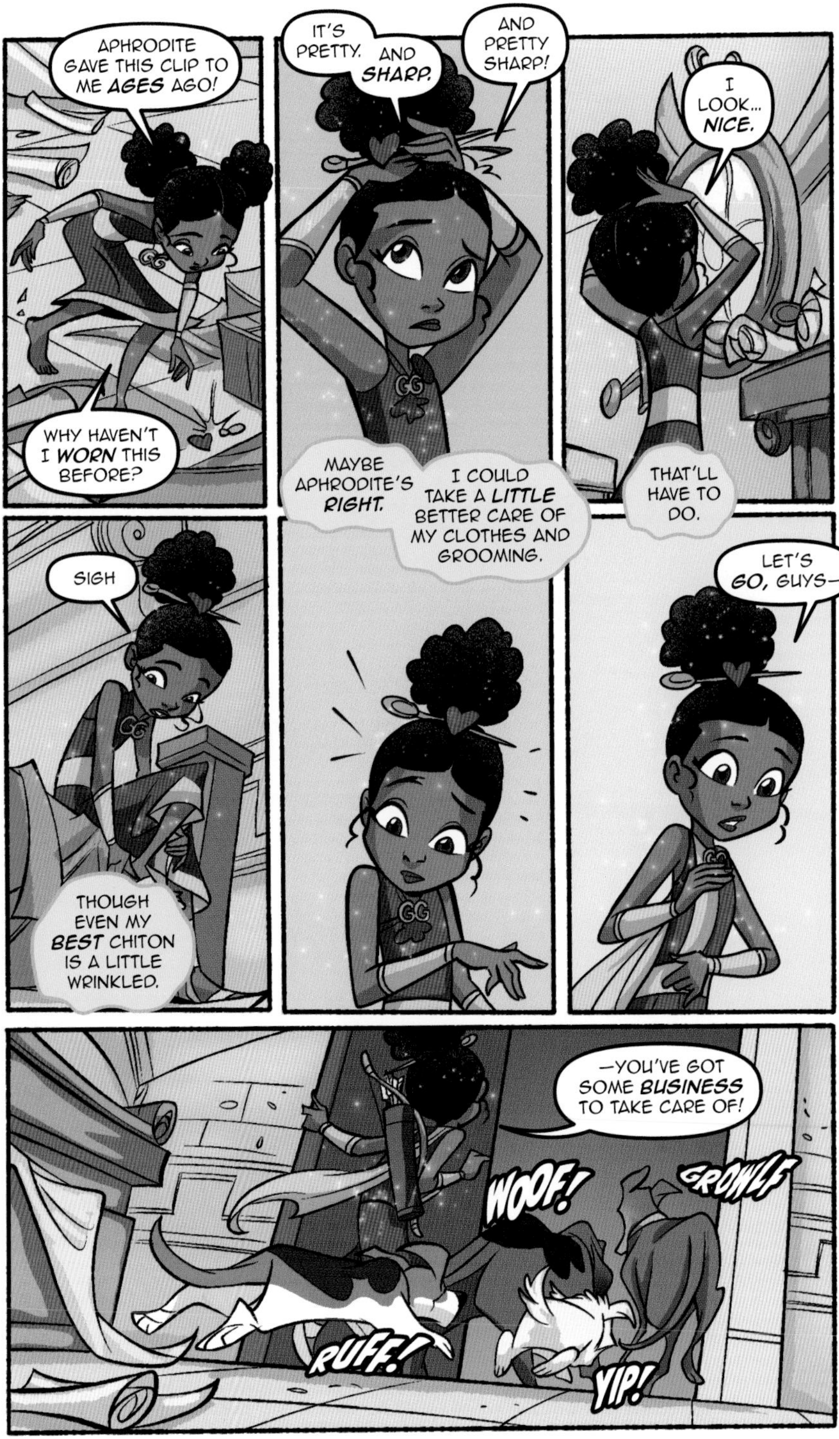
APHRODITE GAVE THIS CLIP TO ME AGES AGO!
WHY HAVEN'T I WORN THIS BEFORE?
IT'S PRETTY.
AND SHARP.
AND PRETTY SHARP!
MAYBE APHRODITE'S RIGHT.
I COULD TAKE A LITTLE BETTER CARE OF MY CLOTHES AND GROOMING.
I LOOK... NICE.
THAT'LL HAVE TO DO.
SIGH
THOUGH EVEN MY BEST CHITON IS A LITTLE WRINKLED.
LET'S GO, GUYS—
—YOU'VE GOT SOME BUSINESS TO TAKE CARE OF!
WOOF!
GROWLF
RUFF!
YIP!

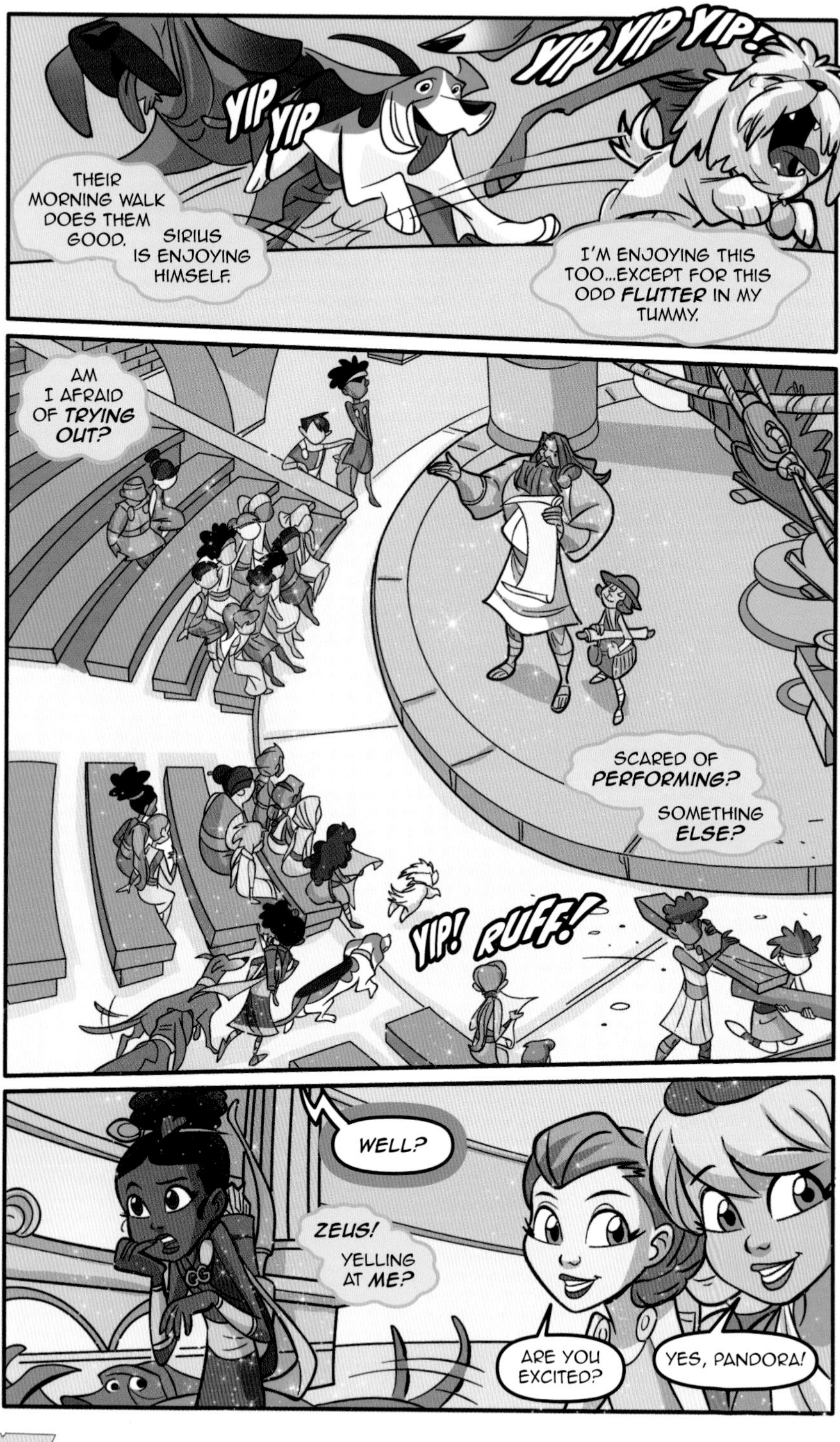

YIP YIP
YIP YIP YIP!
THEIR MORNING WALK DOES THEM GOOD.
SIRIUS IS ENJOYING HIMSELF.
I'M ENJOYING THIS TOO...EXCEPT FOR THIS ODD FLUTTER IN MY TUMMY.
AM I AFRAID OF TRYING OUT?
SCARED OF PERFORMING?
SOMETHING ELSE?
YIP! RUFF!
WELL?
ZEUS!
YELLING AT ME?
ARE YOU EXCITED?
YES, PANDORA!

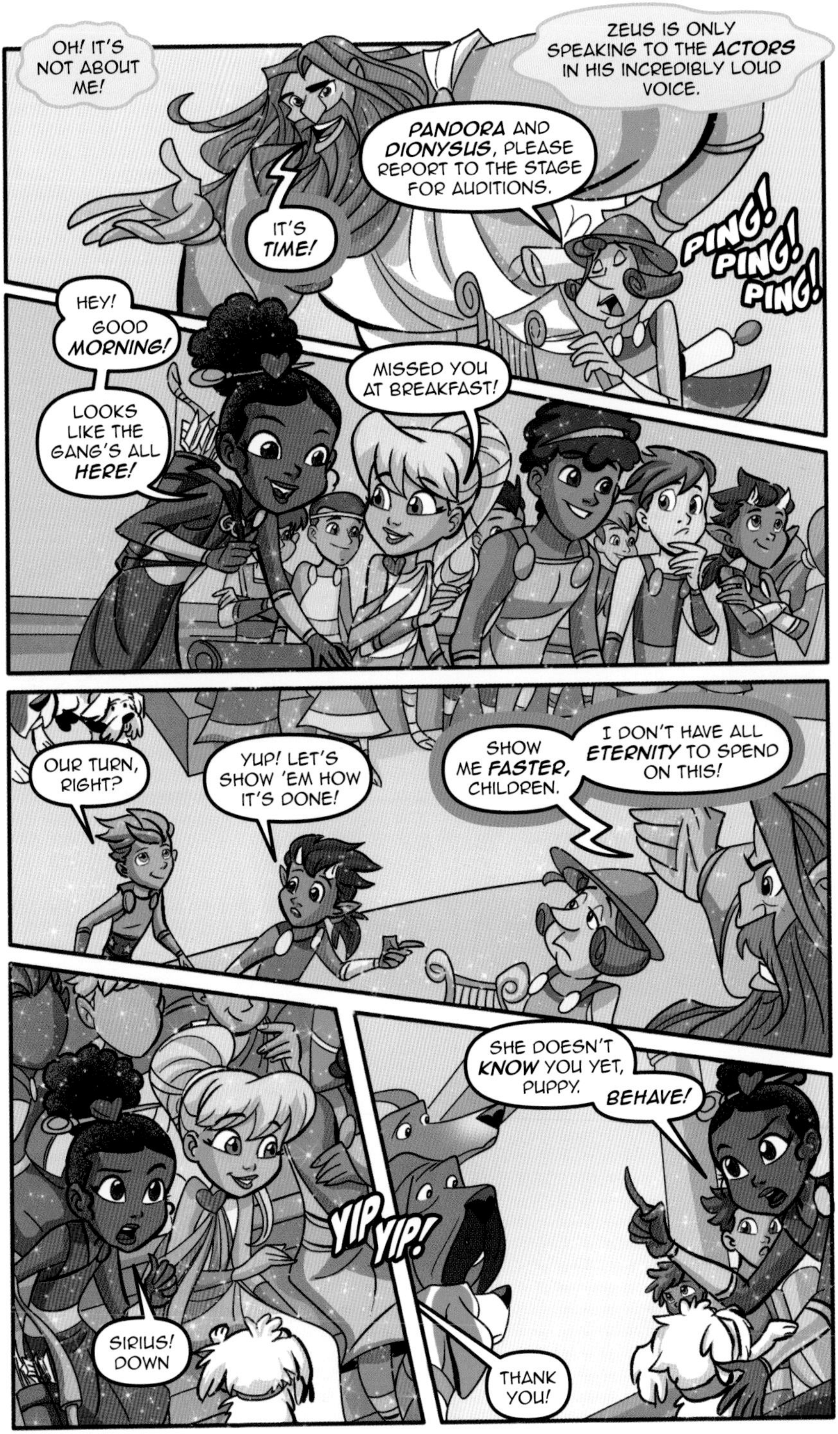

OH! IT'S NOT ABOUT ME!
ZEUS IS ONLY SPEAKING TO THE ACTORS IN HIS INCREDIBLY LOUD VOICE.
PANDORA AND DIONYSUS, PLEASE REPORT TO THE STAGE FOR AUDITIONS.
IT'S TIME!
PING! PING! PING!
HEY! GOOD MORNING!
LOOKS LIKE THE GANG'S ALL HERE!
MISSED YOU AT BREAKFAST!
OUR TURN, RIGHT?
YUP! LET'S SHOW 'EM HOW IT'S DONE!
SHOW ME FASTER, CHILDREN.
I DON'T HAVE ALL ETERNITY TO SPEND ON THIS!
YIP YIP!
SIRIUS! DOWN
SHE DOESN'T KNOW YOU YET, PUPPY.
BEHAVE!
THANK YOU!

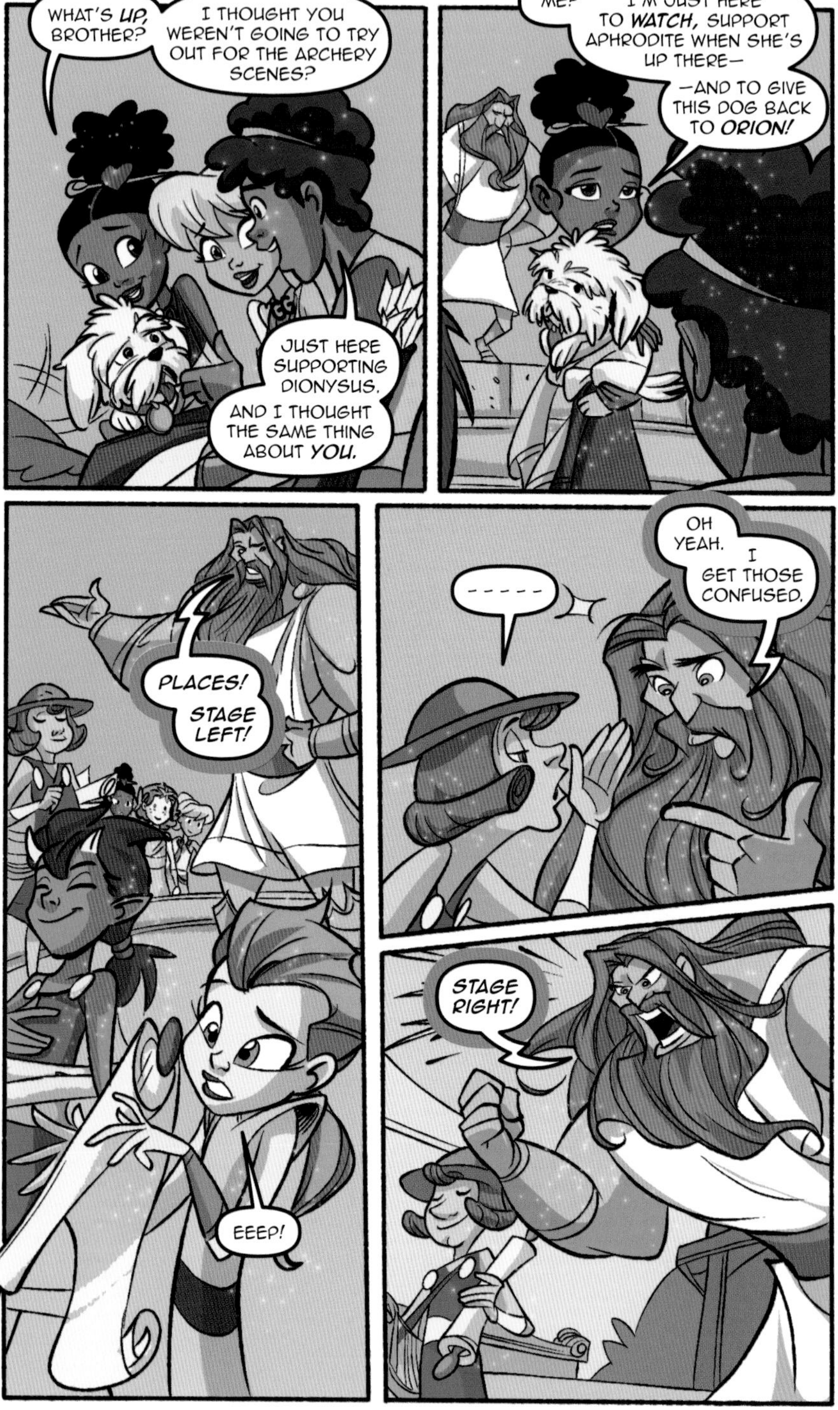

WHAT'S UP, BROTHER?
I THOUGHT YOU WEREN'T GOING TO TRY OUT FOR THE ARCHERY SCENES?
JUST HERE SUPPORTING DIONYSUS.
AND I THOUGHT THE SAME THING ABOUT YOU.
ME?
I'M JUST HERE TO WATCH, SUPPORT APHRODITE WHEN SHE'S UP THERE—
—AND TO GIVE THIS DOG BACK TO ORION!
PLACES!
STAGE LEFT!
EEEP!
- - - - -
OH YEAH.
I GET THOSE CONFUSED.
STAGE RIGHT!

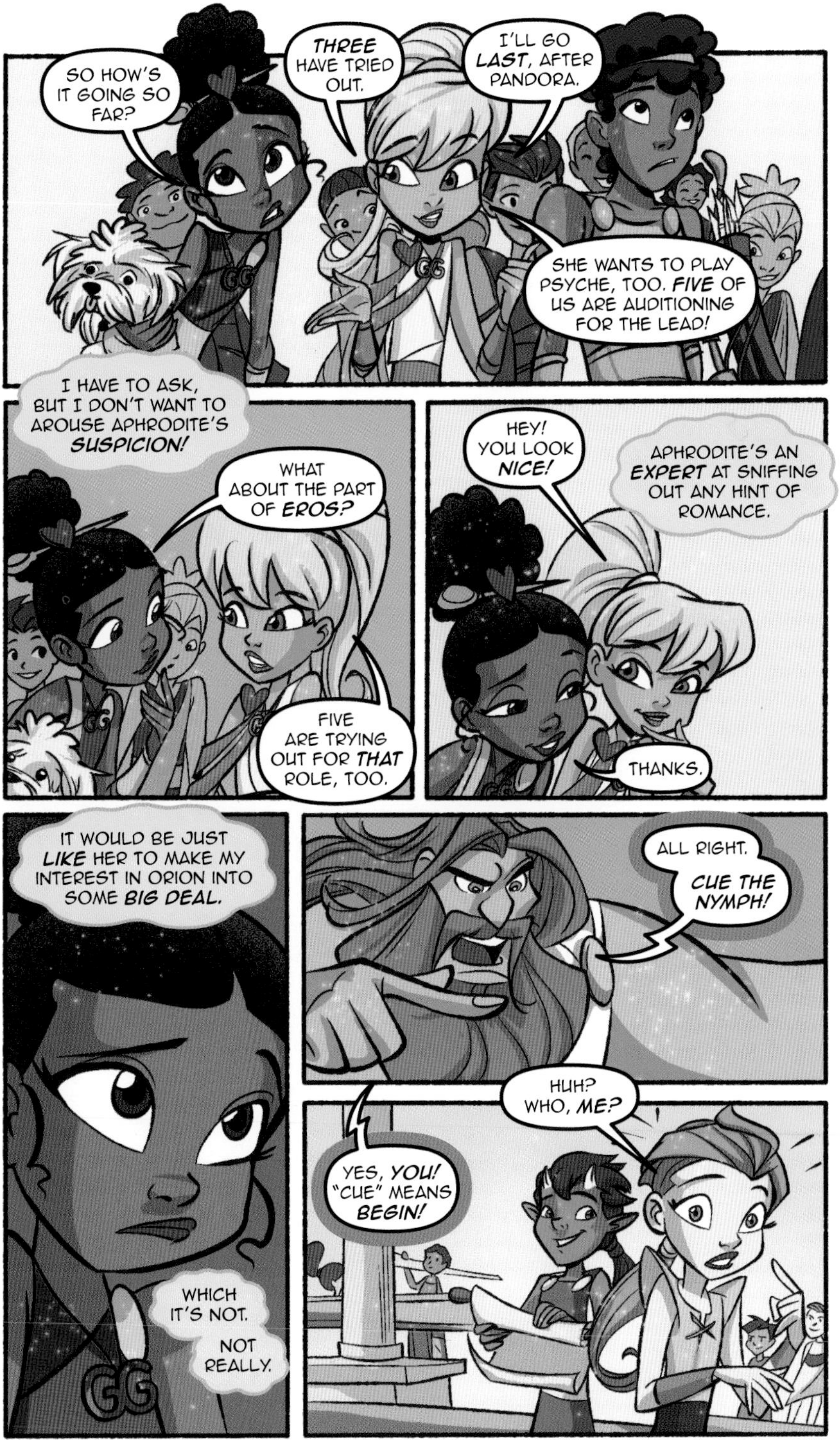
SO HOW'S IT GOING SO FAR?
THREE HAVE TRIED OUT.
I'LL GO LAST, AFTER PANDORA.
SHE WANTS TO PLAY PSYCHE, TOO. FIVE OF US ARE AUDITIONING FOR THE LEAD!
I HAVE TO ASK, BUT I DON'T WANT TO AROUSE APHRODITE'S SUSPICION!
WHAT ABOUT THE PART OF EROS?
FIVE ARE TRYING OUT FOR THAT ROLE, TOO.
HEY! YOU LOOK NICE!
APHRODITE'S AN EXPERT AT SNIFFING OUT ANY HINT OF ROMANCE.
THANKS.
IT WOULD BE JUST LIKE HER TO MAKE MY INTEREST IN ORION INTO SOME BIG DEAL.
WHICH IT'S NOT.
NOT REALLY.
ALL RIGHT.
CUE THE NYMPH!
HUH? WHO, ME?
YES, YOU! "CUE" MEANS BEGIN!

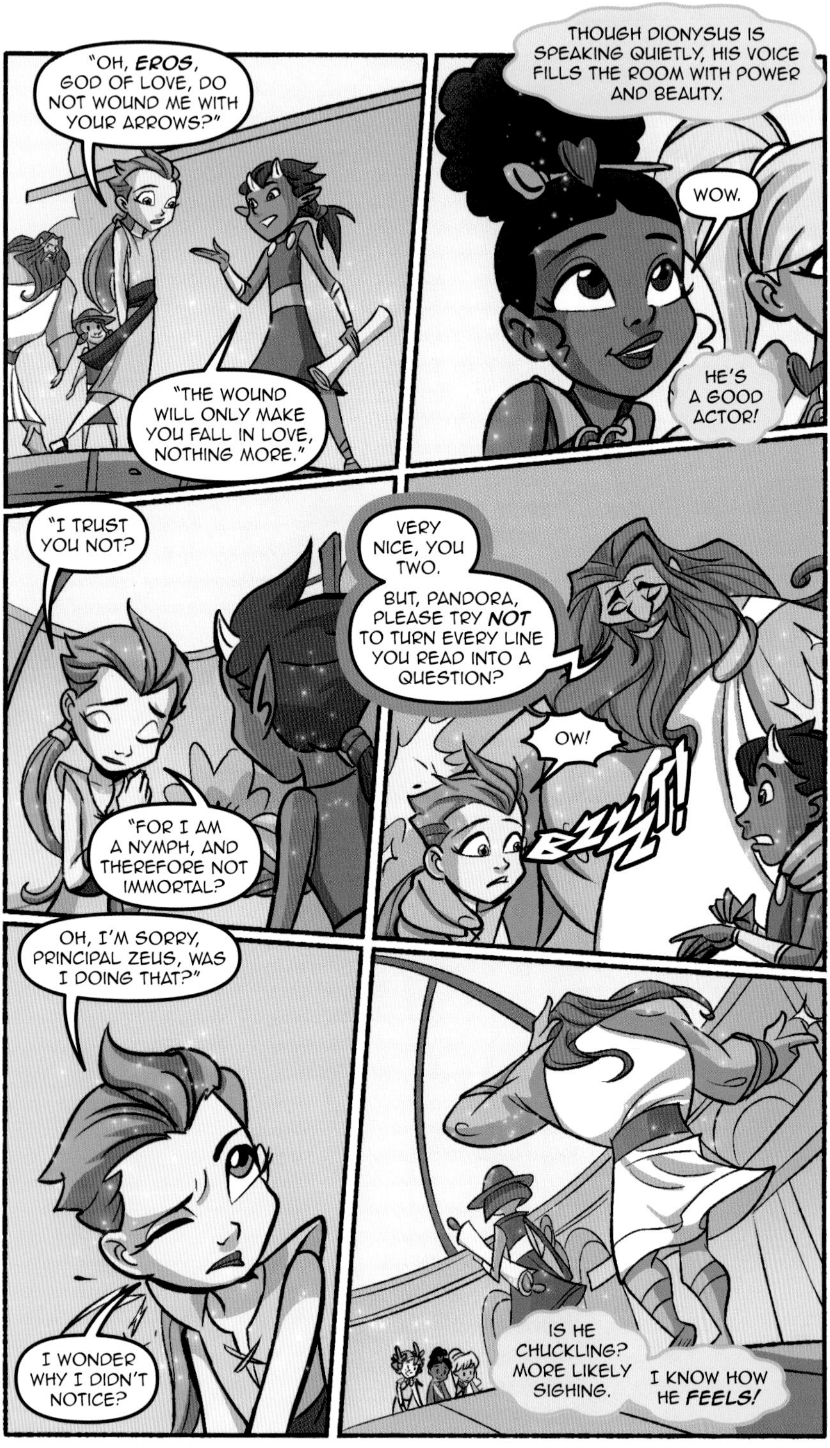
"OH, *EROS*, GOD OF LOVE, DO NOT WOUND ME WITH YOUR ARROWS?"
"THE WOUND WILL ONLY MAKE YOU FALL IN LOVE, NOTHING MORE."
THOUGH DIONYSUS IS SPEAKING QUIETLY, HIS VOICE FILLS THE ROOM WITH POWER AND BEAUTY.
WOW.
HE'S A GOOD ACTOR!
"I TRUST YOU NOT?
"FOR I AM A NYMPH, AND THEREFORE NOT IMMORTAL?
VERY NICE, YOU TWO.
BUT, PANDORA, PLEASE TRY *NOT* TO TURN EVERY LINE YOU READ INTO A QUESTION?
OW!
BZZZT!
OH, I'M SORRY, PRINCIPAL ZEUS, WAS I DOING THAT?"
I WONDER WHY I DIDN'T NOTICE?
IS HE CHUCKLING? MORE LIKELY SIGHING.
I KNOW HOW HE *FEELS!*

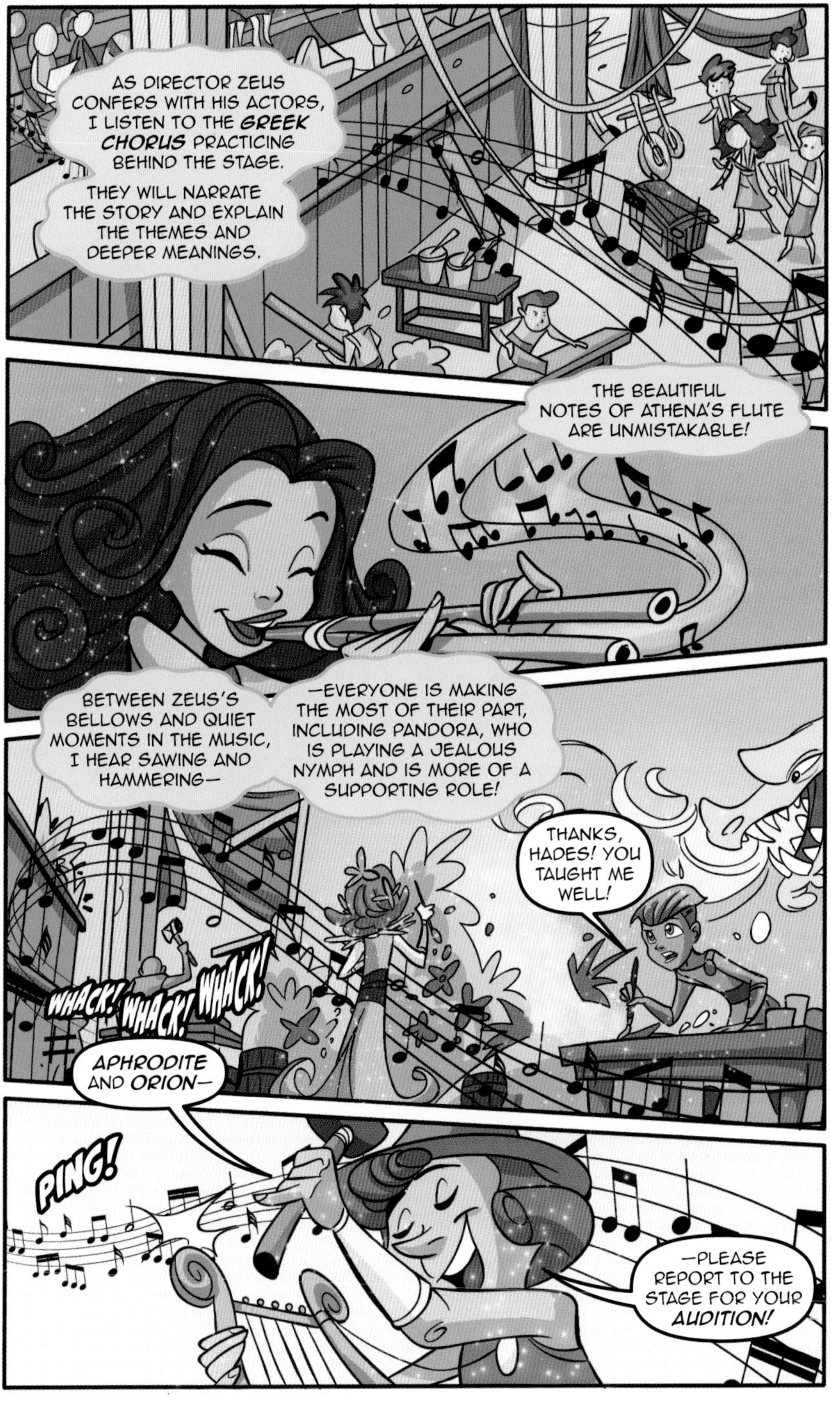
AS DIRECTOR ZEUS CONFERS WITH HIS ACTORS, I LISTEN TO THE *GREEK CHORUS* PRACTICING BEHIND THE STAGE.
THEY WILL NARRATE THE STORY AND EXPLAIN THE THEMES AND DEEPER MEANINGS.
THE BEAUTIFUL NOTES OF ATHENA'S FLUTE ARE UNMISTAKABLE!
BETWEEN ZEUS'S BELLOWS AND QUIET MOMENTS IN THE MUSIC, I HEAR SAWING AND HAMMERING—
—EVERYONE IS MAKING THE MOST OF THEIR PART, INCLUDING PANDORA, WHO IS PLAYING A JEALOUS NYMPH AND IS MORE OF A SUPPORTING ROLE!
THANKS, HADES! YOU TAUGHT ME WELL!
WHACK! WHACK! WHACK!
APHRODITE AND *ORION*—
PING!
—PLEASE REPORT TO THE STAGE FOR YOUR *AUDITION!*

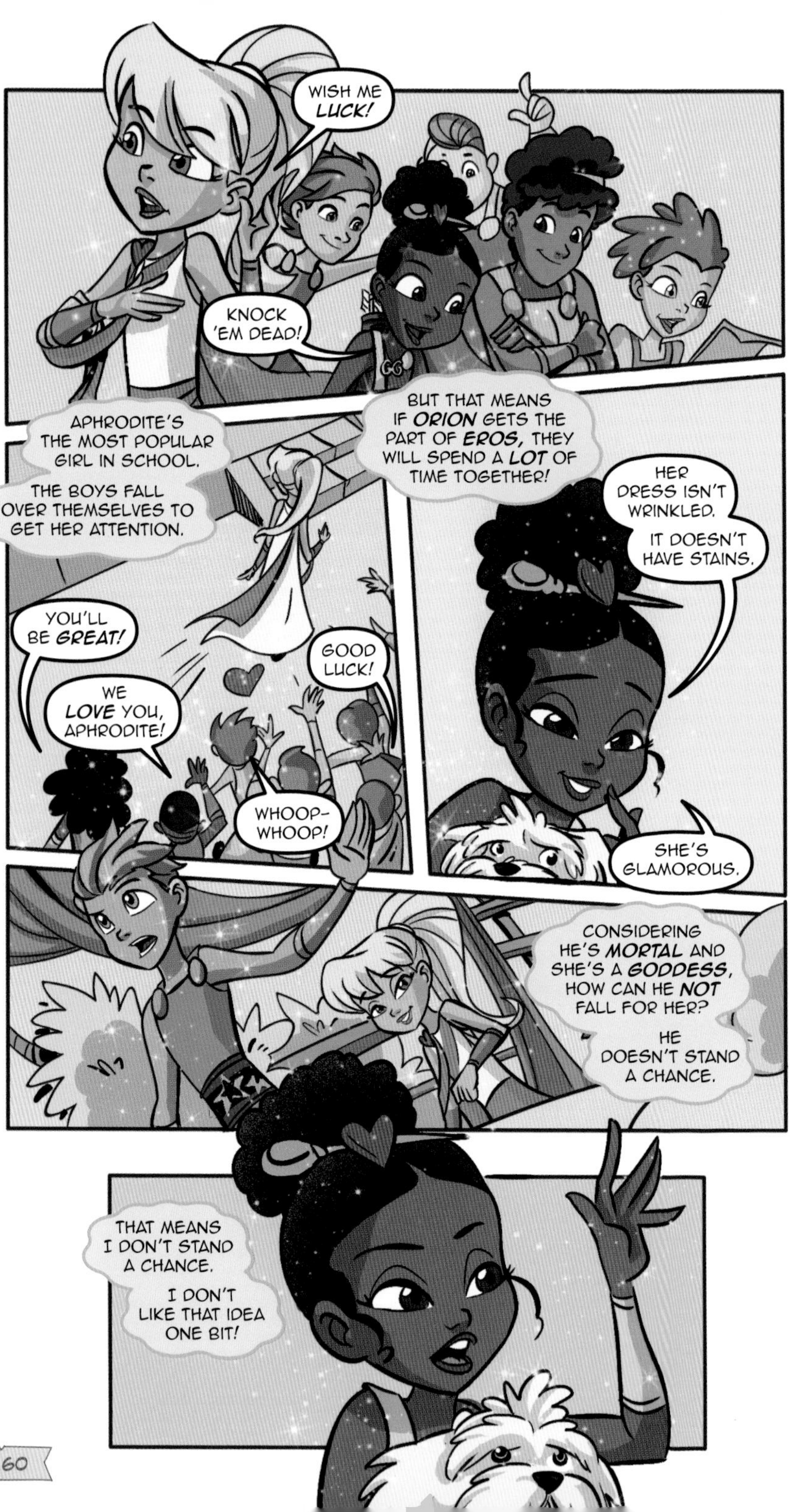
WISH ME LUCK!
KNOCK 'EM DEAD!
APHRODITE'S THE MOST POPULAR GIRL IN SCHOOL.
THE BOYS FALL OVER THEMSELVES TO GET HER ATTENTION.
BUT THAT MEANS IF ORION GETS THE PART OF EROS, THEY WILL SPEND A LOT OF TIME TOGETHER!
YOU'LL BE GREAT!
GOOD LUCK!
WE LOVE YOU, APHRODITE!
WHOOP-WHOOP!
HER DRESS ISN'T WRINKLED.
IT DOESN'T HAVE STAINS.
SHE'S GLAMOROUS.
CONSIDERING HE'S MORTAL AND SHE'S A GODDESS, HOW CAN HE NOT FALL FOR HER?
HE DOESN'T STAND A CHANCE.
THAT MEANS I DON'T STAND A CHANCE.
I DON'T LIKE THAT IDEA ONE BIT!

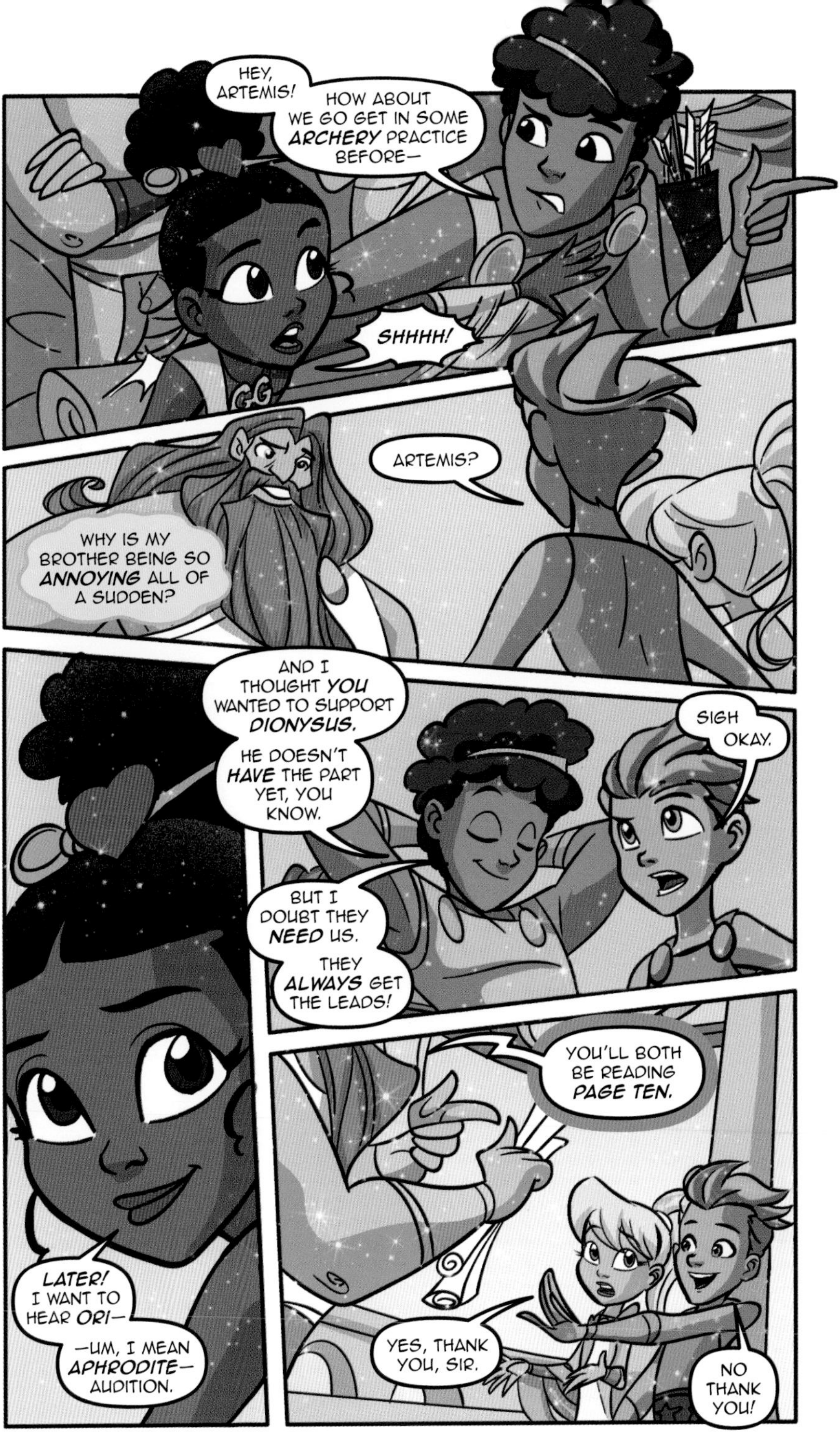
HEY, ARTEMIS!
HOW ABOUT WE GO GET IN SOME ARCHERY PRACTICE BEFORE—
SHHHH!
ARTEMIS?
WHY IS MY BROTHER BEING SO ANNOYING ALL OF A SUDDEN?
AND I THOUGHT YOU WANTED TO SUPPORT DIONYSUS.
HE DOESN'T HAVE THE PART YET, YOU KNOW.
SIGH
OKAY.
BUT I DOUBT THEY NEED US.
THEY ALWAYS GET THE LEADS!
LATER! I WANT TO HEAR ORI—
—UM, I MEAN APHRODITE— AUDITION.
YOU'LL BOTH BE READING PAGE TEN.
YES, THANK YOU, SIR.
NO THANK YOU!

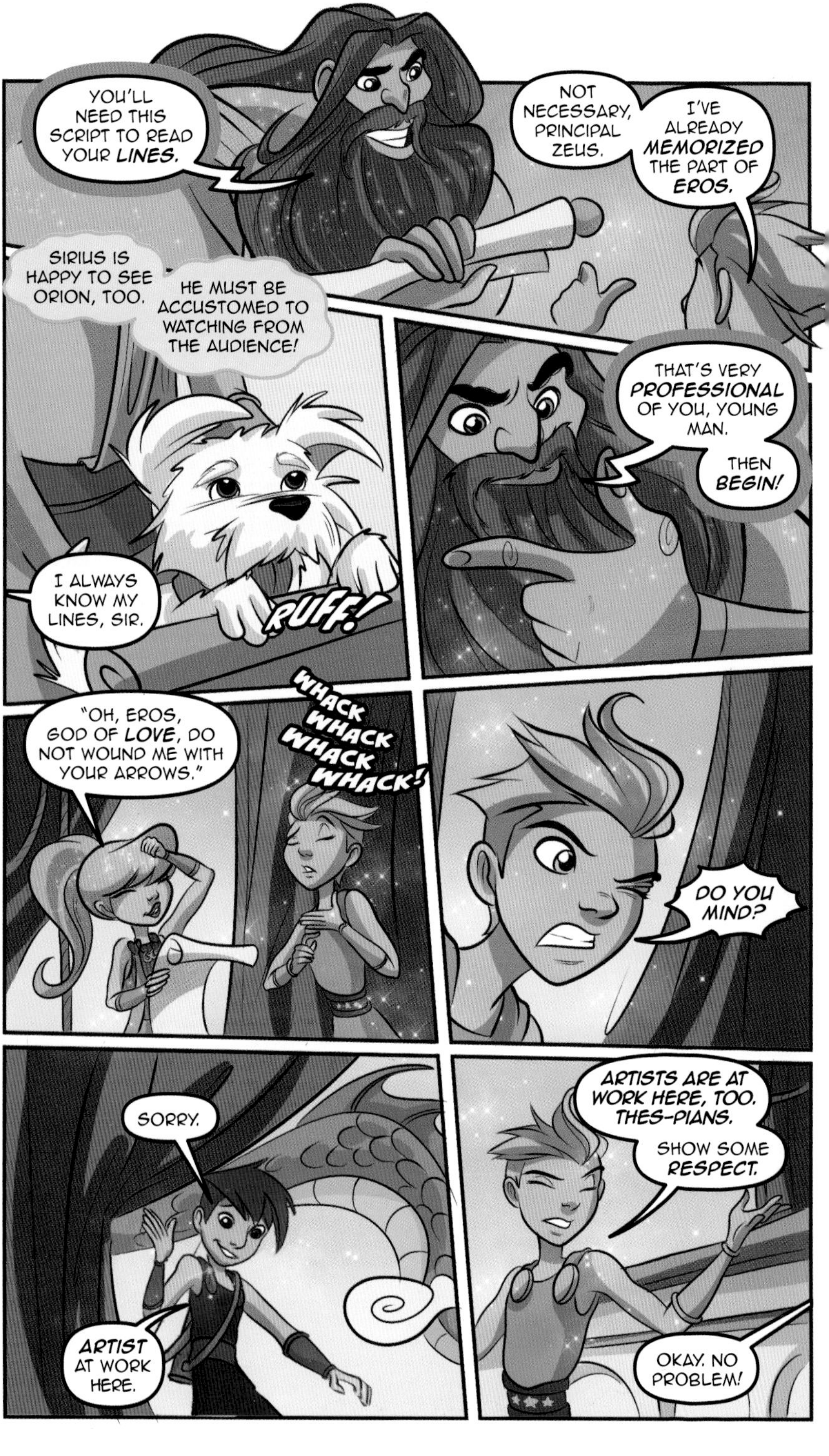
YOU'LL NEED THIS SCRIPT TO READ YOUR LINES.
NOT NECESSARY, PRINCIPAL ZEUS.
I'VE ALREADY MEMORIZED THE PART OF EROS.
SIRIUS IS HAPPY TO SEE ORION, TOO.
HE MUST BE ACCUSTOMED TO WATCHING FROM THE AUDIENCE!
THAT'S VERY PROFESSIONAL OF YOU, YOUNG MAN.
THEN BEGIN!
I ALWAYS KNOW MY LINES, SIR.
RUFF!
"OH, EROS, GOD OF LOVE, DO NOT WOUND ME WITH YOUR ARROWS."
WHACK WHACK WHACK WHACK!
DO YOU MIND?
SORRY.
ARTIST AT WORK HERE.
ARTISTS ARE AT WORK HERE, TOO. THES-PIANS.
SHOW SOME RESPECT.
OKAY. NO PROBLEM!

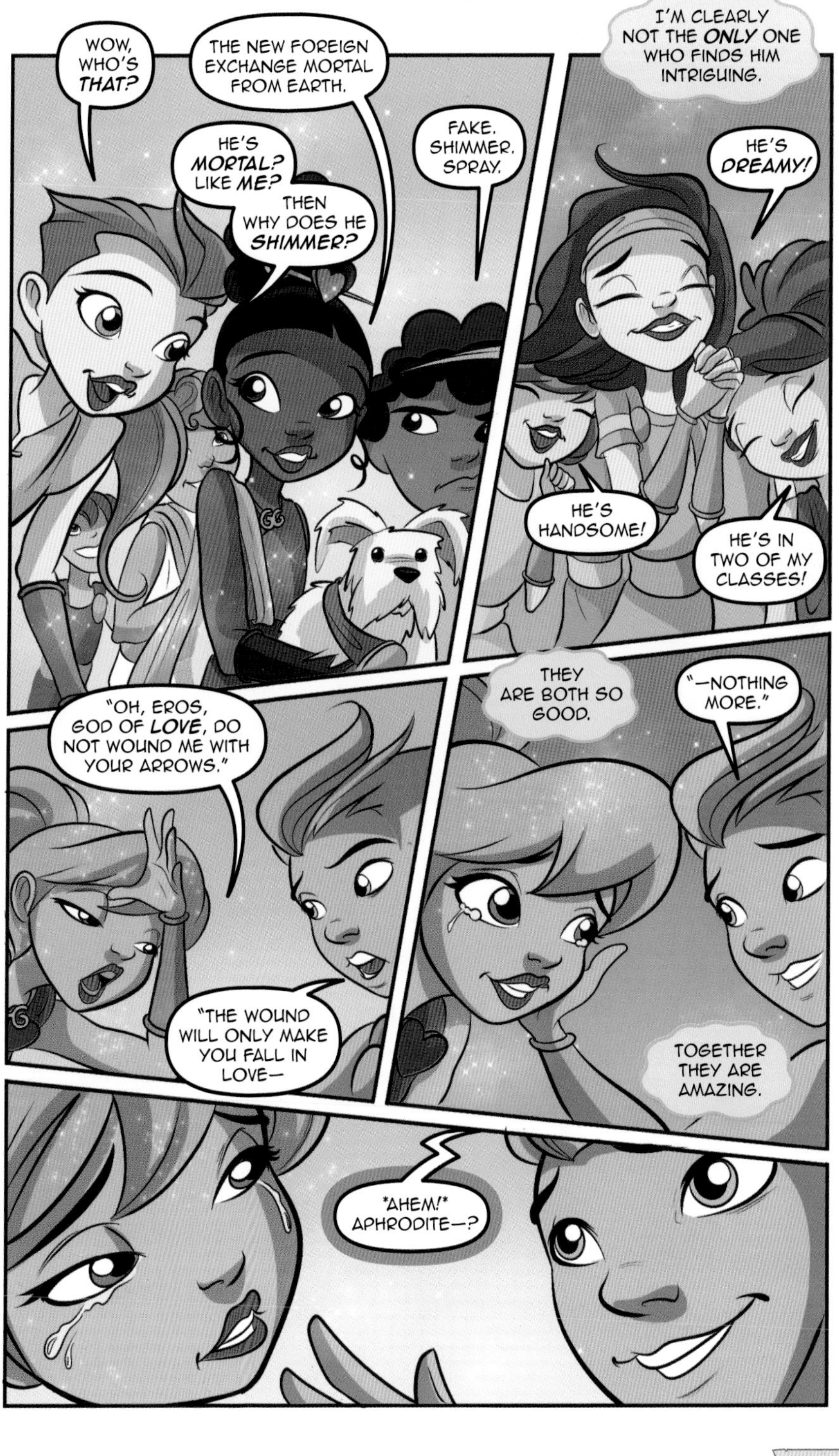
WOW, WHO'S *THAT?*
THE NEW FOREIGN EXCHANGE MORTAL FROM EARTH.
HE'S *MORTAL?* LIKE *ME?*
THEN WHY DOES HE *SHIMMER?*
FAKE. SHIMMER. SPRAY.
I'M CLEARLY NOT THE *ONLY* ONE WHO FINDS HIM INTRIGUING.
HE'S *DREAMY!*
HE'S HANDSOME!
HE'S IN TWO OF MY CLASSES!
"OH, EROS, GOD OF *LOVE*, DO NOT WOUND ME WITH YOUR ARROWS."
"THE WOUND WILL ONLY MAKE YOU FALL IN LOVE—
THEY ARE BOTH SO GOOD.
"—NOTHING MORE."
TOGETHER THEY ARE AMAZING.
AHEM! APHRODITE—?

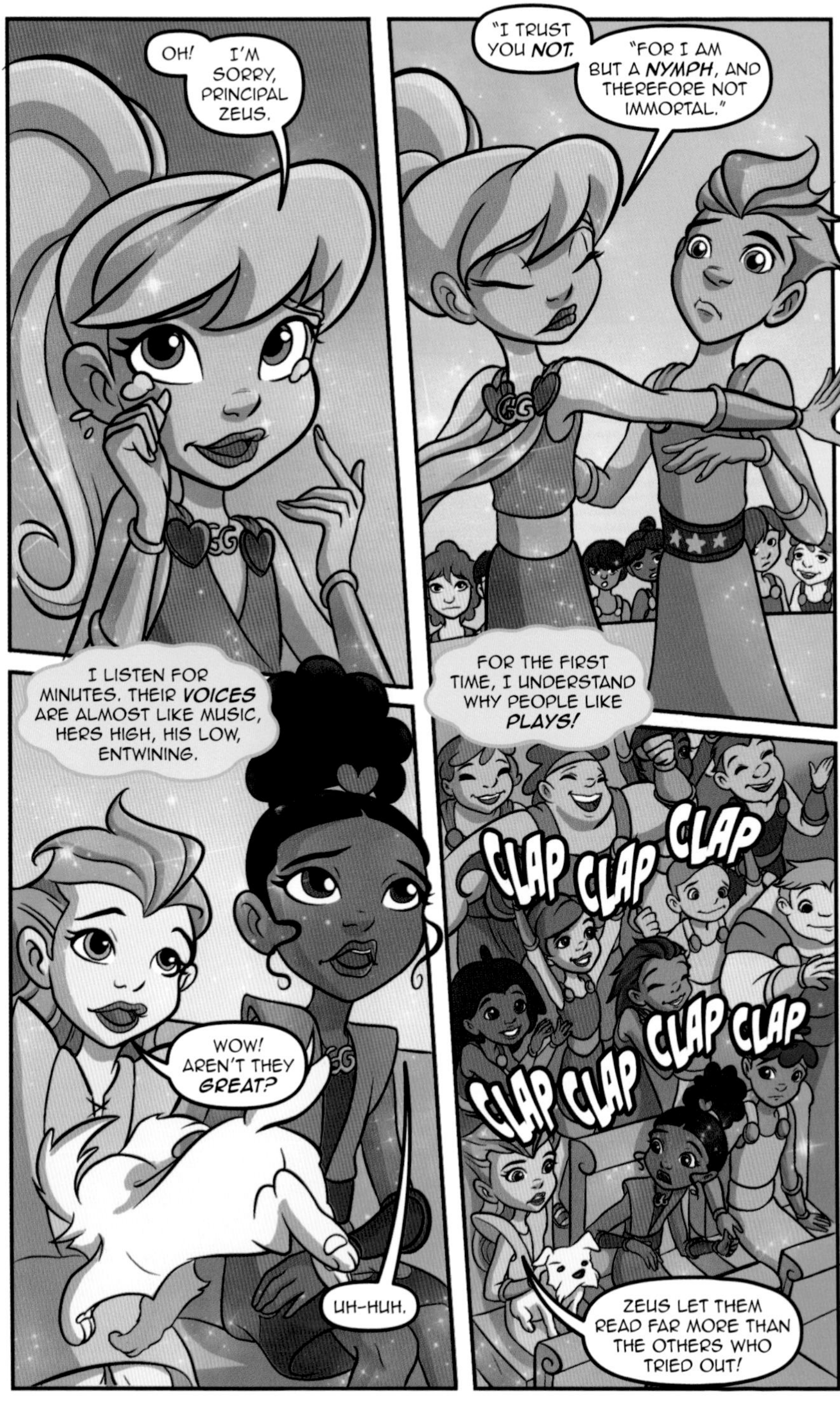
OH!
I'M SORRY, PRINCIPAL ZEUS.
"I TRUST YOU NOT.
"FOR I AM BUT A NYMPH, AND THEREFORE NOT IMMORTAL."
I LISTEN FOR MINUTES. THEIR VOICES ARE ALMOST LIKE MUSIC, HERS HIGH, HIS LOW, ENTWINING.
WOW! AREN'T THEY GREAT?
UH-HUH.
FOR THE FIRST TIME, I UNDERSTAND WHY PEOPLE LIKE PLAYS!
CLAP CLAP CLAP
CLAP CLAP CLAP CLAP
ZEUS LET THEM READ FAR MORE THAN THE OTHERS WHO TRIED OUT!

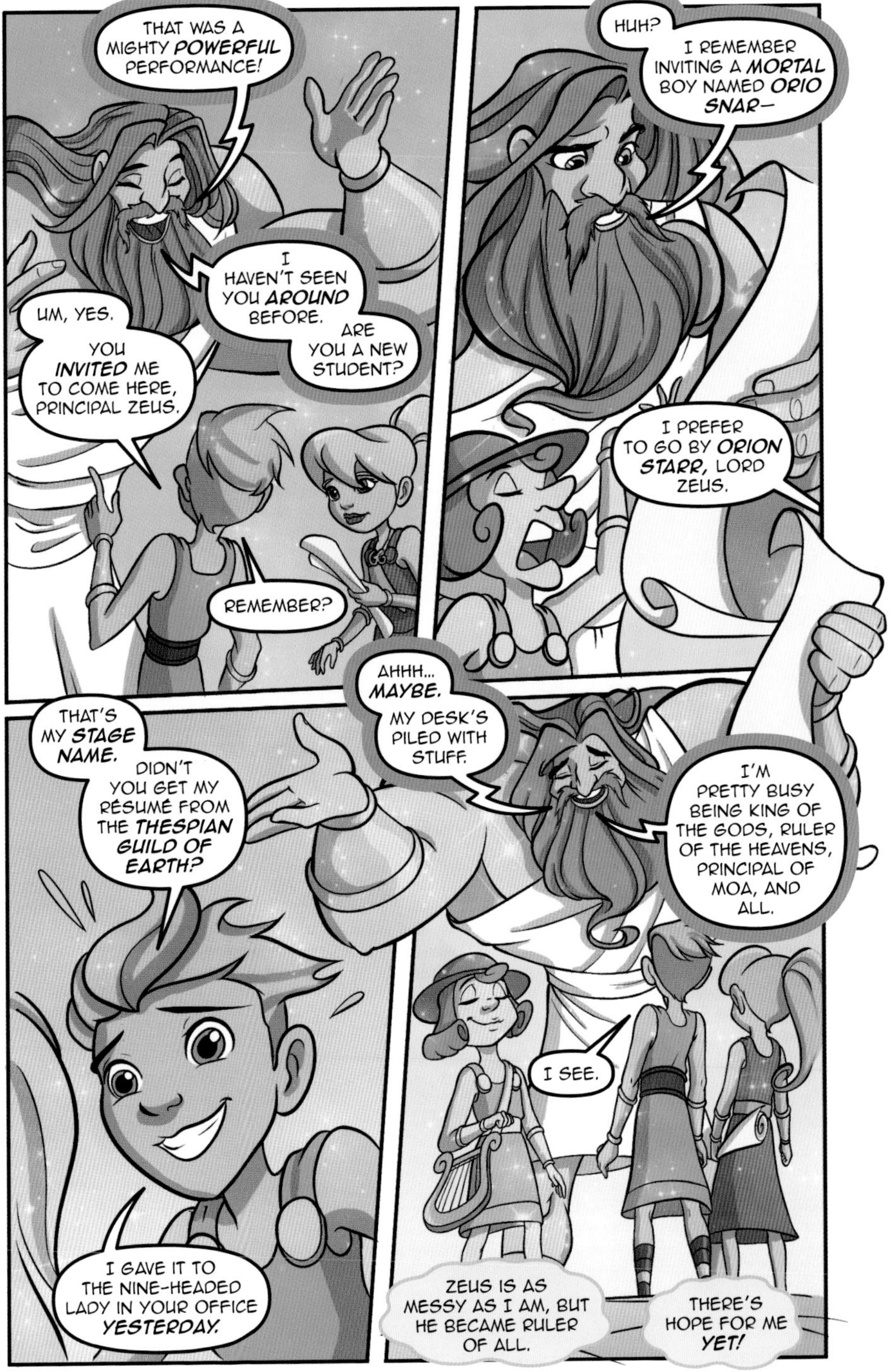
THAT WAS A MIGHTY POWERFUL PERFORMANCE!
I HAVEN'T SEEN YOU AROUND BEFORE.
ARE YOU A NEW STUDENT?
UM, YES.
YOU INVITED ME TO COME HERE, PRINCIPAL ZEUS.
REMEMBER?
HUH?
I REMEMBER INVITING A MORTAL BOY NAMED ORIO SNAR—
I PREFER TO GO BY ORION STARR, LORD ZEUS.
THAT'S MY STAGE NAME.
DIDN'T YOU GET MY RÉSUMÉ FROM THE THESPIAN GUILD OF EARTH?
I GAVE IT TO THE NINE-HEADED LADY IN YOUR OFFICE YESTERDAY.
AHHH... MAYBE.
MY DESK'S PILED WITH STUFF.
I'M PRETTY BUSY BEING KING OF THE GODS, RULER OF THE HEAVENS, PRINCIPAL OF MOA, AND ALL.
I SEE.
ZEUS IS AS MESSY AS I AM, BUT HE BECAME RULER OF ALL.
THERE'S HOPE FOR ME YET!

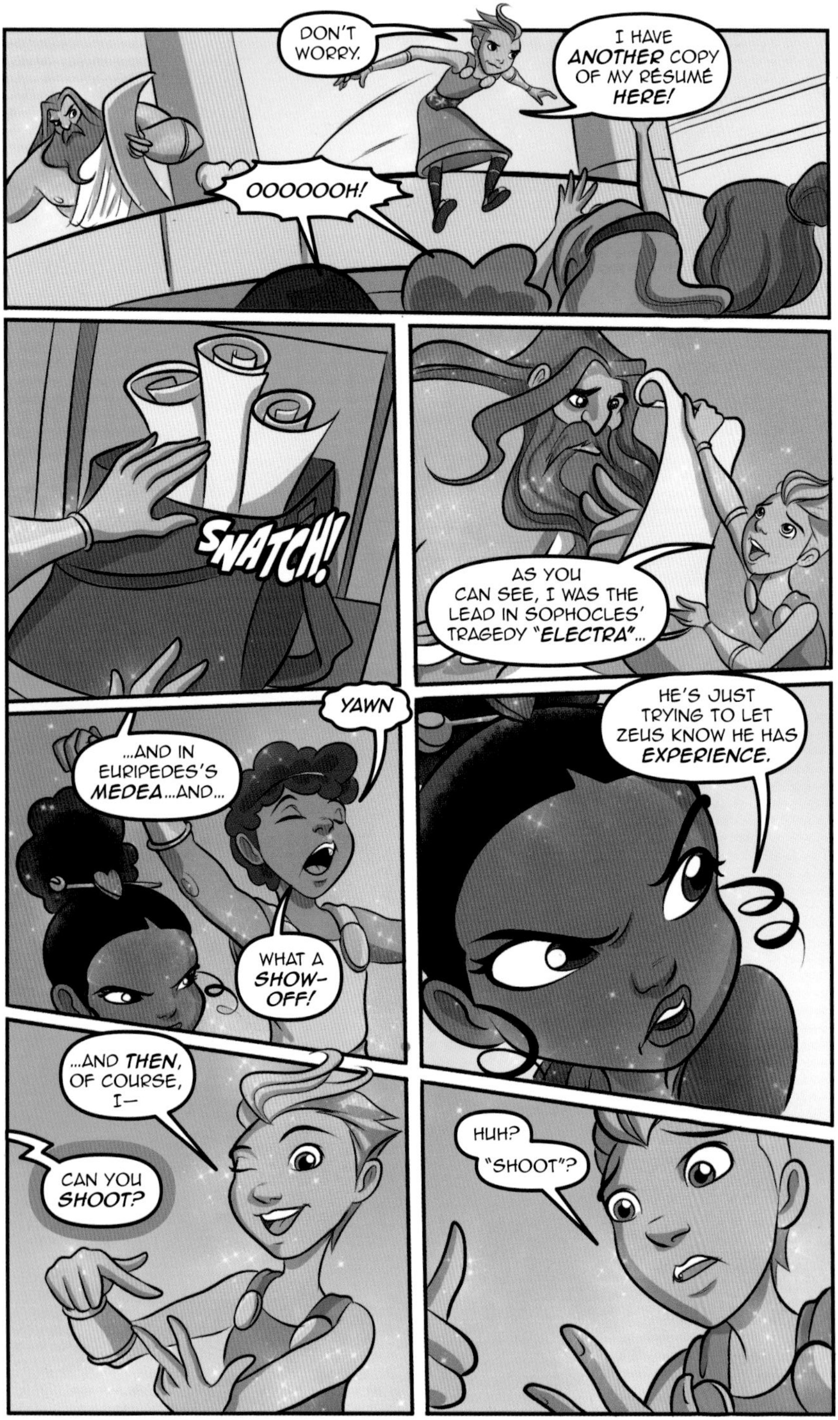
DON'T WORRY.
I HAVE ANOTHER COPY OF MY RÉSUMÉ HERE!
OOOOOOH!
SNATCH!
AS YOU CAN SEE, I WAS THE LEAD IN SOPHOCLES' TRAGEDY "ELECTRA"...
...AND IN EURIPEDES'S MEDEA...AND...
YAWN
WHAT A SHOW-OFF!
HE'S JUST TRYING TO LET ZEUS KNOW HE HAS EXPERIENCE.
...AND THEN, OF COURSE, I—
CAN YOU SHOOT?
HUH? "SHOOT"?

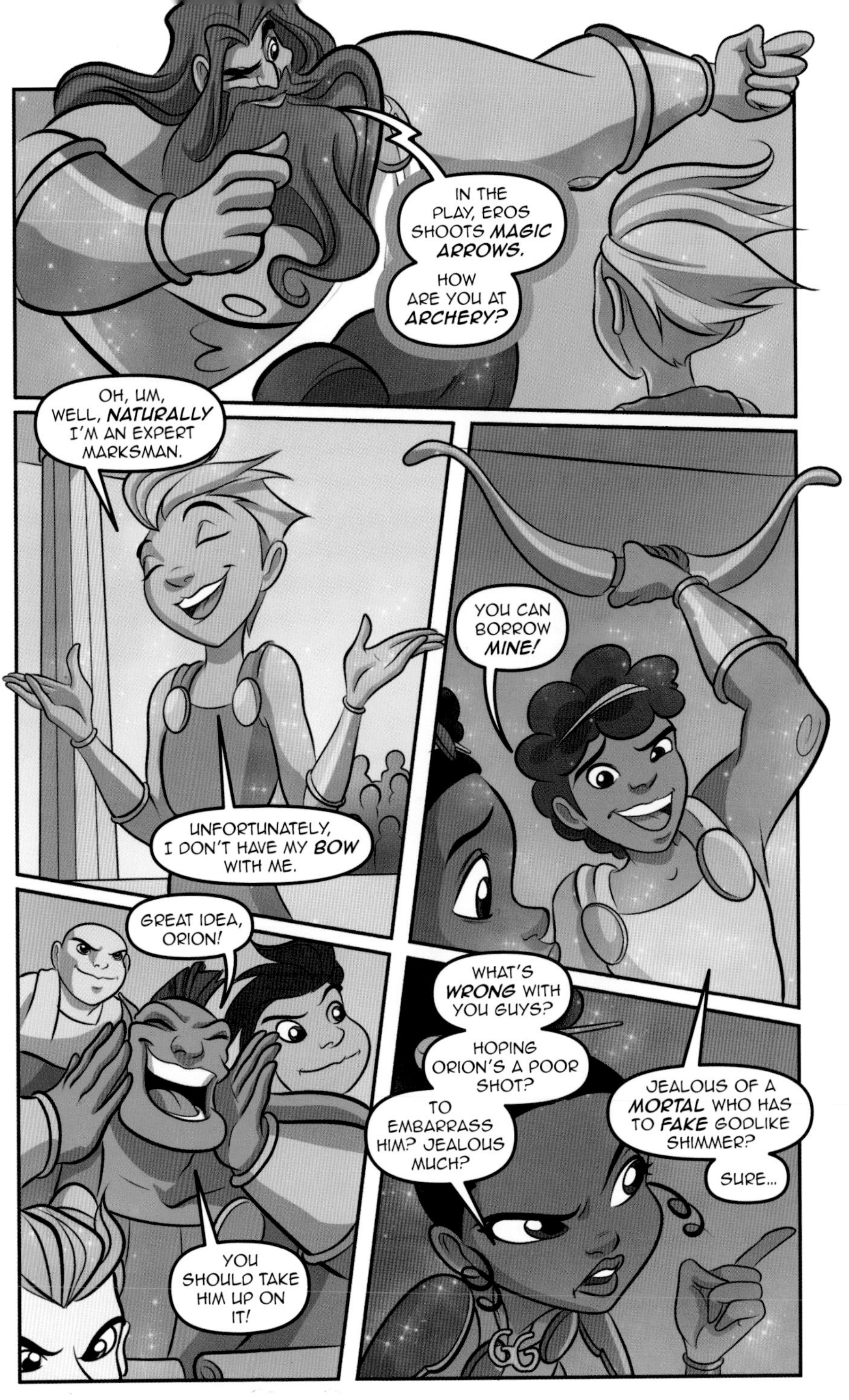
IN THE PLAY, EROS SHOOTS MAGIC ARROWS.
HOW ARE YOU AT ARCHERY?
OH, UM, WELL, NATURALLY I'M AN EXPERT MARKSMAN.
UNFORTUNATELY, I DON'T HAVE MY BOW WITH ME.
YOU CAN BORROW MINE!
GREAT IDEA, ORION!
YOU SHOULD TAKE HIM UP ON IT!
WHAT'S WRONG WITH YOU GUYS?
HOPING ORION'S A POOR SHOT?
TO EMBARRASS HIM? JEALOUS MUCH?
JEALOUS OF A MORTAL WHO HAS TO FAKE GODLIKE SHIMMER?
SURE...

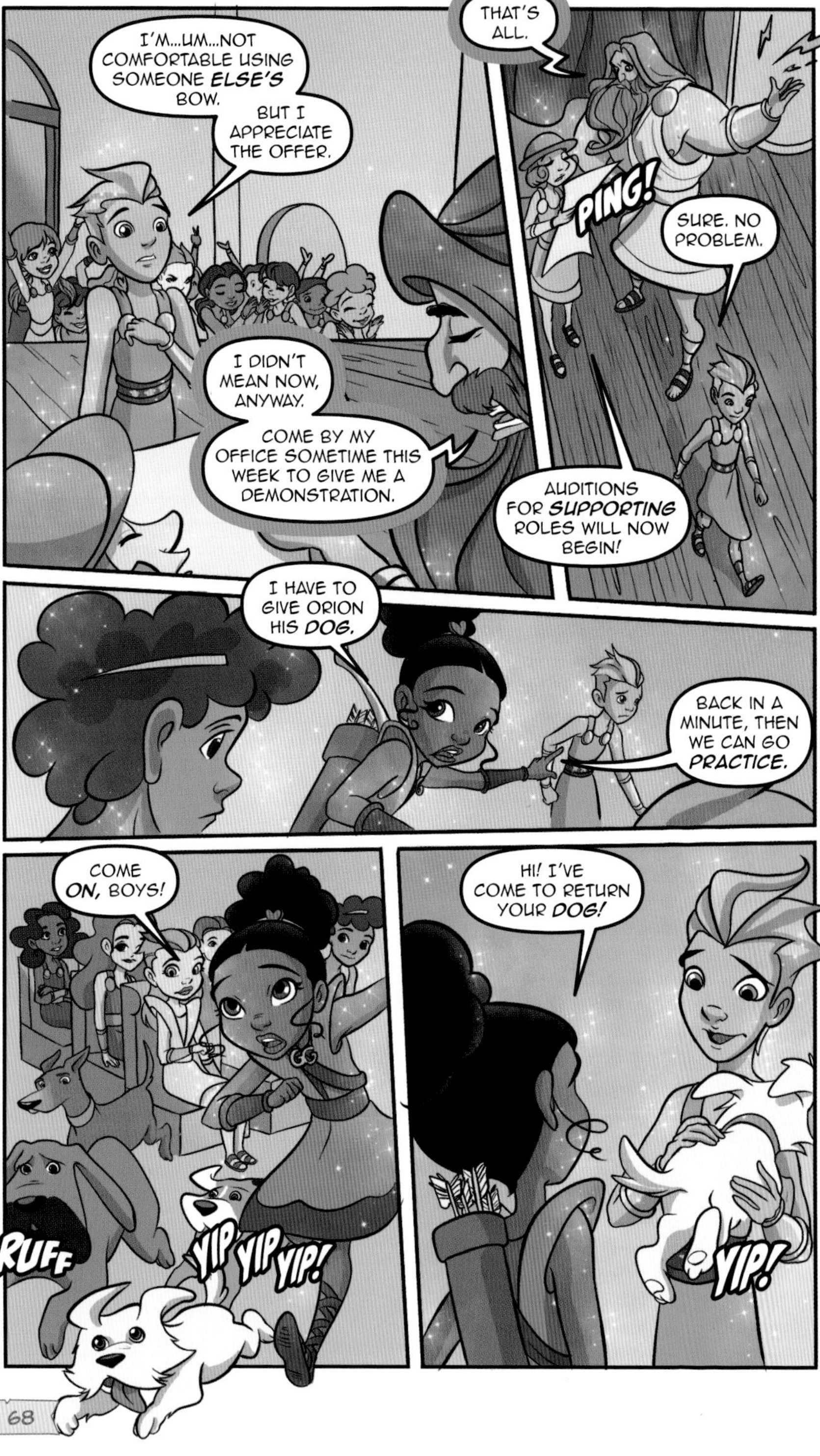

I'M...UM...NOT COMFORTABLE USING SOMEONE ELSE'S BOW.
BUT I APPRECIATE THE OFFER.
I DIDN'T MEAN NOW, ANYWAY.
COME BY MY OFFICE SOMETIME THIS WEEK TO GIVE ME A DEMONSTRATION.
THAT'S ALL.
PING!
SURE. NO PROBLEM.
AUDITIONS FOR SUPPORTING ROLES WILL NOW BEGIN!
I HAVE TO GIVE ORION HIS DOG.
BACK IN A MINUTE, THEN WE CAN GO PRACTICE.
COME ON, BOYS!
RUFF
YIP YIP YIP!
HI! I'VE COME TO RETURN YOUR DOG!
YIP!

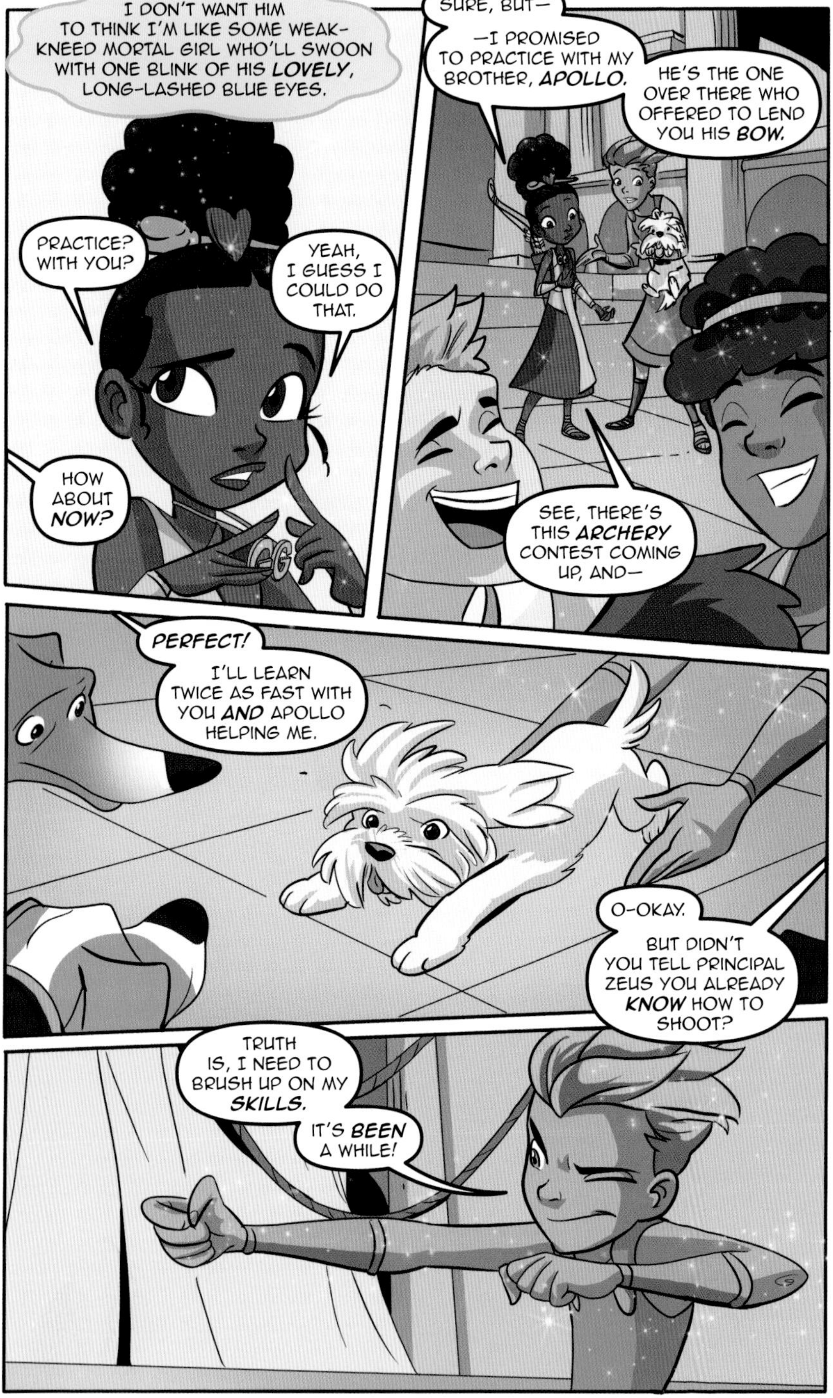
I DON'T WANT HIM TO THINK I'M LIKE SOME WEAK-KNEED MORTAL GIRL WHO'LL SWOON WITH ONE BLINK OF HIS *LOVELY*, LONG-LASHED BLUE EYES.
PRACTICE? WITH YOU?
YEAH, I GUESS I COULD DO THAT.
HOW ABOUT *NOW?*
SURE, BUT—
—I PROMISED TO PRACTICE WITH MY BROTHER, *APOLLO.*
HE'S THE ONE OVER THERE WHO OFFERED TO LEND YOU HIS *BOW.*
SEE, THERE'S THIS *ARCHERY* CONTEST COMING UP, AND—
PERFECT!
I'LL LEARN TWICE AS FAST WITH YOU *AND* APOLLO HELPING ME.
O-OKAY.
BUT DIDN'T YOU TELL PRINCIPAL ZEUS YOU ALREADY *KNOW* HOW TO SHOOT?
TRUTH IS, I NEED TO BRUSH UP ON MY *SKILLS.*
IT'S *BEEN* A WHILE!

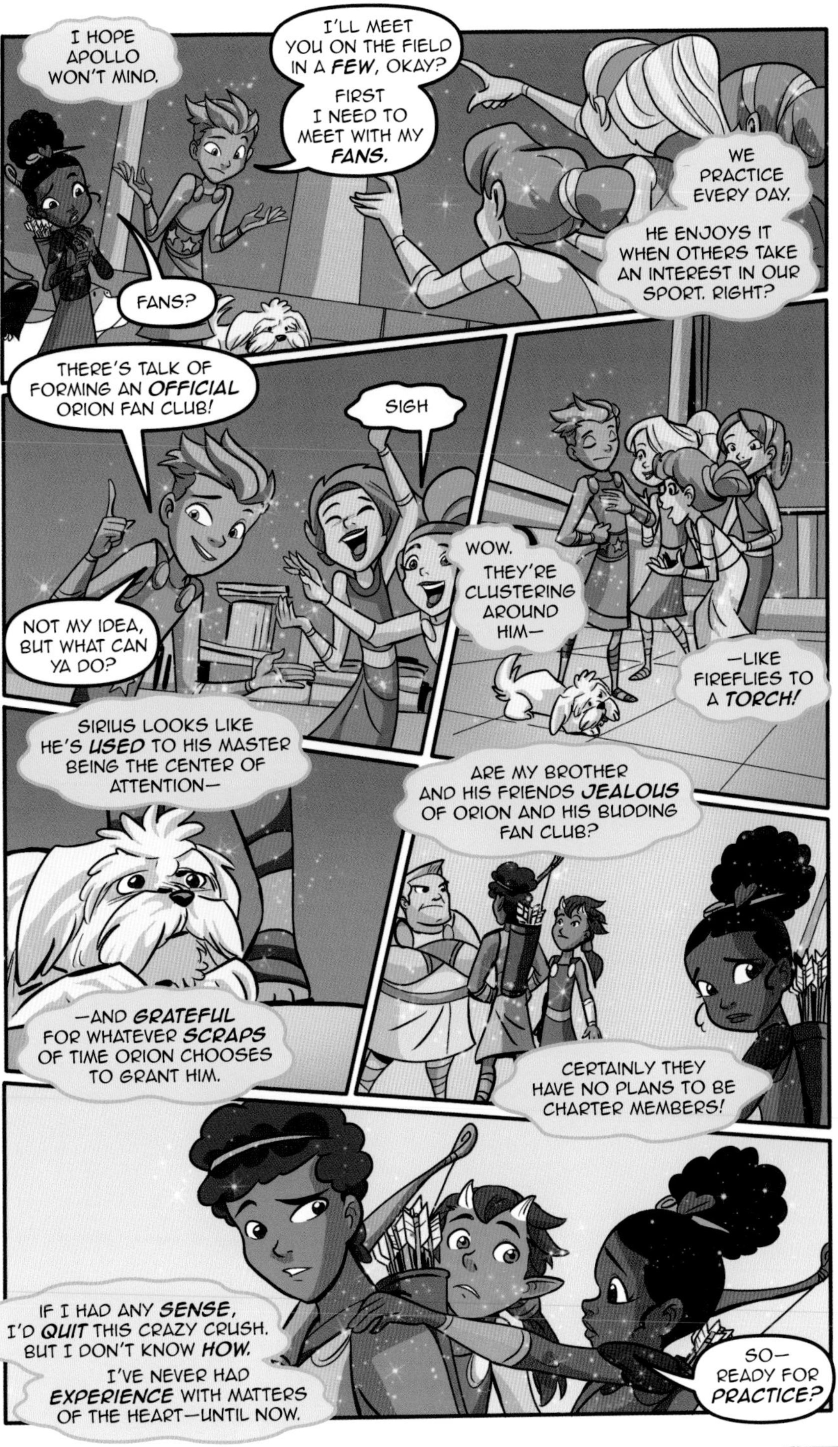

I HOPE APOLLO WON'T MIND.
I'LL MEET YOU ON THE FIELD IN A *FEW*, OKAY?
FIRST I NEED TO MEET WITH MY *FANS*.
WE PRACTICE EVERY DAY.
HE ENJOYS IT WHEN OTHERS TAKE AN INTEREST IN OUR SPORT. RIGHT?
FANS?
THERE'S TALK OF FORMING AN *OFFICIAL* ORION FAN CLUB!
SIGH
NOT MY IDEA, BUT WHAT CAN YA DO?
WOW. THEY'RE CLUSTERING AROUND HIM—
—LIKE FIREFLIES TO A *TORCH!*
SIRIUS LOOKS LIKE HE'S *USED* TO HIS MASTER BEING THE CENTER OF ATTENTION—
—AND *GRATEFUL* FOR WHATEVER *SCRAPS* OF TIME ORION CHOOSES TO GRANT HIM.
ARE MY BROTHER AND HIS FRIENDS *JEALOUS* OF ORION AND HIS BUDDING FAN CLUB?
CERTAINLY THEY HAVE NO PLANS TO BE CHARTER MEMBERS!
IF I HAD ANY *SENSE*, I'D *QUIT* THIS CRAZY CRUSH. BUT I DON'T KNOW *HOW*.
I'VE NEVER HAD *EXPERIENCE* WITH MATTERS OF THE HEART—UNTIL NOW.
SO— READY FOR *PRACTICE?*

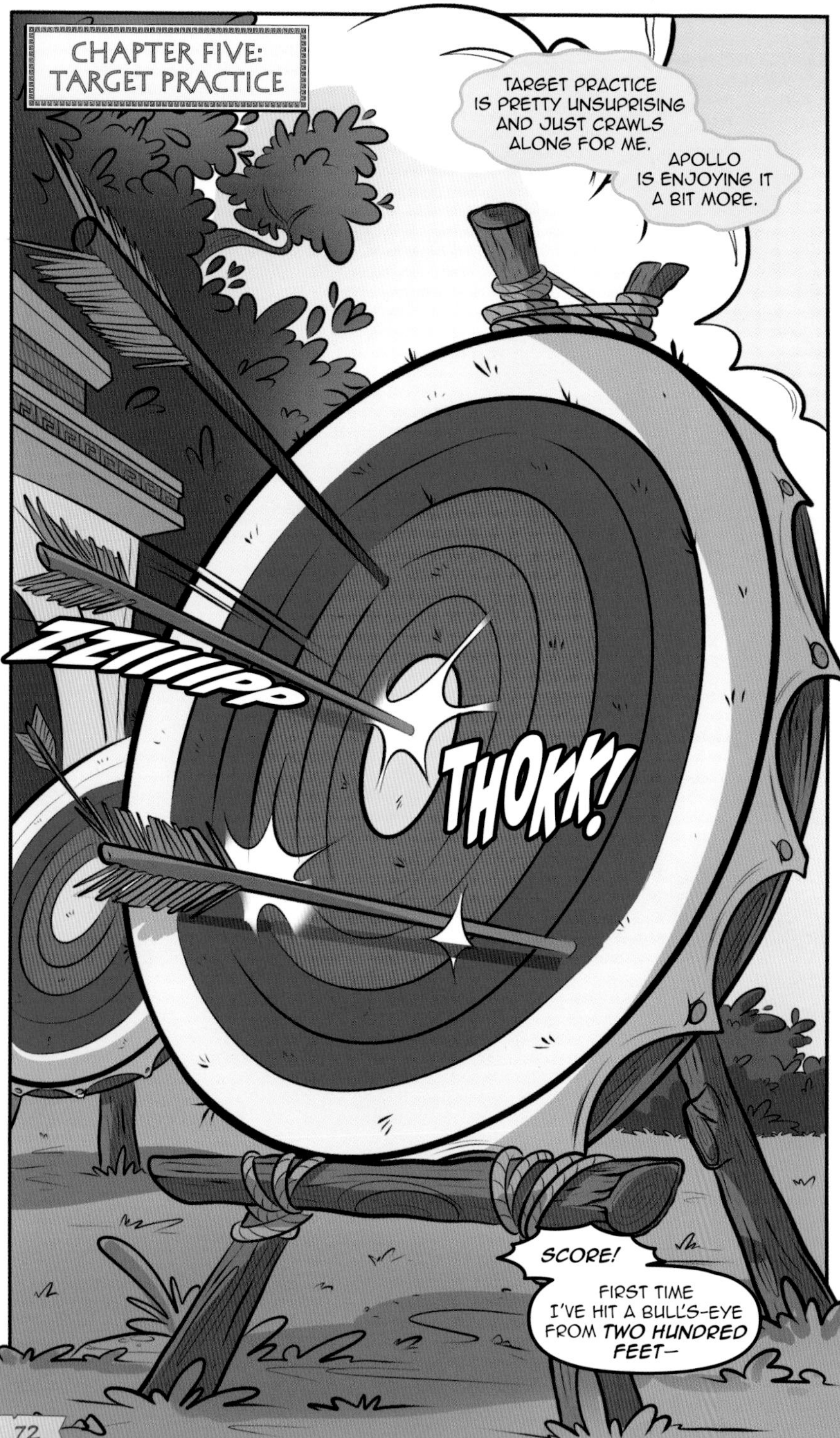

CHAPTER FIVE:
TARGET PRACTICE
TARGET PRACTICE IS PRETTY UNSUPRISING AND JUST CRAWLS ALONG FOR ME.
APOLLO IS ENJOYING IT A BIT MORE.
ZZIIIIPP
THOKK!
SCORE!
FIRST TIME I'VE HIT A BULL'S-EYE FROM *TWO HUNDRED FEET*—

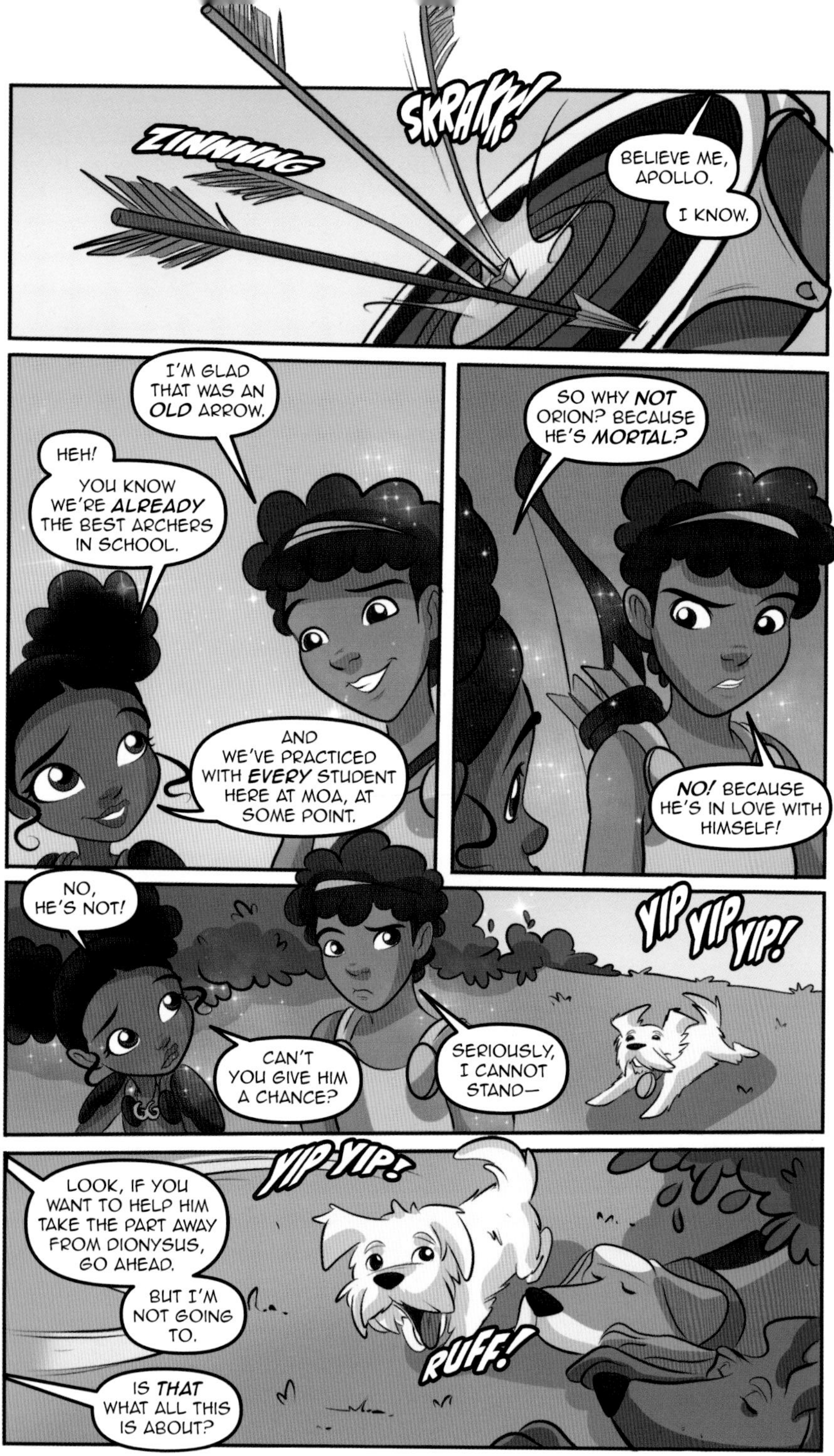
ZINNNNG
SKRAKK!
BELIEVE ME, APOLLO.
I KNOW.
I'M GLAD THAT WAS AN OLD ARROW.
HEH!
YOU KNOW WE'RE ALREADY THE BEST ARCHERS IN SCHOOL.
AND WE'VE PRACTICED WITH EVERY STUDENT HERE AT MOA, AT SOME POINT.
SO WHY NOT ORION? BECAUSE HE'S MORTAL?
NO! BECAUSE HE'S IN LOVE WITH HIMSELF!
NO, HE'S NOT!
CAN'T YOU GIVE HIM A CHANCE?
SERIOUSLY, I CANNOT STAND—
YIP YIP YIP!
LOOK, IF YOU WANT TO HELP HIM TAKE THE PART AWAY FROM DIONYSUS, GO AHEAD.
BUT I'M NOT GOING TO.
YIP YIP!
RUFF!
IS THAT WHAT ALL THIS IS ABOUT?

I **KNOW** YOU AND DIONYSUS ARE GOOD FRIENDS **AND** BANDMATES.

ORION ONLY WANTS A CHANCE TO **PRACTICE** A LITTLE BEFORE SHOWING ZEUS WHAT HE'S **GOT.**

UH-HUH. WHATEVER. I'M OUTTA HERE.

AM I INTERRUPTING?

I WAS JUST **LEAVING.** YOU TWO HAVE **FUN.**

TWINS AND BEST FRIENDS SINCE BIRTH.

IT FEELS **WEIRD** ARGUING WITH HIM!

HEY, I BROUGHT MY OWN **ARROWS**—

—BUT CAN I STILL USE YOUR **BOW,** APOLLO, IF YOU DON'T NEED IT RIGHT NOW?

HMM?

HE NEVER REALLY LETS **ANYONE** BORROW HIS BOW. NOT EVEN **ME.**

THAT'S OKAY.

GIRLS ALWAYS SEEM TO WARM TO ME MORE THAN BOYS. I'VE NEVER UNDERSTOOD IT.

YOU MAY FIND THIS HARD TO BELIEVE—

—I KNOW I DO—

—BUT NOT EVERYONE'S A FAN OF O.

UMMM... "O"?

ARES TALKS LIKE THAT SOMETIMES. I'VE ALWAYS THOUGHT HIM **CONCEITED.**

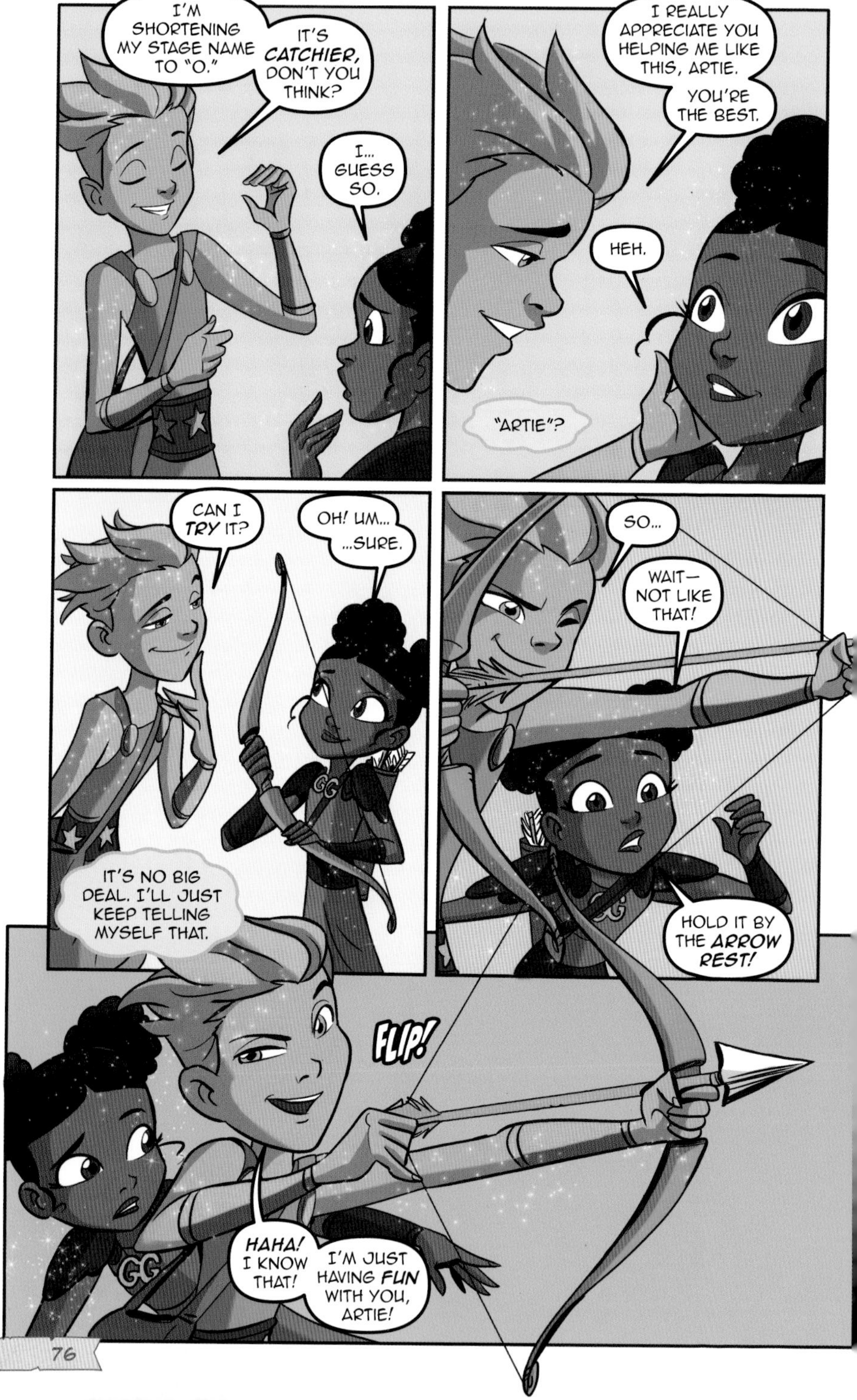
I'M SHORTENING MY STAGE NAME TO "O."
IT'S CATCHIER, DON'T YOU THINK?
I... GUESS SO.
I REALLY APPRECIATE YOU HELPING ME LIKE THIS, ARTIE.
YOU'RE THE BEST.
HEH.
"ARTIE"?
CAN I TRY IT?
OH! UM... ...SURE.
IT'S NO BIG DEAL. I'LL JUST KEEP TELLING MYSELF THAT.
SO...
WAIT— NOT LIKE THAT!
HOLD IT BY THE ARROW REST!
FLIP!
HAHA! I KNOW THAT!
I'M JUST HAVING FUN WITH YOU, ARTIE!

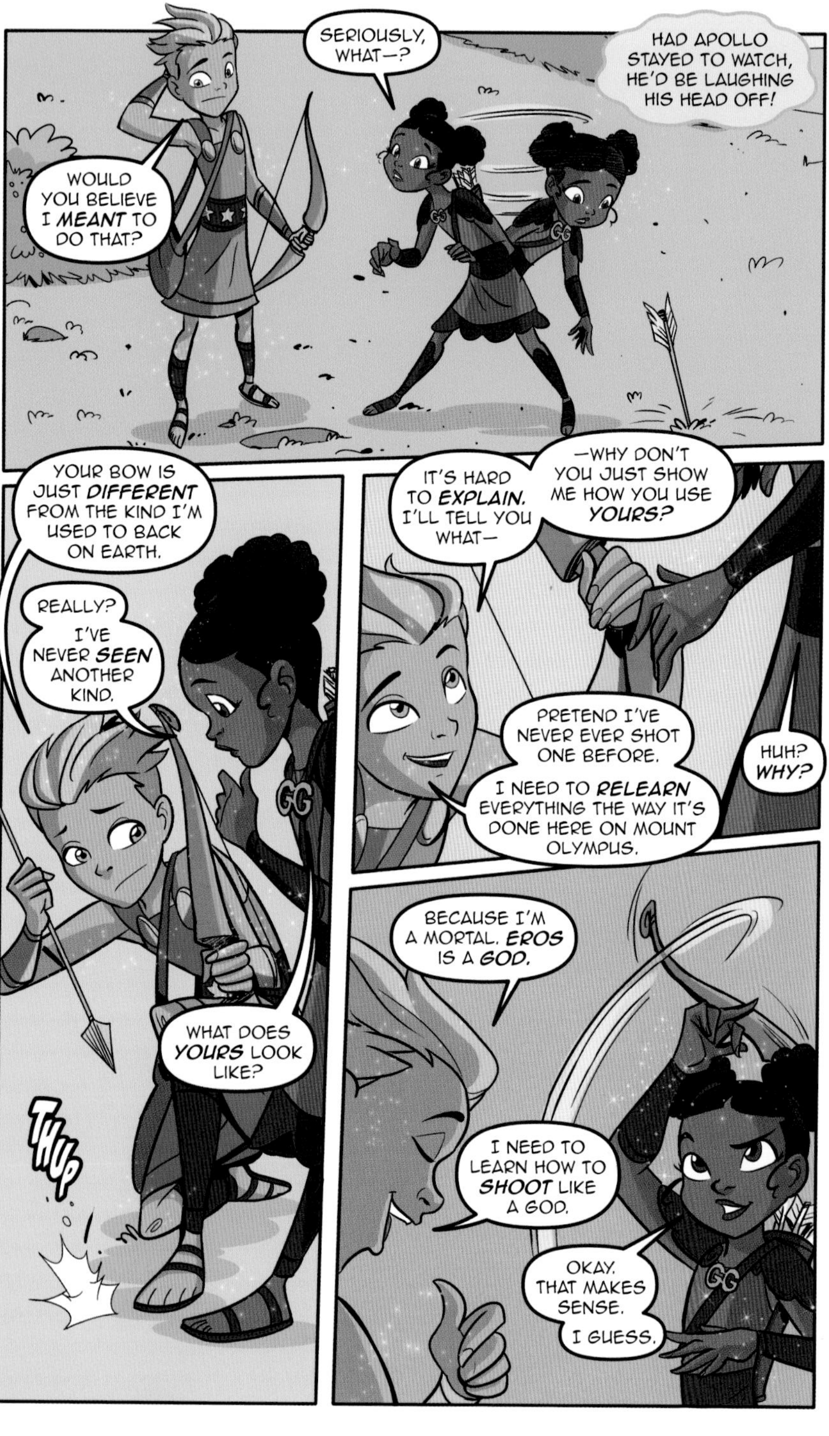
SERIOUSLY, WHAT—?
HAD APOLLO STAYED TO WATCH, HE'D BE LAUGHING HIS HEAD OFF!
WOULD YOU BELIEVE I *MEANT* TO DO THAT?
YOUR BOW IS JUST *DIFFERENT* FROM THE KIND I'M USED TO BACK ON EARTH.
REALLY?
I'VE NEVER *SEEN* ANOTHER KIND.
WHAT DOES *YOURS* LOOK LIKE?
THUP
IT'S HARD TO *EXPLAIN.* I'LL TELL YOU WHAT—
—WHY DON'T YOU JUST SHOW ME HOW YOU USE *YOURS?*
PRETEND I'VE NEVER EVER SHOT ONE BEFORE.
I NEED TO *RELEARN* EVERYTHING THE WAY IT'S DONE HERE ON MOUNT OLYMPUS.
HUH? *WHY?*
BECAUSE I'M A MORTAL. *EROS* IS A *GOD.*
I NEED TO LEARN HOW TO *SHOOT* LIKE A GOD.
OKAY. THAT MAKES SENSE.
I GUESS.

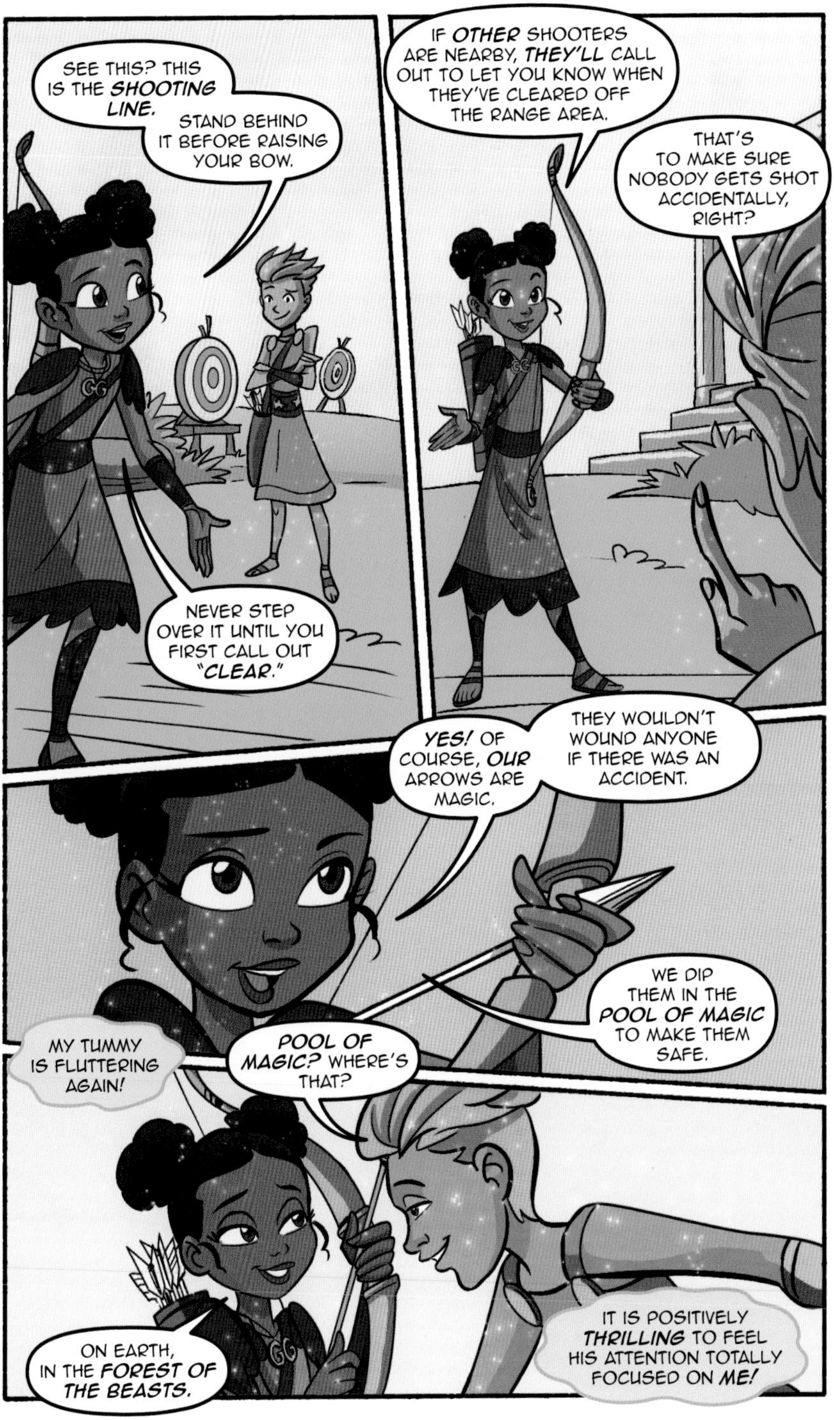
SEE THIS? THIS IS THE *SHOOTING LINE.*
STAND BEHIND IT BEFORE RAISING YOUR BOW.
NEVER STEP OVER IT UNTIL YOU FIRST CALL OUT *"CLEAR."*
IF *OTHER* SHOOTERS ARE NEARBY, *THEY'LL* CALL OUT TO LET YOU KNOW WHEN THEY'VE CLEARED OFF THE RANGE AREA.
THAT'S TO MAKE SURE NOBODY GETS SHOT ACCIDENTALLY, RIGHT?
YES! OF COURSE, *OUR* ARROWS ARE MAGIC.
THEY WOULDN'T WOUND ANYONE IF THERE WAS AN ACCIDENT.
WE DIP THEM IN THE *POOL OF MAGIC* TO MAKE THEM SAFE.
MY TUMMY IS FLUTTERING AGAIN!
POOL OF MAGIC? WHERE'S THAT?
ON EARTH, IN THE *FOREST OF THE BEASTS.*
IT IS POSITIVELY *THRILLING* TO FEEL HIS ATTENTION TOTALLY FOCUSED ON *ME!*

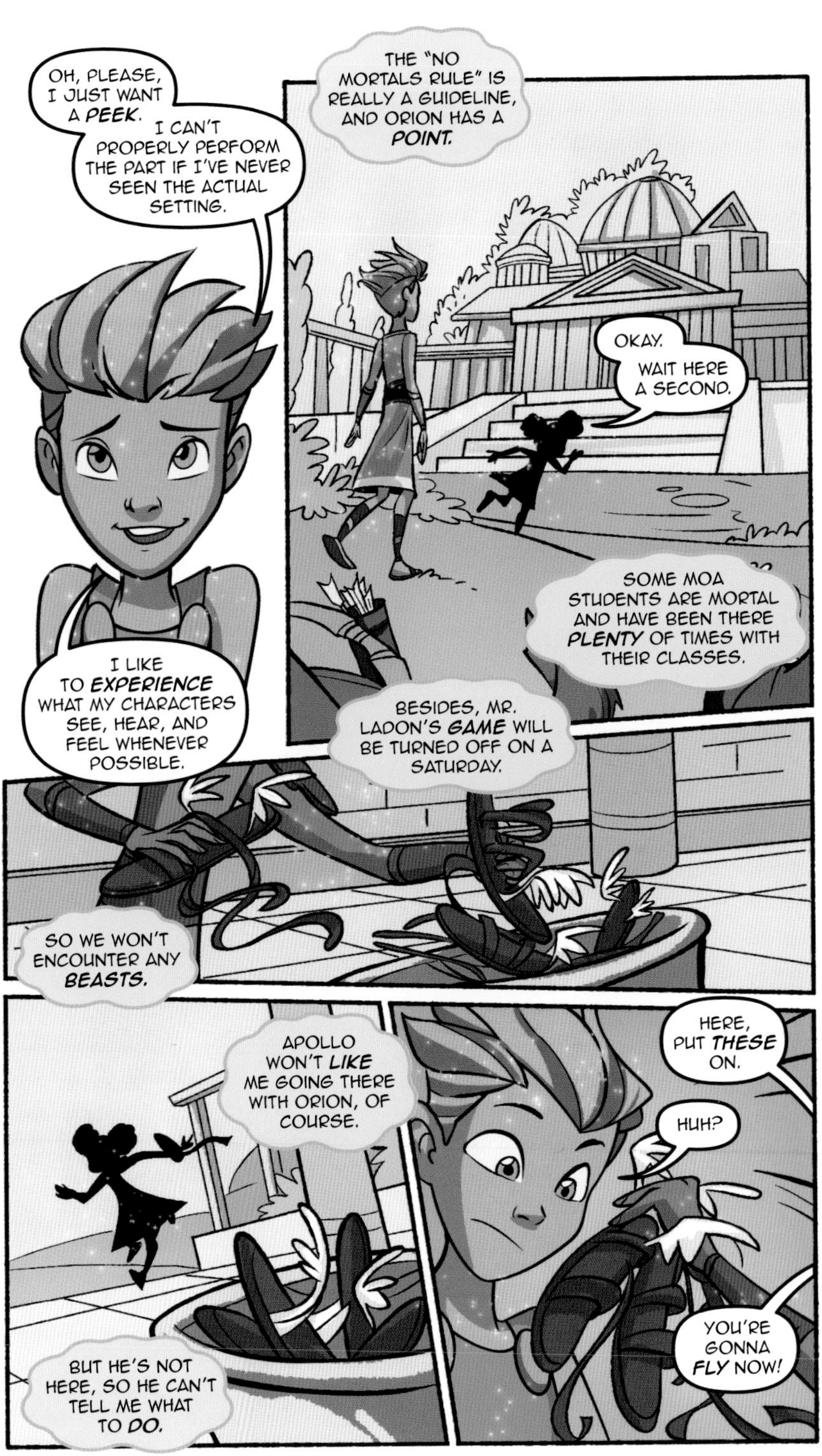
OH, PLEASE, I JUST WANT A *PEEK*.
I CAN'T PROPERLY PERFORM THE PART IF I'VE NEVER SEEN THE ACTUAL SETTING.
THE "NO MORTALS RULE" IS REALLY A GUIDELINE, AND ORION HAS A *POINT.*
OKAY.
WAIT HERE A SECOND.
I LIKE TO *EXPERIENCE* WHAT MY CHARACTERS SEE, HEAR, AND FEEL WHENEVER POSSIBLE.
SOME MOA STUDENTS ARE MORTAL AND HAVE BEEN THERE *PLENTY* OF TIMES WITH THEIR CLASSES.
BESIDES, MR. LADON'S *GAME* WILL BE TURNED OFF ON A SATURDAY.
SO WE WON'T ENCOUNTER ANY *BEASTS.*
APOLLO WON'T *LIKE* ME GOING THERE WITH ORION, OF COURSE.
BUT HE'S NOT HERE, SO HE CAN'T TELL ME WHAT TO *DO.*
HERE, PUT *THESE* ON.
HUH?
YOU'RE GONNA *FLY* NOW!

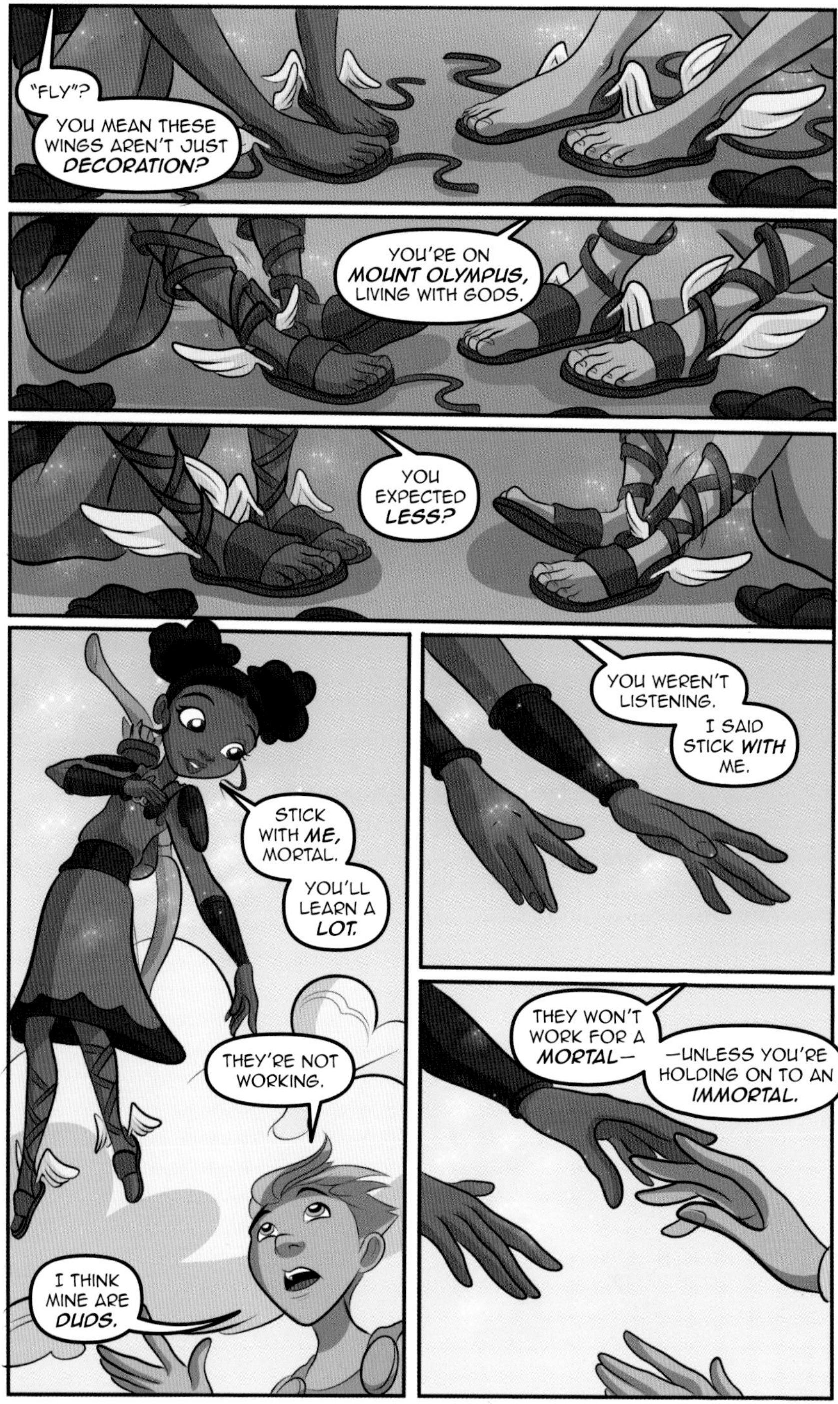
"FLY"?
YOU MEAN THESE WINGS AREN'T JUST DECORATION?
YOU'RE ON MOUNT OLYMPUS, LIVING WITH GODS.
YOU EXPECTED LESS?
STICK WITH ME, MORTAL.
YOU'LL LEARN A LOT.
THEY'RE NOT WORKING.
I THINK MINE ARE DUDS.
YOU WEREN'T LISTENING.
I SAID STICK WITH ME.
THEY WON'T WORK FOR A MORTAL—
—UNLESS YOU'RE HOLDING ON TO AN IMMORTAL.

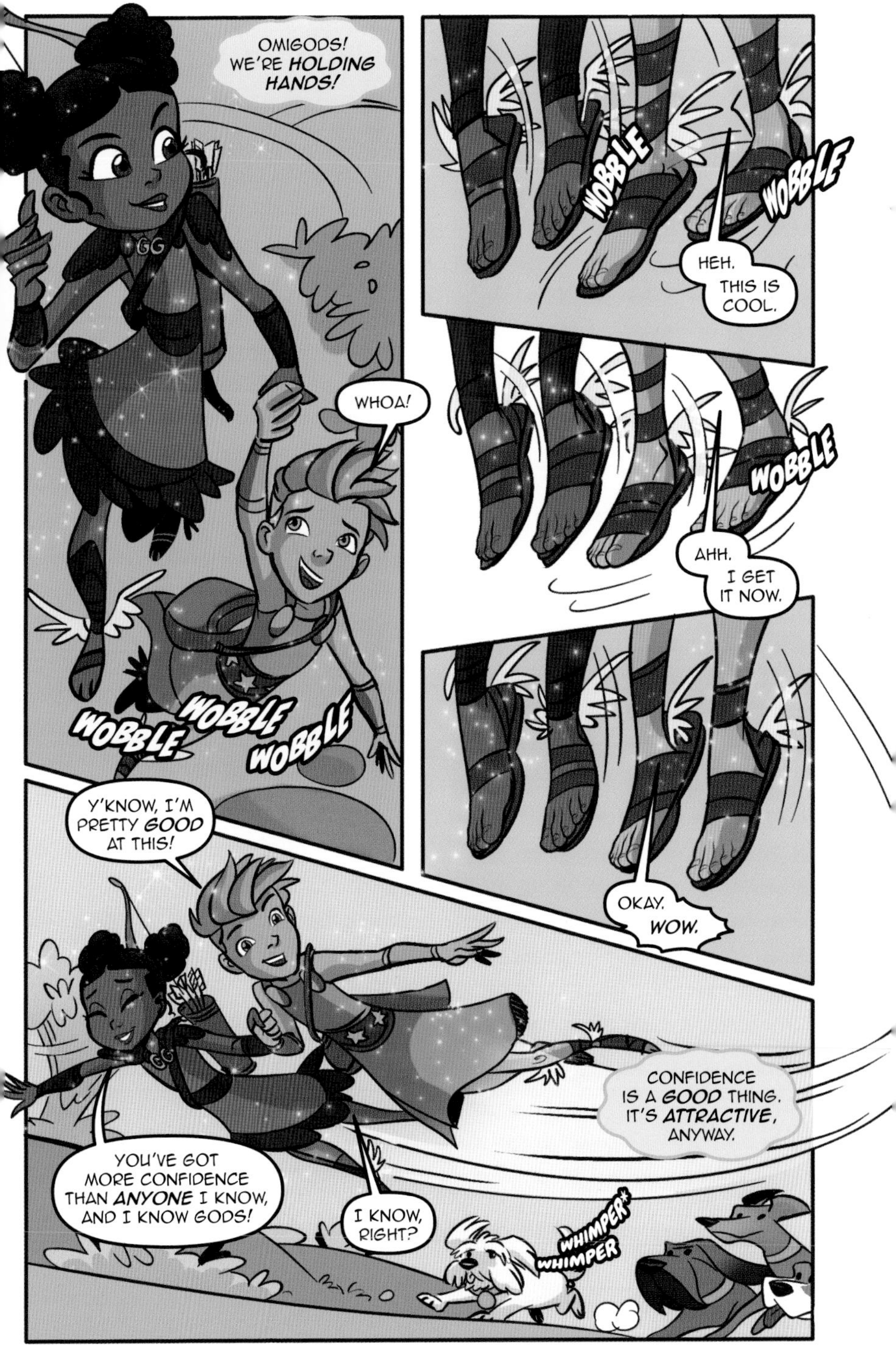
OMIGODS! WE'RE HOLDING HANDS!
WHOA!
WOBBLE
WOBBLE
WOBBLE
WOBBLE
WOBBLE
HEH. THIS IS COOL.
WOBBLE
AHH. I GET IT NOW.
OKAY. WOW.
Y'KNOW, I'M PRETTY GOOD AT THIS!
CONFIDENCE IS A GOOD THING. IT'S ATTRACTIVE, ANYWAY.
YOU'VE GOT MORE CONFIDENCE THAN ANYONE I KNOW, AND I KNOW GODS!
I KNOW, RIGHT?
WHIMPER*
WHIMPER

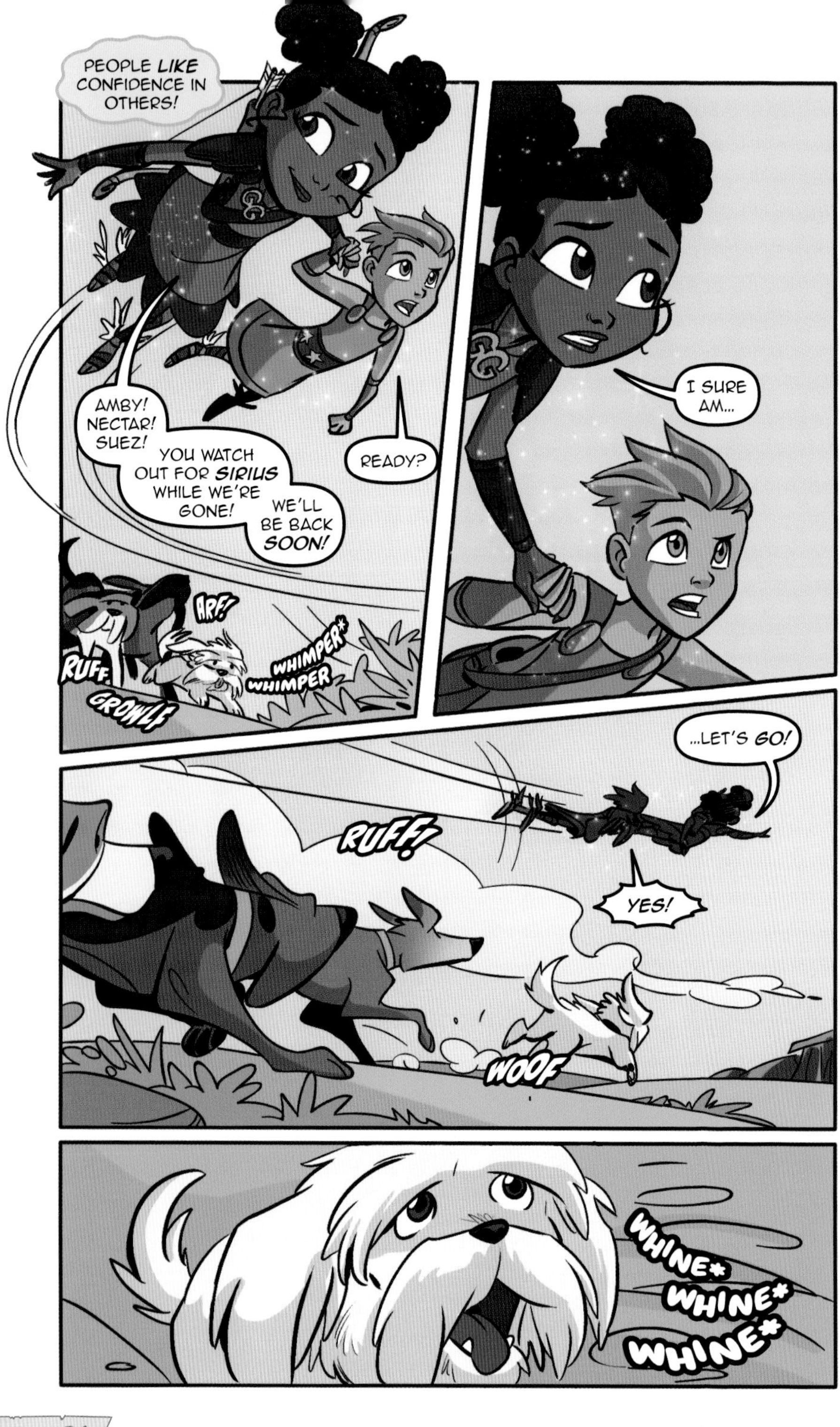

PEOPLE LIKE CONFIDENCE IN OTHERS!
AMBY! NECTAR! SUEZ!
YOU WATCH OUT FOR SIRIUS WHILE WE'RE GONE!
WE'LL BE BACK SOON!
READY?
ARF!
RUFF
GROWLF
WHIMPER* WHIMPER
I SURE AM...
...LET'S GO!
RUFF!
YES!
WOOF
WHINE* WHINE* WHINE*

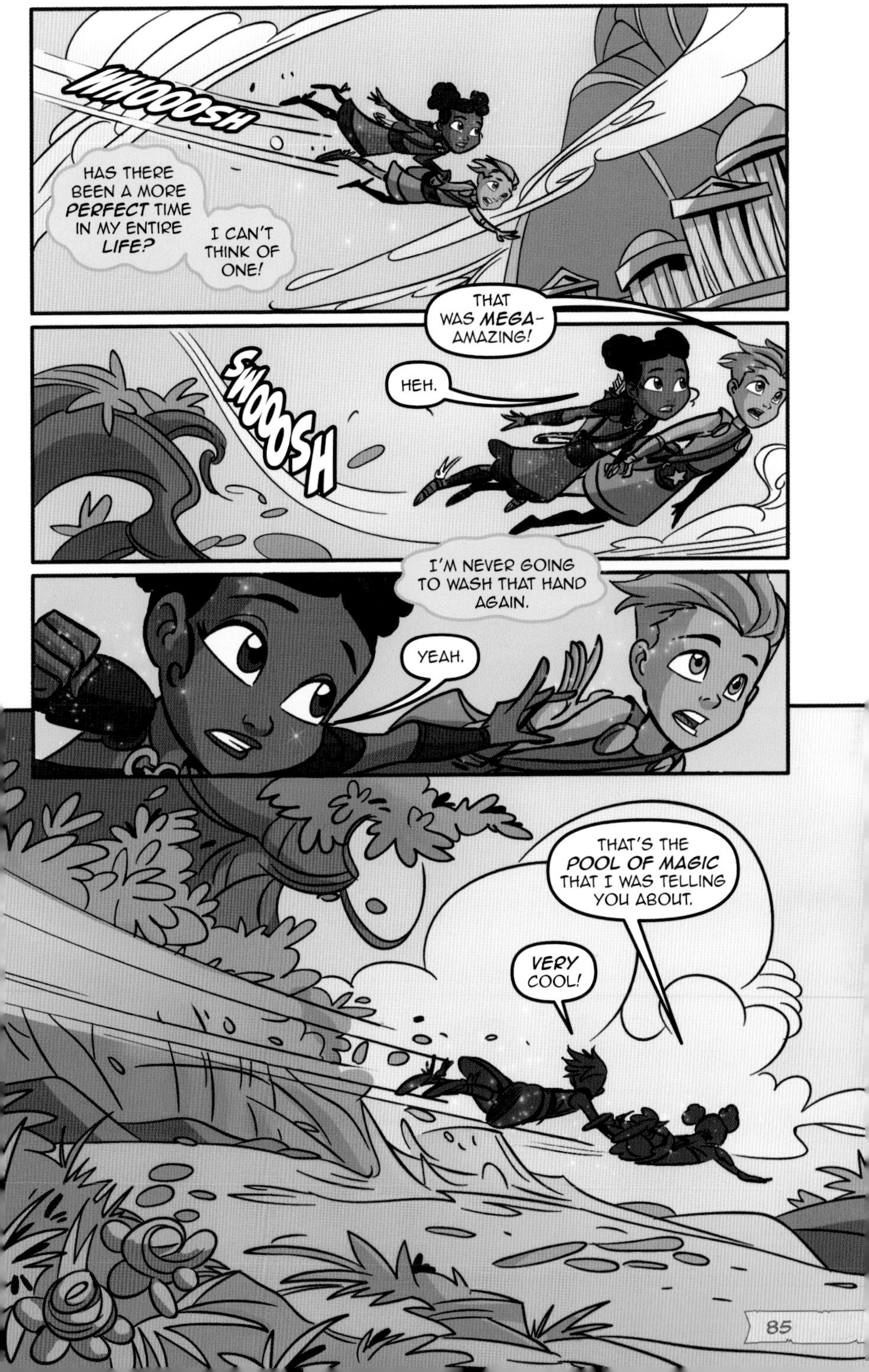
WHOOOOSH
HAS THERE BEEN A MORE PERFECT TIME IN MY ENTIRE LIFE?
I CAN'T THINK OF ONE!
THAT WAS MEGA-AMAZING!
SWOOOSH
HEH.
I'M NEVER GOING TO WASH THAT HAND AGAIN.
YEAH.
THAT'S THE POOL OF MAGIC THAT I WAS TELLING YOU ABOUT.
VERY COOL!

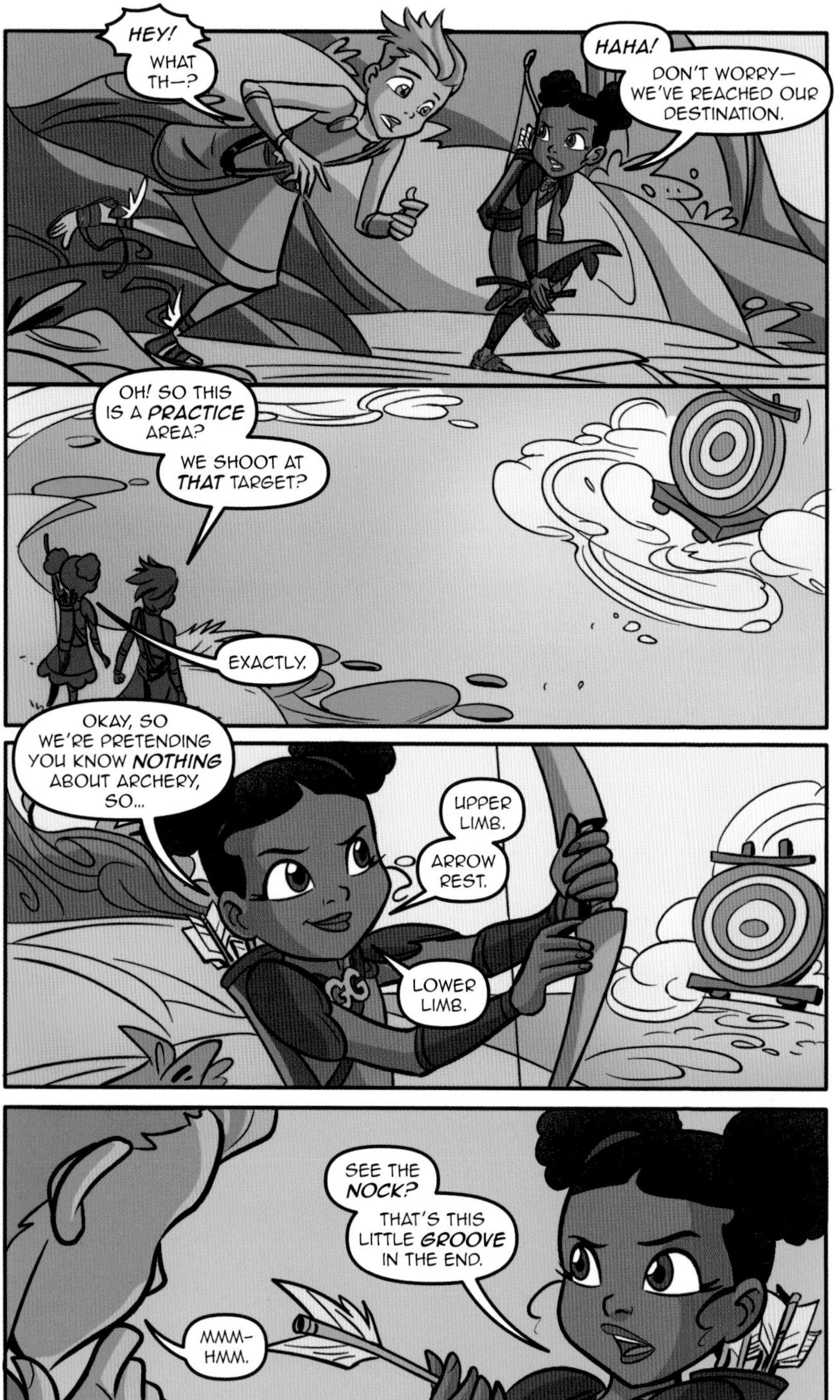
HEY! WHAT TH—?
HAHA! DON'T WORRY— WE'VE REACHED OUR DESTINATION.
OH! SO THIS IS A PRACTICE AREA?
WE SHOOT AT THAT TARGET?
EXACTLY.
OKAY, SO WE'RE PRETENDING YOU KNOW NOTHING ABOUT ARCHERY, SO...
UPPER LIMB.
ARROW REST.
LOWER LIMB.
SEE THE NOCK?
THAT'S THIS LITTLE GROOVE IN THE END.
MMM-HMM.

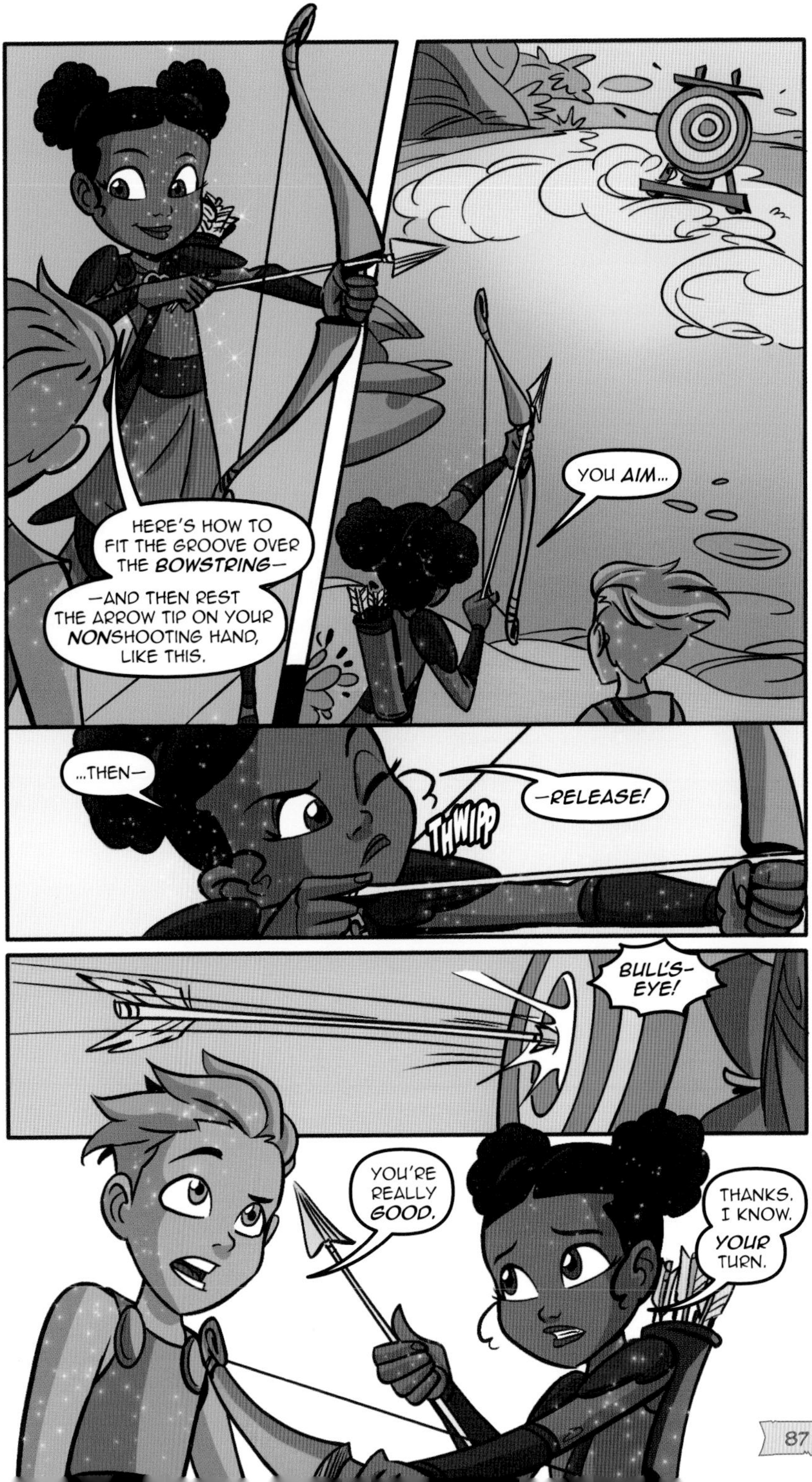
HERE'S HOW TO FIT THE GROOVE OVER THE *BOWSTRING*—
—AND THEN REST THE ARROW TIP ON YOUR *NON*SHOOTING HAND, LIKE THIS.
YOU *AIM*...
...THEN—
—*RELEASE!*
THWIPP
BULL'S-EYE!
YOU'RE REALLY *GOOD.*
THANKS. I KNOW. *YOUR* TURN.

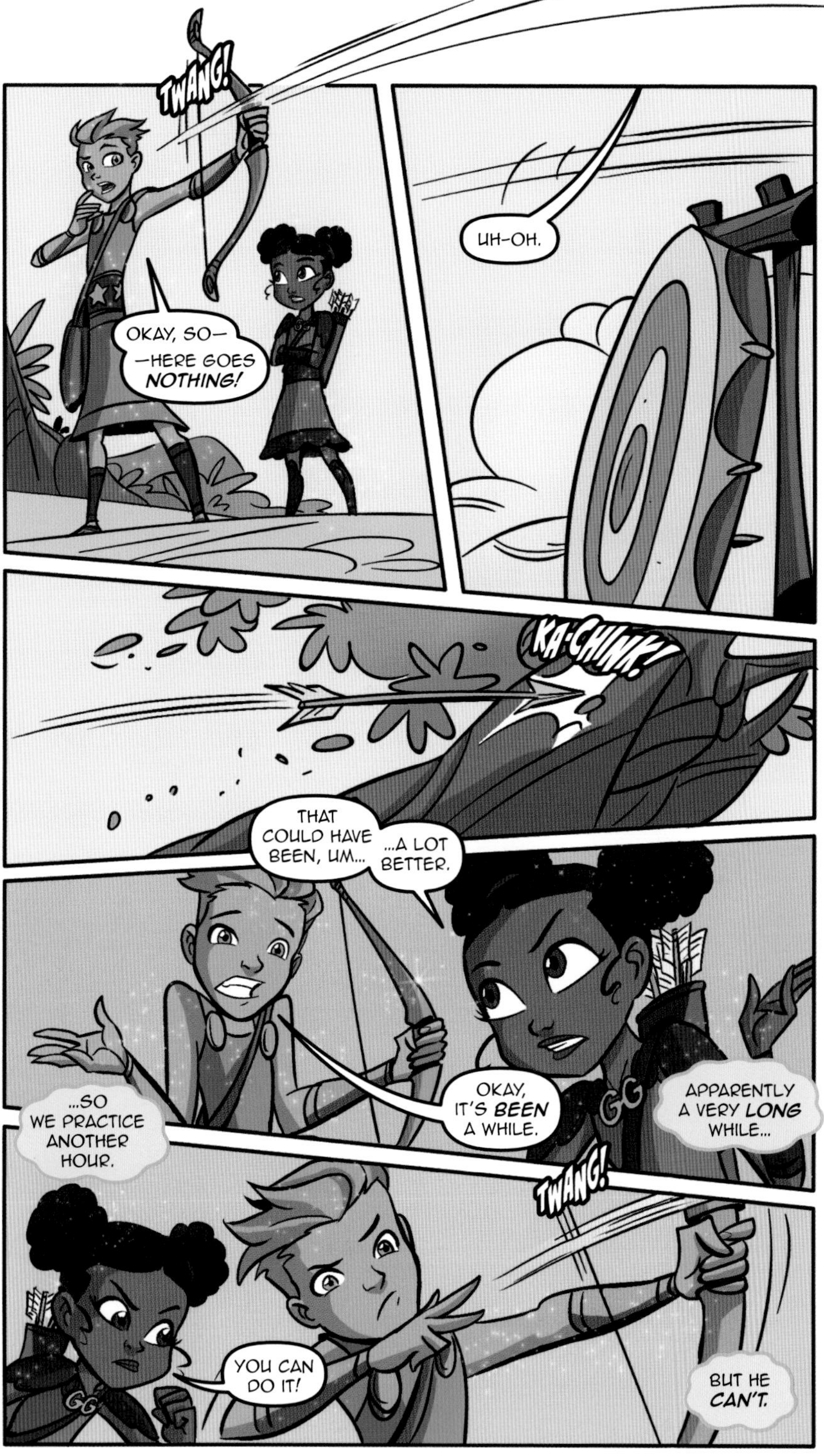
TWANG!
OKAY, SO—
—HERE GOES NOTHING!
UH-OH.
KA-CHINK!
THAT COULD HAVE BEEN, UM...
...A LOT BETTER.
OKAY, IT'S BEEN A WHILE.
APPARENTLY A VERY LONG WHILE...
...SO WE PRACTICE ANOTHER HOUR.
TWANG!
YOU CAN DO IT!
BUT HE CAN'T.

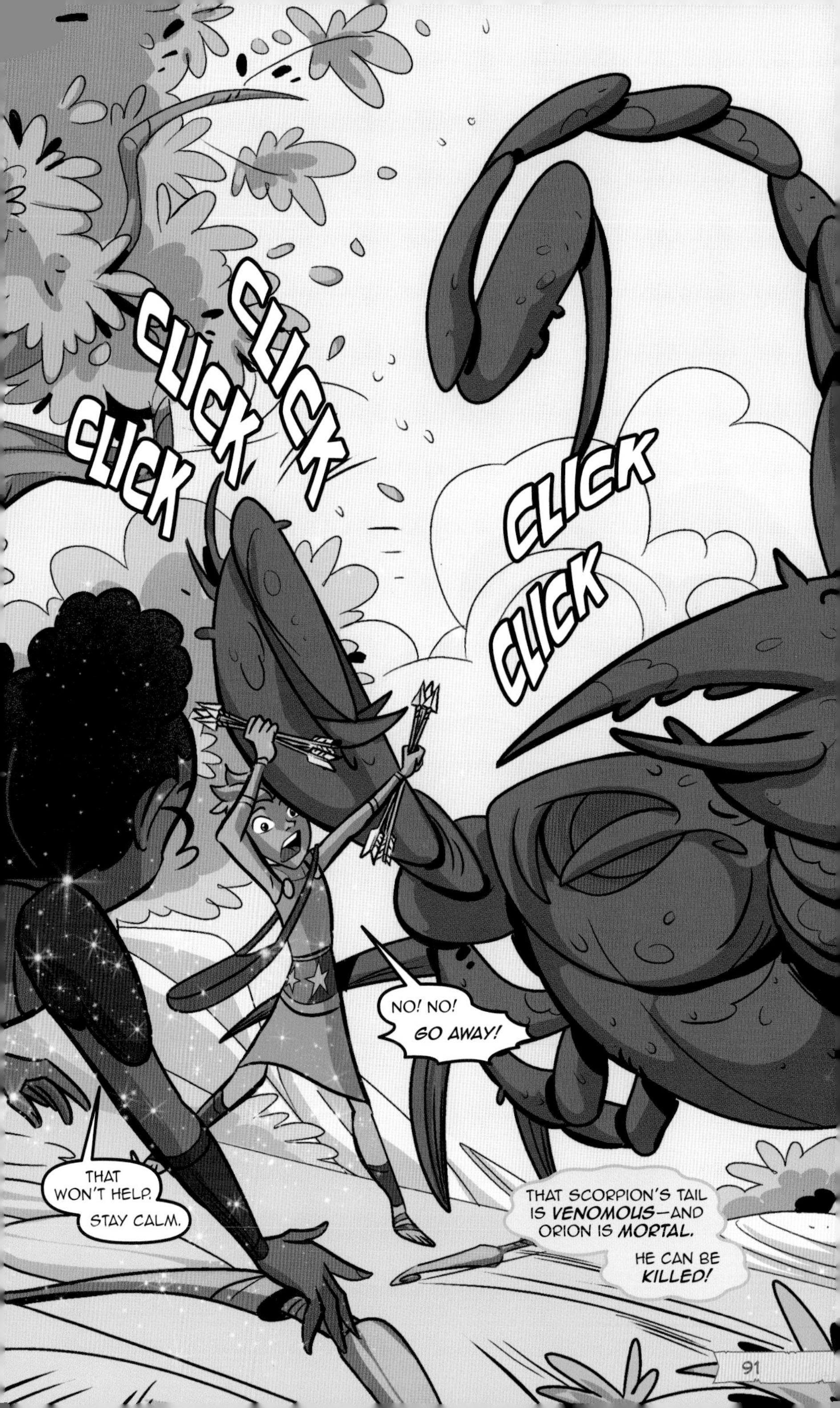
CLICK
CLICK
CLICK
CLICK
CLICK
NO! NO!
GO AWAY!
THAT WON'T HELP.
STAY CALM.
THAT SCORPION'S TAIL IS VENOMOUS—AND ORION IS MORTAL.
HE CAN BE KILLED!

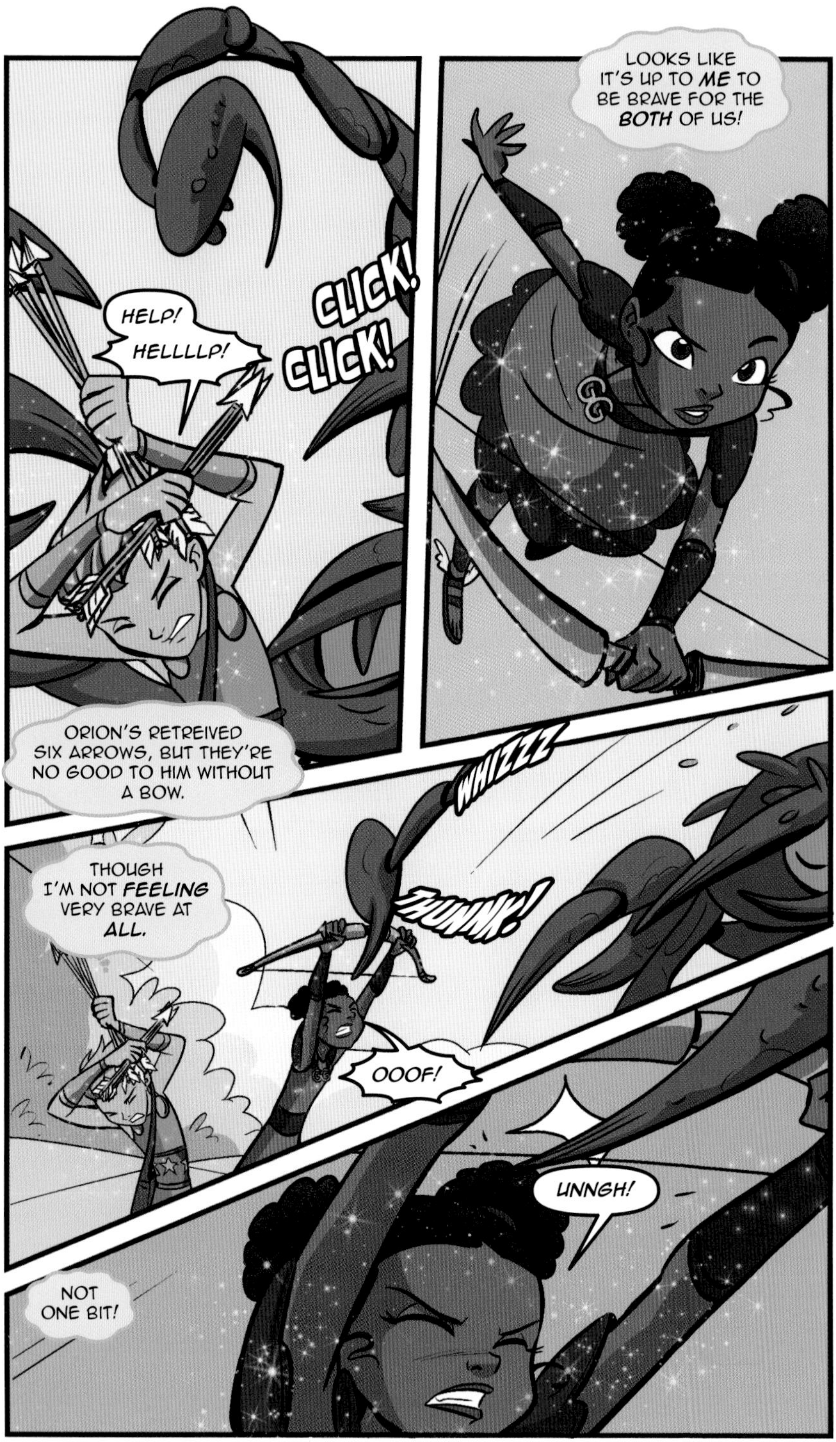
HELP!
HELLLLP!
CLICK!
CLICK!
LOOKS LIKE IT'S UP TO *ME* TO BE BRAVE FOR THE *BOTH* OF US!
ORION'S RETREIVED SIX ARROWS, BUT THEY'RE NO GOOD TO HIM WITHOUT A BOW.
WHIZZZ
THOUGH I'M NOT *FEELING* VERY BRAVE AT *ALL.*
THUNK!
OOOF!
UNNGH!
NOT ONE BIT!

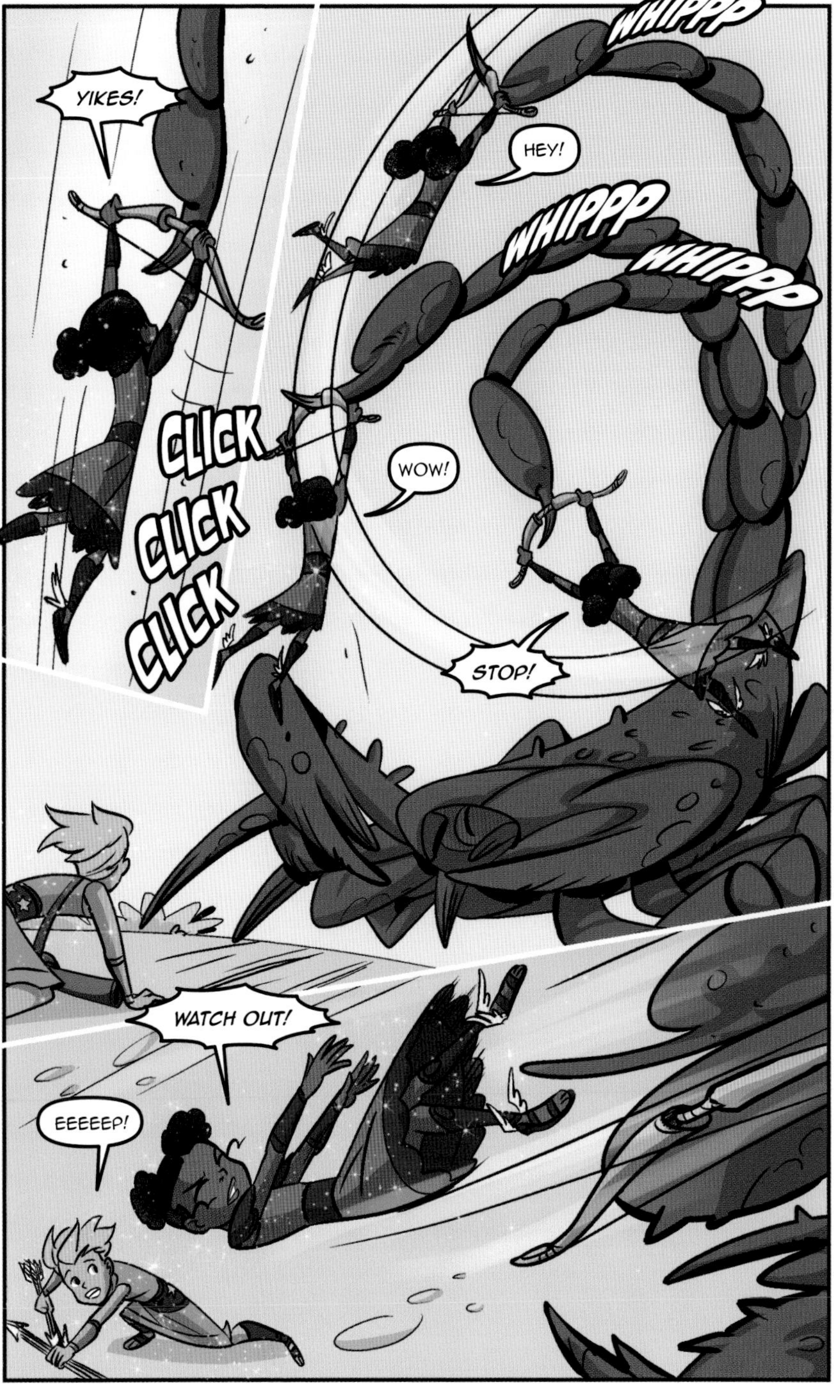
YIKES!
CLICK
CLICK
CLICK
WHIPPP
HEY!
WHIPPP
WHIPPP
WOW!
STOP!
WATCH OUT!
EEEEEP!

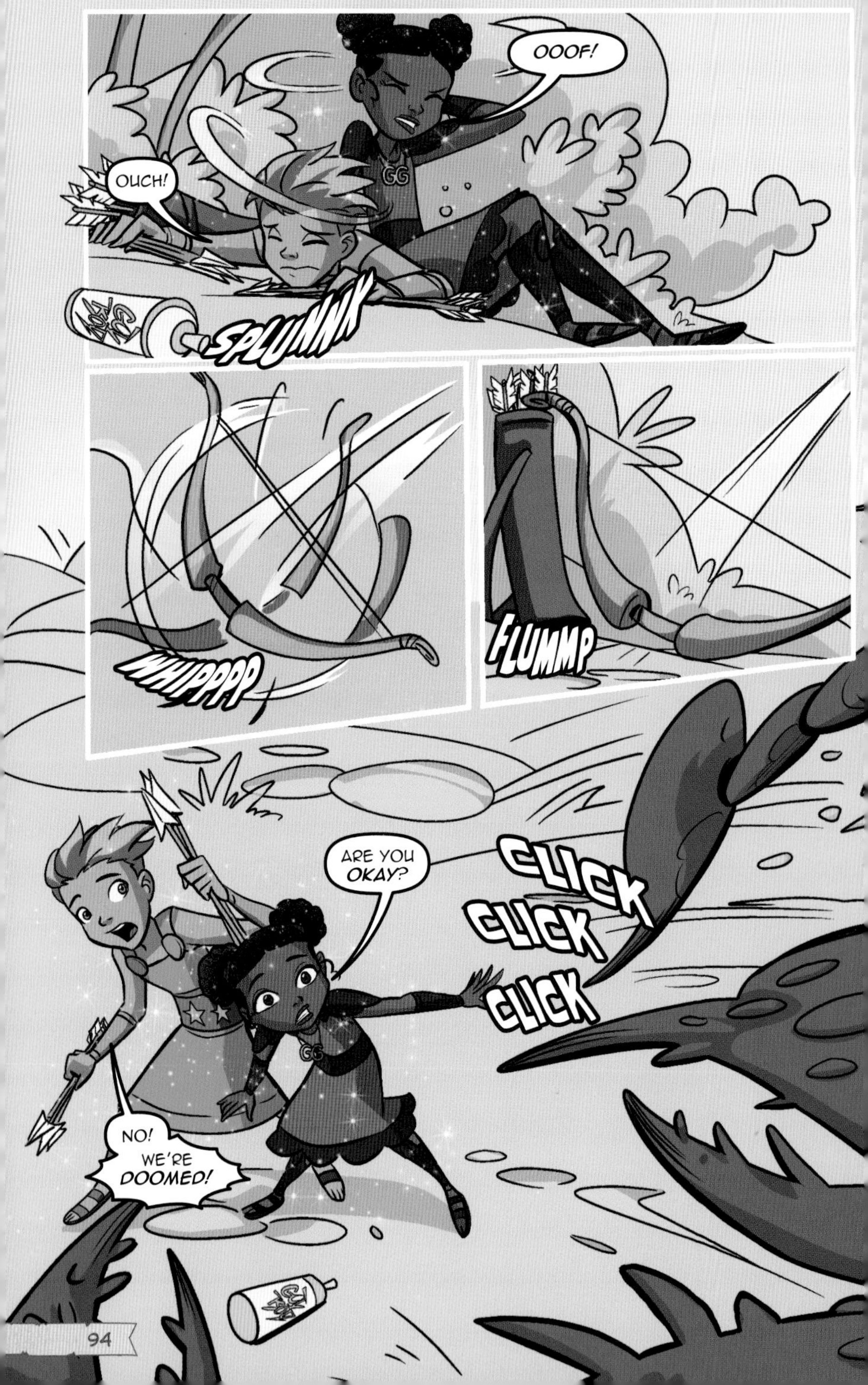
OOOF!
OUCH!
SPLUNNNK
WHIPPPP
FLUMMP
ARE YOU OKAY?
CLICK
CLICK
CLICK
NO! WE'RE DOOMED!

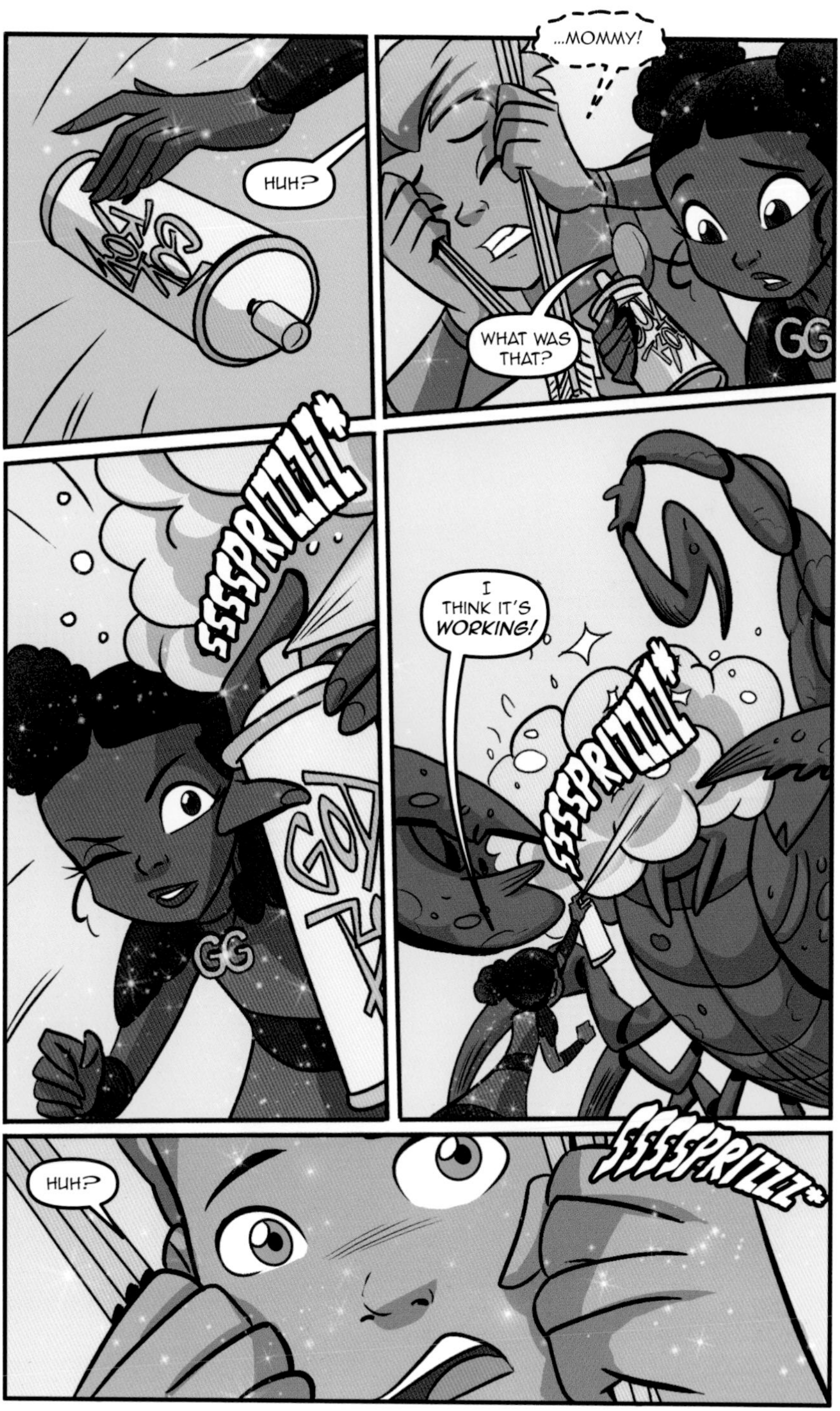
HUH?
...MOMMY!
WHAT WAS THAT?
SSSSPRIZZZZ*
I THINK IT'S *WORKING!*
SSSSPRIZZZZ*
HUH?
SSSSPRIZZZZ*

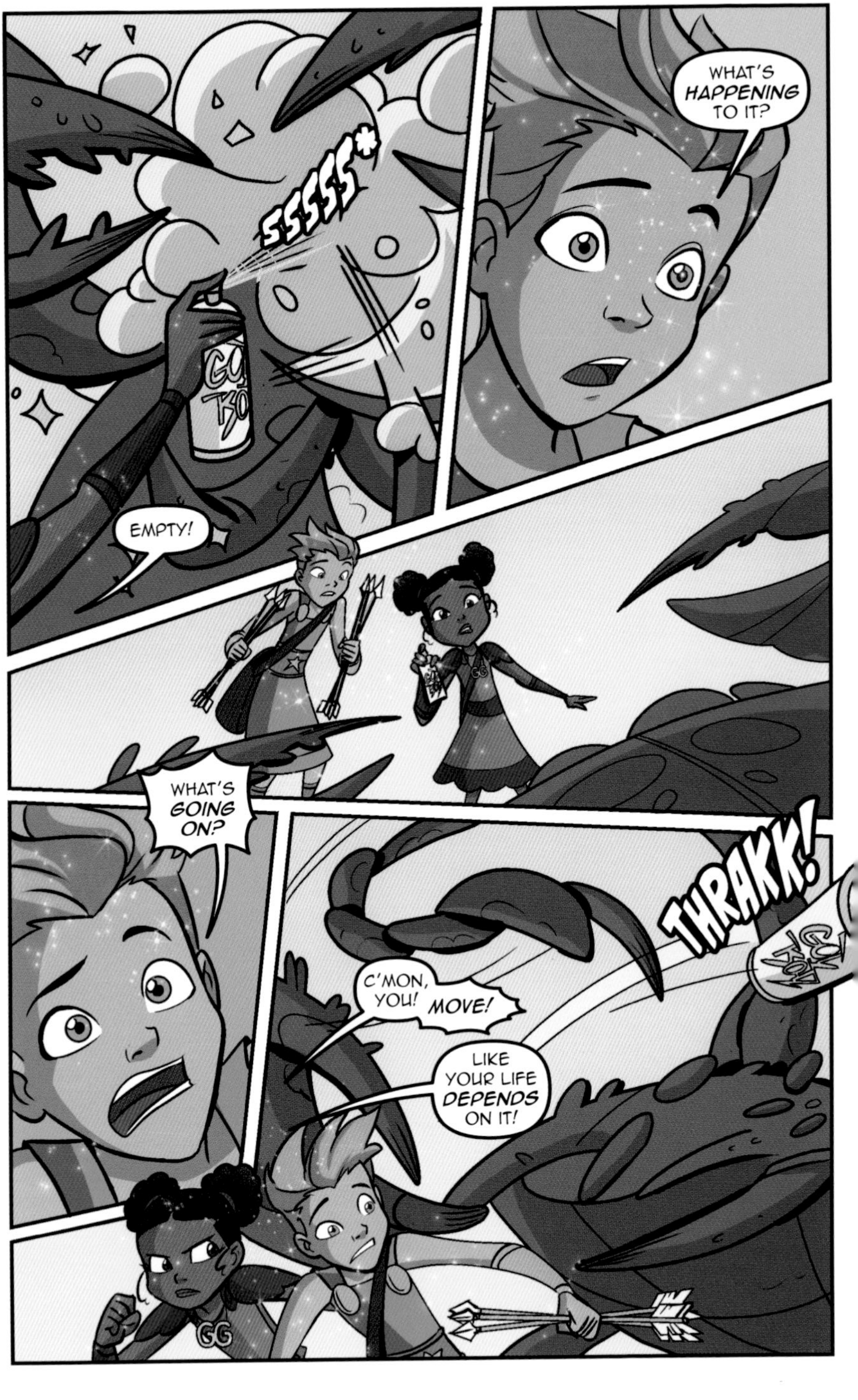
SSSSS*
WHAT'S HAPPENING TO IT?
EMPTY!
WHAT'S GOING ON?
THRAKK!
C'MON, YOU! MOVE!
LIKE YOUR LIFE DEPENDS ON IT!

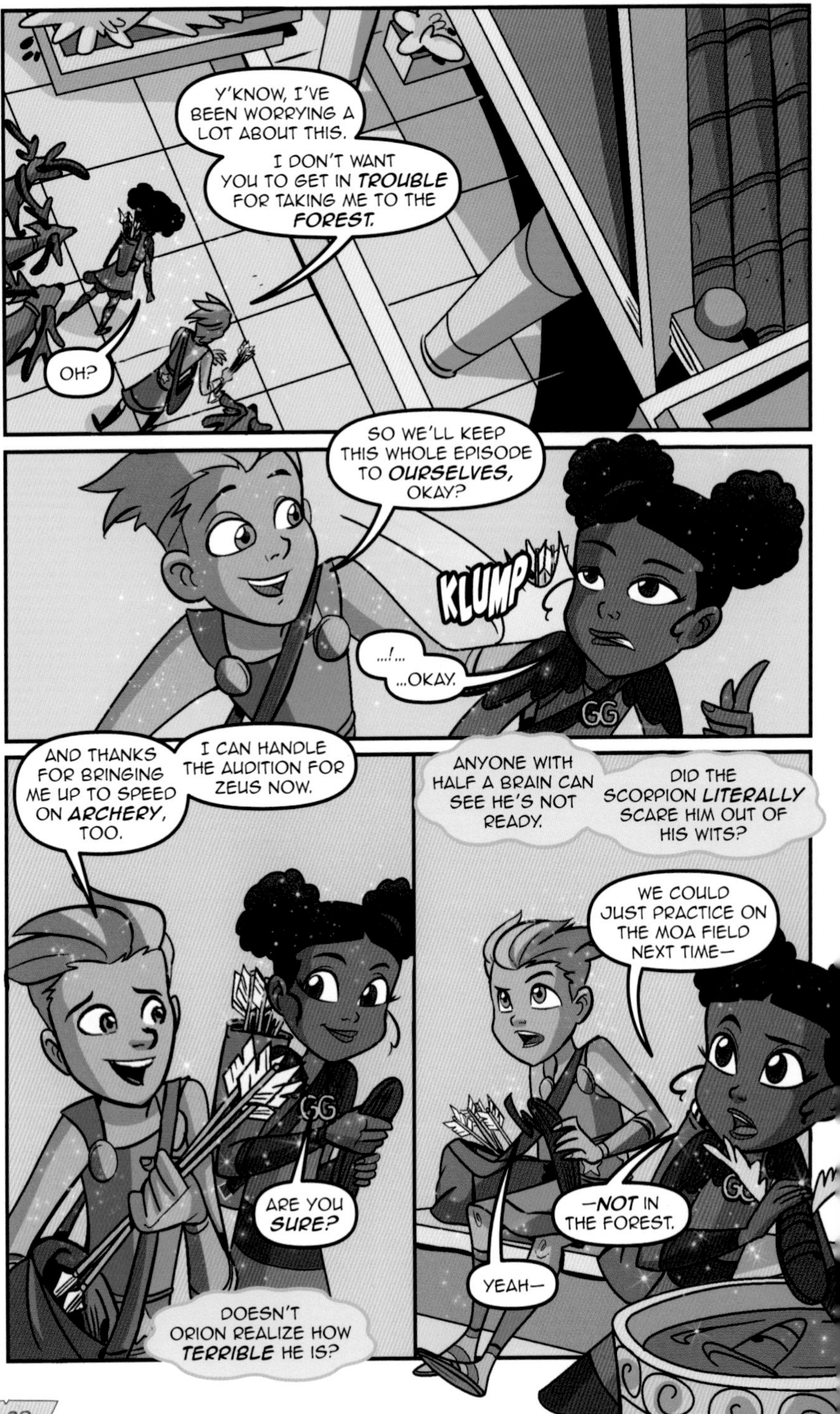
Y'KNOW, I'VE BEEN WORRYING A LOT ABOUT THIS.
I DON'T WANT YOU TO GET IN *TROUBLE* FOR TAKING ME TO THE *FOREST.*
OH?
SO WE'LL KEEP THIS WHOLE EPISODE TO *OURSELVES,* OKAY?
KLUMP
...!...
...OKAY.
AND THANKS FOR BRINGING ME UP TO SPEED ON *ARCHERY,* TOO.
I CAN HANDLE THE AUDITION FOR ZEUS NOW.
ARE YOU *SURE?*
DOESN'T ORION REALIZE HOW *TERRIBLE* HE IS?
ANYONE WITH HALF A BRAIN CAN SEE HE'S NOT READY.
DID THE SCORPION *LITERALLY* SCARE HIM OUT OF HIS WITS?
WE COULD JUST PRACTICE ON THE MOA FIELD NEXT TIME—
YEAH—
—*NOT* IN THE FOREST.

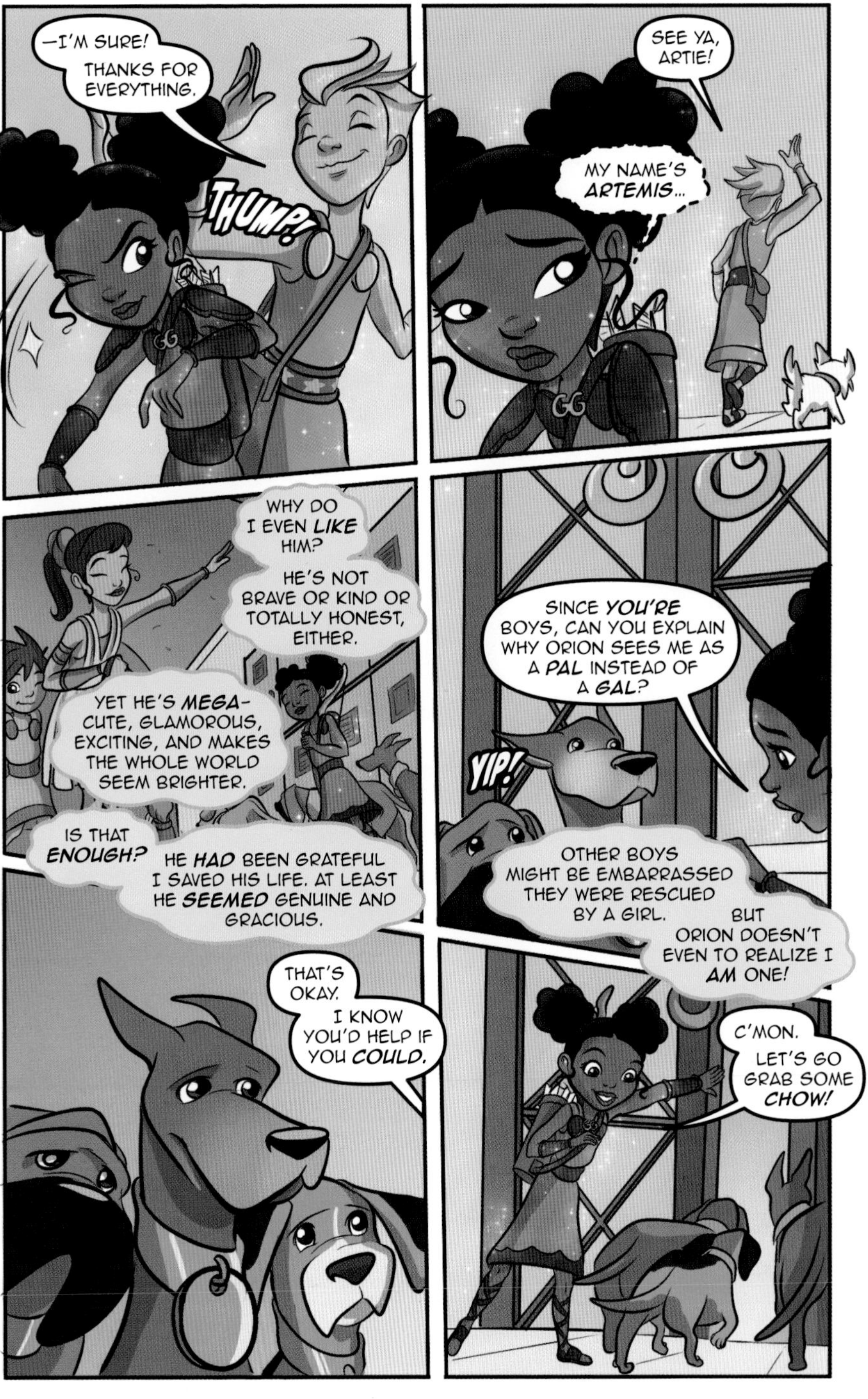

—I'M SURE!
THANKS FOR EVERYTHING.
THUMP!
SEE YA, ARTIE!
MY NAME'S ARTEMIS...
WHY DO I EVEN LIKE HIM?
HE'S NOT BRAVE OR KIND OR TOTALLY HONEST, EITHER.
YET HE'S MEGA-CUTE, GLAMOROUS, EXCITING, AND MAKES THE WHOLE WORLD SEEM BRIGHTER.
IS THAT ENOUGH?
SINCE YOU'RE BOYS, CAN YOU EXPLAIN WHY ORION SEES ME AS A PAL INSTEAD OF A GAL?
YIP!
HE HAD BEEN GRATEFUL I SAVED HIS LIFE. AT LEAST HE SEEMED GENUINE AND GRACIOUS.
OTHER BOYS MIGHT BE EMBARRASSED THEY WERE RESCUED BY A GIRL.
BUT ORION DOESN'T EVEN TO REALIZE I AM ONE!
THAT'S OKAY.
I KNOW YOU'D HELP IF YOU COULD.
C'MON.
LET'S GO GRAB SOME CHOW!

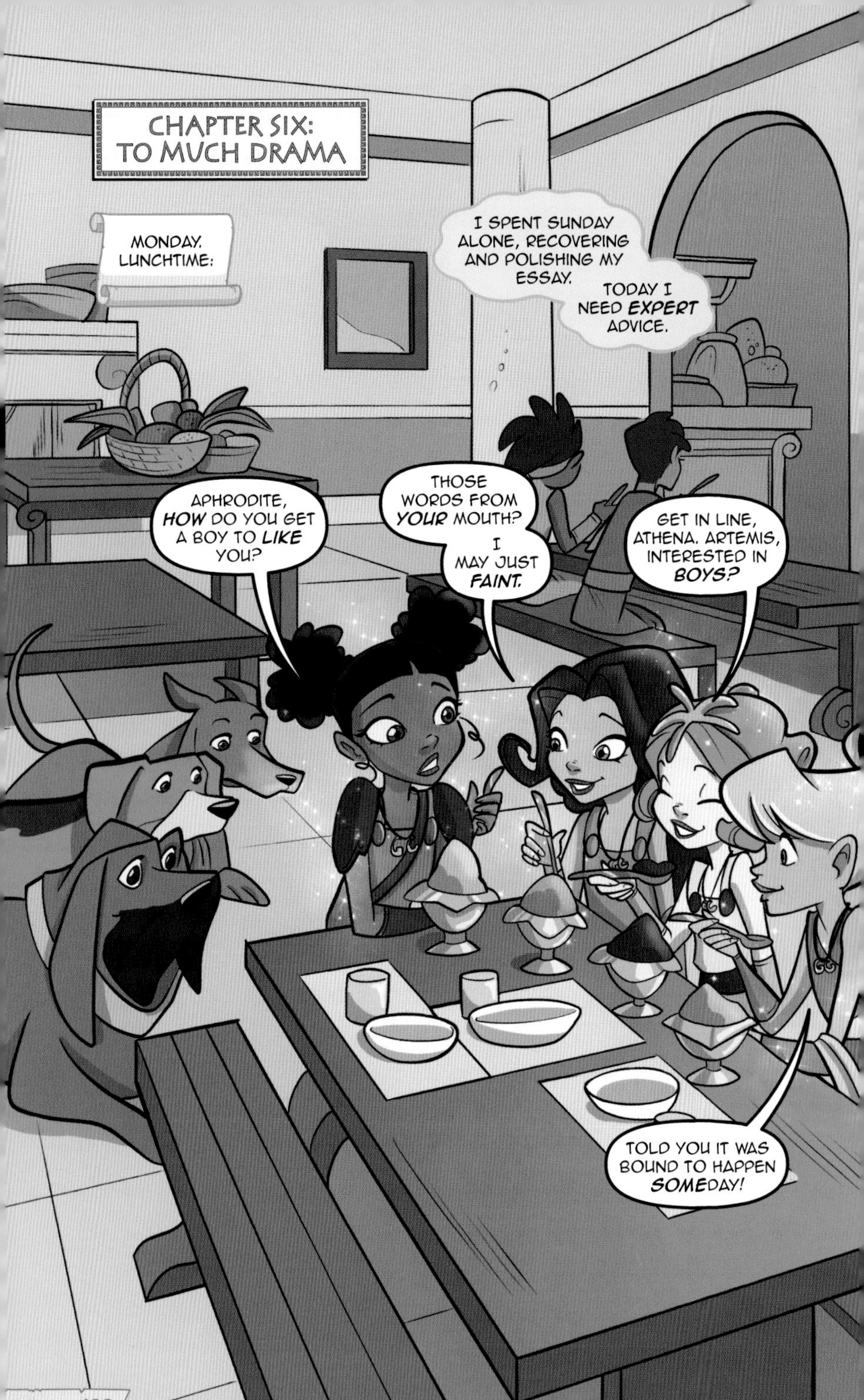
CHAPTER SIX:
TO MUCH DRAMA
MONDAY. LUNCHTIME:
I SPENT SUNDAY ALONE, RECOVERING AND POLISHING MY ESSAY.
TODAY I NEED EXPERT ADVICE.
APHRODITE, HOW DO YOU GET A BOY TO LIKE YOU?
THOSE WORDS FROM YOUR MOUTH?
I MAY JUST FAINT.
GET IN LINE, ATHENA. ARTEMIS, INTERESTED IN BOYS?
TOLD YOU IT WAS BOUND TO HAPPEN SOMEDAY!

SIGH

THE PROBLEM IS, HE DOESN'T SEEM TO NOTICE THAT I'M A *GIRL* NO MATTER HOW CUTE I DRESS.

HE EVEN CALLS ME "*ARTIE.*"

YIKES!

I'LL BE *GLAD* TO GIVE YOU SOME TIPS ON BOYS.

PING! PING! PING!

HE SLAPS ME ON THE BACK LIKE APOLLO AND HIS FRIENDS DO WITH ONE ANOTHER.

THAT WON'T WORK.

WHY SHOULD HE CHOOSE PLAIN OLD *ME* WHEN HE COULD HAVE *ANY* GIRL?

HE'S GOT A *FAN CLUB* FULL OF THEM! AND LIKE I SAID, HE THINKS I'M A *GUY!*

HERE'S THE FIRST ONE:

WHEN YOU'RE AROUND ORION, *DON'T* ACT STARSTUCK.

JUST RELAX AND BE YOUR OWN WONDERFUL SELF.

Y'KNOW, HADES LIKED *ME* BETTER WHEN I STOPPED ACTING *FAKE* AROUND HIM.

DON'T LOOK AT *ME!*

I'VE NEVER *HAD* A BOYFRIEND.

I THINK APHRODITE'S *RIGHT.*

BUT I HAVE NOTICED THAT BOYS ADMIRE GIRLS WHO CAN *DO* THINGS....

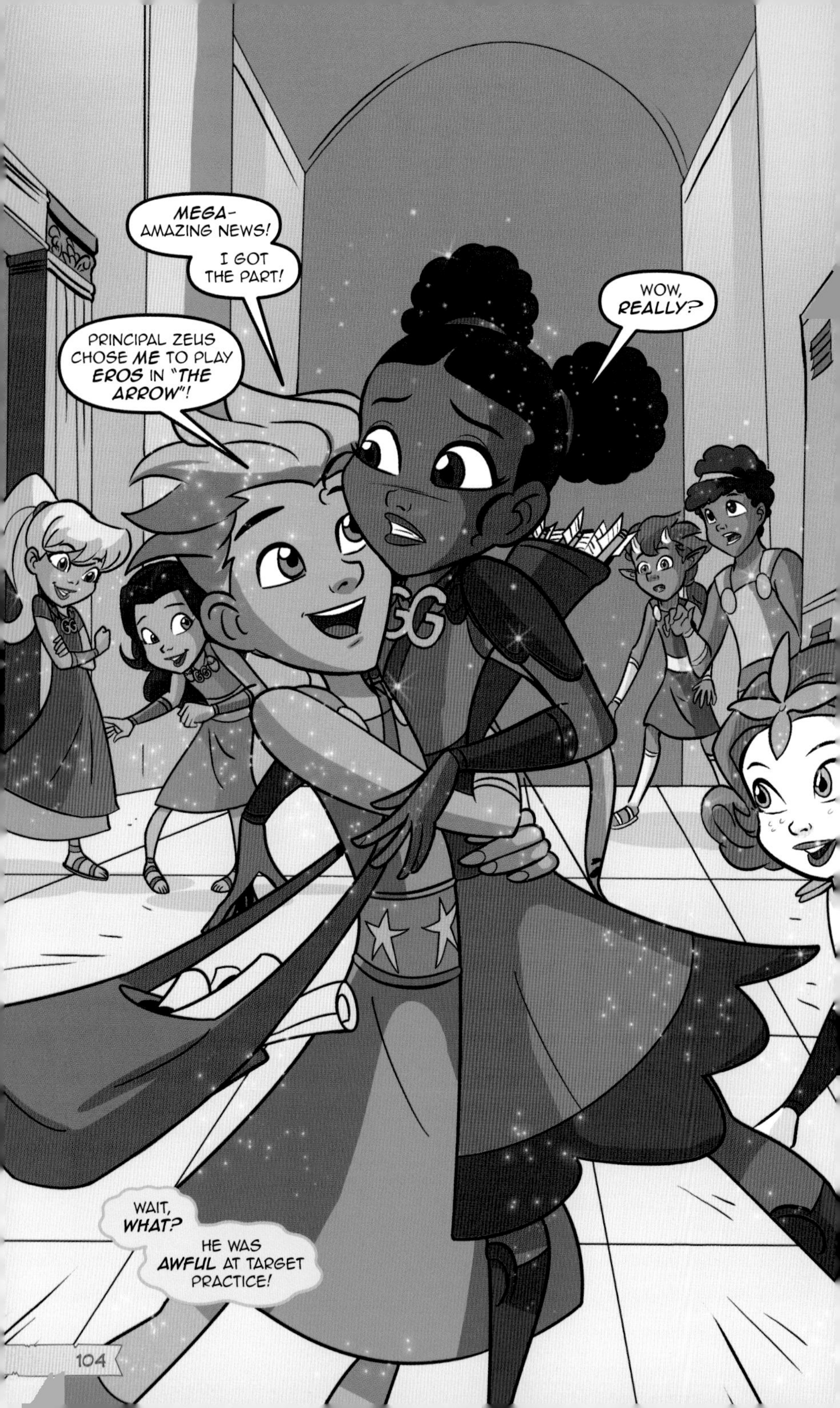
MEGA-AMAZING NEWS!
I GOT THE PART!
PRINCIPAL ZEUS CHOSE ME TO PLAY EROS IN "THE ARROW"!
WOW, REALLY?
GG
GG
WAIT, WHAT?
HE WAS AWFUL AT TARGET PRACTICE!

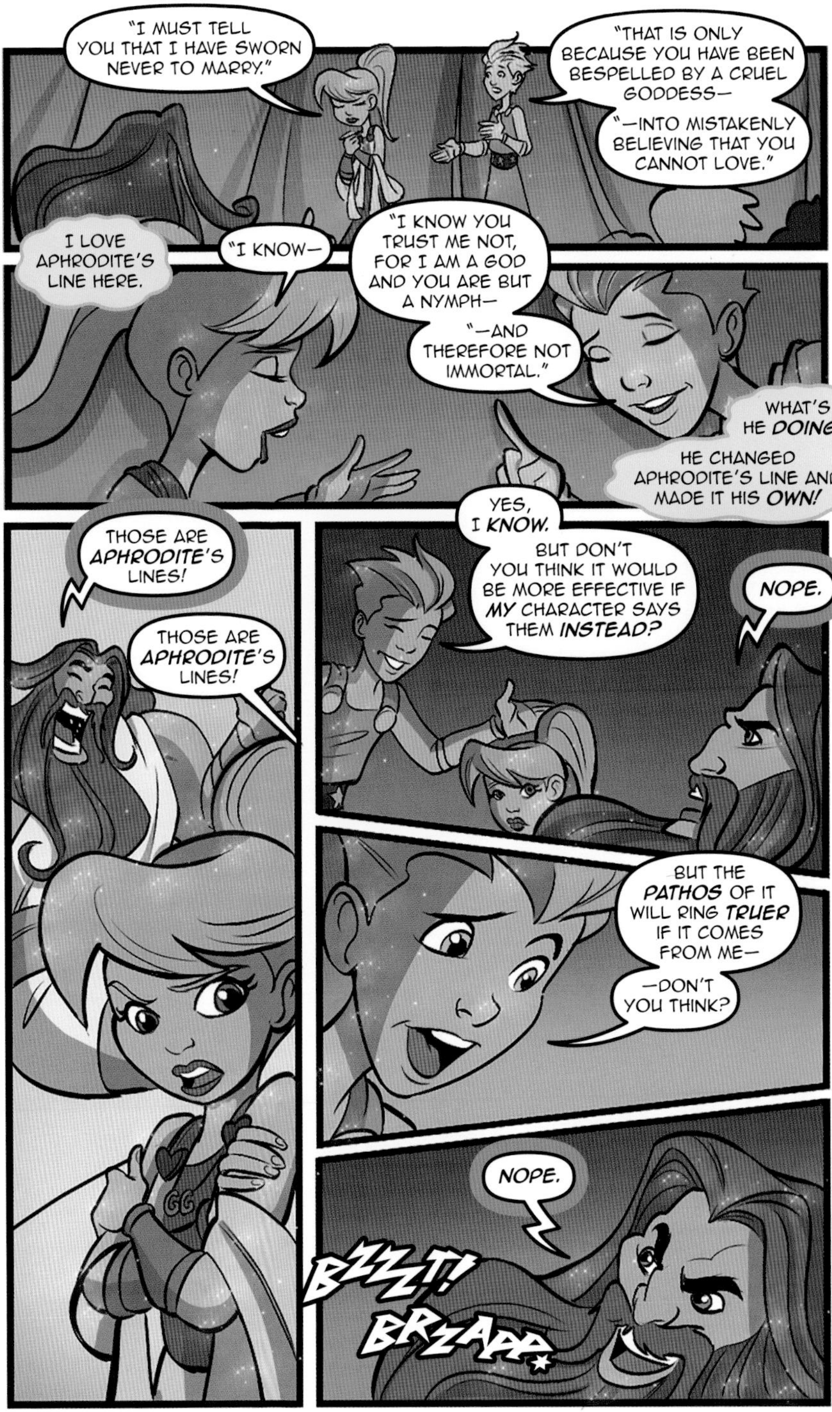

"I MUST TELL YOU THAT I HAVE SWORN NEVER TO MARRY."
"THAT IS ONLY BECAUSE YOU HAVE BEEN BESPELLED BY A CRUEL GODDESS—
"—INTO MISTAKENLY BELIEVING THAT YOU CANNOT LOVE."
I LOVE APHRODITE'S LINE HERE.
"I KNOW—
"I KNOW YOU TRUST ME NOT, FOR I AM A GOD AND YOU ARE BUT A NYMPH—
"—AND THEREFORE NOT IMMORTAL."
WHAT'S HE *DOING?*
HE CHANGED APHRODITE'S LINE AND MADE IT HIS *OWN!*
THOSE ARE *APHRODITE*'S LINES!
THOSE ARE *APHRODITE*'S LINES!
YES, I *KNOW.*
BUT DON'T YOU THINK IT WOULD BE MORE EFFECTIVE IF *MY* CHARACTER SAYS THEM *INSTEAD?*
NOPE.
BUT THE *PATHOS* OF IT WILL RING *TRUER* IF IT COMES FROM ME—
—DON'T YOU THINK?
NOPE.
BZZZT!
BRZAPP

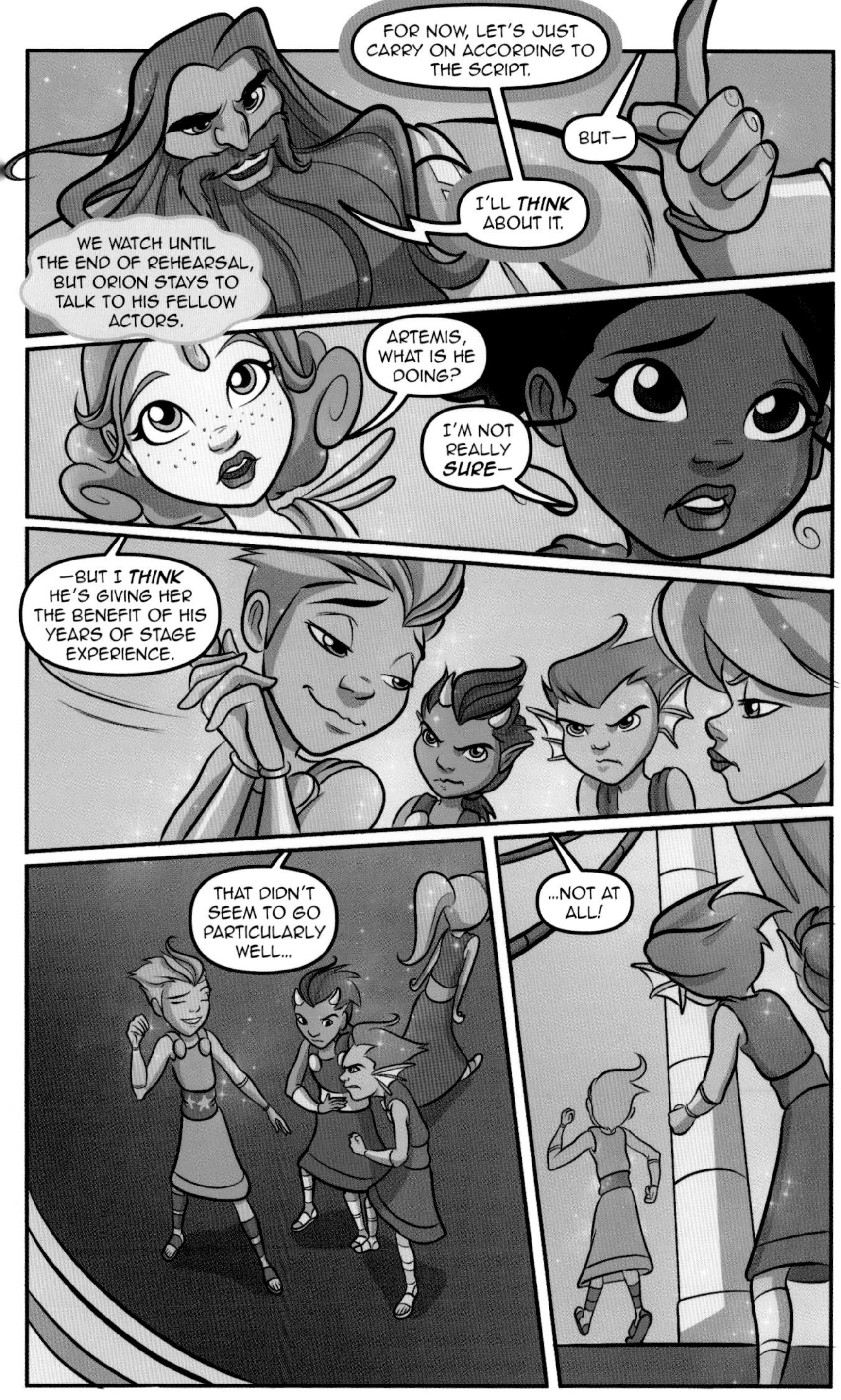
FOR NOW, LET'S JUST CARRY ON ACCORDING TO THE SCRIPT.
BUT—
I'LL *THINK* ABOUT IT.
WE WATCH UNTIL THE END OF REHEARSAL, BUT ORION STAYS TO TALK TO HIS FELLOW ACTORS.
ARTEMIS, WHAT IS HE DOING?
I'M NOT REALLY *SURE*—
—BUT I *THINK* HE'S GIVING HER THE BENEFIT OF HIS YEARS OF STAGE EXPERIENCE.
THAT DIDN'T SEEM TO GO PARTICULARLY WELL...
...NOT AT ALL!

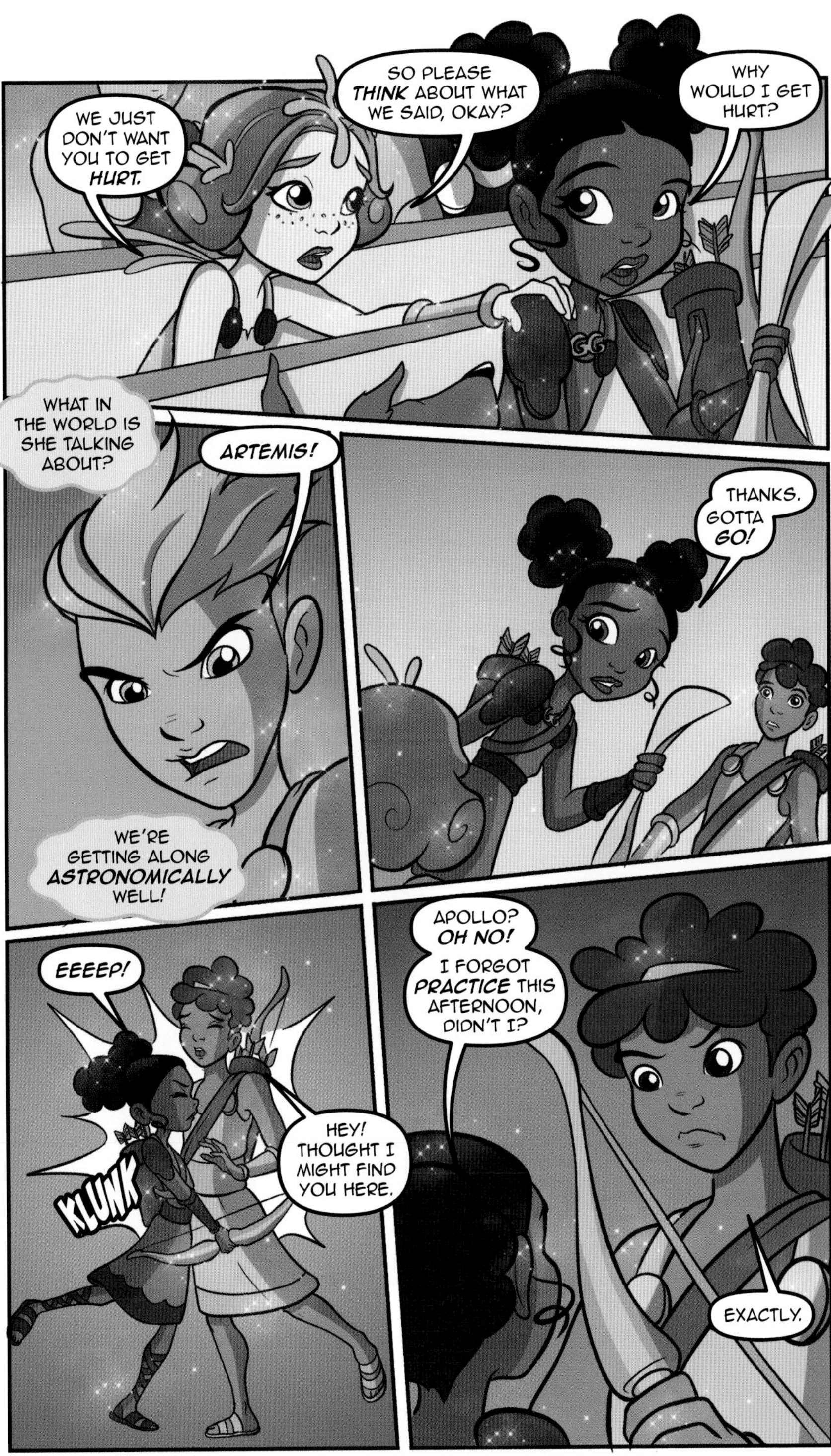
WE JUST DON'T WANT YOU TO GET HURT.
SO PLEASE THINK ABOUT WHAT WE SAID, OKAY?
WHY WOULD I GET HURT?
WHAT IN THE WORLD IS SHE TALKING ABOUT?
ARTEMIS!
THANKS. GOTTA GO!
WE'RE GETTING ALONG ASTRONOMICALLY WELL!
EEEEP!
KLUNK
HEY! THOUGHT I MIGHT FIND YOU HERE.
APOLLO? OH NO!
I FORGOT PRACTICE THIS AFTERNOON, DIDN'T I?
EXACTLY.

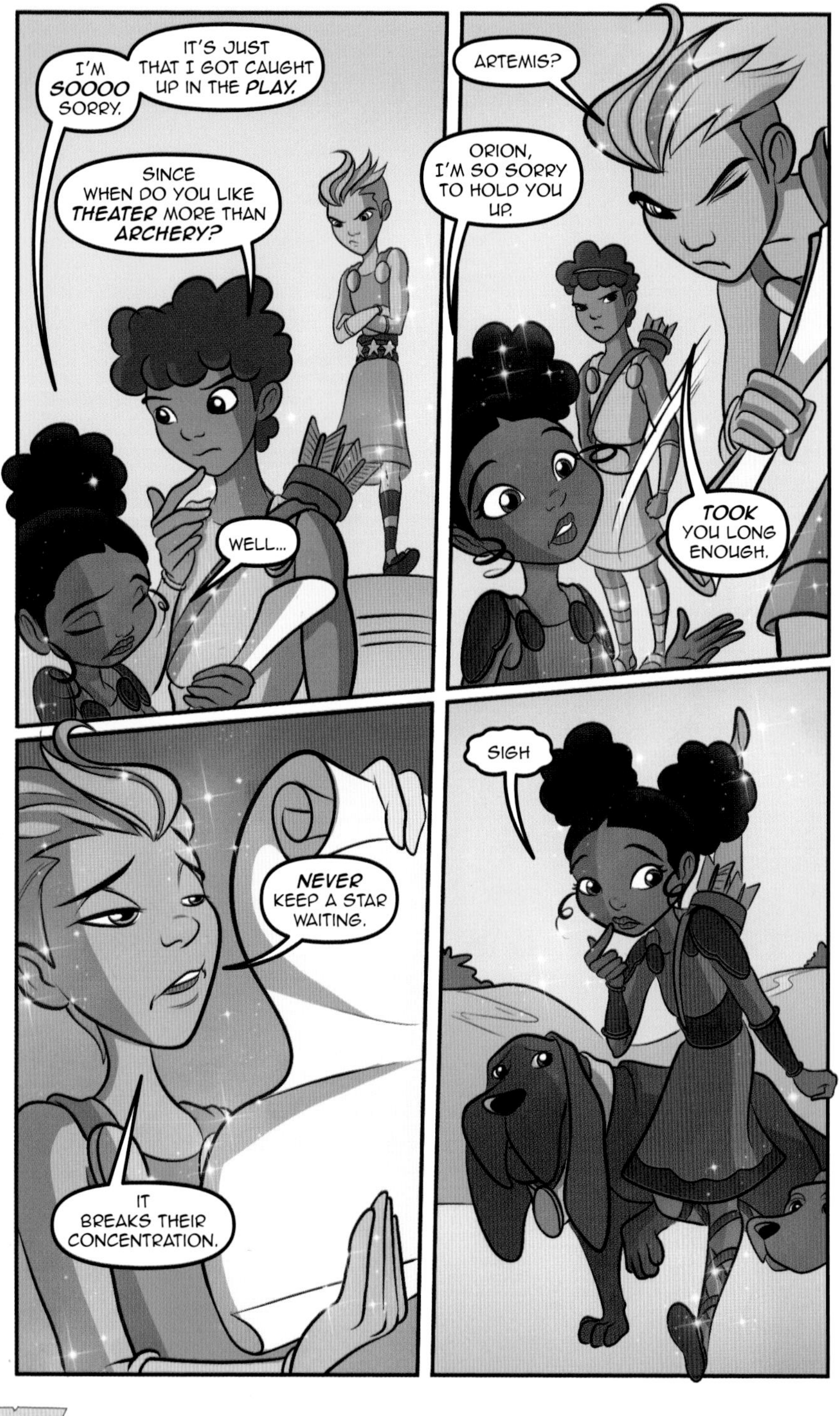
I'M *SOOOO* SORRY.
IT'S JUST THAT I GOT CAUGHT UP IN THE *PLAY.*
SINCE WHEN DO YOU LIKE *THEATER* MORE THAN *ARCHERY?*
WELL...
ARTEMIS?
ORION, I'M SO SORRY TO HOLD YOU UP.
TOOK YOU LONG ENOUGH.
NEVER KEEP A STAR WAITING.
IT BREAKS THEIR CONCENTRATION.
SIGH

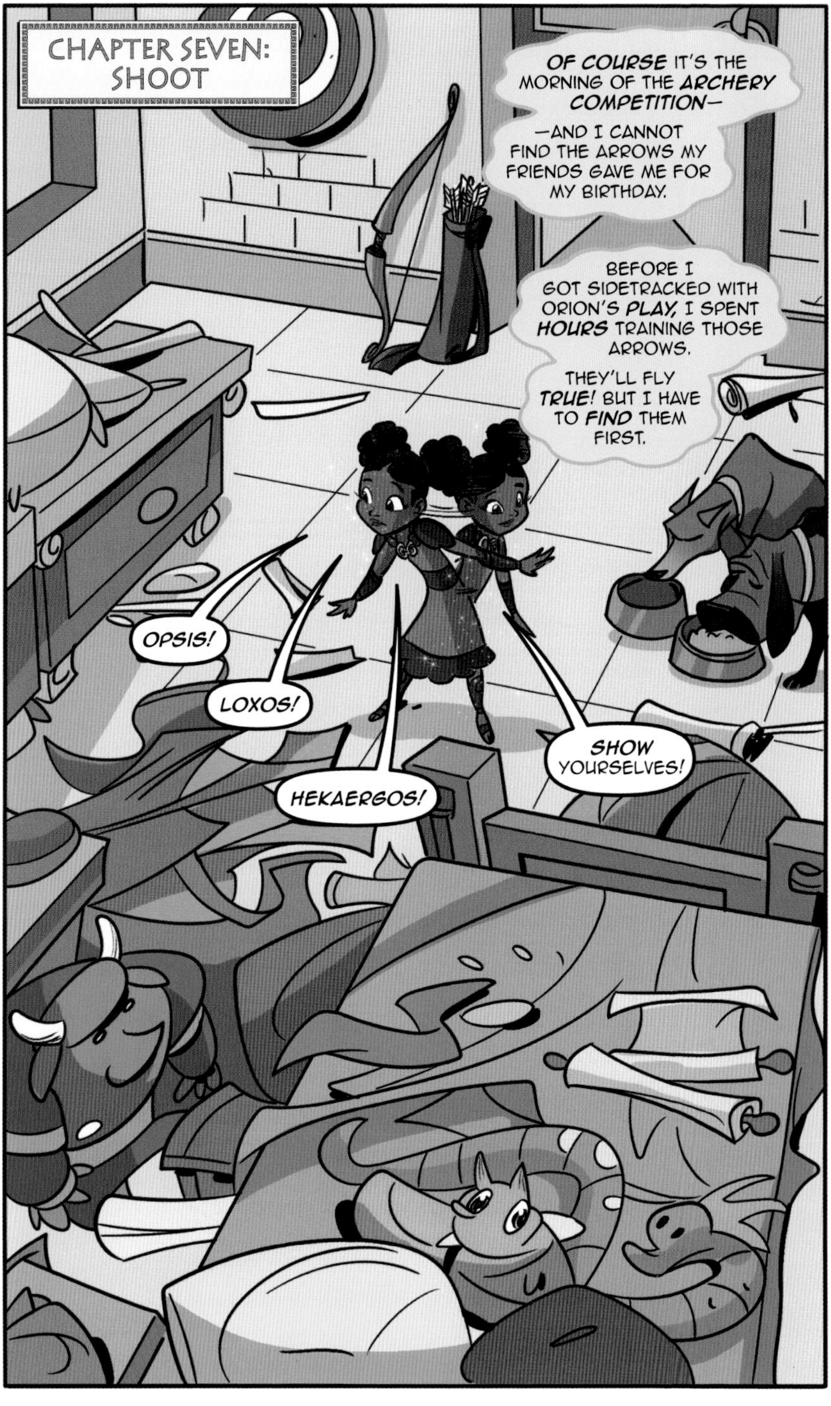

CHAPTER SEVEN: SHOOT
OF COURSE IT'S THE MORNING OF THE ARCHERY COMPETITION—
—AND I CANNOT FIND THE ARROWS MY FRIENDS GAVE ME FOR MY BIRTHDAY.
BEFORE I GOT SIDETRACKED WITH ORION'S PLAY, I SPENT HOURS TRAINING THOSE ARROWS.
THEY'LL FLY TRUE! BUT I HAVE TO FIND THEM FIRST.
OPSIS!
LOXOS!
HEKAERGOS!
SHOW YOURSELVES!

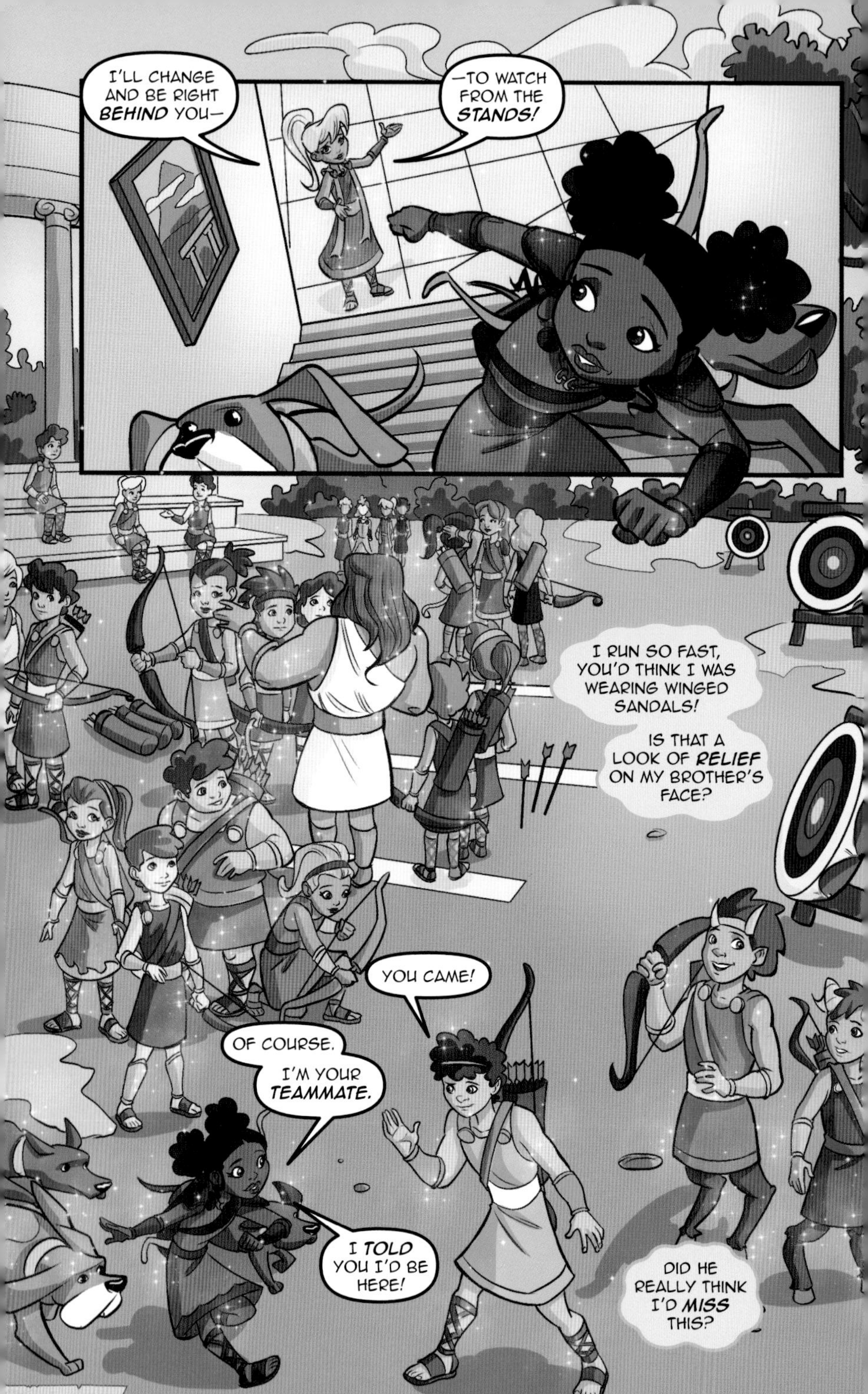

I'LL CHANGE AND BE RIGHT *BEHIND* YOU—
—TO WATCH FROM THE *STANDS!*
I RUN SO FAST, YOU'D THINK I WAS WEARING WINGED SANDALS!
IS THAT A LOOK OF *RELIEF* ON MY BROTHER'S FACE?
YOU CAME!
OF COURSE.
I'M YOUR *TEAMMATE.*
I *TOLD* YOU I'D BE HERE!
DID HE REALLY THINK I'D *MISS* THIS?

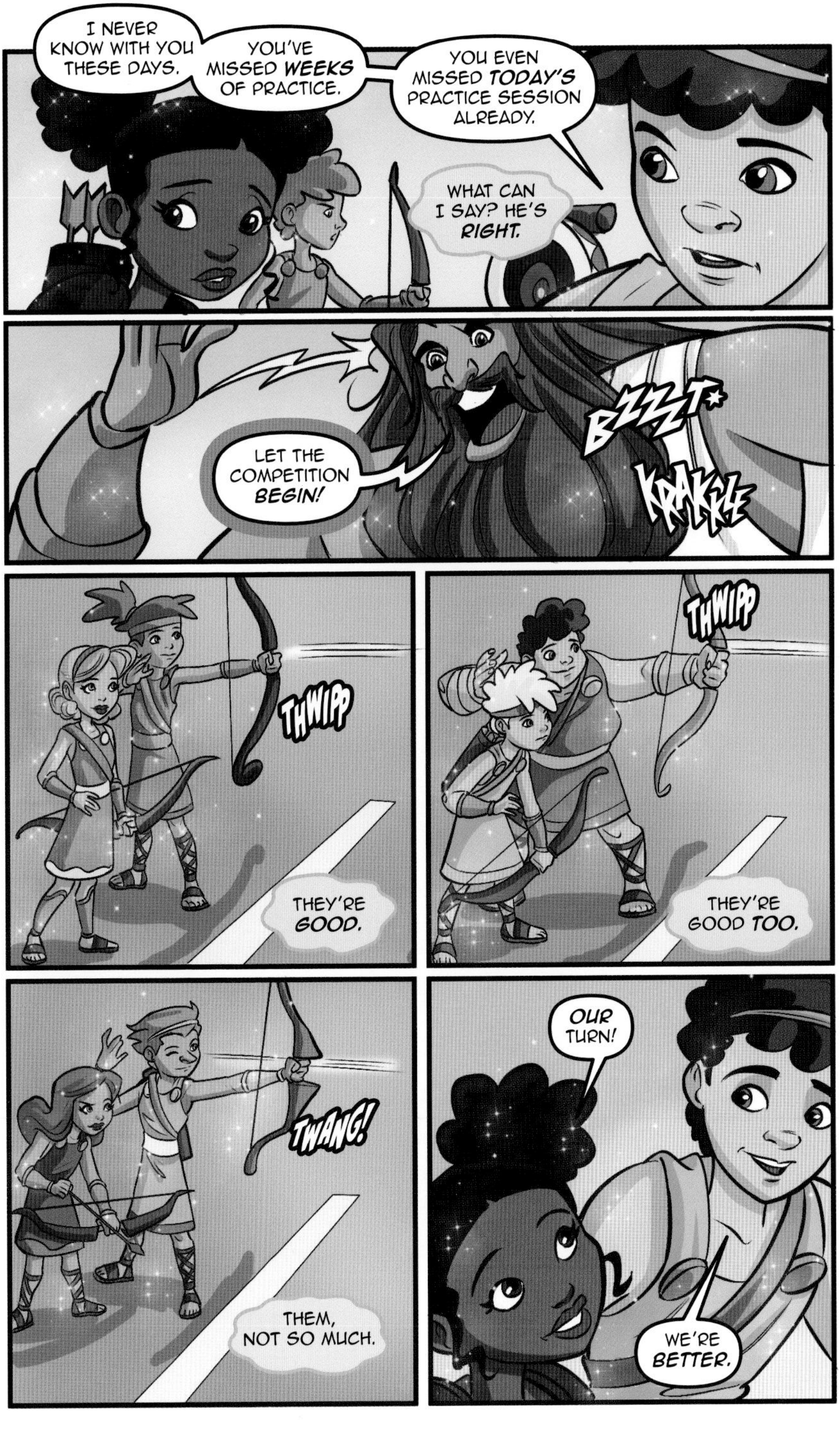
I NEVER KNOW WITH YOU THESE DAYS.
YOU'VE MISSED **WEEKS** OF PRACTICE.
YOU EVEN MISSED **TODAY'S** PRACTICE SESSION ALREADY.
WHAT CAN I SAY? HE'S **RIGHT.**
BZZZT
KRAKKLE
LET THE COMPETITION **BEGIN!**
THWIPP
THEY'RE **GOOD.**
THWIPP
THEY'RE GOOD **TOO.**
TWANG!
THEM, NOT SO MUCH.
OUR TURN!
WE'RE **BETTER.**

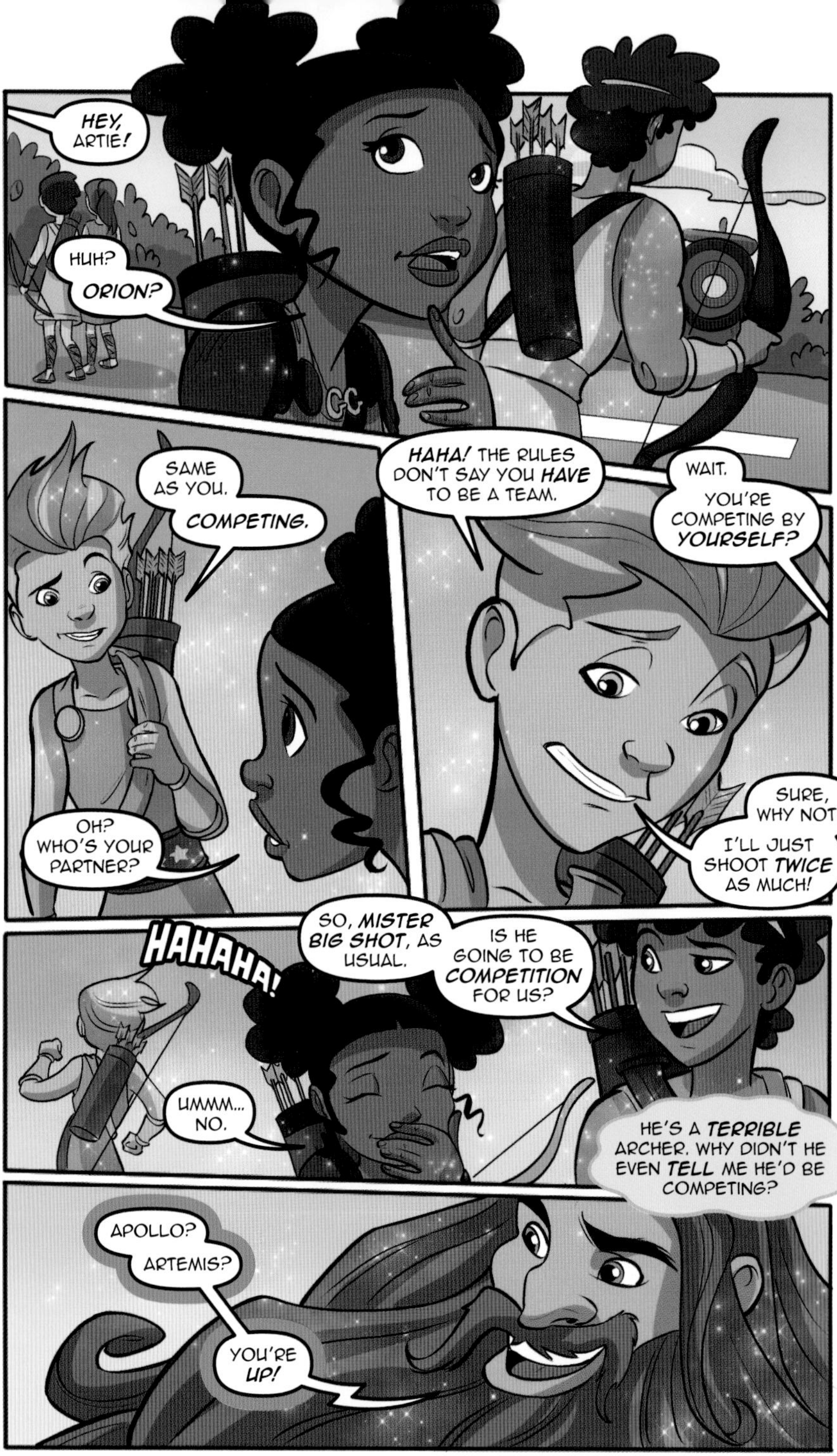
HEY, ARTIE!
HUH? ORION?
SAME AS YOU. COMPETING.
OH? WHO'S YOUR PARTNER?
HAHA! THE RULES DON'T SAY YOU HAVE TO BE A TEAM.
WAIT. YOU'RE COMPETING BY YOURSELF?
SURE, WHY NOT? I'LL JUST SHOOT TWICE AS MUCH!
HAHAHA!
SO, MISTER BIG SHOT, AS USUAL.
IS HE GOING TO BE COMPETITION FOR US?
UMMM... NO.
HE'S A TERRIBLE ARCHER. WHY DIDN'T HE EVEN TELL ME HE'D BE COMPETING?
APOLLO? ARTEMIS?
YOU'RE UP!

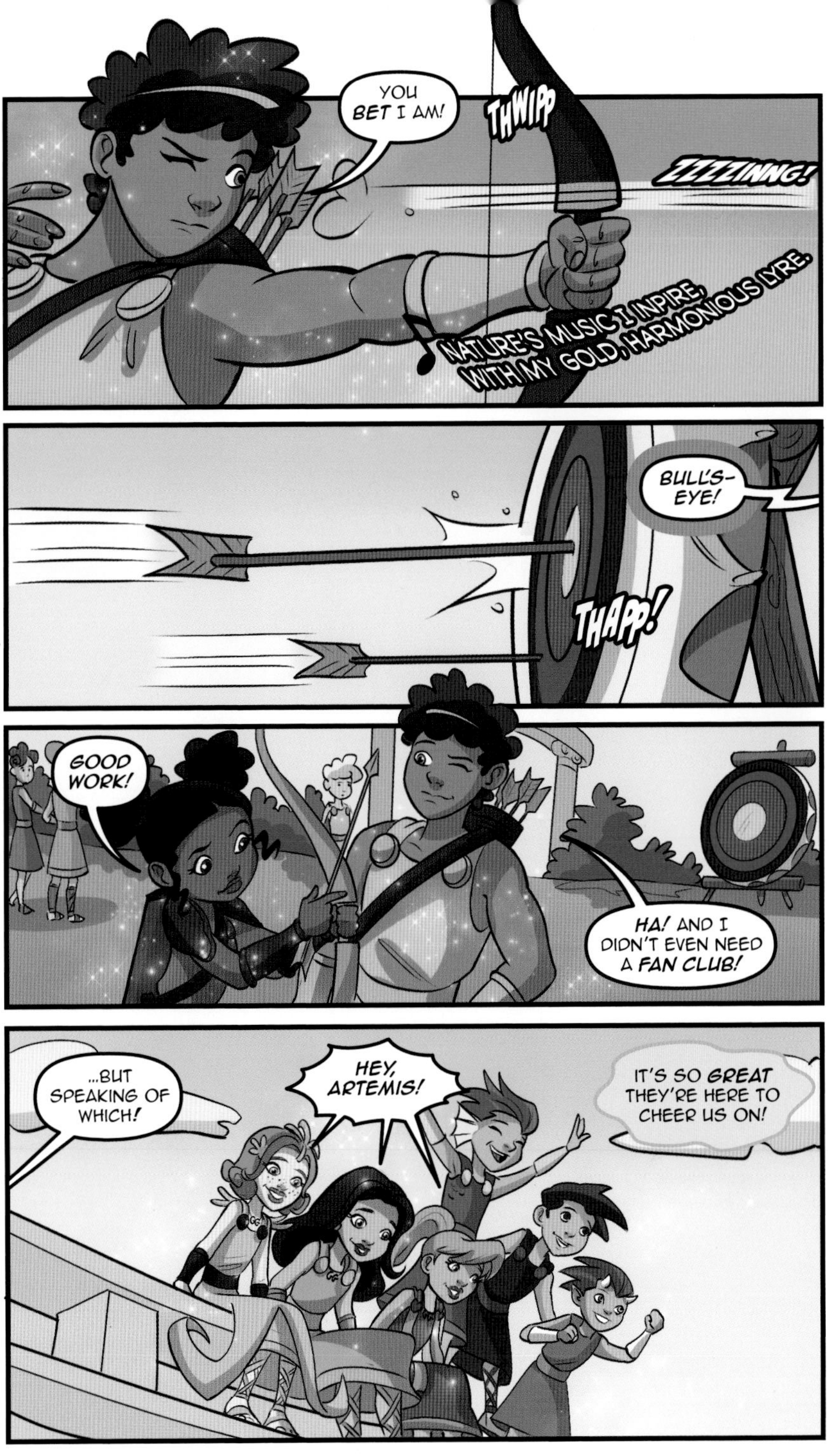
YOU BET I AM!
THWIPP
ZZZZINNG!
NATURE'S MUSIC I INPIRE, WITH MY GOLD, HARMONIOUS LYRE.
BULL'S-EYE!
THAPP!
GOOD WORK!
HA! AND I DIDN'T EVEN NEED A FAN CLUB!
...BUT SPEAKING OF WHICH!
HEY, ARTEMIS!
IT'S SO GREAT THEY'RE HERE TO CHEER US ON!

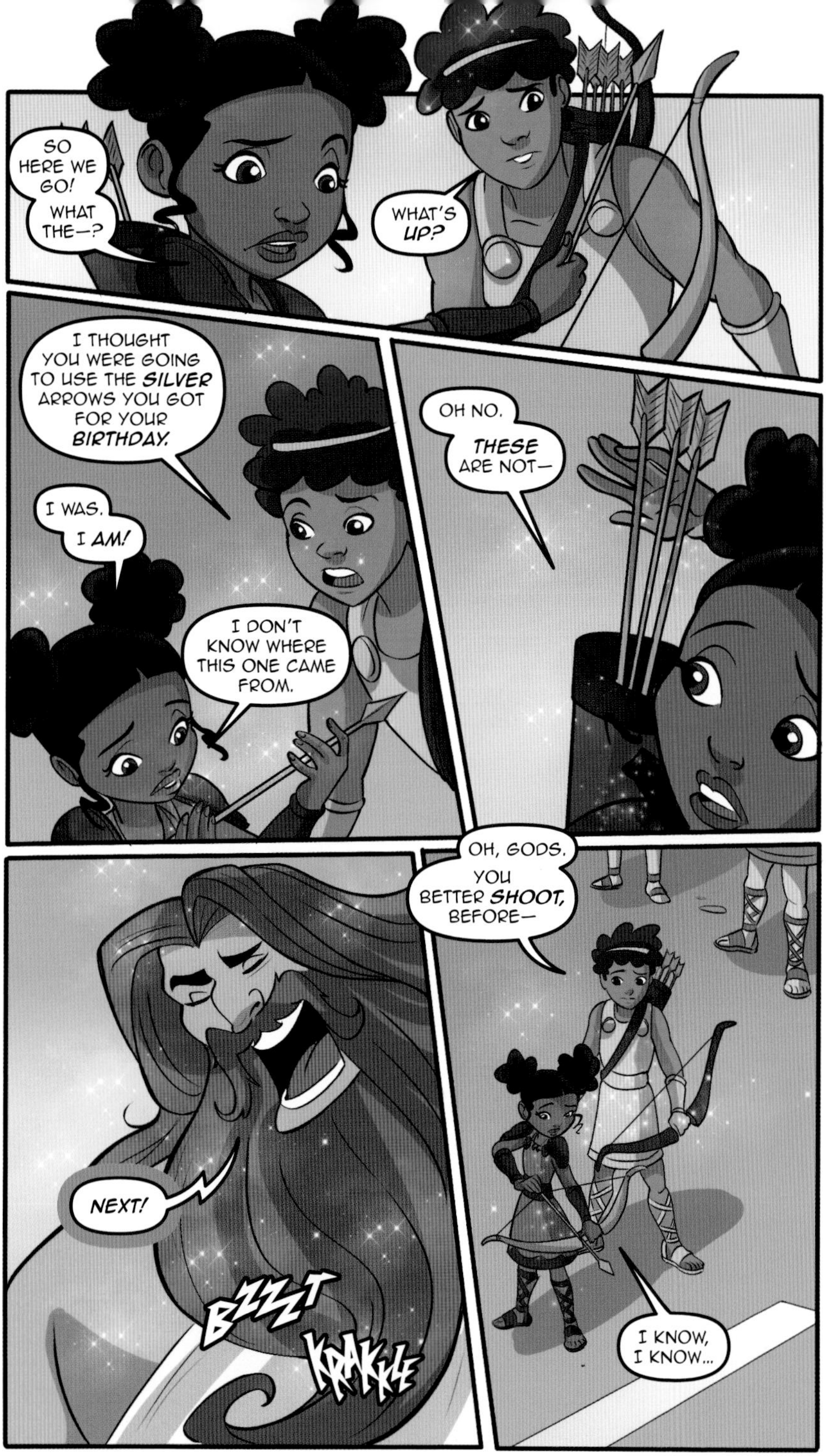
SO HERE WE GO!
WHAT THE—?
WHAT'S UP?
I THOUGHT YOU WERE GOING TO USE THE SILVER ARROWS YOU GOT FOR YOUR BIRTHDAY.
I WAS.
I AM!
I DON'T KNOW WHERE THIS ONE CAME FROM.
OH NO.
THESE ARE NOT—
NEXT!
BZZZT
KRAKKLE
OH, GODS.
YOU BETTER SHOOT, BEFORE—
I KNOW, I KNOW...

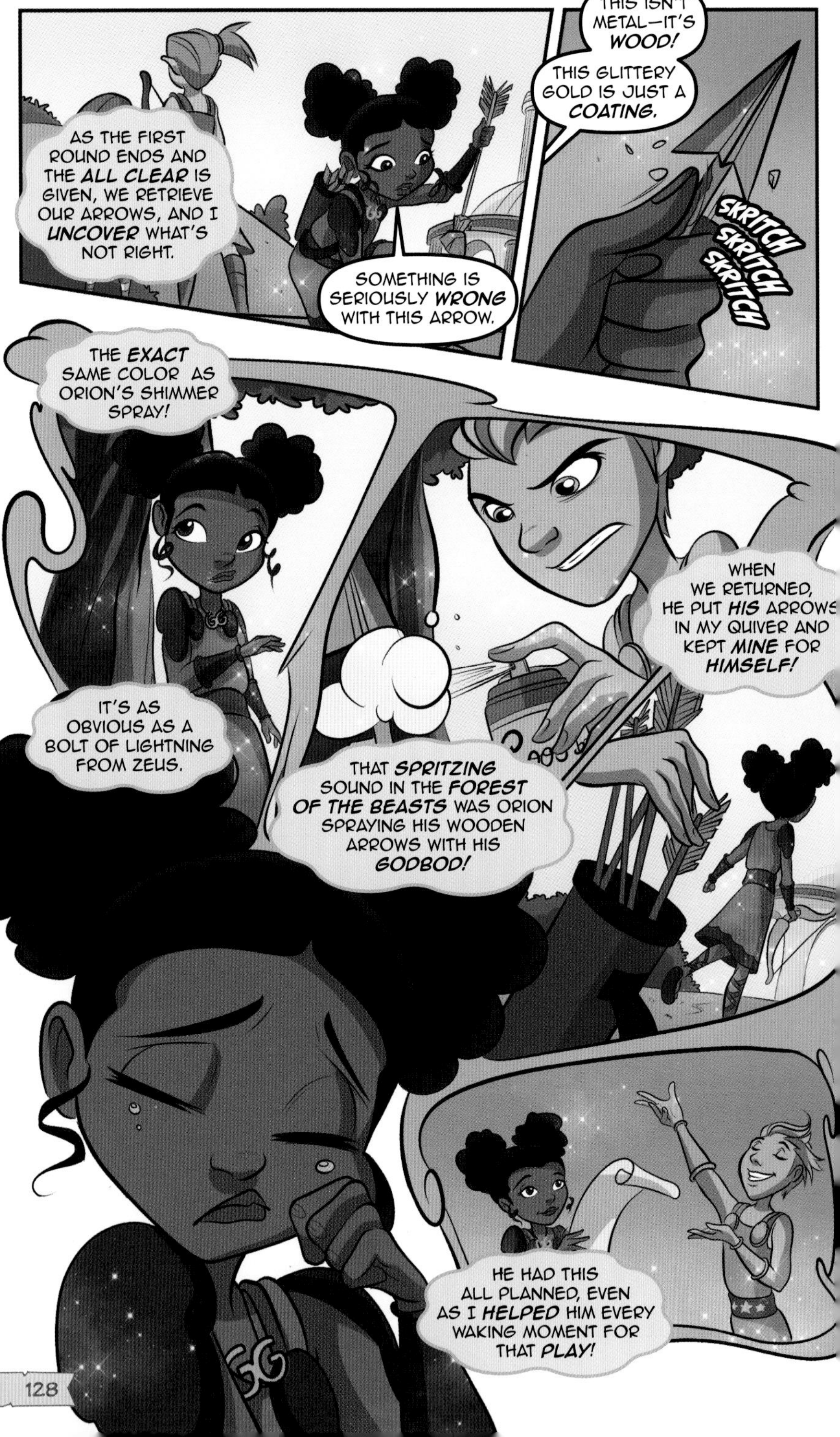

AS THE FIRST ROUND ENDS AND THE ALL CLEAR IS GIVEN, WE RETRIEVE OUR ARROWS, AND I UNCOVER WHAT'S NOT RIGHT.
SOMETHING IS SERIOUSLY WRONG WITH THIS ARROW.
THIS ISN'T METAL—IT'S WOOD!
THIS GLITTERY GOLD IS JUST A COATING.
SKRITCH SKRITCH SKRITCH
THE EXACT SAME COLOR AS ORION'S SHIMMER SPRAY!
WHEN WE RETURNED, HE PUT HIS ARROWS IN MY QUIVER AND KEPT MINE FOR HIMSELF!
IT'S AS OBVIOUS AS A BOLT OF LIGHTNING FROM ZEUS.
THAT SPRITZING SOUND IN THE FOREST OF THE BEASTS WAS ORION SPRAYING HIS WOODEN ARROWS WITH HIS GODBOD!
HE HAD THIS ALL PLANNED, EVEN AS I HELPED HIM EVERY WAKING MOMENT FOR THAT PLAY!

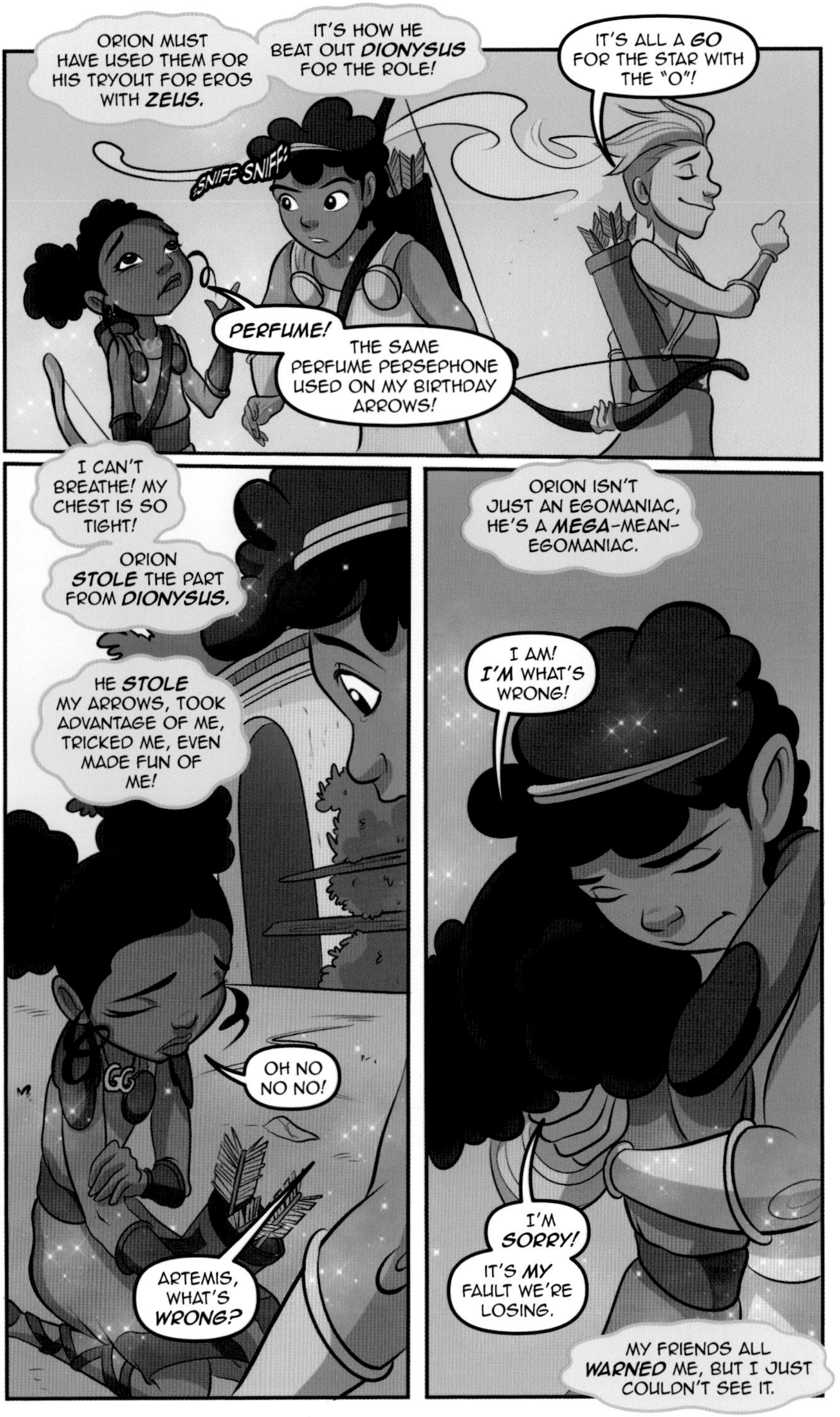
ORION MUST HAVE USED THEM FOR HIS TRYOUT FOR EROS WITH ZEUS.
IT'S HOW HE BEAT OUT DIONYSUS FOR THE ROLE!
IT'S ALL A GO FOR THE STAR WITH THE "O"!
SNIFF SNIFF
PERFUME!
THE SAME PERFUME PERSEPHONE USED ON MY BIRTHDAY ARROWS!
I CAN'T BREATHE! MY CHEST IS SO TIGHT!
ORION STOLE THE PART FROM DIONYSUS.
HE STOLE MY ARROWS, TOOK ADVANTAGE OF ME, TRICKED ME, EVEN MADE FUN OF ME!
OH NO NO NO!
ARTEMIS, WHAT'S WRONG?
ORION ISN'T JUST AN EGOMANIAC, HE'S A MEGA-MEAN-EGOMANIAC.
I AM! I'M WHAT'S WRONG!
I'M SORRY!
IT'S MY FAULT WE'RE LOSING.
MY FRIENDS ALL WARNED ME, BUT I JUST COULDN'T SEE IT.

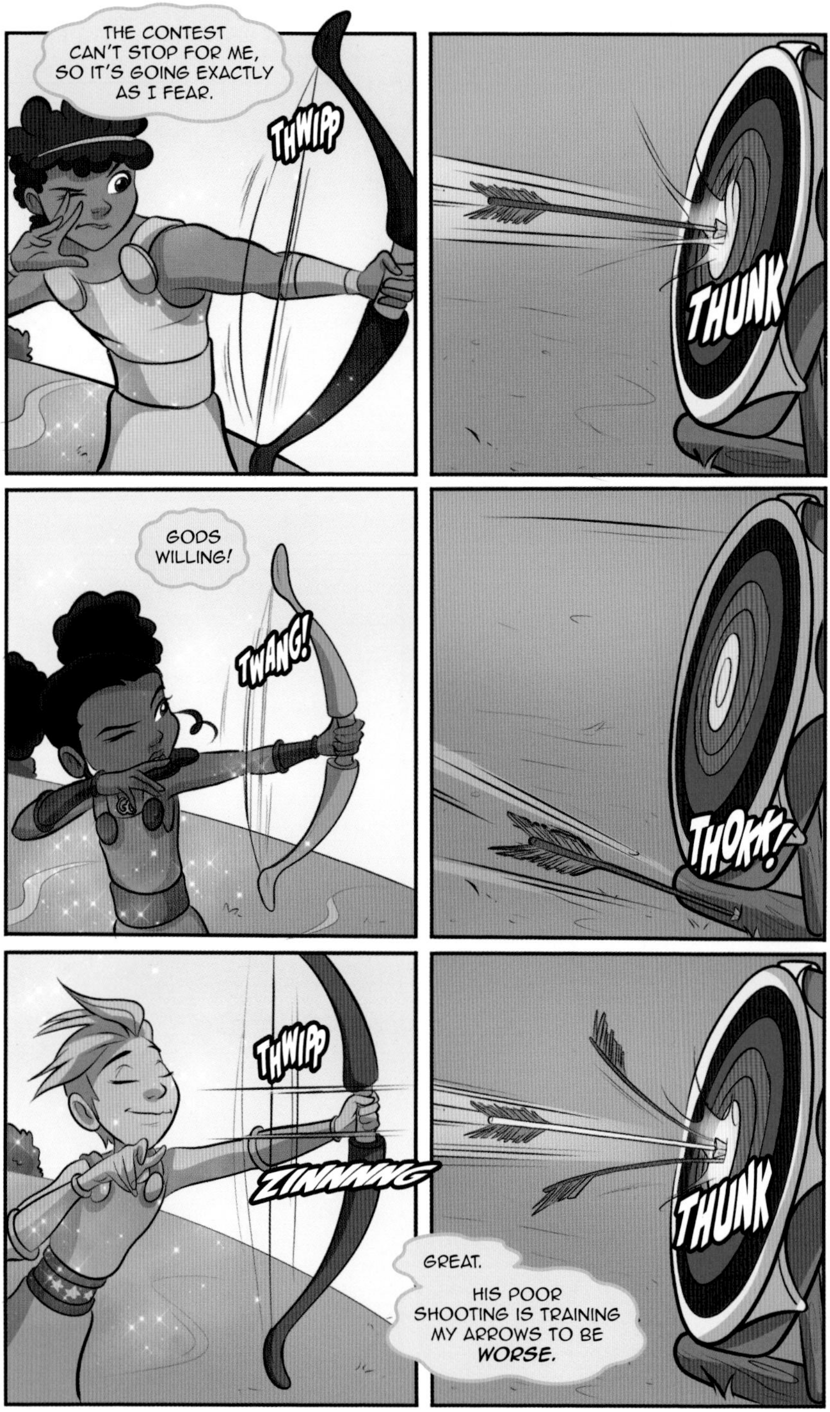
THE CONTEST CAN'T STOP FOR ME, SO IT'S GOING EXACTLY AS I FEAR.
THWIPP
THUNK
GODS WILLING!
TWANG!
THOKK!
THWIPP
ZINNNNG
THUNK
GREAT.
HIS POOR SHOOTING IS TRAINING MY ARROWS TO BE *WORSE.*

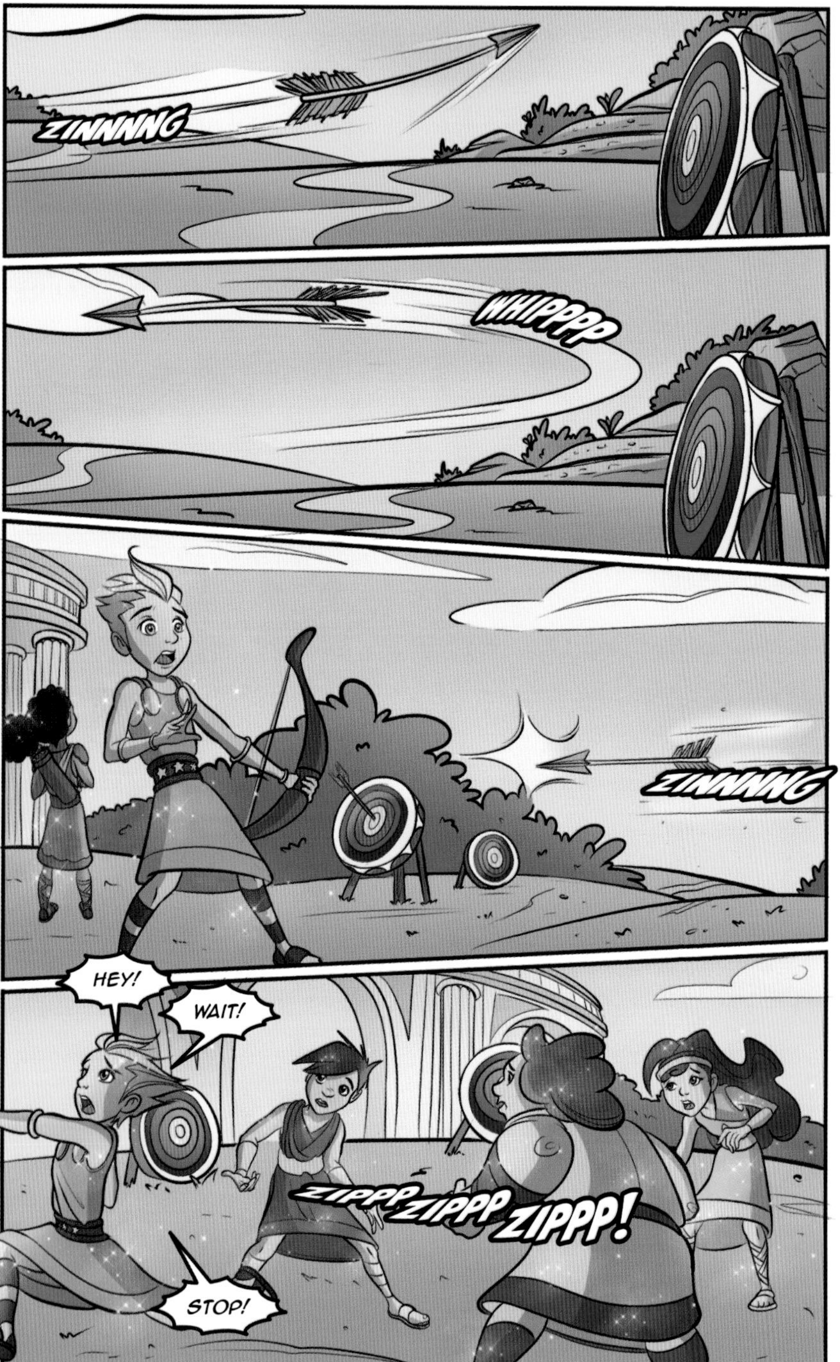
ZINNNNG
WHIPPPP
ZINNNNG
HEY!
WAIT!
ZIPPP ZIPPP ZIPPP!
STOP!

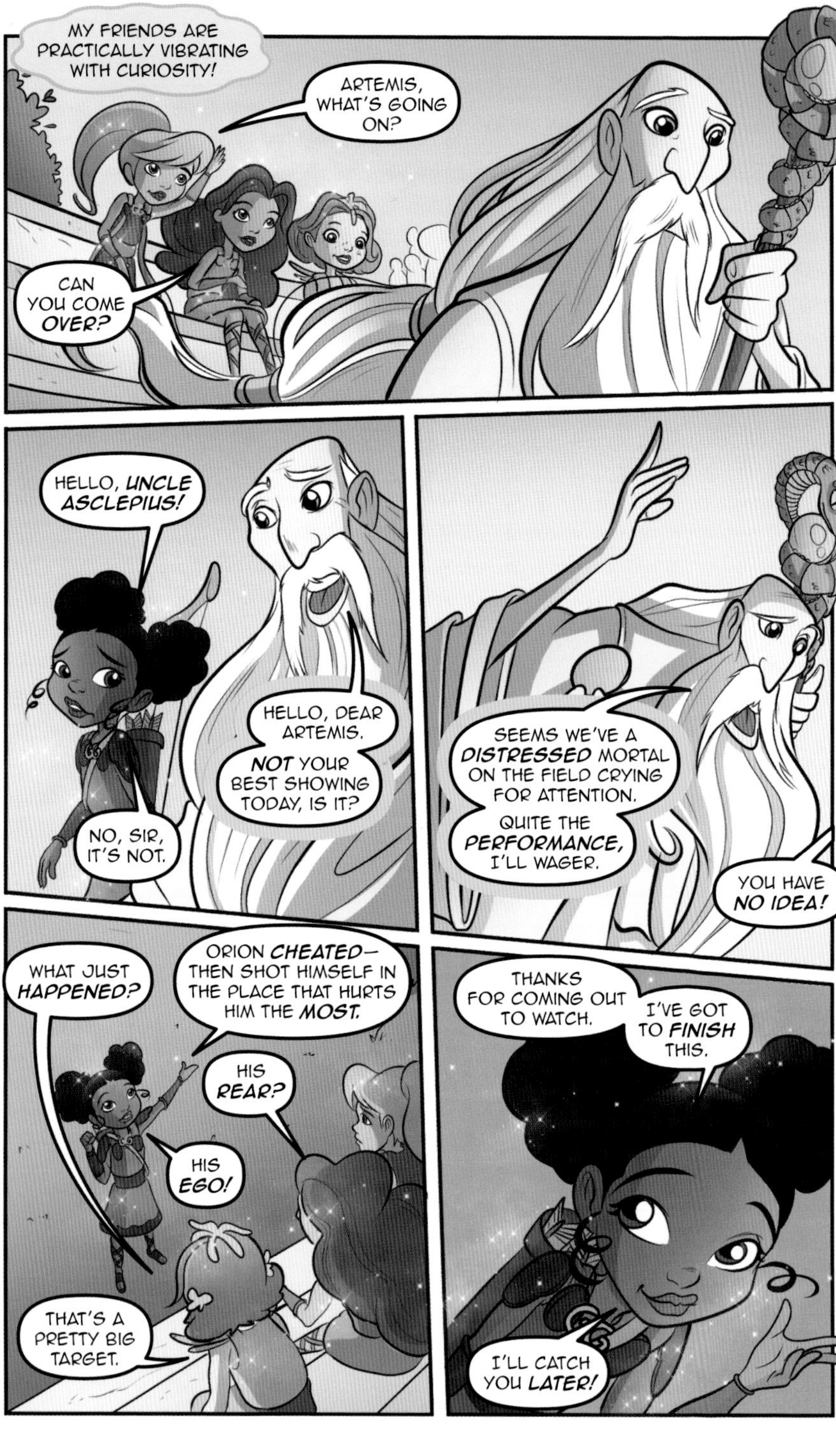
MY FRIENDS ARE PRACTICALLY VIBRATING WITH CURIOSITY!
ARTEMIS, WHAT'S GOING ON?
CAN YOU COME OVER?
HELLO, UNCLE ASCLEPIUS!
HELLO, DEAR ARTEMIS.
NOT YOUR BEST SHOWING TODAY, IS IT?
NO, SIR, IT'S NOT.
SEEMS WE'VE A DISTRESSED MORTAL ON THE FIELD CRYING FOR ATTENTION.
QUITE THE PERFORMANCE, I'LL WAGER.
YOU HAVE NO IDEA!
WHAT JUST HAPPENED?
ORION CHEATED—THEN SHOT HIMSELF IN THE PLACE THAT HURTS HIM THE MOST.
HIS REAR?
HIS EGO!
THAT'S A PRETTY BIG TARGET.
THANKS FOR COMING OUT TO WATCH.
I'VE GOT TO FINISH THIS.
I'LL CATCH YOU LATER!

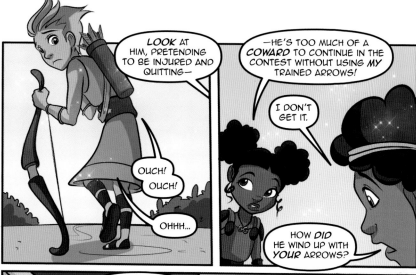

LOOK AT HIM, PRETENDING TO BE INJURED AND QUITTING—

—HE'S TOO MUCH OF A COWARD TO CONTINUE IN THE CONTEST WITHOUT USING MY TRAINED ARROWS!

I DON'T GET IT.

OUCH! OUCH!

OHHH...

HOW DID HE WIND UP WITH YOUR ARROWS?

I TOOK HIM TO THE FOREST OF THE BEASTS.

WHAT? WHY?

IT'S COMPLICATED.

YEAH. I'LL BET.

I'M SORRY. TRULY.

YEAH. YOU SHOULD BE.

WE'VE ALWAYS SUPPORTED, DEFENDED, AND ENCOURAGED ONE ANOTHER.

I'VE MESSED THIS UP AND DON'T KNOW HOW TO FIX IT.

BUT I DO KNOW THAT FIGHTING OVER SOMEONE LIKE ORION IS ABSOLUTELY DUMB!

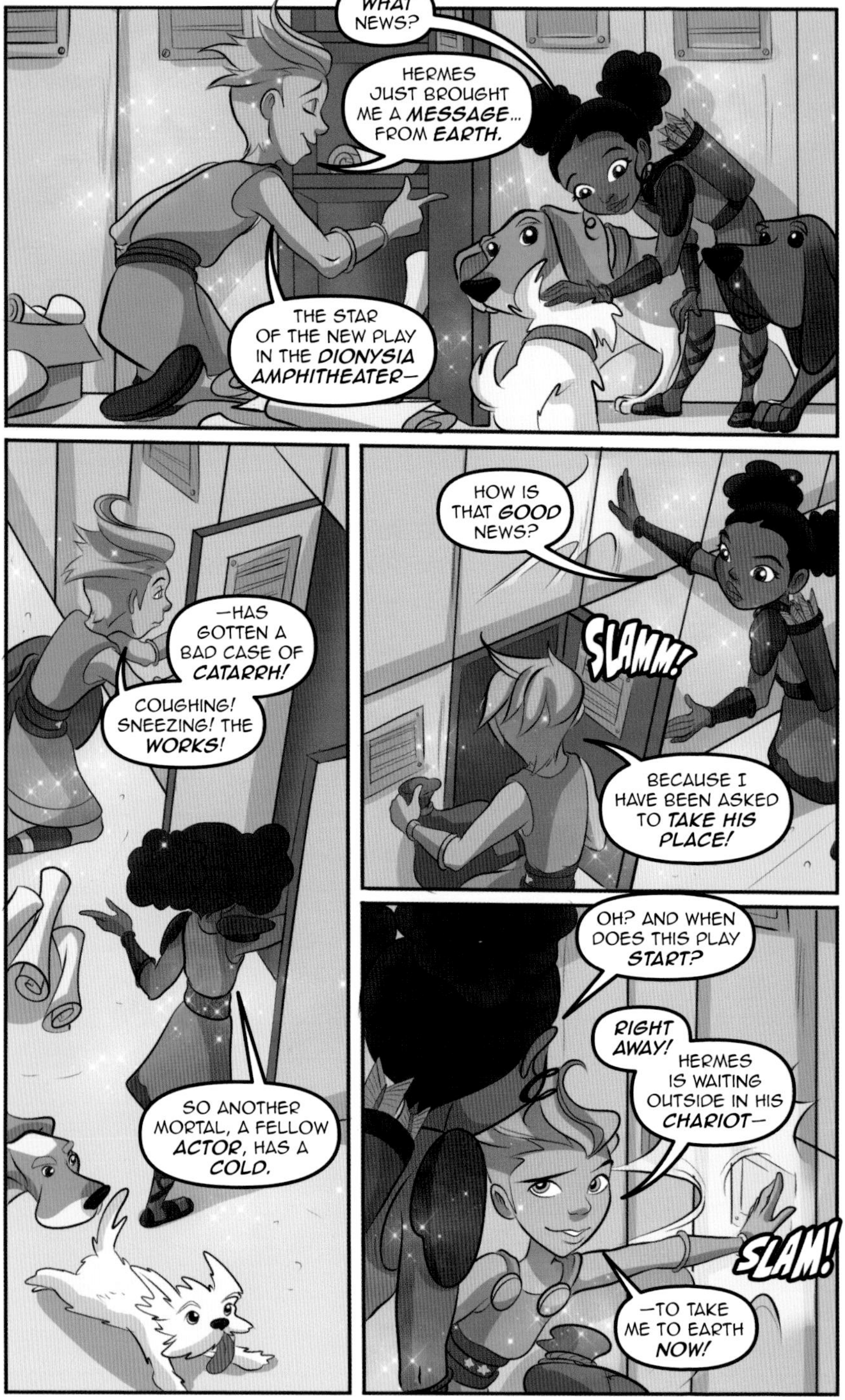
WHAT NEWS?
HERMES JUST BROUGHT ME A MESSAGE... FROM EARTH.
THE STAR OF THE NEW PLAY IN THE DIONYSIA AMPHITHEATER—
—HAS GOTTEN A BAD CASE OF CATARRH!
COUGHING! SNEEZING! THE WORKS!
SO ANOTHER MORTAL, A FELLOW ACTOR, HAS A COLD.
HOW IS THAT GOOD NEWS?
SLAMM!
BECAUSE I HAVE BEEN ASKED TO TAKE HIS PLACE!
OH? AND WHEN DOES THIS PLAY START?
RIGHT AWAY!
HERMES IS WAITING OUTSIDE IN HIS CHARIOT—
SLAM!
—TO TAKE ME TO EARTH NOW!

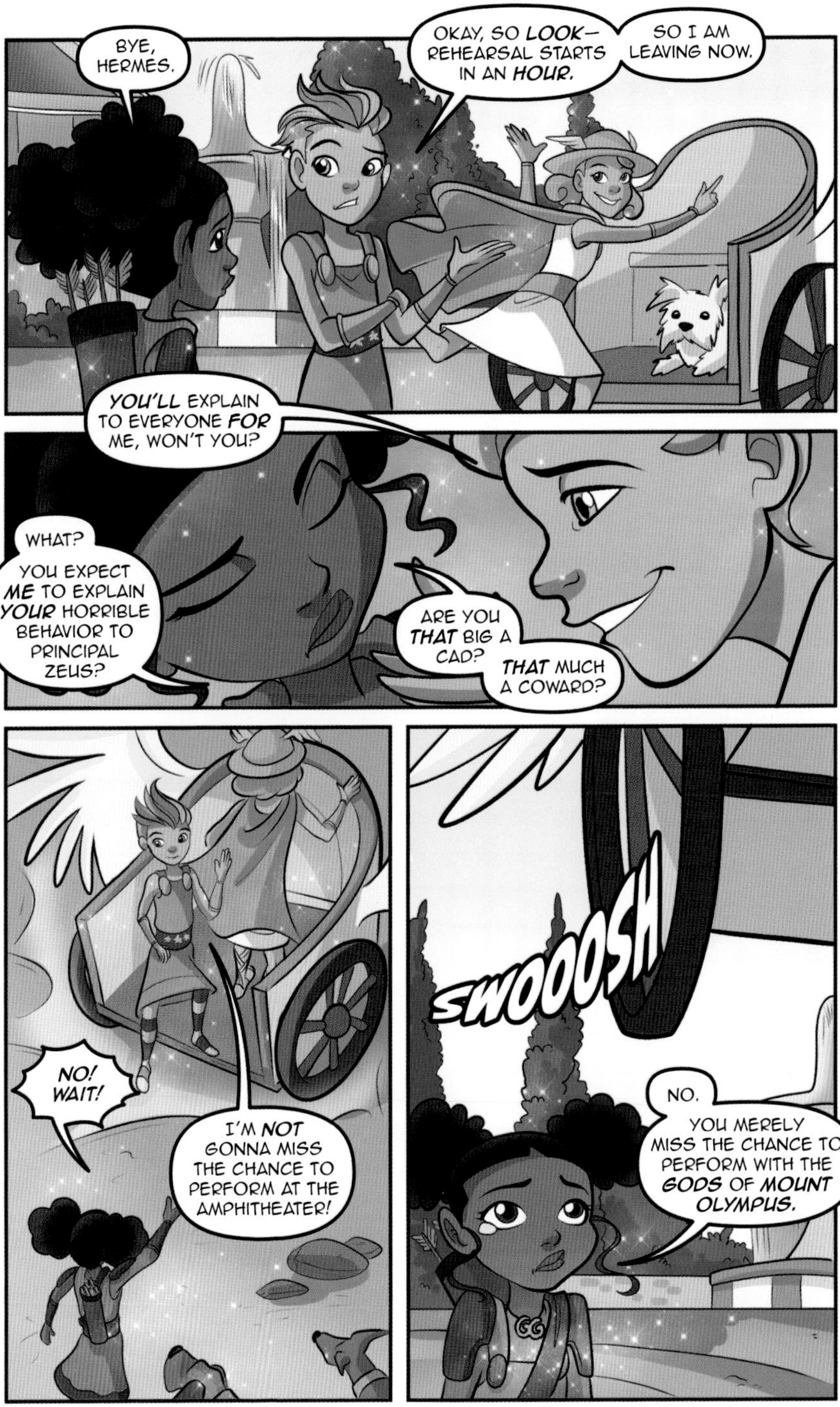
BYE, HERMES.
OKAY, SO LOOK— REHEARSAL STARTS IN AN HOUR.
SO I AM LEAVING NOW.
YOU'LL EXPLAIN TO EVERYONE FOR ME, WON'T YOU?
WHAT?
YOU EXPECT ME TO EXPLAIN YOUR HORRIBLE BEHAVIOR TO PRINCIPAL ZEUS?
ARE YOU THAT BIG A CAD?
THAT MUCH A COWARD?
NO! WAIT!
I'M NOT GONNA MISS THE CHANCE TO PERFORM AT THE AMPHITHEATER!
SWOOOSH
NO.
YOU MERELY MISS THE CHANCE TO PERFORM WITH THE GODS OF MOUNT OLYMPUS.

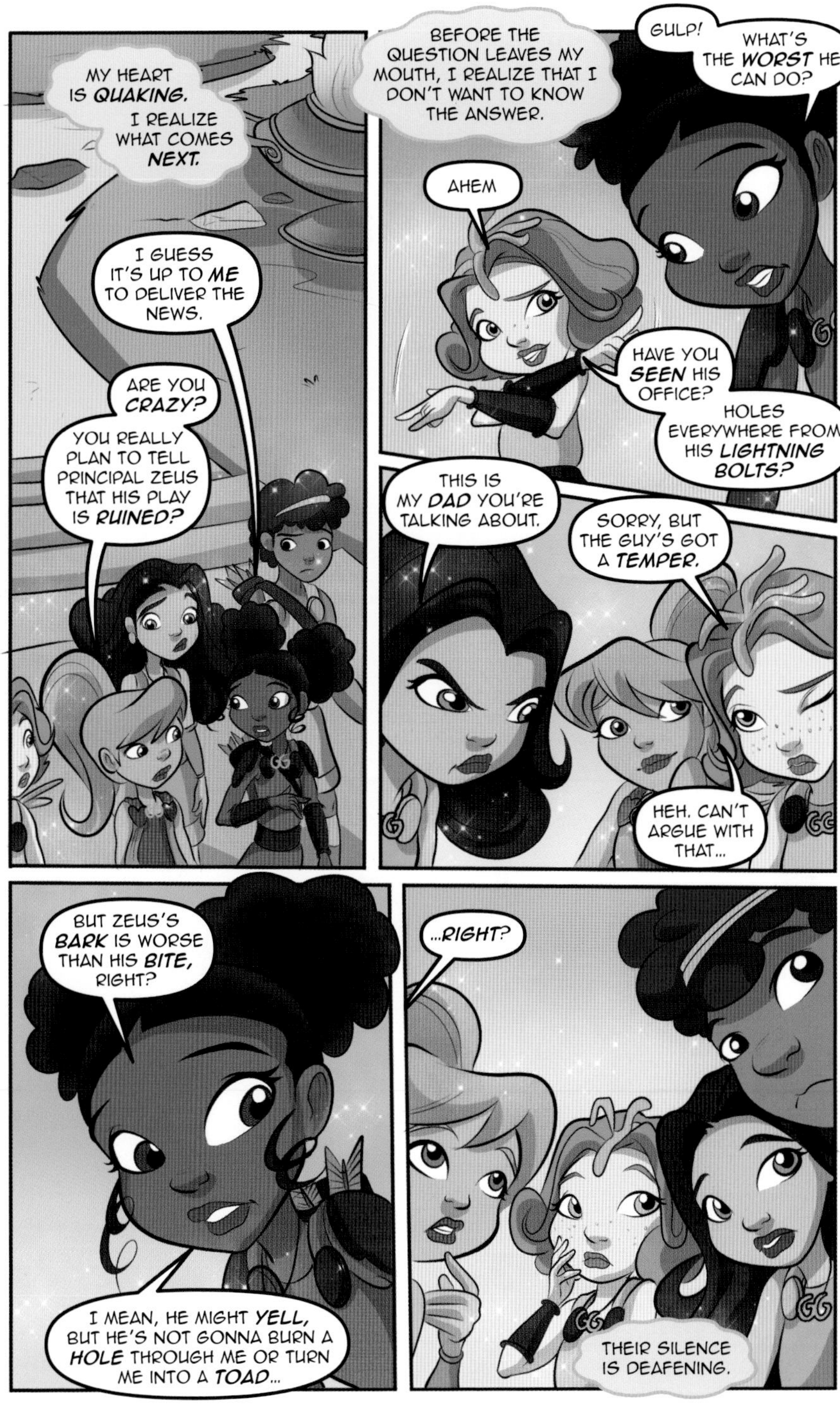
MY HEART IS QUAKING.
I REALIZE WHAT COMES NEXT.
I GUESS IT'S UP TO ME TO DELIVER THE NEWS.
ARE YOU CRAZY?
YOU REALLY PLAN TO TELL PRINCIPAL ZEUS THAT HIS PLAY IS RUINED?
BEFORE THE QUESTION LEAVES MY MOUTH, I REALIZE THAT I DON'T WANT TO KNOW THE ANSWER.
GULP!
WHAT'S THE WORST HE CAN DO?
AHEM
HAVE YOU SEEN HIS OFFICE?
HOLES EVERYWHERE FROM HIS LIGHTNING BOLTS?
THIS IS MY DAD YOU'RE TALKING ABOUT.
SORRY, BUT THE GUY'S GOT A TEMPER.
HEH. CAN'T ARGUE WITH THAT...
BUT ZEUS'S BARK IS WORSE THAN HIS BITE, RIGHT?
I MEAN, HE MIGHT YELL, BUT HE'S NOT GONNA BURN A HOLE THROUGH ME OR TURN ME INTO A TOAD...
...RIGHT?
THEIR SILENCE IS DEAFENING.

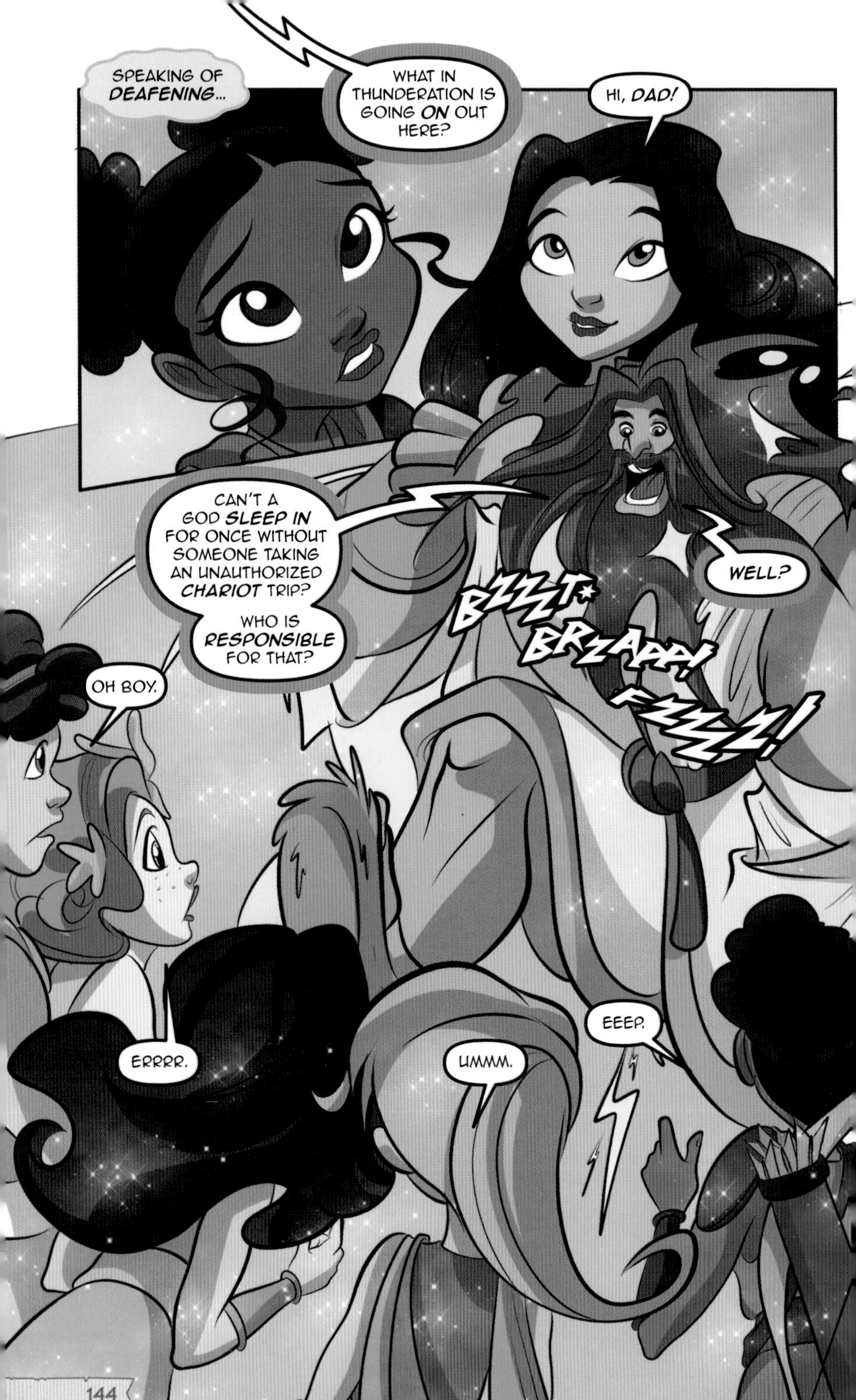
SPEAKING OF *DEAFENING*...
WHAT IN THUNDERATION IS GOING *ON* OUT HERE?
HI, *DAD!*
CAN'T A GOD *SLEEP IN* FOR ONCE WITHOUT SOMEONE TAKING AN UNAUTHORIZED *CHARIOT* TRIP?
WHO IS *RESPONSIBLE* FOR THAT?
WELL?
BZZZT*
BRZAPP!
FZZZZ!
OH BOY.
ERRRR.
UMMM.
EEEP.

CHAPTER NINE:
WILD BEASTS

I'M *DREADING* THIS RETURN TO THE *FOREST OF THE BEASTS*, BUT IT'S OUR CLASS ASSIGNMENT.

MAYBE I SHOULD'VE PLAYED *SICK?*

NO, I CAN'T LET MY FRIENDS DOWN. OR *MYSELF*.

LET'S LAND *HERE*, MY DEER!

SWOOSH

WE ALL NEED TO SCORE A'S ON THIS SECOND PART OF THE TEST TO REACH THE NINTH AND FINAL LEVEL OF THE ARROW.

TODAY WE MUST VANQUISH *ECHIDNA* THE SHE-DRAGON AND THE GOAT-HEADED *CHIMERA*.

149

WAIT—WHY ARE THERE SO *MANY*?

WHY ARE THEY SO *PRETTY*?

I *READ* THAT THEY CAN CHANGE FORMS TO *LURE* THEIR PREY!

IT'S N-NOT WHAT'S ON A MONSTER'S *OUTSIDE* THAT COUNTS!

COME SSSSEEE USSSS!

YESSSSS.

USSSS!

WAIT!

W-WHAT'S HAPPENING *NOW*?

THEY'RE HICCUPING!

AND *TRANSFORMING* AGAIN!

HIC!

HIC!

HIC!

HIC!

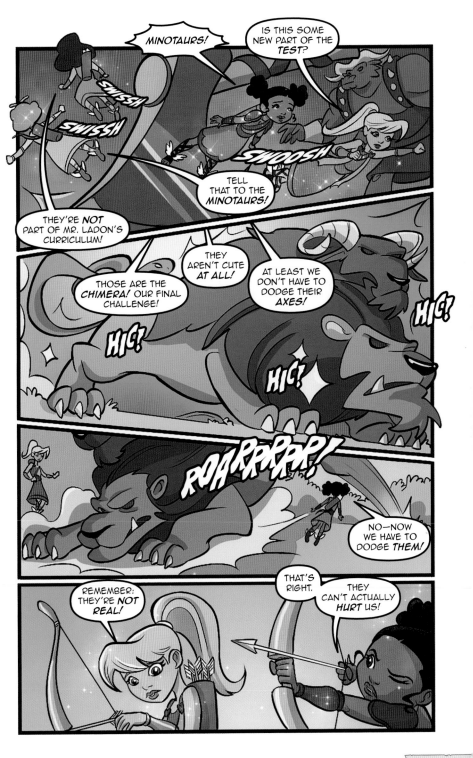

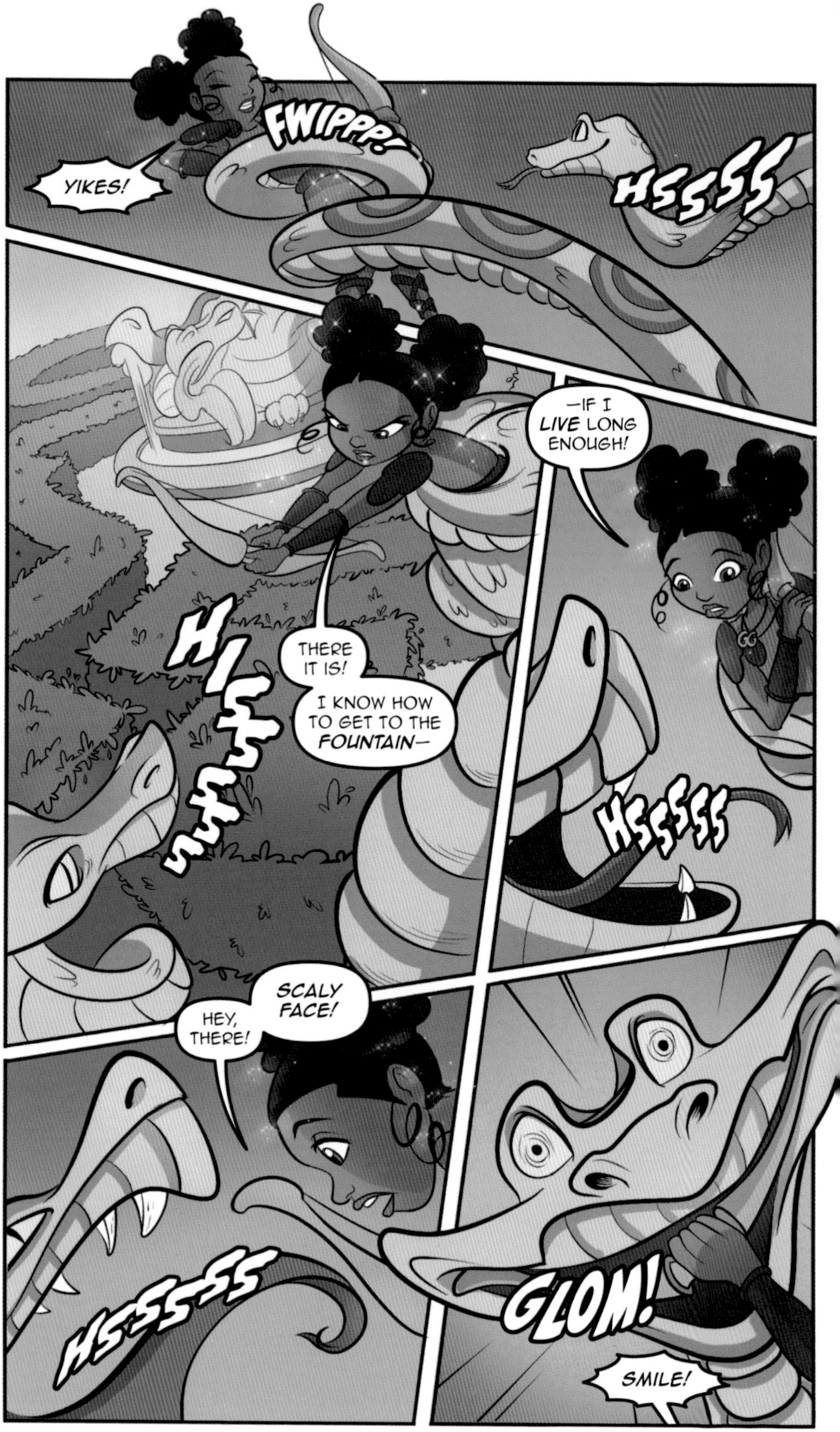

YIKES!
FWIPPP!
HSSSS
THERE IT IS!
I KNOW HOW TO GET TO THE FOUNTAIN—
HISSSSSS
—IF I LIVE LONG ENOUGH!
HSSSSS
HEY, THERE!
SCALY FACE!
HSSSSS
GLOM!
SMILE!

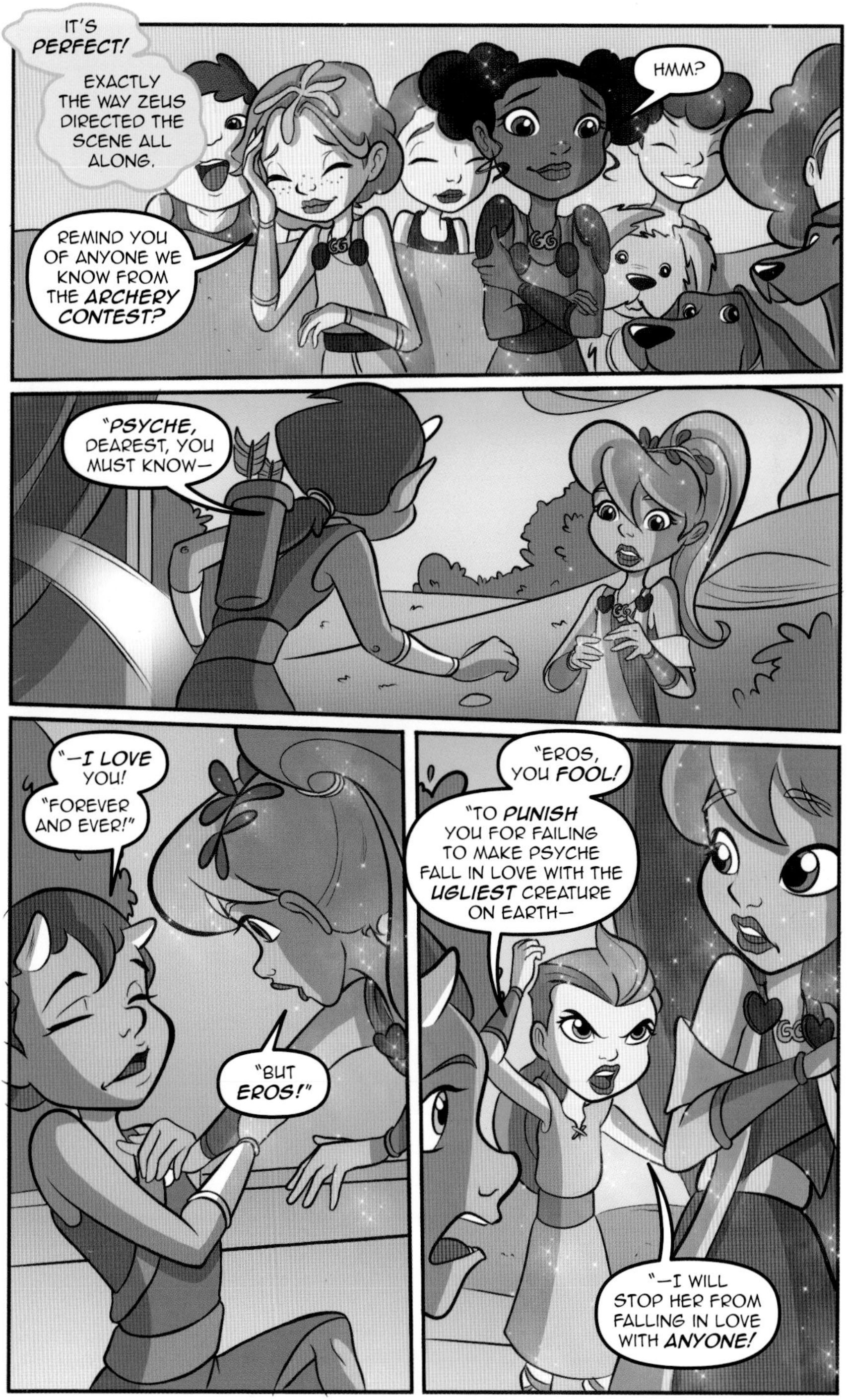
IT'S *PERFECT!*
EXACTLY THE WAY ZEUS DIRECTED THE SCENE ALL ALONG.
HMM?
REMIND YOU OF ANYONE WE KNOW FROM THE *ARCHERY CONTEST?*
"*PSYCHE,* DEAREST, YOU MUST KNOW—
"—*I LOVE* YOU!
"FOREVER AND EVER!"
"BUT *EROS!*"
"EROS, YOU *FOOL!*
"TO *PUNISH* YOU FOR FAILING TO MAKE PSYCHE FALL IN LOVE WITH THE *UGLIEST* CREATURE ON EARTH—
"—I WILL STOP HER FROM FALLING IN LOVE WITH *ANYONE!*